PRAISE FOR OSGOOD AS DEAD

"An epic, aesthetic entry in the imminently enjoyable Spectral Inspector series. *Osgood as Dead* is wickedly paced and intricately plotted, and Beckett's use of elements of mental health struggles is always authentic and empowering. Peopled with engaging characters and making excellent use of Chicago's geography and history, Beckett's latest installment is a helluva good time."

Laurel Hightower, author of *The Day of the Door*

"A sensual, surreal mindfuck that pins your eyelids open! Fair warning: you'll be red-eyed and hungover after staying up all night to finish this book."

Isaac Thorne, author of *Tab's Terrible Third Eye*

"We all know that when we're craving outrageous queer antiheroes, the creepiest of urban legends, and inappropriate quips we want Beckett. What? No not that Beckett. The other one."

BP Gregory, author of *Flora & Jim*

"Sharp as a knife, this is horror that lingers, wrapping itself around guilt, grief, and the shadows we leave behind. *Osgood as Dead* doesn't just haunt—it consumes."

Shane Hawk, author of *Anoka*

"Witty, sexy and creepy as hell. Beckett's writing is modern and stylish; his talent for building imperfect yet relatable and absolutely lovable characters is truly magnificent. Consider me an instant Osgood fan — I want to slurp up every drop of the Osgoodness!"

Dalton Primeaux, author of *Tales From Beyond The Closet*

"A haunting, relentless journey into the supernatural and the human psyche, *Osgood as Dead* masterfully blends horror, mystery, and emotional depth. Prudence Osgood is the kind of protagonist who lingers with you long after you close the book — flawed, haunted, and deeply human. Equal parts heart-wrenching and horrifying, this story will grip you, shake you, and refuse to let go. Prepare to lose sleep over this one."

Amber Dean, author of *Hysterical*

"Beckett delivers the goods in Osgood as Dead, the fourth action-packed outing for Prudence Osgood, his flawed but feisty protagonist, handling the mayhem with panache and keeping a light touch even when things are at their darkest. Prepare yourself for a wild ride to hell and back again."

David Demchuk, author of *RED X* and *The Bone Mother*

"Raw, sexy, and fucking scary!"

Harlinn Draper, author of *Roughneck*

"Chapters drop one after the other like bombs leaving debris of terror and pleasure in equal parts!"

Alana K. Drex, author of *Oops, I Killed My Boyfriend*

OSGOOD AS DEAD

"Masterfully written, terrifyingly creepy, seductively entertaining, and chilling to the bone ... *Osgood as Dead* is Beckett at the top of his game!"

Vince Rogers, author of *Terror Zone*

"*Osgood as Dead* is **Osgood as Hell**! Prepare to enjoy Paranormal Horror at its finest with a dynamic lineup of quirky and endearing characters that will leave you laughing while exploring a disturbed landscape with a unique plot."

Sarah DeRosa, author of *Mortifier*

"*Osgood as Dead* is deliciously brutal. A nonstop horror coaster that will make your stomach drop at every twist and turn."

Heather Chuon, *Demo Nation*

"A foul-mouthed and rip-roaring ride, there's no place that *Osgood as Dead* won't go—including the deepest caverns of demon-hunter Osgood's twisted, trauma-laced, filthy mind. Hilarious quips punctuate the action to perfect effect; a cinematic adventure for (very) grown-up fans of *Buffy, the Vampire Slayer.*"

Lindz McLeod, author of *Love, Happiness, And All The Things You May Not Be Destined For*

"Brimming with energy, fluid prose, amazing characters, and a gripping plot, *Osgood as Dead* fires on all cylinders. High stakes, spectral forces, trauma, shaky relationships, possession; this book has everything you need."

Pedro Iniguez, author of *Fever Dreams of a Parasite*

COOPER S. BECKETT

"Seamlessly bouncing between tones of sexy and gripping, humor and grief, Beckett's noir-thriller-meets-supernatural romp expands the series' uniquely-crafted otherworldly universe, blending genres and bending minds on its way to a wild finale."

Joey Powell, author of *Nightmares From the Gray*

"Sex, mass destruction, paranormal universal secrets and a Very Special Episode of *Diff'rent Strokes*? Yup! The Spectral Inspectors gang is back in *Osgood as Dead*, with the wit and bite you love. From battling demons named Yoko to existential crises to threesomes, Os is always up for action. Dig into this bitchin new adventure - it's a humdinger!"

Julia Marchese, host of *The Horror Movie Survival Guide*

OSGOOD AS DEAD

THE SPECTRAL INSPECTOR, BOOK IV

COOPER S. BECKETT

HORROR & CARNAGE PRESS

Interior Illustrations by Watchful Eye aka Lucas Gardner

Book Design by Cooper S. Beckett

1 2 3 4 5 6 7 8 9 10

Published Internationally by Horror & Carnage Press

ISBN: 978-1-946876-35-5

BISAC: Fiction / Horror / Mystery

Horror & Carnage Press - Chicago, Illinois

CooperSBeckett.com

PREVIOUSLY ON THE
SPECTRAL INSPECTOR

A UTHOR'S NOTE: EVERYBODY NEEDS a refresher from time to time, and if you're new here, there's a bit of stuff to catch up on. Here are recaps for the first three books in Prudence Osgood's saga.

Osgood As Gone

Once, Prudence Osgood and Audrey Frost were up-and-coming stars of the burgeoning paranormal investigation TV show craze before a hoax put an end to their friendship, partnership, and television careers. Now, over a decade later, Osgood is a barely functioning alcoholic ghosthunter for hire, her body broken by a car accident that killed her for a full 8 minutes and haunts her every night when she closes her eyes, her heart broken by all of those she's pushed away, especially former friend, partner, and girlfriend, Audrey Frost. But when she receives a cryptic, untraceable email, her yearning for mystery and adventure is reignited.

This mysterious email leads Osgood and (partner? assistant?) Zack to a rest stop with hundreds of posters of missing teenagers, including Audrey's sister, forcing an icy reconciliation and a temporary truce. They find themselves on the trail of a band that was once as popular as the Beatles, but somehow faded into absolute obscurity. These mysteries collide with the realization that the band made a deal with the devil for power and that power came with consequences, but for the band's fans instead. In the end, their investigation leads to a world outside of space and time, where an ancient entity rules over his beloved followers. Turning the crowd on the entity saps its power and ultimately destroys it. But an attack by the creature makes Osgood vulnerable and just when she thinks it's over, she disappears from our world without a trace.

***

Osgood Riddance

After vanishing for fifteen months, Osgood's return confuses her almost as much as her friends. She has no memory of her time away, only knowing that she went somewhere unearthly. While Osgood goes into a state of denial, pretending to be fine, Audrey and Zack cannot, and go about investigating. In an effort to distract herself (and *not* be the subject of an investigation), Osgood hooks up with Sam Goddard, an old boyfriend, for some great sex and horrifying afterglow. An orchidlike creature beyond earthly description claws its way out of her chest and attacks her lover. Her escape from the creature leads her to the hospital where she discovers that she has a teratoma, a brain tumor with eyes and teeth, possibly planted there during her time outside this world.

When the creature that has taken control of Goddard's body comes for her at the hospital, killing staff without regard, Osgood and the teem flee north to Donald Albrecht's house. Osgood's frail former mentor is happy to give them shelter, but isn't sure he can join the fight. When the Goddardmonster attacks the house, it's nearly unstoppable, until the arrival of Osgood's estranged aunt Eliza, who has some power of her own. This wild group attempts to expel the creature from Goddard as well as stop a doorway between worlds from opening and letting countless other monsters and creatures into our world. The fight requires Osgood to step into the strength of the powerful women along the Osgood family lineage, like her aunt Eliza and great grandmother Lil, but in the end, while the creatures are expelled, Goddard dies, and our heroes are broken.

***

Osgood As She Gets

A few years and a pandemic have passed since the events of the previous book. When Prudence Osgood sees a young woman leap in front of a subway train, Osgood and the Spectral Inspectors begin to look into a disturbing trend. Kids and teens around Chicago are being murdered at an alarming rate by someone the cops are calling the North Side Ripper. Concurrently, teenage suicide is way up.

A grief counselor with secrets of her own, Dr. Remy Yeagher, says that there is no North Side Ripper, and the suicides and murders are connected to an internet game these kids are playing called the Graveyard Game: look into the eyes of a hooded statue in Chicago's Rosehill Cemetery to see your death. Even those who don't play along still seem to end up dead. A winding path drags Osgood through her own depression and suicidal trauma as she tries to stop the needless deaths of countless young people.

Their investigation ultimately leads to an ancient woman kept alive by the magic of this hooded statue and sustained by the souls of the dead children. The Spectral Inspectors decapitate the statue and take down the woman in a showdown that leaves them all bruised and battered.

Left with a newfound appreciation for those around her, Osgood reconnects with Nora, a girlfriend she hasn't been honest with and has been avoiding. While on an El ride, though, there's a terrible crash. Nora is cut in half by the flying windshield. The other passengers endure similar horrors, and Osgood is flung straight out the front of the train onto the tracks and gravel, where she waits to die.

An Author's Note on Triggers

M ILD SPOILERS TO BE found below, as sometimes mentioning triggers does spoil plot points. Feel free to skip over the rest of this note if you'd rather not read it. If, for whatever reason, its presence, or the idea of triggers offends you, feel free to fuck right off.

Osgood As Dead contains scenes and themes of suicide and murder, alcoholism, drug and opioid addiction, implied child molestation, implied sexual assault, homophobia, and toxic masculinity as well as extreme violence, gore, and torture. If you would like to read the book but are uncertain if these things will be too much for you, please ask a friend to read it first.

If you or someone you know is experiencing suicidal thoughts or a crisis, please reach out immediately to the **Suicide Prevention Lifeline at 800-273-8255** or text **HOME** to the Crisis Text Line at **741741**. In North America, you can dial **988** to receive quick help from a suicide or crisis counselor. These services are free and confidential and are not limited to suicide, but to mental illness as well.

No shame. No stigma. Get help if you need it.

Also, I call J.K. Rowling a cunt. If that triggers you, well, maybe you're a cunt, too.

One last thing, as I'm finishing this book just after the 2024 election. If you voted for *him*, to paraphrase Tim Curry. "I didn't make her *for you!*"

For David Lynch
who taught me
how to dream

And as he said
to the villains
of this world

Fix Your Hearts
Or Die.

ONE

*W*HAT FRESH HELL... THOUGHT Osgood before an entirely new level of pain coursed through her body, a knife cutting through her as through butter, its blade catching and ripping skin and tissue here and there, moving with indifference and alacrity. This knife could flay her to the bone. Perhaps it was doing just that. She wanted to scream, tried to scream, as her skin prickled everywhere, like each hair follicle and pore yawned open and swallowed battery acid. Her right leg (the "good" one, as far as that could be said about any part of Osgood's body) throbbed, swollen, an overinflated inner tube, ready to burst at any moment. Pain was such an abstract concept to most people; a scraped knee, a headache that they say is a migraine without understanding the true horror of the word, a paper cut, maybe a broken bone on a ski trip that had confined them to the lodge. But Osgood knew from pain. There was nothing like the pain of a compound fracture or a gaping wound deep enough to see the gleam of bone. There was the ache of pain, the pulse of pain, the stab of pain, but something more atop it all. Pain at this level was heat, fire, an endless pulsing agony shooting through nerves right to the center of you.

Pain at this level was hell. Burning, boiling, rending, and eternal.

She could only see directly above her. Couldn't move. The world was a blur without her glasses, but she'd forgotten them enough in her life that she could fill in the visual gaps. A tiled drop ceiling, fluorescent tubes, a fire or carbon dioxide alarm, its LED blinking lazily. Sound emerged, quiet murmuring of conversations a room over or outside the door. The endless droning *beep beep beep* that Osgood realized matched her heart, causing it to *beep* faster. A suction *shush* matched by a release that repeated and repeated.

It's breathing for me, realized Osgood.

"Good morning!"

The voice belonged to a young man, perhaps. Cheerful, calm. He must not be surprised by the state she's in. He must have seen her before.

Osgood couldn't turn her head, and the breathing apparatus made speaking impossible, so she could only wait until the young man appeared above her. His hair was a little wild, short, and delicate light brown. He smiled, baby face only betraying his adulthood by a scratchy bit of a two to three-day-old beard. There was something in his eyes, though, that suggested age.

"Hi!" he said, in that tone that salesmen use, which says, "You're the most important person I'm meeting all day!" He waited a moment, sizing her up with his gaze. "Oh, don't worry about saying it back." He moved away. "Your heart rate is elevated, Prudence." Then he came back and leaned down. "Are you fucking someone in there?"

Osgood wanted to respond, to ask him what the fuck was happening, to demand answers, to—

"Become belligerent? Become pain-in-the-ass Prudence Osgood?" The young man smiled and put his hand on her shoulder. No, not put, *pressed,* a gesture that ignited a pain so searing she felt tears squeeze out and roll down her cheeks. "Oh my," he said, then leaned down and licked her right cheek. "Salty!"

She felt a growing horror in her stomach as he smiled at her. She couldn't move, and this man above her was going to... What? Rape her? No, his face said something different. He wasn't here for that. He was here—

"You'll never guess," he said, and moved away. She heard a sweep, and the air pressure in the room changed. She could feel it in her ears. The conversation beyond the room went quiet. He'd closed the door.

Osgood wondered if she could silence the pain in her head, drift away, disassociate. Could she go to the crossroads, her kingdom, here and now? Let this ... thing ... have his way.

"*Thing*?" he asked with a laugh, reappearing above her face and leaning close. Even his breath on her skin seared her flesh. "You have no idea what I am!" This pleased him immensely. Osgood thought she heard him titter. His eyes were vivid brown and seemed liquid; his irises moved, churned, an eddy swirling toward the black drain of pupils. "You're almost there...." He leaned closer. "Oh! Wait!" He let out an expulsive laugh, then disappeared, fumbling beside him. A drawer opened and closed.

He slid something onto her face, causing her temples to burn, catching and yanking out hair. The blurry image above her became clear; he'd returned her glasses. Seeing him, though, she realized that she didn't know him at all. His coat was white, and the name pinned to it seemed to be Dr. Castor. But Osgood's attention kept being drawn to the face she didn't recognize and that strange smile that seemed to strain him, the muscles in his jaw and cheeks throbbing. She saw his eyes weren't brown, but orange. They were fire. Orange like—

"You got this."

The eye in the sky, thought Osgood.

He snapped his fingers. "I thought it about time we became acquainted."

New tears rolled down Osgood's face. The eye in the sky; present in her life and dreams since her car accident decades ago. Sometimes a quasar, sometimes a black hole, sometimes an eddy of pure malice just out of sight, out of reach. But she always felt it, knew it was there. Watching. Waiting. Waiting for today, perhaps.

"Obviously, I'm more than an eye," he said.

He can hear my thoughts, Osgood realized.

"That's a bingo," he said.

Well then, thought Osgood, *you should know I have very little patience for guys like you.*

"Oh, why? Because patriarchy? Believe women? Hashtag metoo?" With that last one, he crossed each hand's index and middle fingers to make the hashtag. He laughed. "Shall we pretend I'm an incel? MAGA? What do you prefer? Who's your ghoul *du jour,* Pru?" He stared at her for a moment, not waiting for a response but seeming to consider his options, drawing the tip of his tongue over his lips in the simplest of gestures that seemed utterly obscene. Then his smile drew in as he pursed his lips. "I've got it." He called over his shoulder, "Alice, could you come in here?" He turned back to Osgood. "BRB." Then, his face was gone from her view.

Osgood felt relief, not from the agony as that was still very much present, but from the absence of that face. That simulacrum of humanity, hanging out in the uncanny valley just beyond the realm of reality. Her brain found it challenging to connect thoughts, and though a nagging idea of what was happening here attempted to take hold, she found herself pushing it away.

Can't ignore reality forever, her mother's voice told her. She knew that, of course, but *at* this moment, she had to focus *on* this moment. Unfortunately, that moment brought the pain back to the forefront, and she again wanted to scream until her voice gave out.

Just avoid it, she thought, *find a distraction.*

A distraction was provided by a freckled young woman, straw-colored hair framing a face that seemed to be primarily eyes.

"Are you alright?" asked Alice. The Pooh Bear characters on her scrubs suggested she belonged in the children's ward and was moonlighting wherever Osgood resided.

Osgood stared at her, wondering how the woman wanted her to respond, frozen with a respirator in her throat, after all.

It didn't take long for Alice's expression of concern to begin to sag away. What was first sincere and helpful drifted into a smile — *that* smile — as she leaned in. Her eyes flickered in a blink and became orange fire. "How's this for your patriarchy?" she asked.

Osgood understood. And it annoyed her. *A shapeshifter.*

"Nothing so pedestrian," said Alice. "I wear them like clothing."

Straightforward, thought Osgood.

"Why beat around the fucking bush at this point?" asked Alice. Her grin became a leer. "Unless that's what you want."

You've reached me at a bad time, and I think my pussy is closed at the moment.

Alice giggled. "Even through the pain, you are a treasure, Prudence."

Pain has been my companion longer than you have, thought Osgood.

"Ya sure about that?"

Then fill me in. Who are you?

"Ah, well..."

And none of that "I have so many names" bullshit.

"Fair enough," said Alice. "Call me Yoko."

Here to break up the Spectral Inspectors?

"Aww," said Yoko. "I thought that was your job."

You're the eye in the sky.

Yoko nodded.

And the quasar?

"One and the same."

Then I'll bite, thought Osgood. *The critical question isn't* who *you are but* what *you are.*

"Even that's pretty rote," said Yoko. "*What* I am is inconsequential. What matters is, *I am.*"

Are we implying we're God?

"Oh, Jehovah? The long-dead big G? Thankfully not," said Yoko. "Enough of this. It's not what I've come to talk with you about."

Oh good, thought Osgood. *Frankly, the conversation was becoming rather dull.*

"Ah, the perpetually petulant Prudence Osgood. You should be flattered, you know."

Should I?

"Of all the people in the world. No, of all the beings in the universe, in the outside..." Yoko trailed off, the grin leaving her face.

You picked me.

"No!" exclaimed Yoko. She reached up and drew her hand down Osgood's face in a caress that felt like coarse grit sandpaper. "I didn't have to pick you, you *are!*"

What the fuck does that mean?

"Something happened when you died, at that place you call crossroads. That moment sent out waves into the universe. Little bits, like breadcrumbs, drawing some of us toward this petty little planet from across the cosmic sea."

Bullshit.

"It's why *he* was there," said Yoko.

The Lord of the Hinterlands, thought Osgood. The being made of shimmering light and smoke who'd consumed dozens upon dozens of young people, including Audrey's sister, Caroline Frost.

"'Lord,'" Yoko scoffed. "Nothing but a borrowed title playing at borrowed importance in a borrowed tower on borrowed land."

Alright, thought Osgood. *So we're playing the power hierarchy game? Remember that thing you thought was big and scary? I'm bigger and more horrifying.*

Suddenly, Yoko coughed, then again and again, real hacking coughs that would make you cross the street to get away if you heard them out on a walk. Alice disappeared from view. When she returned, wiping her mouth, she looked ashen. "Let me cut to the chase."

Please do.

"I want you," said Yoko. Was that a bit of a plea in her voice?

You're moving a little fast there, Yoko.

"Please, be serious."

Why? This is absurd! You're a figment of my imagination. Probably because of the drug cocktail I'm on as I lie here in the hospital after— Osgood remembered all at once. The dancing fireflies. The subway car stopping

(crashing)

abruptly. Nora, bisected by glass. Osgood, thrown from the car onto the gravel below the tracks.

"What was that about fireflies?" asked Yoko. The grin had gone, and her face looked older and darker. Deadly serious.

I saw fireflies, a circle, a dance...

"An ... eye?" Yoko winked one of those flaming orange eyes at Osgood.

You caused the crash.

Yoko shrugged.

So you "want" me. I assume not for sex.

"It can be a delightful distraction," said Yoko, "but no."

Then you want to wear me? Like poor Alice here.

At the question, Alice seemed to have an orgasm right there. Her eyes rolled back; her mouth hung open. A long line of saliva dripped from between her teeth. Then Yoko snapped back. "Intensely," she growled.

Then why don't you?

Yoko's grin vanished, her eyes narrow, fury growing. She stood tall above Osgood, almost seeming to touch the ceiling, at least from this bizarre perspective. "Not going to make this easy, are you?"

Osgood wished she could laugh, but inside her head would have to do. *Sorry,* she thought.

"Alright," said Yoko through clenched teeth. She momentarily fumbled off to the side and brought up a long plastic tube.

And that is?

"Your life," said Yoko. She pinched the tube.

In an instant, Osgood couldn't breathe. Her chest locked up. No oxygen would come, nothing. She tried to reach out and scramble, to do something, but couldn't; she could only look into Yoko's flaming orange eyes burning in Alice's face. *Please!*

Yoko released the tube. Oxygen rushed back into Osgood, burning all the way, adding a whole new level to her pain. "So, listen, you stupid bitch..."

Wow, dropping all pretense now.

"You are in an awful position here," said Yoko wearing the Alice costume.

Seems like, Osgood conceded.

Alice walked away. Osgood heard a clatter and a crunch, then Alice returned holding a whiteboard that she must have yanked off the damned wall. "I want to make this crystal clear for you."

She held the whiteboard over Osgood's head. On it was written a doctor's name, a nurse's name, a date,

(March?!)

and then an acronym that horrified Osgood for reasons she couldn't understand.

Yoko tapped the acronym's letters as she said, "Locked-in syndrome." Her voice caused the words written on the board to become ferocious. She tossed the whiteboard away. "You've been here for four fucking months and haven't moved a muscle on your own." Yoko, speaking through Alice, sounded manic, a little feral.

No, no, no, no, pled Osgood, wishing, like Scrooge had, that this foul shade could sponge away the writing on that board and make it somehow not so.

Yoko took out Alice's cell phone. "I wish I knew her passcode; I'd—" A *click*. "Wow. Face unlock. It is astonishing what magic y'all have created and still find time to gripe about desert handymen."

Osgood didn't acknowledge. She found herself laser-focused on the words "locked-in syndrome." She'd only heard them in documentaries, maybe a made-for-TV movie. It was rare and horrifying. To be able to see, feel, and experience everything, but not communicate at all.

"Alright," said Yoko. "Looks like fewer than a thousand people in the US have or have had LIS. Mazel! And there are something like 300 million people in the US?" Yoko's fiery eyes went up and to the left. Calculating? "That's fucking *rare*. Well, you always thought you were special."

Why don't you just take me?

"Is that an offer?"

Panic rose in Osgood, but she couldn't do anything about it. She couldn't move at all. No fingertips, no mouth. All beholden to the breathing tube in—

"Prudence!" shouted Yoko, clapping her hands above Osgood's face. "Stay with me."

No. Osgood felt her defiance rising. *No, I'm not offering.*

Yoko sighed. "Well," she said. "My shift is almost up."

What does that mean?

"We're going to try plan B."

What does that *mean?*

"I want you to know I tried the easy way," said Yoko, leaning down until her lips nearly touched Osgood's eyes. "And that you shouldn't get too comfortable. All alerts stop if I disconnect the machines from the nursing station. I could do *anything* I wanted to you."

Ah, the rape threat.

"Is everything about your quim, Pru?" asked Yoko. Her tone felt playful, but her face didn't match. "Because I could kill you. For real. Forever." Yoko moved to Osgood's ear. "You know that you've always kinda wanted that. You put that semicolon on your wrist," Yoko tapped, and Osgood felt but couldn't see, "and you say it's to show that you're a survivor, but really, it's a target. So when you look down at it, you know that you could dig that X-ACTO knife you keep in your desk right into those scars and trace that T all the way down." The word "down" dragged on as though Yoko was stuck on it. Alice's chin hit her chest, and that seemed to snap the thing inside her back.

More tears ran down Osgood's cheeks.

Yoko produced a syringe and stuck it into Osgood's hanging IV bag. As she did it, her head twitched violently.

What's that? asked Osgood of the liquid making its way into her body.

But the world was already growing swimmy, the view above her narrowing, narrowing, narrowing, like the iris closing at the end of a silent film. The world grew dark. *No, please...* Osgood begged. She knew what lurked in the dark.

"You may be hard to kill, Prudence Osgood," said Yoko as Osgood drifted away. "But you can still fucking die."

Two

"THERE'S A LOT TO that question," says Osgood. "Are you sure you wanna hear it?"

He nods.

"Alright. I'll be honest, things have fucking sucked." Prudence Osgood sucks the dregs of a Bahama Mama through her straw and then considers. "Well, I was gonna say the last couple of years, but..."

Virgil, across the bar, wipes a glass and nods at her. The benevolent blankness of his face makes him a perfect bartender, the kind of face you can look into and say literally anything without fear of judgment. Why? Because Virgil will understand. She felt terrible about ribbing him for his name when they met, her first evening on The Isle. "My mother was a poet," he'd intoned solemnly, then winked.

"A good deal of my life has sucked." Osgood slides the glass across the varnished cut-bamboo bar.

Virgil takes the glass with one hand and replaces it with another in a flash and a wink of one rich caramel-brown eye. Osgood grins at him. He returns to wiping glasses with his cloth.

"Once upon a time, I died," she says. She shuffles on the stool, switching from one ass cheek to the other as today her body has decided she'll find no comfort in sitting. The thin fabric of her bikini bottoms slides up the crack of her ass, and it takes every iota of self-control to not go digging in the canyon for it.

Nice girls don't pick their behinds, her mother's voice reminds her.

"Eight and a half minutes, I was dead. Car crash. I was only 19. I met, well ... something ... in the dark. I still don't know if he... if *it* was a demon, a demigod, or something else we may not have a name for. I was halfway to the morgue when I woke up in that body bag. Zipped over my face and everything. They said I terrified the EMTs. Can you imagine?"

Virgil's face suggests that he can't, in fact, imagine.

"I clawed my way out of that bag. The boy, or man, I guess, attending my body, fainted right there in the ambulance. The woman screamed. The driver swerved and nearly crashed. Yeah, I was almost in a *second crash* the night I died. God knows how I could move enough to get the zipper down... So much of my body's been broken. Spinal fractures, pelvic fractures, broken legs. A crack in my fucking skull. You used to be able to see the scar under my hairline," she leans forward, pulling at the neon green curls on the right side of her head. "But now my only skull scar is from when I had a brain tumor removed." A tap on the crown of her head indicates where Virgil could find that scar should he be so motivated ... or so close.

Her new Bahama Mama is icy, crystalizing cold, and Osgood relishes it. She sighs for a moment, taking in the breeze, the heat. The Isle is the perfect temperature. That temperature and humidity where you almost don't feel any difference between your body and the world. Not so hot you're sweaty, nor so cold you need to bundle. She's topless, as The Isle allows "all the nudity you like." She'd be naked but is unsure how the humans she might want to fuck would feel about her 19s bush. She wonders if Virgil has checked out her tits yet. Surely, when he slid the drink across the bar. They're not subtle, after all.

"There was rehab and surgeries, and I got *a little* bit better, but not a day has gone by since then that I haven't felt that accident in some way. Twenty-six years." She raises her glass, and Virgil dips his head in return. "I walk with a cane when it's bad. At least then, people can *see* my 'infirmity.' Otherwise, I look normal, and they'll say, 'Oh, you should take some Aleve or something,' or 'Have you tried CBD?' As though the only reason I wasn't feeling perfect was I hadn't done any fucking research. They're trying to be helpful, I know. But it's so fucking insulting. Worse is when you can tell they don't quite believe your pain. Bosses are like that.

"That's the one way I'm lucky, I guess. I haven't had a real boss in maybe five years. No longer have to explain that sometimes I simply *can't* come in and fuck you for not reading the HR file about Prudence Osgood's chronic misery." She knocks her knuckles against the bartop. "I betrayed the love of my life. I don't know if you've ever done anything monumentally stupid that made someone you care about give you that 'I can't trust you ever again' look, but... I still see it. Audrey's face. When that stupid special effect almost killed her. Ruined our relationship. Our partnership. Our show. My reputation. Jesus. I'll tell you what, Virgil. I may be a pretty mediocre person in general, but I will work my pale, pimpled ass off to *never* hurt her like that again. She did give me another chance. It took a decade, but still. She didn't have to. No one had to."

Osgood wishes Audrey was here with her, on the seat next to hers, just so she could turn and look into her beloved's blue eyes. She's sure they'd match the color of the sky and the water down here in the Tropic of Cancer.

"We found out what happened to her sister. But we kinda..." How does one explain this to a layperson? Layperson nothing, a *normal* human. "In the process, we went someplace ... other. And that thing I mentioned, the thing I met at the crossroads when I died, was there, and it poked a hole in me." She taps her chest between her tits. Virgil's burnt sienna eyes acknowledge but don't linger. Such a professional. "And I fell into that hole. A hole in the world. For fifteen months. I wish I could better explain that, but I can't. The mercy is that I don't remember much from my time there, so I guess those fifteen months were worse for my friends than for me. But the me that came back out..." Osgood laughs. "Well, the me that came back out had a brain tumor. Have you heard of a teratoma?"

Virgil hasn't.

"Don't google it. But that's what it was. I'd also been gifted a gateway from the realm of monsters. I fucked an old friend. Well, he was once a lover. An important one, too. And just as I was cumming," she laughs again at the absurdity, "a *monster* came out of my chest. There really is no other way to put that. And whatever ridiculous thing you've conjured in your head at the word 'monster,' I assure you that the thing that emerged from me was even more ridiculous than that. And that *thing* consumed him ... or inhabited him."

(wore him like clothing)

Osgood stops, unable to place the thought. It draws her focus, but only for a moment before she again smiles at Virgil and continues. "Whatever it did turned *him* into a monster. One that had to be stopped. And not to belabor the point... He died. And he never would've been in that situation without me."

Osgood stops for a moment and looks into her drink. Bits of muddled mango float like orange juice pulp, spinning in an eddy that she must've created with her straw. She doesn't look over, down the bar, because she knows, without question, that if she does, Sam Goddard will be sitting there, most certainly dead, his head lolling and his martyr eyes looking up at her. She clears her throat and changes the subject. "I got Covid, of course. Twice. My immune system didn't stand a chance. Even got the bonus Long Covid booby prize. As if I wasn't tired enough already! As if my brain functioned regularly above the median. Then a particularly difficult case that made me do this..." She shows Virgil her left wrist, displaying the raised, jagged scar left over from the night she beheaded a statue and nearly took her hand off. "Well, after that, my ... well, she wasn't my girlfriend at that point. Someone special? She died. Another accident. This one..."

She waits, wondering if Virgil will chime in. Opine. But he doesn't. So she laughs and raises her drink. "Well, let's just say it's shocking I survived it."

Virgil smiles at that. The same bare smile that feels warm and friendly, but Osgood knows is a mask he wears for visitors on The Isle. People confide any number of things to this man, she knows, and his job is to reflect back the island ethos of relaxation without judgment. That in itself is some kind of absolution or forgiveness, isn't it? With his absurd ancient name, Virgil is here to let them know that all is well, that they are forgiven of their sins, and that they can step outside themselves. Let others take the proverbial wheel. When Virgil swaps out her depleted glass again for a new drink, Osgood feels a delightful tipsy swimminess. The filing down of pain lines, rounding them off, making them less likely to snag on something. Forcing that relaxation, no matter how unwilling her body might be. The very idea of relaxation is foreign to Osgood. Downtime has always been marked either in the hospital, on bed rest, or, hell, blacked out from booze or any number of extracurricular drugs. Even when movement is excruciating, she finds sitting still tricky, and not only because of the pain that holds dominion over nearly every bit of her body.

Realizing that Virgil's job is not to converse but absorb, and Osgood has astonishingly run low on woes, she gives the bartender a smile and wink (both of which he returns) and slides off the bar stool, turning away toward the boardwalk that skirts the beach on The Isle. The dark wood planks give way to brilliant white powder, the type of sand she thought only existed in brochures and magazines. But, no, The Isle offers both white sand beaches and warm turquoise water, which grows to cerulean and azure as it moves further from the surf before reaching that glorious phthalo blue that Bob Ross used to adore. She stands at the rail and looks across the sea. A tiny thought hovers in her margins, like a gnat buzzing around her ear. It's little more than a hum, without context or content, slipping into the background, though occasionally it gets close enough. Osgood closes her eyes and breathes in through the nose, out through the mouth. In through the nose, out through the mouth. The gnat quiets.

She opens her eyes again, squinting at the blazing orange sun hanging over the horizon, its brilliance reflected in the water beneath, which has begun to cast The Isle's white stucco buildings in similar tones. Even knowing that it's Sol, Earth's very own star, she feels uncomfortable as its color blazes deeper, reminding her of the horrid red sun that held dominion over the sky of the Hinterlands. She turns away with a shiver as the ocean breeze draws up goose pimples on her arms and tits.

A ways down along the boardwalk walks a couple sporting a tan from many days on The Isle. Both wear swimsuits: him, bright orange board shorts, and her, a navy bikini adorned with matching orange polka dots. Osgood takes a breath and drops her bottoms; nothing ventured, after all. She wonders if she can get them both to go rubbernecking as they walk by. They near, both of them almost inhumanly attractive. He's tall with broad shoulders and arms that are toned but not overtly muscular. Even though her preference for men usually trends toward twink, Osgood's ancient lizard brain awakens. The woman fits her type. One of her types, anyway. Although, Osgood wonders if she really has a type. Often "wants to fuck me" is her type.

Also muscular and toned, the woman is sharp featured with thin lips that seem to be in perpetual smirk mode. Osgood definitely catches the man's attention, and it comes with a wink. The woman is more of a mystery, and as they move past, they seem to move into flirty conversation with each other.

She hears a rustle in the underbrush, and a small orange cat oozes into view. It regards Osgood with dispassionate feline eyes, gives her a single *mrow* of acknowledgment, then darts down the path and around the corner as though late for a very important date, as a rabbit was once upon a time. Osgood sighs. Animals have never been very fond of her.

She gives the water a last look, the burning sun nearing the horizon now. Soon it'll be dark, and the sky will be spatter painted with stars, showing a depth to the universe that, at once, excites and deeply frightens her. The constellations will be familiar, of that she's (nearly) certain, and she can lie on a beach chair and look up, perhaps seeing a meteor or two. A shower is starting this week, after all. Perseids. Geminids? She can't remember. She knows that one dominates winter and the other summer, so she *should* know which is which, right?

She shakes her head and turns from the boardwalk's rail; her crimson bikini bottoms hang off a crooked pointer finger. With unearned confidence, she throws them over her shoulder to dangle like Sinatra's coat, then swaggers as best as possible up the path toward her bungalow between the overgrown trees. The individual buildings are squat and simple, built close together but not touching, long enough along the water that they all had their own personal view. Her bungalow is on an end flanked by a path, number 312, same as the prefix for her family's first phone number in their Chicago home where she'd spent her childhood. One path leads from the beach, the other to the pool, with a branch off shortly before the restaurants.

Steak tonight, she thinks. *Bloody as they'll allow.* When life gives you steak, you eat steak, and when life gives you an all-inclusive resort, well, you suck the marrow from life's bones.

The bracelet she'd received on arrival, a beaded thing that looks fancier than any she's ever worn, has an NFC chip embedded that unlocks her door with a swipe of her hand across the panel. She regards it as magic but is sure that if Zack were here, he'd go into why it's all straightforward and mundane. Inside the bungalow, white marble flooring leads to a white platform topped with a white mattress clad in white sheets and a white comforter flanked by sheer white curtains tied to white columns. When Osgood first opened the door — Had that been this morning? Yesterday? She can't remember — her first thought had been how easily the entire setup would stain. Immediately after, she'd wanted to order a bottle of something red. A nice Barbera. A big Amarone. Something full-bodied. She sees that the bed has been made inside the dim room, and a towel animal sits atop it. She cocks her head and stares but can't resolve what on earth it's supposed to be. The *third* googly eye adds to the mystery.

As she steps forward, her bare big toe hits a folded piece of paper. Osgood reaches down and plucks it up with crimson fingernails that match her swimsuit. It's a piece of The Isle's stationery folded in two. Osgood had giggled when she first saw the stationary bearing The Isle's logo, which looked like an alien smiley face emoji. The woman who'd checked her in had told her its meaning, but she couldn't remember what it was. Just now, she's distracted. Because upon unfolding the note, she sees words written below that logo. She knows the handwriting in an instant. She's seen it throughout her life, of course, on notes both happy and not, on an angry "Don't contact me" note slipped under her door once, on a Christmas card that said how glad she was that Osgood was in her life again. On everything.

Because Audrey is everything to Osgood. And this note, written by Audrey Frost, concerns her.

"'We need you,'" Osgood reads aloud, then traces her finger over the letters, inked in blue pen, and watches as a small trail of blue smudges across the page. She rereads it to herself. Then again, aloud. While it's nice to feel needed, it seems an odd sentiment while she's on vacation. She never goes on vacation, after all. It's also strange that the ink is somehow still wet. And odd that Audrey's somehow gotten this stationery and sent a personally written note to the resort almost fifteen hundred miles from Chicago... All of these oddities concern Osgood. But what concerns her most is the sudden ache in her chest upon reading it, the ache in the area between her breasts where that deity or demigod had punched a hole in her. It throbs in a way it hasn't for years.

And the three simple words on that note, written in a steady hand, hint at desperation.

At once, Prudence Osgood is afraid.

THREE

O SGOOD STARES AT HER phone, something she hasn't done since she arrived on The Isle — however long ago that'd been — but sees no new messages. The reason, of course, could be the empty triangle at the top. No bars. No signal. She turns on wifi, and while she sees one named **The Isle**, she has no idea what the password might be. She sighs, tries *fuck me*, then sighs again when she's denied access. Her performance is awfully theatrical, considering she sits alone in her room, and the sound echoes off the marble floor and the stucco walls. She throws the phone on the white linen of the bed behind her and looks again at the note.

We need you.

Audrey isn't one to throw that sort of statement around lightly. She doesn't believe in needing people, as needing is a desperate act (a sentiment she shares with Osgood), and thinks *choosing* and *wanting* people is far more essential. So, in this note, Osgood senses urgency even without an exclamation point. Osgood sighs again, then stands. Fuck it. She'll go to the lobby. Find out the wifi password. Figure this whole thing out.

She snatches a wrap covered in gigantic hibiscus blooms and wraps herself in it, momentarily proud of her ability to origami the sarong into a workable piece of clothing. The Isle may be permissive, but no nudity is allowed in the lobby.

On The Isle, said lobby looms over a courtyard: a two-floor structure of glass, stucco, and thatch with sliding doors that open as soon as you near them, blasting the chill of the lobby's air conditioner out into the courtyard. The rare internal voice of her father asks, *Are we trying to air condition the whole resort?* Osgood enters, her bare feet chilly against the off-white marble flooring. The faintest background music plays inside, a steel drum rendition of The Beach Boys' *Kokomo*, a song that always struck her as sad, like nostalgia for something, someplace, that never really existed. The music may as well be blaring, though, as the lobby is devoid of life and otherwise silent as the grave. The mirrored wall behind the front desk reflects a screensaver back at her. That same smiley logo for The Isle bounces around the screen.

Above that reflection is her own. She's momentarily surprised by herself. Why? She looks rested for a change. Her hair, curly on the right and buzzed on the left, looks professionally done, with layers and tone shifts in the neon greens, not just a single layer of rapidly fading Manic Panic. *I'm hot!* she thinks. Osgood snickers to herself, forgetting everything else for a moment. But she can't forget for long. The note intrudes back into her momentary reverie. *We need you.*

"Hello?" she asks. Her voice echoes off the marble of the lobby.

No answer.

She scowls. Where was the customer service here? However, she supposes that few people want to enter the lobby during their trip. Have to put on clothes after all. The doors have a sign asking, "Did You Remember to Dress?" a sentiment she's sure is on all the doors of Valentine Michael Smith's ... commune? cult? ... in *Stranger in a Strange Land*. Osgood sees a bell tucked behind an advertisement for a massage service and smacks it. The ring echoes around the space, and a woman appears, hair black, skin tan, smile warm, and eyes ... beguiling.

The name tag pinned to her crisp white polo introduces her as Maria. Osgood immediately smiles back, a reflex without thought.

"*¡Hola!*" says Maria.

Osgood repeats it, though feels mildly embarrassed by her use of Spanish. How many tourists come here with the barest understanding of a handful of Spanish words and try to make them their vocabulary for the week? Surely, it must annoy the staff.

"How can I help you, *Señorita* Osgood?"

"Just—" begins Osgood, a reflexive response to being addressed as anything but her last name and overall distaste for gendered honorifics, but she surprises herself by letting it go. "My phone has no signal."

"*Sí,*" says Maria. "Our cell signals go in and out."

"And right now..."

"They are out." Maria smiles again, winking one of her gorgeous brown eyes and flashing two rows of perfect teeth in a grin.

Osgood nods. "And the wifi is—"

"Working perfectly," finishes Maria.

A laugh escapes Osgood. She wonders where it came from but knows that she feels calm. Relaxed. She almost can't think of the reason for her concern anymore. She looks down at her hands, both empty. Why had she come here? Oh, yes. "Password!"

"Simple! *The Isle.* Capital T, capital I."

Osgood confirms. "The wifi name is..."

"*The Isle.* Capital T, capital I."

"And the password is the same."

Maria nods, continuing to smile. Osgood mirrors it back again, though she reflexively covers her teeth with her lips to keep from showing her own, yellowed by age, smoking, and, let's be honest, neglect. They stand silently, smiling at each other, until Osgood grows self-conscious and thanks the woman.

"Can I help you with anything else, *Señorita*?"

Osgood can't think of a single thing. She looks toward the deep teal-tinted glass doors, knowing that not far beyond them, the ocean lazily laps at the white shore. She sighs. Comfort. Such a rare sensation for Prudence Osgood, but here it is. Why is she trying so hard to connect with someone outside this place?

We need you.

Right! It isn't just *someone*; it's Audrey. And the "we" means Zack as well. Essential. That's what he is. As much as it might upend her comfort here on The Isle, she does need to connect with those back home. Maybe it'll be as simple as, "Don't run away to a beach somewhere for good, Pru, we need you!" and she can assure them that she is indeed (if unfortunately) returning home once this trip ends on... Well, when it ends, at least. When Osgood turns back to Maria, she finds the lobby empty once again. Osgood puffs out a small laugh. She didn't even hear the woman leave.

Osgood hears a rumble, and a fresh breeze of cool, scented air blushes over her. Nearly every indoor space on The Isle smells the same. She can't place the scent, but she's sure it comes in a bottle that they pump into some massive diffuser somewhere on the property. Whatever it is, it brings her a profound calm. She wonders if she could get a bottle for the apartment on Clark Street. Not that the wafting scents of Mary's burgers coming up from below don't please her greatly. It's more in the late evenings to overnights when that smell turns to rancid leftover French fries that have been boiling in grease all afternoon. That's when she could use this. She closes her eyes and breathes deeply, and the less-desired scents of Mary's Diner and Bar vanish, replaced by *The Scent of The Isle*™. Osgood honest-to-god grins from ear to ear, surprising even herself.

"You seem thrilled."

The voice startles her so much she shoves herself backward, her eyes still closed. She collides with a table and opens her eyes just in time to see a massive pot crash to the floor, sending dirt, peat, and a handful of gorgeous pink and white orchids across the marble. "Oh, fuck."

"I'm sorry, I didn't mean to—"

She turns, surprised to find the man from earlier, the handsome one from the couple, standing before her in only his board shorts, chest gleaming with the finest layer of sweat. His hair is effortlessly styled. There's a day or two's growth of fine light brown hair on his cheeks and chin, and she immediately notices the shorter hairs around his neckline and upper cheeks. This beard is styled to be "unshaven." He takes her arm in his hand, not hard, just support-ing, perhaps to ensure she won't fall atop those orchids. She looks back at them and, for a moment, doesn't see flowers. Instead, she sees ... things. Creatures. They roil in the dirt, leaving streaks as they push their petals across the floor, dragging themselves toward her. They want her, don't they? Because she knows what they are. The babies of that horrid thing that had climbed from her chest and consumed the humanity of Sam Goddard in the Heartland Motel on Peterson Avenue one winter that seemed like ages ago.

"Are you alright?" ask the man.

Osgood blinks at the absurd question. No, she isn't alright. She knocked over a pot of monsters, and now here they come! But of course, they don't. They aren't. After all, they're only orchids. "Oh," says Osgood. She turns to him. "I just got a little..." What? Light-headed? Blown away by how attractive he is? Sure, he'd like that line.

Judging by the pitch of his board shorts, though, Prudence Osgood doesn't need a line.

Maria's reappearance with a broom and dustpan breaks the silence. Despite Osgood's protestations, Maria assures them that she doesn't need help, that this isn't a big deal, and, absurdly, that this "happens all the time."

"Why don't we get out of her way?" suggests the man. His smile gleams in the way that only someone who's won the enamel lottery can.

Osgood covers her smile with her lips again.

Near the courtyard fountain, an abstract creation of marble and cascading water, she encounters the woman, sitting in a plastic rattan chair next to a plastic rattan couch, resting her feet and drink on a plastic rattan coffee table. The woman looks up at Osgood and smiles, flashing deep brown eyes and a smile so beautiful Osgood wonders if she'll again be knocked off her feet. The man sits on the arm of the chair, and both halves of the couple seem to wait for her.

For what? wonders Osgood. *To make a move?* She's not sure she even has a move in her; these two beguile her so.

"Hi," says the woman in a voice deep and velvety, like Kathleen Turner as Jessica Rabbit. Osgood's heart skips a beat. But it's the throb of her pussy that gets her attention more. Sure, the man is hot. But ... that woman. That voice. Osgood notices that the woman's bikini bottoms again match the man's board shorts, and her bare chest matches his glistening sheen. They're both perfectly tan from head to toe, clearly from hours of careful toning in the sun.

"Osgood," says Osgood.

"Excuse me?" asks the woman with a laugh.

"That's me," says Osgood. She coughs, trying to sound nonchalant. "Osgood."

"Hello, Osgood," says the man.

"Or Os," says Osgood.

"Os," says the woman with a smile. "I'm Rebecca, and my husband, who can't take his eyes off you, is Simon."

"Oh, he, uh..." Osgood looks at Simon, who gazes at her with a lustful hunger that excites and frightens her. How long has it been since she'd had sex? A while, certainly. Car masturbation with Dr. Ramona Yeagher doesn't count, either. "I hadn't noticed."

"Well," says Rebecca, "We both know that's not true. Don't worry, though, we're open."

Aha, thinks Osgood. *Open. That word that the normies use to indicate that they'd enjoy a threesome.* But why judge this? This is a hot AF couple who seem *really* into her. And here in paradise, without a care in the world, why on Earth would she turn that down? So she cocks an eyebrow. "Oh really?" she asks rhetorically as she pulls one loop of the knot in her sarong, causing it to unravel and drop to the polished cement ground. Standing nude before them, she looks directly into Rebecca's deep umber eyes. This is Osgood challenging them, of course. Asking, *Can you handle me?* without speaking.

But what she sees in those eyes frightens her a little. The hunger for sex, the lust, yeah, but within it a yearning, the kind Osgood is sure she must project when she looks at Audrey but has rarely seen directed at herself.

"How would you like to see our villa," proposes Simon, moving behind Osgood and putting his hands on her upper arms. His palms and fingers are both soft and not warm, but hot, though Osgood knows she always runs cold. She reaches up and puts her pale right hand atop his, squeezing it. Looking back to Rebecca, she finds that there's little she wants more than to see their villa. Perhaps there's little she's *ever* wanted more.

As the trio walks a palm-lined path to the other side of The Isle, Osgood has a fleeting thought that she'd left her room for a specific purpose.

Oh well, surely it doesn't matter as much as this...

Four

R EBECCA TURNS TO OSGOOD at the door of their villa and smiles, beckoning her with a perfectly manicured crimson fingernail. Osgood again sees the hunger in the woman's eyes and feels helpless to resist it, stepping out of Simon's hands and up to Rebecca, nude, save her bikini bottoms. She reaches out both arms, resting them momentarily on Osgood's shoulders, which causes Osgood to realize that they're nearly the same height — quite a feat as she stands 6-foot sans shoes. The woman turns her hands and finds the almost bare nape of Osgood's neck, then slides into the bushy thatch of curls she'd dyed bright green just before

(when?)

she got here.

A sudden tug at the roots causes Osgood's eyes to roll back and a tuning fork to sound all through her body. Someone knows the buttons to push. When she refocuses her eyes on Rebecca's, the woman wears a mischievous smirk. Osgood hungrily dives into a kiss that Rebecca returns. As a general habit, Osgood doesn't linger on kisses in encounters with people she doesn't know well. In fact, only Audrey's lips hold enough sway over Osgood to keep her focused there for an extended period. She always figures there's so much to do and so little time. And if you kiss strangers too much up front, sometimes they want to kiss you again after licking your asshole. But as she presses her face into Rebecca's, their tongues mingling back and forth like a fencing match, she feels a desire to devour this woman in every way she can. She slides her hands down Rebecca's back and into her bikini, taking whole handfuls of ass. Then the fabric pulls away, and Osgood notices Simon sliding it down Rebecca's legs.

"Thought I'd help," he says.

"Thank you, my love," says Rebecca. She holds Osgood at arm's length, fixing her with an appraising look that lasts long enough for Osgood's discomfort levels to rise. "I think, Simon," she begins, without looking away from Osgood, "I'd like some time just for her and me."

"As it pleases you, my love," says Simon.

Internally, Osgood rolls her eyes at the pet names and repetition, but she's surprised she feels more wistful than annoyed. If only. She can count on one hand the number of people who've had pet names for her and on two fingers the number who'd called her their *love*. Most people see her as hard or abrasive, she knows, but would it be so bad?

Rebecca pulls Osgood close with one arm until her lips tickle Osgood's ear, and Rebecca's warm breath causes shivers down her spine. "I want to fuck you until you forget who you are," whispers the woman.

"I. Yes. Also. That. I want." Osgood whispers back, cringing at her sudden inability to string together a coherent sentence. She feels Rebecca's hyperbolic statement pinging at the actual truth lurking just below Prudence Osgood's surface.

Do you have to be so ... you?

No one has ever actually asked her that question. "So queer," yes. "So difficult," also. Still, many have implied or outright said that Osgood's "Osgoodness" is a primary cause of their pain, drama, heartache, disappointment, and enough other awful things she can't count them.

"You have a lot of stuff," Rebecca says as she leads Osgood up the stairs to the bedroom loft.

Osgood nods, feeling déjà vu, but she can't place it. Instead, she agrees with the word: "Stuff."

"Maybe we can erase some of that."

They reach the upper level, and the enormous picture windows lining one wall of the villa cast the brilliant midday sun into the room. Somehow, the linens and fixtures here seem even whiter than in Osgood's room. She notices a toy spread on a table along one wall. Accoutrements galore.

Wait, thinks Osgood. A tiny voice within her. A voice shouting to get her attention. Osgood believes she knows what it is. The bitter, uncomfortable truth. She can never erase her "stuff," only work through it. To erase it would be to lose a part of herself. While she's sure some people in her life would be thrilled for her to, at the very least, sand down her edges a bit, she's spent 45 years crafting this human called Osgood, and while she rarely likes her, she's more than comfortable being her.

The pain! exclaims that tiny voice. Osgood hushes it. The pain isn't overt today, so why on earth would she want to focus on it? Especially as Rebecca sits on the bed and traces fingernails up and down Osgood's sides as she stands nude before her. A ripple of gooseflesh moves across her, and she giggles. At the sound, she presses her hand to her mouth, feeling the heat of embarrassment in her cheeks. That embarrassment moves to pleasure as Rebecca's hands pull Osgood's pelvis forward, and her tongue parts Osgood's lips.

The first wave of pleasure is intense, extreme, and all at once, Osgood feels like a 16-year-old boy touching a boob for the first time and loosing a geyser of jizz inside his tighty whities. But her orgasm doesn't drown Rebecca, thankfully, only encourages the woman whose tongue winds its way farther inside.

We need you.

"I want to put my hand in you," says Rebecca, muffled by bush and labia.

"Alright," says Osgood, head tilted back, her fingers in Rebecca's hair.

"Wear you like a puppet."

"What did you say?" Osgood looks down at the woman, her extraordinary eyes peering through the patch of bush suggest she's smiling. Osgood is about to ask again when Rebecca's tongue is joined by a finger, then two. The shivers return, and Osgood's legs threaten to strike, but Rebecca guides her to the bed, where she flops without breaking the connection.

On the ceiling above Osgood hangs a nearly six-foot wide round mirror, framed with ornate festoonery, likely plaster but meant to look like marble. She sees the wildness of her green curls spread out on the blinding white duvet, her right hand gripping the linens above her head, her left hand in Rebecca's hair. As she watches, she sees herself orgasm before she feels it, and then the waves come crashing over and over.

"Aaand five," says Rebecca. She leans back to meet Osgood's eyes in the mirror on the ceiling. Her hand has vanished inside Osgood's lower half. "I'm wearing you."

"...like clothing," finishes Osgood. Then she lifts her head up and meets Rebecca's eyes in real life. Osgood's about to say more, to... What? Protest? ...when Simon appears behind them, nude, his cock jutting straight out like the literal eggplant that inspired the emoji.

Osgood's eyes widen at the sight, and she's completely forgotten what she wanted to say.

"How are we doing?" asks Simon.

Rebecca turns to her man with mischief on her face. "I think she may be ready to—"

"Fuck me!" says Osgood, at once an exclamation at the sheer size of Simon's member and a request to the man, who climbs atop her and obliges.

That little voice inside her reminds her of the note and points out the odd familiarity of the phrase "wear like clothing," but Osgood ignores it, shoving it deep within, covering its face with a pillow, and snuffing it right the fuck out. Because that voice doesn't matter, does it? Nothing before or since, either. Only The Isle matters. Only The Isle can satisfy her. Only The Isle will consume her thoughts. Only The Isle can give Osgood what she wants. What she's always wanted. Unconditional affection and acceptance. The ability to live her queer-do life out and about without question.

As Simon's grunting and thrusting become manic and he explodes within her, Osgood realizes something profound.

The Isle *is* home.

FIVE

O SGOOD AWAKENS WITH A start.

The world around her is dark, but turning her head to the left, she sees a crescent moon hanging above the horizon through the wall of windows, casting a shimmering smear of white across the dark waters. In the deep purple-blue of the sky, the moon illuminates puffs of clouds. The sounds of the world, of The Isle, return to her, and she hears wind rustling through palm fronds, rattan roofs, and waves lapping at the shore. The rest is oddly quiet. Sitting up, she sees the barest phantom of a room come into focus. The loft bedroom of the villa belonging to Simon and Rebecca, now empty, save her.

"Maybe they went to get dinner," she suggests to herself in a voice that seems entirely too loud.

Like a baby deer, Osgood rises on shaky legs, stabilizing herself by grabbing first the bed, then the wardrobe, then the staircase railing. She wonders where her cane is. Back in the room?

Had she even brought it to The Isle?

But this unsteady gait isn't due to the usual suspects. The familiar pains in her legs are quiet. No, this is a bit of freshly-fucked disorientation. After all, she'd been fisted and then fucked by a dick the size of her arm. Shaky legs are to be expected. But why didn't Simon and Rebecca wake her if they wanted to get dinner? And more importantly, when had she fallen asleep? Osgood's cheeks redden. Had she really been so overwhelmed with an orgasm that it knocked her out cold? Nah, she must have a smidge of the brain scramblies. It wouldn't be the first time Osgood had a reel missing from her memory. Usually, she could chalk the gap up to drink, but she doesn't think that's the case this time.

Holding the brass banister with both hands, she squeaks her way down to the first floor, finding it just as dark and barren as the upper. A peek at the table offers a pad of The Isle's stationery. The alien smiley logo seems to leer. She stands, staring at that pad and logo, and can almost see other words scrawled out on it. Words that exist on a different sheet of this paper, on a sheet back in her bungalow, are only locked in quantum entanglement here.

She looks out of the massive picture windows that reveal a private hot tub and pool, both glimmering aqua, illuminated from below by large saucers of light. Beyond the tub and the infinity pool's termination at a glass wall barrier are the sand and the sea. The crescent moon seems to have adjusted its positioning, now looking like the luminous grin of the Cheshire Cat sans cat. She walks to the sliding doors and presses first her palms, then her forehead against the cool glass. As she breathes, the glass fogs and clears. She holds it for a moment, looking closer at the

(wine-dark)

sea.

Osgood pulls her forehead from the glass, noting with a mild sense of shame that the oils in her skin have left a print. But that shame is short-lived as she parses the interjection, unaware of where or whom it had come from. She remembers listening to Albrecht once, in the days just after he'd been her professor, three sheets to the wind as usual, bloviating about the notion that colors were perceived differently in the time of the ancient Greeks, *i.e.*, Homer mentioning a "wine-dark sea" in his epic works wasn't referring to a sea that was actually red, but to different ideas of color. As she hadn't been as deep into the bourbon as her old professor, the idea hadn't interested her much nor made much sense. But here, looking at a wine-dark yet intensely blue sea, she understands, and it makes her intensely uncomfortable.

She notices something on the horizon, lit only by the scant light of that leering moon. A structure. A boat, perhaps? But why no lights? It appears both very close and massive and small and far away at the same time. The domed roof is familiar, like a building she first saw when barbecuing on the peninsula that led to it — the Adler Planetarium, back in Chicago. Young Prudence had stared up at the dome, fascinated, while her father tried desperately not to overcook the burgers.

"That's the sky theater," said Basil Osgood when she'd asked him about it. "That's where we'll tour the universe without ever leaving the city." He'd stood, looking at it with her for a moment, then returned to his small Weber grill, which had started to smoke.

Little Prudence had been overcome by some of the first stirrings of existential dread in her young life. She'd wondered how vast the universe might be and how much could be seen from within that building.

A knock at the door of the villa distracts her. She fumbles around, looking for her clothes, but ultimately isn't sure she'd worn any there. The knock's second triple rap is louder. "I'm coming," she calls, unable to hide the annoyance in her voice. Not her villa, after all; why should she answer the door? On the first attempt, she's stymied by the bar lock. The question of how her recent fuck buddies left the room with it locked from within appears in her mind, but it can't gain purchase and is gone just as quickly.

When she finally opens the villa door, she's greeted by ... nothing. Ahead of her are large leaves from the greenery surrounding the villas, and the cobblestone path leading to the left and right is devoid of life. She purses her lips, her growing annoyance pushing away the existential dread that seems desperate to take hold within her gut. She leans back inside but pauses before closing the door.

"That's interesting," says Osgood, noting that the room number is three identical zeroes. She's sure it wasn't that when she got to this villa, and anyway, what kind of resort would have a zero room?

Finally, the dread begins to catch up to her.

Six

Prudence Osgood strolls along the concrete path, formed to mimic cobblestones, that bisects The Isle, certain she should be more concerned. After all, this is a resort that had been full of people just hours ago. People like the gorgeous couple Simon and Rebecca, who'd fucked her senseless. But now, on the path, at the pool, around every hidden corner, she finds no one.

The *shuuuush* of the waves blends with warm breezes blushing through the palm tree fronds and the grass roofs. Below it is a nondescript thumping beat from speakers far away, a place Osgood is nearly confident she'll never reach. When she rounds a corner, though, she stops with a start. There in the courtyard is a bar, and behind the bar is Virgil, his deeply tanned face cast downward as he wipes clean glasses.

"Alright," says Osgood to herself, adding an absurd number of *l*s to the word.

She bellies up to the bar. Virgil doesn't address her. She coughs, then "ahem"s. Now, he looks up. His brown eyes have turned fiery orange, and the smile on his face is intense. The expression is sharp enough, in fact, that Osgood slides back, nearly falling backward off the seat.

"What can I get you, *Señorita* Osgood?"

"How about some information, Verge? I'm *beginning* to suspect that this resort might not be a real place." Osgood fixes her eyes on him, hoping the fear doesn't show on her face. Then, almost by rote habit, she adds: "Also bourbon. And not the cheap shit. I want top shelf."

"I'm afraid there's an extra charge for that," says Virgil, wiping the glass in his hands. His eyes don't waver from hers, as though issuing a challenge.

Osgood accepts that challenge and volleys her own. "Charge it to the room."

Virgil replaces the leering smirk with what seems a genuine grin. Genuine enough that it surprises Osgood. Then he reaches behind a row of liquor and retrieves a half-filled bottle of Pappy Van Winkle's Family Reserve.

Eyes wide at the bottle that certainly isn't real (and if it is, it's worth thousands), Osgood attempts a nonchalant shrug. "If I'm gonna drink imaginary bourbon, I may as well drink the best, right?"

Virgil pours, then slides the small glass across the bar to her. Throughout this action, he doesn't break eye contact. Osgood doesn't either until she sips it, and her eyelids flutter as she shudders in ecstasy. It tastes richer than the best she's ever had, though there is, of course, the caveat that having been a destitute ghost hunter, she hasn't had the opportunity to try the greats. That said, she's had several men try to impress her over the years; some of them had wine cellars, some had bourbon collections, and, well, there are just some bottles she's willing to drop her panties for.

Though, she thinks, *I'm pretty sure that's not what Virgil's after.*

"I'm not," he says. Now, he breaks eye contact and returns to the glasses.

Osgood purses her lips and nods. "Virgil."

"Yes?"

"I'm just saying your name."

"Alright."

Nodding, Osgood repeats his name. "Unusual. More of a reference than a name."

"Poet mother," reminds Virgil.

"Right," says Osgood, then adds: "Simon, Rebecca."

"Who might they be?" asks Virgil.

"Shush," says Osgood, dismissing the bartender's question with a wave. "Maria. Mary." She stares daggers into Virgil's forehead. "Biblical names."

"Those are." Virgil returns his eyes to her, lit with an orange blaze over a contented grin. "Fun coincidence. What do you suppose it means?"

Osgood reflects on her past, and the times she's found herself trapped in a manufactured reality. Manufactured by her, of course, but

(as I built my kingdom)

manufactured nonetheless. That reality, that space: the crossroads, where, in real life, her 1982 Buick Skylark had met its fate being t-boned by a semi, and her life had been extinguished briefly. But that space was more than just the crossroads. If she wanted to believe the demigod who'd told her that, anyway. It was a shared creation in the end. Built by her and

(so have you built yours)

enhanced ... by someone. Some*thing*.

Looking at the bourbon in her glass, she wills it to move, to swirl and eddy, but it doesn't. "I guess I'm not in charge," she says under her breath.

"You can be," says Virgil.

Osgood rolls her eyes and knocks back the bourbon, taking two full fingers of Pappy Van Winkle, a sipping bourbon if ever there was one, down her throat with a burn. Emboldened by the (surely fake, right?) booze, Osgood puts her hands flat on the bartop and pushes herself up until she meets Virgil's eyeline. She sees surprise in his eyes as she nears him but takes only a moment to enjoy it before pulling back and loosing her right fist into Virgil's left eye. She hears a crack and wonders which broke, her fingers or Virgil's face. Either way, the pain flashes knives up her arm, a welcome sensation, almost comforting to Osgood. It shows her that she still can feel, wherever this is, even if her chronic pain has been extracted.

Before she slides back onto her stool, Osgood reaches over the bar, scoops a handful of ice into one of the cloth napkins beside her, and holds it to her knuckles. The interaction took only a moment, and she was back where she'd been, as though nothing had happened. But Virgil knew. He took the brunt, and now his ass is parked on the cushioned mesh floor behind the bar. He looks up at her, and his face no longer looks human, just a mask. His eyes have lost all white, and she's almost sure she can see the flames of his irises scorching his eyebrows. The creature before her is angry now. Authentic and genuine anger.

"Now," says Osgood. She reaches over the bar again and nabs the Pappy Van Winkle bottle, then scoops up one of the glass tumblers Virgil had been washing and unceremoniously pours the rest into that glass. She tips the glass at him, takes a sip, then relishes the silence before she continues. "I think we can dispense with the bullshit dance. How about you tell me what's going on?"

Still furious, Virgil pulls himself back to a stand and leans against a post behind the bar. As though trying to appear nonchalant, he scratches his chin. She can hear the bristling of the few days' growth of beard.

"Such a poser," she says. "Were you even listening when I told you that story earlier?"

"I didn't need to," he replies. His voice has lost all semblance of civility and became a guttural growl.

"I really got you with that punch, didn't I?" asks Osgood with a grin. She takes a deep slug of her bourbon.

"You're not able to hurt me."

"Funny, I literally just knocked you down," says Osgood.

"This body ... is not ... me." The voice seems to come from all around her.

Osgood tries to shake it off, putting on her own mask of nonchalance. "When I said I'm not playing your game—"

"You will."

"Trying to be ominous, are you?" Osgood shakes her head and frowns at him. She's not sure how long her blasé attitude will work, but she's going to drill it all the way the fuck down because it's definitely bothering whatever Virgil is. "Simon. Was that you?"

He says nothing.

"I suppose Simon *and* Rebecca were you. Nice cock you gave yourself. Telling about how you're *really* endowed." She holds up her left hand and wiggles her pinky demonstratively.

Still, he says nothing. This makes Osgood a bit nervous because she knows that, beyond this, she doesn't have many other cards to play. Talking could be her undoing. It certainly has been in the past. Running her mouth long enough could talk her deeper into trouble. Instead, she sits, silently waiting, a cocked eyebrow to challenge Virgil, a bourbon to sip.

"You and I have already had this conversation," Virgil says. "A version of it, at least."

Osgood says nothing, folding her arms over her tits.

"I was excited to finally meet you, Prudence." Virgil winks at her. "It's like actually meeting the ant in the colony who just won't stop hurting the others."

Osgood raises the left side of her mouth, cocking an eyebrow and rolling her eyes at the same time.

"But you're right," he says, putting his hands flat on the bar top. "May as well get to the point."

Again, she says nothing. She notes that her silence also seems to irritate him. He may not overtly show it, but his tell is the slightest twitching at the corners of his eyes. She also finds it amusing that the eye she punched has begun to swell.

"You are a *wretched* creature."

"Oh, I coulda told you that," says Osgood.

"Sarcastic deflections aside, I know you agree with that assessment."

"I do," says Osgood. She shrugs for good measure.

"Endless drinking binges, often driving afterward. Flagrant abuse of those around you. You claim it's because of your upbringing, but we know it's just you. Your parents *did* love you, after all; they loved you until you made yourself unlovable. Not because of your 'queerness,' which is how you always present it so those around you will feel sorry for the poor outcast, but because you're just a chore to be near. You have pushed people away since time immemorial, and those few you deem worthy of keeping in your orbit, you alternate between taking them for granted like staff and shoving them out the door for daring to love you."

"This is what you've got for me?" interrupts Osgood. "Psych 101?"

He ignores her. "Yes, Osgood, as you blathered on and on about when you first met *this* me, I'll concede that you've had a rough go. That car accident was bad, and I, of course, don't envy anyone having to live with the physical pain you've endured. But let's set facts straight, as it's just you, me, and Pappy here at the moment. The reason you crashed is because you were desperate for a distraction. Because when you were finished seeing your one and only beloved Audrey, you stopped at a bar and picked up a seventeen-year-old with a fake ID who fingered you in the bathroom. Stumbling away because you discovered she had hygiene issues when you tried to eat her jailbait pussy. You probably don't remember her name. Don't worry, I do. Leslie."

Osgood gulps, hoping he doesn't notice.

But he had noticed. "Never told anyone that, didja? After all, it got lost in the morass of aftermath, because once you became broken, Osgood, you finally had an excuse to allow your hideous insides to spill out. Your pain let you break your entire life. With your parents, with your friends. Plural! Remember your friends, Osgood? Bernadette, Helen? Gary, Allison, Cassidy? You narrowed your aperture to one person, Audrey Frost, desperate that she would take care of you and be your everything, your world, your life. That note she got in — and I'm still trying to figure out exactly how that happened — is a lie, by the way. They don't need you. They did just fine without you. In fact, without you, the 'Spectral Inspectors' will experience a whole new level of stability. But you could never walk away, could you? Because it's yours, isn't it? And walking away would be admitting that you don't *deserve* it. Instead, you go along your selfish merry way, making your selfish merry plans, knowing that when the chips are down, you can always claim pain or heartache, and they'll come running back because they so desperately *want* to love you." Virgil accentuates his period by slamming a glass on the bar and pouring his own drink, not from the bottles on shelves but from an overtly arcane bottle that could only contain an elixir or potion.

Osgood's silent again, not in defiance but in shock. She can almost hear her ears ringing. *Leslie.* She'd shoved that little nugget about her accident down so deep inside her that she hadn't thought about it in decades, almost to the point where it only lived on in myth. But remembering it now, she can see why she didn't want it to linger. Virgil licks his lips hungrily, and she's sure he'll launch back in if she gives him the leeway. Despite her icy indifference to her past and her brio in suggesting that she knows she's wretched, there's only so much a person can take.

But then something strange happens. Virgil's face melts into a mockery of compassion, and he reaches a hand out to ... touch her arm? She recoils, stumbling back a couple feet.

"I didn't want this, Os."

"My friends call me Os," she says.

"I wanted to share my optimism with you. To share my view of the future. Mine. Yours. Ours!"

"And you are not my friend."

"But I could be," he offers.

Osgood feels rage and, for a moment, actually imagines a red flashing light above him. "You know. As I mentioned, I've met monsters, and every single one has something in common."

A wide smirk fills his face. "And what's that?"

"Delusion."

"Oh," he says. His eyes spark as he leans back and folds his arms across his chest. "Do go on."

"Because you might be right, I might be a wretch. I might even be an awful human. But that's the thing. I *know* who I am."

"Self-awareness does not a good person—"

"How about you shut your fucking mouth?" Osgood waits, daring him to continue. When he doesn't, she feels the most tenuous of upper hands. "Monsters ... like you ... are the dregs. Like shit left over once the good stuff has gone."

"Not much different than me calling you a wretch," he mumbles.

"No, you're right. I *am* a wretch," Osgood spits at him. "And I've been a horrorshow. But every monster I've met had some plan to be ... not better ... because that's not it. Wanting to be better or improve is the trait of someone looking to grow in a positive direction. No, monsters want to take up space. Be seen. To spill their bile everywhere they can and bring everyone down. Because they're not actually bigger or better, they've just grabbed enough people and shoved them under."

"As much as I do love this repartee..."

"This isn't repartee," corrects Osgood.

"Are you not having fun?"

"Want your right eye to match?"

Virgil sighs theatrically. "Again, I remind you that this is *not* my body."

"Alright."

"It hardly does you any good to beat me — him — down. He's not real." Virgil lifts his arms, gesturing to the courtyard. "None of this is." Then, his voice takes on a strange tone. "But it could be."

Osgood frowns and stares at him. She cocks her head to the side and feels her green curls tickling her shoulder. "State your proposal."

"It's just that. *The Isle*. It may not be real, and it may not be sustainable when only I create it."

"So you *did* create it," Osgood nods.

"But if you help..."

"It could be my new kingdom," says Osgood, realizing the offer. No, this isn't real, any of it. But it's a damn far sight better than the crossroads, and she didn't even know how many eons she'd spent there.

"Populated with an unending stream of new and sexy people, with dicks even bigger than Sampson."

"Simon," says Osgood, bristling. Sampson was Sam Goddard, the man she'd killed. Or, at the very least, the man she'd gotten killed.

"Yes," says Virgil. Perhaps he *had* meant Sampson.

"What's the catch?"

"You haven't figured that out yet?" he asks, offering a strange titter.

"Thrill me."

Virgil's smile glistens, and his eyes blaze. "Why, I get to be you."

SEVEN

"AND WHAT DO I get?" Osgood asks Virgil. Her question is rife with faux confidence and indifference, as though considering which banana bunch to buy. She raises her hands to gesture at the resort. "All this?"

"Anything," he says with a wink.

The gesture makes her stomach lurch. How could something so innocuous feel so ugly? She pushes her nausea back down and asks for clarification, annoyance in her tone.

"Must I spell everything out for you, Os?"

"You're not my friend," she reminds him.

"Osgood, then, for fuck's sake." His sigh seems genuine rather than theatrical. At least Osgood hasn't broken her habit of annoying *everyone* around her. "You can have *The Isle*. You can have this island *en toto*. Or you can make it something else. Some*where* else. Where have you always wanted to go, to be? It can be that place. Time isn't an issue here. And it doesn't have to be forever, see. You get bored of *The Isle* ... maybe you spend a week touring the highlands of Scotland and drinking some truly superior Scotch."

"Your pitch needs work," she tells him.

But does it?

Deep down, Osgood can feel the tug inside, asking her if she doesn't want to just acquiesce here. Take the deal. "None of it would be real. And I'd probably get immolated in a wicker man in Scotland."

"What does 'real' mean, Prudence? Was the realm of the Lord of the Hinterlands 'real?'"

"Yes," she says. "We got hurt."

"Is that what makes something real?"

He snaps his fingers, and her wrist breaks, the bone tearing its way out just between the ends of her semicolon tattoo in a compound fracture. Osgood screams and instinctively grabs at it, sending furious pain rocketing through her body. She looks at his fiery eyes and massive grin in horror. But then, another snap of his fingers and her wrist mends. The pain vanishes as quickly as it arrived.

"But," gasps Osgood, "that's not real hurt."

"You felt it," he says. "Would you like to feel it again?"

"I— I feel when..." She struggles to get control of her breathing again. "...Kate Winslet eats me out in my dreams, but that doesn't make it real!"

"Is there any difference between living a life in the so-called 'real world' and one completely in your mind that feels real?"

"Yes!" exclaims Osgood.

"What?"

Unsure how exactly to answer in a way that makes sense to herself, she slaps her hands down on the bar and storms off. As she walks along the path toward the beach, her certainty begins to leave her. When she hits the sand, she can't be sure of anything anymore.

Why are you considering this, Os? The voice in her head is Audrey's, and Osgood feels such relief to hear her, even in her own imagination.

"Because his offer is impressive," she tells the voice, then feels the tears begin to fall. *I'm not in pain, Aud,* she thinks, wishing she could have this conversation with the *real* Audrey Frost and not just the version in her head. "And... *Is* there any difference? That Pappy Van Winkle tasted pretty fucking real."

Much of Osgood's life has been consumed with plotting various escapes, from relationships, from family, from friends, from criticism, from pain, from consciousness. She isn't sure if she can escape The Isle or whatever it is for real, though. Or should she regard her arrival here as an escape?

Looking beyond the beach, she realizes she should've seen the signs so much earlier. The moon hasn't moved, still reflected on the water. The planetarium has been replaced by other improbable objects on the horizon: a single spinning wind turbine and a monstrous skeletal oil pumping platform. Looking into the sky, the constellations don't make sense, as though they're randomized, and every time she tries to pick out a known star or pair, the others are simply ... missing. But the cool late-night sand feels real between her toes. The breeze makes her arm hair stand on end in a flush of goose pimples.

The Audrey in her mind has gone silent, and she's alone on the beach. Perhaps alone in the "resort," if Virgil, or whatever he is, has left her to think. She sits on one of the beds that flank the water line. Then she lies flat. She looks at the sheer fabric billowing around the dark wood-slatted roof over the bed. The curtains on the sides flutter in the breeze. She feels the linens below her, soft, smooth.

Must have a high thread count, she thinks.

Osgood sits back up.

"No," she says to the ocean. She jumps off the bed and looks into the sky. "No! There is no fabric, there is no thread count. Because none of this is fucking real! No matter how much you brainwash me to think it is, it's *not real*, and I'm *not* taking the fucking blue pill."

Silence.

Absolute true silence. Osgood looks around, stunned by the dropout, wondering momentarily if she's gone deaf. But no, the world truly has gone silent. Turning her eyes to the ocean, she realizes it's more than that. The water has stopped. A wave hangs mid-crash just before the shoreline. The shimmer of the moon's reflection is now a jagged image on a pock-marked pane of glass. Looking back at the bed behind her, she sees the linens are also mid-billow, their flutter arrested. She takes a step and stubs her toe on...

"The sand?" she asks in disbelief.

She crouches down and tries vainly to push the sand in any direction, to press her hand into it, but it sits as hard as the concrete below her. She looks back to the water and is sure that if she were to try pulling a Jesus and walking on the water, she could.

Maybe I'm *the god,* thinks Osgood.

A shimmer on the glassy surface. Glimpses of reds and yellows in the light. Osgood slowly turns her face toward the sky and immediately wishes she hadn't. There, above her, is the quasar from her nightmares. The quasar from the skies above the crossroads. A swirling mass of billowing gasses that couldn't possibly be as close to her as it seems. The disc of the quasar spans half the sky, and the twin beams of energy belching from the center cover the rest. For a moment, she cowers from it, wishing it away. Hoping it away. Trying desperately to do whatever it had been she could do in her kingdom at the crossroads and atop the tower of the Lord of the Hinterlands.

But she cannot. She's forced to bear witness to the horrible thing in the sky. As it turns, it pulses, spitting gasses from its disc in all directions and colors, swirling faster and faster. Osgood closes her eyes as she becomes dizzy. She collapses to the unmoving sand, and her knees scrape against it, drawing blood. She feels tears rushing down her cheeks. But the sound is even more horrid than the view. It had begun so gradually that she hadn't noticed at first, but grew louder and louder. At first, the tone was high, but it sank lower as it grew in volume. Now, the thrumming bass smashes into her eardrums and chest like punches, distorting as it deepens. She feels it so deeply in her guts that nausea hits. She expels from both ends onto the concrete sand, then shoves herself away from the putrid mess, shredding several layers of skin off her ass on the uneven ground as she goes. The pulsing has intensified, and now the accretion disc undulates as though the whole thing is some sort of fever dream helicopter from the dawn of flight. The gas jets coalesce, and the center becomes a black hole. The disc's cloud of gasses begins to burn in multi-colored flame thousands of light-years high as the monstrous abomination above her transforms into something even more horrible.

The eye in the sky.

STAND, it commands in a voice so loud it ruptures her eardrums, and she feels blood trickle down the sides of her face.

Unable to resist or even think about resisting, she grasps the edge of one of the beach beds, pulling on the linen until it snaps off the opposite side, but by then, she's moved to a crouch. She slowly unbends her body, feeling the symphony of her life's agony returning to her back and limbs. She fumbles toward a standing position, fumbling around her sanity and losing her grip. A migraine thumps through her head, so loud she's afraid it might collapse her skull inward before the horrible flaming eye in the sky blows it out.

NOW BOW.

Osgood gasps and laughs through the pain. She can't formulate much rational thought, but she knows one thing: she'll sooner die than give this monstrosity the pageantry of her bow.

"You didn't say, 'Simon says.'"

She cringes in anticipation of the attack she's sure is coming, but nothing comes. She casts her eyes tentatively back up to the sky and sees the black hole narrow for a moment, then flash open wide, almost to the edges of the fiery iris. No sound comes from it for one second, two, and then just before three, she feels the sonic boom shockwave as a blare, like the largest brass instruments playing their deepest notes.

And Osgood blows away, tumbling and crashing into the beach furniture, then the wall separating The Isle's bungalows until she reaches the courtyard. She manages to turn her head away from the eye in the sky just long enough to see the plate glass windows of the lobby race toward her ... or her toward them ... until she hits, and the glass, along with her body, shatters.

Eight

T HE FIRST THOUGHT IS of pain, and the next is of fear. The third and juiciest feeling is rage.

Osgood opens her eyes. She stands on the shore of an unfamiliar body of water, wine dark again. *It may as well be blood,* she thinks. The sky above her is the blackest of chasms, wholly devoid of stars. Even the unseeing void is better than that eye in the sky, though. Her ability to hear slowly returns, bringing the sound of waves crashing in. They're violent, the water roiling with foam, and in the foam, slimy things lie mostly unseen just below the surface. But there's enough above the surface to horrify.

Before her is a cragged mass of rock and dirt shooting into the air, taller than the tower she'll always call Sears back home in Chicago. *Where my body is,* she thinks. But in the center of it, about twenty paces up the jagged hill, is the carved maw of a cave, gaping hungrily for her.

"What should I do here?" she asks herself. "It's all fake... A dream, a hallucination, a mirage."

That fact cannot be denied. Nothing here is real. She's... reasonably confident of that anyway. *The Isle* wasn't real. This, however... Well, she's been to places before with obscene angles and cliffs that defy geometry and mathematics.

"So you're gonna treat it as real?" she asks herself.

Her other option is to sit down, close her eyes, and wait. She supposes treating this hallucination, this jaunt outside of reality, as real is undoubtedly the more exciting choice. Nodding, she staggers forward, feeling every footfall as her plantar fasciitis and twice broken first three toes on the right foot scream. Her ankles join the chorus, one damaged by the accident, one during an ill-fated single game of roller derby. Her derby career had both begun and ended on that same night in August, too many years ago to count. She snickers, remembering her derby name: "Osgood Goddamn."

But the snicker is short-lived, and the pain immense. Every inch of her is on fire, reminding her of the pain of her life. She's broken both legs in multiple places, her pelvis fractured, some vertebrae fused, a literal broken neck, and a repeatedly damaged skull that has even been sawn open.

Maybe this is hell.

Suits you, says Cynthia Osgood in her head.

She tells the mimic of her mother to fuck off and continues to plod her way up the incline.

A sickly tree covered in thorns grows off to the side, its roots digging into the rock. It's shed one branch, and against her better judgment, Osgood grabs for it, grasping loosely enough to nearly drop it the first time but then getting a good hold, strengthened by the thorns impaling her hand.

"What's three … four more wounds?" she grumbles, using the thorny branch as a makeshift cane. It helps, but only barely.

She screams toward the cave: "Is this what I get if I say no? Is my new kingdom a personal hell?" The word *hell* echoes back to her, like a response to her question, and again, she snickers at the absurdity of it all.

"Make no mistake, Os," says Virgil, coming into view at the mouth of the cave. "I *will* hurt you. But physical pain has been your companion for too long. That's not where the torment lies."

"I'd rather have the motherfucking eye over you," says Osgood, snapping her jaw shut so hard to punctuate it that the crown on her left rear molar shatters and sends her into a coughing fit that forces her to bend over, inflaming her agony further.

"Oh, hadn't you guessed? We're the—"

"Yeah," says Osgood in a harsh whisper, feeling blood coating her tongue and throat. "None of this shit you're saying is a surprise, you know."

"Oh, I do know, *spec*-tral in-*spec*-tor."

Finally, Osgood crests the rise. The cave mouth yawns before her, far more massive than she'd expected, dwarfing Virgil standing in the center, wrists clasped behind his back, a malicious grin on his face.

"Why don't you just *take* my body?" Osgood asks. "You wouldn't be the first." She hacks and spits out a shard of crown that cuts her lower lip on its way out. A new trickle of blood drips down her chin.

"Where's the fun in that?"

"You can't, can you?" She stops moving toward him, slamming the tip of her stick of thorns against the rock beneath her feet. The action causes some of the flesh on her hand to rip as the thorns dig deeper. But the moment is satisfying because, again, Virgil looks frustrated.

"I can do *anything*," he tells her.

"A lotta guys tell me that, but usually they give up after ten minutes of trying to get me off and stick their sad dick inside me, while I can roll over and do it in thirty seconds with the wand. A minute with my own fingers."

"Your lewdness. Does it make you feel—"

"Powerful?"

He cocks his head at the response.

"If you can do anything, just do it." She waits, allowing the pause to become pregnant, but doesn't carry it to term. "But see, I don't think you can. Because if you could, you wouldn't have made me a resort. You wouldn't have populated it with people, and I wouldn't be here now. After I pissed off that stupid eye of yours, I'd be brain-dead, wouldn't I?" She watches his face vacillate between anger, bemusement, and something else. Something that Osgood *almost* thinks is respect. Looking Virgil directly in his burning eyes brings understanding and confirmation. "No, you *can't* kill me. And you can't have me brain-dead because then you can't use me as your little puppet for your puppet show, can you? And moreover, you actually need *me*, right? There's something special about this wretch here, and you're desperate to get it."

Virgil purses his lips.

Now it's Osgood's turn to smile. Smile through the pain. Smile a bloody red gash. "But you can't. Without my agreement."

"No," says Virgil quietly, performing a theatrical sigh. And even though he's at least ten feet away at the mouth of the cave, she hears him perfectly. "I can. But it's messy."

"Aha."

"And you'd wind up here anyway. In whatever kingdom your mind builds. But it'd be a destroyed mind. Mad. Functioning like a candle, when it used to be a blaze. And I'd have only a little corner as well." Virgil folds his arms. "So, since you're gonna be here one way or another, whaddya say you just... lemme have it? So much better for you. For me. For everyone."

She looks down at her bare feet, realizing she's still naked. And her body bears the scars of brambles, the rock-hard glassy sand, and, well, everything she's ever put it through. Wouldn't it be nice to rest?

"So nice," says Virgil.

"Get the fuck out of my head!" Osgood screams at him before bursting out with a laugh at the absurdity. "Just... stop listening."

Virgil smirks as well, but his fiery eyes remain paradoxically cold. "Fair enough."

She feels the smallest of weights lifting, and her migraine goes from a fourteen on the pain scale down to a ten. It's the most minor relief, to be sure, but it feels like a balm for her soul. *He could do that,* she thinks. *He could take the pain away again.*

Why can't you? comes a calm voice in the distance, one she can't quite hear clearly. She's about to chase the thought when she returns to his benevolence, living essentially forever in a world of her own fucking pure imagination. Where she could eat and drink anything. Where she could fuck anyone. Where she—

Prudence! That voice is loud. She flicks her eyes to Virgil, but he doesn't hear it. The sound of a *clap* echoes off the rock.

Yes? she answers in her head. But that is all. Momentarily, she feels as if she can recognize the voice and maybe follow it to its source, but as the moment stretches, she begins to forget she even heard it.

"As you haven't agreed," says Virgil, walking over to her and grabbing her hand, "I'll assume you still need convincing." She pushes against his arm feebly. "C'mon." He begins to drag her toward the cave, grumbling in some odd language that doesn't seem to even share phonemes with human language. When they reach the cave, he turns to her, and she flinches away at his gaze.

He slaps her across the face. "Look." He points up above their heads.

She doesn't. Since his hand touched her, she's felt the same nausea that already once made her spill her bowels down her legs. He puts both hands on her cheeks and turns her head up. As he does, his hands squeeze her face, and his middle finger seems to press through her cheek, directly into the crevasse of her deposed tooth. She feebly tries not to cry out at this new pain and at the horror of his touch and decides if she must shit herself, she'll do her damnedest to shit on him.

When she finally acquiesces and looks above her, she sees Latin. "'Abandon all hope, ye who enter here,'" she reads aloud, despite not knowing the language.

Mercifully, Virgil releases her and does a giddy half-jig. "I put that there for you."

"And *that's* where Virgil came from. I get it," she said, rolling her eyes at him. "You know *Inferno* isn't actually biblical, right?"

Virgil just smiles, rubbing his hands together like the maniacal villain in some cartoon.

"It's an allegorical poem that criticizes the faith and political leaders of the time. It's like if someone wrote now about a trip through hell and Trump and Pope Francis were there." She shrugs. "But I'd have to believe in hell for it to matter. And I don't."

"Oh," says Virgil, his smile straining his cheeks. "Of course you do. I know atheism is all very—"

"I'm agnostic," says Osgood.

His smile vanishes, and again, his face looks like a mask, drooping and hanging off a scowl.

"But please," she says with faux interest. "Continue."

"—trendy," he finishes, the scowl drooping further and pulling the whole face with it. For a moment, it seems, Osgood can see a line at the crown of his head, full of pulsing white-hot light.

"That's it?" asks Osgood. "*That's* what blows your gasket?"

His eyes blaze at her, and she sees a fury greater than any she's seen before. "You fucking arrogant cunt!" He lunges for her, yanking off her glasses, and Osgood screams as he goes for her eyes, grabbing the sides of her head between his hands and pressing thumbs into her eyeballs. He's so quick, she can't even close them, so she sees, up close, his thumbs in detail. Maggots crawl in and out of holes amid the ripples and ridges of his thumbprints. But that's the last she sees as she hears a wet squelch, and her eyes flicker out. She feels them pop inside her skull, first the right, then the left, and still, he presses his thumbs deeper.

She feels him touch her brain.

ABANDON ALL HOPE
YE WHO ENTER

NINE

IT'S HARD TO DEFINE where she goes next. Osgood is unmoored. She's been *nowhere* before, but this isn't nowhere. It's not nothing. It's almost overwhelmingly *something*. Like TV snow before digital. The space between channels, a roiling cauldron of noise created by microwaves that have sailed through the cosmic seas since the Big Bang itself. Only this noise is everywhere. She doesn't see it, but feels it, smells it, tastes it. It's in her head and in front of her, screaming its unfocused sounds at her while also somehow silent. Crawling into her nooks and crannies. Sending electricity pulsing everywhere. And there, hidden deep within the noise itself, is the signal. Flickering frames. Shimmers. The phantom data that makes up life, us. Perhaps the soul, if one believes in such things. Osgood is alive but isn't. She can hear the roar of the cosmic gulf but also cannot. She can taste copper, like choking on a penny caught in her throat, worsening its discomfort. She can see something, too, but isn't sure what. Perhaps Virgil hasn't destroyed her vision after all.

Do not forget that none of this is real.

She wants to believe that. Tries desperately to believe. But just as she reached her limit pretending to be a good little Catholic girl for her parents, she can't do it any longer. She's seen too much. She's seen backstage of reality, the seams in the fabric that stitch it all together. If *that* cosmic pantomime could be considered authentic, then this certainly can, too. As real as any day in life. Because Virgil is right. What does it matter if something exists or doesn't, as long as your mind goes all in on it? She's pondering this when the noise coalesces, and she can no longer hold her present mind together. Life is flickering on. The signal is breaking through. This signal is vivid, unlike the one received by her seventeen-inch black and white with foil crushed onto the broken rabbit ears. This signal is real.

She is four years old. This many fingers. It's night. The wind echoes through the gangway between their house and the next. They're *very* close, and the window in her bedroom nearly meets the window in her neighbor's. She wishes kids lived there so she could throw across an emptied soup can and some string. Instead, it's only ancient Miss Borse and her *friend*. She's not thinking of that tonight, though, only of her wet pajama bottoms. And the dream. She isn't sure what it had been about, as the moment she'd awakened in a pool of pee, she'd been distracted. Distracted from the specifics but not from the feeling of horror. As she shimmies her way out of the lofted bed over the playhouse her father made for her, she feels the essence of the dream returning to her but tries to push it away. She doesn't want to know what it had been that scared the pee out of her, does she? She has to focus, anyway.

The sound she makes when she hits the floor of her bedroom couldn't be more than the faintest thump, but Pru hears it, and if she does, then...

Then what?

...then any

(thing)

one else could hear it, too. Her mother is just on the *other side of that wall.* The wall her bed is on! She tries to tiptoe around Duplo blocks but steps on the corner of one and yelps. She stands frozen in place, listening for any indication of stirring. Only house sounds. The metronome pendulum of the clock on the wall downstairs, the one her father winds daily. The low hum of the humidifier at the top of the stairs. Drip, drop, drip, drop in the bathroom down the hall. Dad was never sure where the drips came from, but they seemed to go quiet whenever he tried to track them down and then reemerge in the small hours, like death creeping up on you.

Or so he'd said. Mom hadn't liked that. He'd laughed. She hadn't.

She flings herself across the bedroom, leading with her head, trailing her still-dripping PJ pants behind her. Her bolt is so haphazard that it is the closet door itself that stops her, ricocheting her rather gently onto her tush. She looks up at it, then fumbles with the slight indentation until she manages to slide the door to the side. It sounds like chalk scraping down a chalkboard, but only in her mind. It's actually barely audible. But she still struggles to keep it as slow and quiet as possible. When it's open, she dumps the pajama bottoms unceremoniously in the hamper, then covers them with a few wayward bits of clothing from the floor near her closet. The pee will be dry by morning. A quick feel around shows that the wetness on her already is. She tosses her tops in as well; it wouldn't do not to match.

When she has a crisp new set, a *Rainbow Brite and the Star Stealer* tie-in that she'd begged Mom to buy her at *Zayre, she slows her breathing and begins the quiet walk back to her lofted bed.

Pru has made it midway across the room when the floor wakes up and emits a *creeeeeeaaaaaaaaaakkkkkkkkkk* that could wake those dead sneaking up on you. She freezes. Silence again. Except it isn't silent. There's a sound on the other side of her bedroom door. The door is ajar, but nothing is visible through the three-inch crack, almost as though the sound itself is hiding. A rustling, maybe? Papers being shuffled. Perhaps the humidifier is blowing...

No, that's breathing.

She's unsure if she thinks it or if someone has put that thought in her head. She did it, didn't she? She woke up Mom or Dad, and they'll come in and see the wet spot on the mattress. Mom will be angry. Dad'll tell her it's okay, and she'll try to believe him, but she knows big girls don't wet the bed, even if they have a terrible dream. And little Prudence Osgood has evidence that she is definitely not a big girl, tonight at least.

Then there's another sound. A snore. Her dad. Sawing logs, as he'd say. After a few *hoooonks*, she hears the clipped voice of her mom snap a muffled, "Basil!" Her father responds, but his voice is sleepy, and the wall manages to muffle all meaning. Something is comforting, grounding, about hearing them through the wall. She takes a deep breath, thinking that maybe everything will be alright.

But then she remembers, and it brings the sound back to the forefront. That's definitely breathing. And it's definitely coming from outside her door. The adults she lives with, the ones who protect her, are in the next room, likely already falling back to sleep, as their daughter listens to something horrifying breathing just outside her door. Her focus on it makes it clearer, as though amplifying the sound. She can hear the intake's raspy suction and the exhale's breezy whistle. It's not quiet. Not at all.

It wants me to hear.

The thought is hers, but it's weird. It's her voice, but ... deeper?

For the briefest of moments, like an old subliminal message hidden in advertising, she's aware that she isn't a four-year-old girl in the house on Summerdale, less than half a mile from her current home on Clark Street, but a forty-something-year-old woman getting brainfucked by an elder god.

The moment dissipates, though, and leaves young Pru standing, frozen like a doe, listening to the thing breathing outside her door. The sound comes from higher up, so it's not a dog. Not that she has a dog, anyway. 'Cuz Mom's allergic. She says it's Dad, but he'd told her the real truth.

Operating outside all rational thought telling her not to, she moves toward the door. As she does, there comes a noise of the sort that only the oldest of houses can conjure, one that sounds like it originates up on the tar-papered roof and travels all the way down into the house's bowels. That noise, the kind Mom would say is "just the house settling" if she were here, makes the little voices in Pru's head beg her to rush back into bed, wet spot be dammed, and shield herself with her Geoffrey Giraffe quilt.

But she doesn't.

No, feeling perhaps the beginning inklings of a lifelong search for monsters, little Prudence Osgood walks toward the door. When she makes her own creak, less than three feet from the slab of old wood (heartwood, her dad had called it, but she doesn't know what that means), suddenly, the house goes completely silent. The breathing has stopped. So has the dripping. And the sound of the humidifier is gone.

A pop, ozone in the air, and she finds herself in the dark — real dark. She whips her head toward her bedroom window, and even the orange glow of the streetlights is gone. So is the blue canary nightlight in the low outlet in the hall, the one that she can see when her door is ajar.

But we didn't have one of those. Why would we have had one of those? My parents didn't know that song...

The thought feels alien, making Pru's head itch. But the feeling in her chest is more pressing because now, without any glimmer of light, the breathing has resumed, and her eyes are beginning to see things again. She wonders if she's just getting used to the dark because Miss

Newton, her preschool teacher, had promised that would happen, and that's why she shouldn't be afraid of the dark. But no, in the dark is the strangest flickering glow. And that glow is coming from—

It's not real, Prudence.

The assurance doesn't matter as that light grows in intensity at the edge of her door: orange, flickering. The breathing has grown louder and now seems strained. Is that laughter beneath it? Barely stifled laughter? That thing in the hallway, the thing that woke her up—

The Bicycle Man, she thinks, but then doesn't know why that moniker is in her head. She's never heard the phrase or reference before, but she's sure at this moment that the Bicycle Man also came to her in that dream, the one that made her pee herself. And now that *very same* Bicycle Man is standing outside her door, running something along the wood. When pale bits of flesh appear at the door's edge, she realizes they're his fingers, and he's about to pull himself around. If she doesn't hide right now, if she doesn't move right now, she'll see the Bicycle Man's nose, surely long and crooked like a crone's, as he begins to crest the edge of the door and look her way.

If he does that, she'll see him. And she'll … know … him. Another thing that she doesn't understand. Why does she have to be so little? Why can't she just call for her parents? They might not be able to banish the creature, but they could surely get her to move from this spot where she seems to have grown roots. Because mom would tell her she's getting too old for this, that nightmares aren't real, that monsters aren't real. Why does she always sound so angry when she says it? *Most parents,* she thinks, *would want to be reassuring.* But not her mother.

She makes up her little mind to risk it, to call out. They'll come running, concerned she fell out of bed again. But she only did that *one time*, and she isn't a baby anymore! As the fingers slip over the edge of the door onto her side, they seem lit from within. Then she sees it. The point of a nose. It's now or never. She has to call. She has to scream. She opens her mouth...

And nothing comes out.

Ten

L IKE THE SHUFFLING OF the deck, the house on Summerdale is
gone.

Without even an interstitial moment, Prudence sits cross-legged
on an old mottled brown shag rug in their semi-finished basement in
Rolling Meadows in front of an old 19-inch Hitachi color TV, the
kind with the UHF dial and the illuminated channel numbers. They'd
moved from Chicago to the suburbs (where things are safe) when
gang activity and the overarching invented threat of **Stranger Danger**
loomed. She's a teenager. Pre-teen, actually, but eleven is basically a
teenager. And her hormones have made vastly different decisions than
her mother, Cynthia, would like. Their bra-shopping outing (because
her chest hurts *all the time*) had gone very poorly when Cynthia tried
to strap them down, the way someone at school said they'd done to
Judy Garland so she could play Dorothy. But it never made sense to
Prudence that Dorothy was supposed to be eight in that story. Judy
was basically an adult! That Fairuza girl who'd starred in the second
one, now *she* was a little girl.

Pru is spending a rare moment not focused on her soon-to-be
teenagerdom. It's a kind of surrealistic brain blip, a moment of jamais
vu, the lesser-known cousin of déjà vu. In that briefest of moments,
she's uncertain where she is in time, feeling at once as though she is in
her former bedroom on Summerdale, in this basement on Elm Street

(the name had scared ten-year-old Prudence when they'd moved here), driving along a dark and barren road, and also an odd feeling of being somewhere *other*. The moment holds in her mind, like the negative blotch of a particularly impressive fireworks blast, long enough to cause her to wrinkle her freckled nose and purse her lips, a comical exaggeration that one might see entitled *Fig 4. The Thinker*.

Then it's gone. And that weird commercial for Sharkins Insurance plays on the TV, where the man dressed as a shark offers insurance to women who've just had an accident. Prudence thinks it's strange for many reasons. The obvious is that the shark has arms and legs, isn't in the water, and seems to be offering insurance *post*-crash ("Oh no, do you have insurance?" asks Woman One. "Oh no, I don't," says community-theater-reject Woman Two, holding a concerned finger to her lips). But primarily, the strangeness came from the absent focus of the shark's overlarge dark eyes. She can see the sides of the felt peeling up. And then there's the way the shark says, "I'll give you what you need." It gives Prudence the shivers, which she's mildly embarrassed about, but it only seems to come on late at night, in the nether hours when nothing feels quite real. Because of the uncanny valley horror of it all, she'd felt justified enough to tell Audrey from up the street about it. And Audrey hadn't mocked. She'd said, "I know, right!" and touched Prudence's arm.

She's home alone tonight. It's mid-January, and the windows upstairs are glazed over with ice. The basement, often colder than above, has a new vent direct from the furnace that her father had put in while trying to make this unfinished basement into a comfortable area. Perhaps he'd done it because he could see the growing tension between his wife and daughter and wanted to offer a respite for growing Pru. Or maybe he planned to wall it up and live down here himself. She found it difficult to know the whims of Basil Osgood sometimes.

Before coming downstairs, she'd considered starting a fire in the living room fireplace but knew she'd surely catch Cynthia's wrath. Perhaps her father's, too, if only a gentle, "C'mon now, Pru, why can't you just *try* to behave?" She does try. She wants to behave. But things hadn't been the same since Cynthia had walked in on Prudence and Audrey. They'd been in their underwear. Ten years old. What was the big deal? Ten-year-olds play doctor, don't they? They're at least curious! All Prudence had known was she wanted Audrey to come over every day.

The upstairs floorboards creak, not in the way their old house's bones had, but in that slightly-less-well-built way of newer homes. She looks up at the ceiling's exposed crossbeams and waits. She listens to the sound of her breathing paired with an Empire Carpeting commercial, and when the creaking doesn't reoccur, she unclenches, only then realizing she'd been clamped tightly from jaw to butthole.

She wishes Audrey were here. Maybe she should call. But it's late. Nearly eleven. Audrey's parents have also seemed jittery around the two of them lately. Too jittery to allow for late-night phone calls, even on a Saturday.

When the commercials end, *Diff'rent Strokes* returns. Prudence again scrunches her brow. Hadn't she been watching something else? She looks at the TV, which has a series of buttons tracking down beside the screen with channel numbers that glow blue when selected. Right now, the selection sits halfway between 50 and 66, where the old UHF channel 60 had been.

Weird, thinks Prudence.

She hasn't watched this show in ages, not since they got cable anyway. Back in Chicago, all they'd had were 2, 5, 7, 9, 11, 13 (but 13 was for churchies), and 60 for a long while, but then it split and became higher wattage 50 and lower 66. The small selection, and the fact that one was always at the whim of the TV antennae (because only the one in the basement family room got to hook up to the *big* antenna in the attic) meant *Diff'rent Strokes, Facts of Life, Brady Bunch,* and *Barney Miller* were what she'd watched. But *Diff'rent Strokes,* like the others, had occupied a more juvenile time in her life.

And *Saturday Night Live* should be on.

She leans forward and presses the brushed aluminum button next to 5. Vanilla Ice is in the middle of his first set, singing his hit that Osgood's father keeps ranting about and then playing *Under Pressure* loudly on his record player until she rolls her eyes and walks out of the room. She doesn't know why he's so insistent. Her mother doesn't care, and Prudence is *well aware* of the blatant rip-off, as she counts both Bowie and Queen among her most played cassettes. After Ice, there is another commercial, and Prudence zones out.

But the *creak!* upstairs happens again. This time, it comes not from the dining room above her but from the hallway above the staircase. Again, Prudence waits. She returns her attention to the TV when the SNL bumper showing Joe Mantegna appears, but there's a burst of quick static, and the channel light moves back to the space between 50 and 66. Conrad Bain is once again on her TV. When *Diff'rent Strokes* cuts to a new scene, she feels an extraordinary sense of creeping dread. It begins in her bowels and creeps up into a stomach ache, then heartburn, and then her whole head is pins and needles. The moment she sees the bicycle shop, she knows this episode.

This is the über-ep in all "very special episodes" infamy. They'd even talked about it uncomfortably in school the first time it aired. When Arnold and Dudley are brought into the back room of that bicycle shop, and the man gets a little too close, she feels like vomiting. The Bicycle Man. The episode that she and her friends, in their pre-teen detachment, call "Arnold Gets Molested." Of course, he doesn't. He high-tails it out of there, and Conrad Bain comforts him. But the

Bicycle Man on TV sits awfully close to young Gary Coleman, and his hands are on him. Who knows what happens to poor Dudley?

Prudence's stomach lurches. Because the *creak!* upstairs has become footsteps, and the door at the top of the basement stairs whines open. Her parents could be home, sure, but when have they ever returned without calling out, "Prudence, we're home!" mostly to avoid embarrassing incidents like the time she was touching herself to *The Red Shoe Diaries* in the living room upstairs, 'cuz the living room had cable. No, whoever has just opened the door upstairs isn't her parents.

"Hello?" she croaks out, really only hitting the "lo" bit. Silence.

Gary Coleman says, "Whatchoo talkin' 'bout?" to the Bicycle Man, which strikes Prudence as an awfully blasé attitude considering the man's hand has slid inside the child's shirt. Then, the footsteps resume. First stair, then second, closer and closer. Two more, and there's a small landing as the staircase turns for its descent into the basement. Prudence keeps her eyes glued to the screen because looking up raises a primal horror within her. There is a flickering orange glow of fire. She may not have been allowed to start a fire in the fireplace upstairs, but the fire was here nonetheless.

"I'll give you what you need," the Bicycle Man says lecherously to Gary Coleman, but Prudence finds, to her horror, he's speaking to her, staring directly at the camera as his hand slides up the boy's leg. And the footsteps down the stairs resume. Three, then four, and in two more steps, the orange glowing thing will crest the wall and become visible.

Prudence Osgood glimpses another dimension as time folds in on itself like a tesseract contorting. In the tesseract, time is always. She is at once her forty-five-year-old self, lying in a hospital bed, staring at the ceiling; she is her four-year-old self, peeing a fresh stream down her leg as she sees the Bicycle Man; she is here, in her basement, as he peers around the corner, a smile on his face and fire in his eyes; she's in an el train as a swarm of fireflies dances just before her girlfriend is bisected and she's hurled from the vehicle; she's standing in a ballroom watching falling chandelier pieces nearly kill her beloved Audrey while a man in the corner with fiery eyes grins. A giant red sun burns above a crumbling tower that the Lord of the Hinterlands dwells within. But the sun is really orange, isn't it? Orange and angry. Like that quasar burning in deep space. The eye in the sky, the eyes of the Bicycle Man, see all.

And again, Prudence cannot scream.

Eleven

T HE DECK SHUFFLES AGAIN, and the cards dealt are a familiar hand.

She smokes but wishes she could quit. She can still feel Leslie's fingers inside her, a brand-new college student just fumbling at sapphism. Her nails had clipped Pru's vaginal walls once or twice. Thankfully, though, the cigarettes mask the scent and taste of the young woman's infection. Pru doesn't blame her. Easy to get a yeast infection when one is in the blazes of experimentation. She does wish she hadn't tasted it. That taste had put a damper on it all, hadn't it? She can't fuck Audrey right now, so fucking anyone was supposed to be an acceptable alternative. Well, if not sufficient, at least distracting.

Her hand shakes as she brings the cigarette to her lips. It's unlit, but she'll soon change that. She turns up the song on the radio, "The End of What's Real," that old hit single.

> *He'll marry us in the hinterlands,*
> *and we'll never have to return.*
> *Let the world around us crumble.*
> *Let the world around us burn.*

I see you brought the fire, she thinks as a hand lights the cigarette dangling from her mouth.

She's not sure where that thought had come from; she just vaguely remembers reading it in a book when she was in high school, maybe from those Point Horror authors or Christopher Pike. She knows *something* sits beside her in the passenger seat. Not wanting to see it, she looks away, askance, so she's viewing the road ahead out of the corner of her eye, focusing instead on the driver's side window as rows of corn blast past, and her open windows let in the sounds of the rural night. Crickets, cicadas, maybe, and the vague sound of semis on the highway in the distance. But looking this way keeps *him* from her view.

She's seen this man multiple times in her life before, but each time it's been a dream, hasn't it? The man with the fiery eyes. The Bicycle Man. Though she's unsure why she calls him that, she knows that his appearance makes her incredibly uncomfortable. In that shamey way she sometimes feels when someone of authority tries to tell her about sexual health.

It's possible, of course, that she's asleep right now. Doesn't the road feel a little bit too dark? Doesn't the sky have an artificial glow of manufactured night?

The thing beside her sings along with the refrain of "The End of What's Real." His voice feels thin, like a radio signal trapped between overlapping transmitters in a zone of fading reach. She won't look at him. Won't talk to him. Won't acknowledge.

"You can't ignore me, Osgood," says the Bicycle Man as the last verse plays.

He's right. She can't. Because how much longer can she drive like this, turned almost 90 degrees away from the road?

Slowly, she turns back, hearing every sound of the faux leather seat in the Buick Skylark, with nearly 180,000 miles on it. When she's facing forward again, she sees ahead, the amber beacon that marks her turn north. It blinks in the distance, waiting for her.

Will you get there? comes the thought. She shudders involuntarily.

This isn't real, comes the voice. *Don't forget that. This isn't how it happened.*

But he sure looks real as she turns enough to see him. Tall, thin, ashen, with razor teeth and flaming eyes. Seated on his lap is a small rag doll

(show us on the doll)

made from unbleached and undyed linens, with purple yarn hair only on half the head. He turns it toward her, and she immediately recognizes it.

(where he touched you)

When she was in kindergarten, a policeman had come to her class with two rag dolls, a boy and a girl. The class giggled like crazy when they realized that the boy doll had a dangling bit of fabric and a sac between its legs. The girl was more subtle but had a definite slit of a vagina. The policeman, in his gruff Chicago accent, said that they all had private parts, something Prudence already knew, of course, because her mother had shrieked when she'd shown her friend from around the corner her vagina. She wasn't sure why she was in trouble—was it for showing the cool body part she'd discovered or for not wearing underpants? As the policeman pointed out, these dolls were used so kids could demonstrate instead of saying what had been done to them. Kindergarten Prudence had been mortified at the thought of sitting in a small room with this gruff, mustachioed man and both her parents and touching that doll's vagina.

This doll.

The Bicycle Man in the seat next to her does just that. He stares at her, his burning eyes searing into hers, as he slides his index and middle fingers in and out of the doll's nondescript slit. She thinks she may vomit and flicks the cigarette out the window, dry heaving over and over.

"I'll give you what you need," says the Bicycle Man, licking his fingertips. "Or am I going to have to eat this entire banana sundae myself?"

Now, she can't stop it and projects her meager dinner onto the steering wheel and the windshield. She feels the dregs of the vomit dropping down her bottom lip as he touches her cheek, sliding his warm fingers under her hair at the back of her head. His thumb tickles her eyelashes, and she wants to die.

Of course, she does die.

Only seconds later, the Buick Skylark blasts into the intersection with the flashing amber beacon and is met by a semi-truck full of frozen dinners with a front cab that nearly flips entirely onto the Skylark. With her head trapped between the steering wheel and the car's roof, another phantom appears to her, one of shimmering light.

Prudence Osgood dies begging.

TWELVE

THE SOUND OF BREATHING.

A monotonous beep.

Shuffling. Muffled talking.

The ceiling above Osgood was in focus this time, and she could feel the slight pressure of her glasses on her nose. She couldn't move her eyes. She couldn't move her lips. Frozen in place, as she'd oft dreamed as a child, in nightmares where she could not scream. She wanted to scream here and now, but even if there hadn't been a breathing tube in the way, her vocal cords were paralyzed. She could hear voices, but they sounded like they were underwater. Even underwater, though, she knew them. Audrey was here. Somewhere beyond her sight line. And Zack.

She felt a tear roll down her cheek and momentarily marveled that she could cry. And at that marvel, she wondered how she hadn't been doing it all along.

"Is she crying?" That was Zack.

"No, that's not—" Audrey now. "Wait."

Then they were above her.

Audrey's hair was long and hung down far enough to tickle Osgood's cheek before she brushed it away. Her blue eyes, usually an icy color that didn't match her personality, were today a richer hue, the cerulean of a summer sky, or the heart of an iceberg. Zack seemed to have visibly aged and now wore more than just scruff on his face. Sure, his mustache didn't quite connect to the hair on his chin, but it was fuller than she'd ever seen it. She wanted nothing more than to reach up, reach out, touch both of them, hug both of them. Reunite the Spectral Inspectors.

"I'll call the nurse," said Zack.

No! thought Osgood. *We don't need a nurse. Just us! Just us for a moment, please!*

But the nurse, one that Osgood didn't recognize with a Karen haircut and a Karen scowl, came into the room and shined an obnoxiously bright flashlight in each of Osgood's eyes. The purple aftereffect blotted out her ability to see Audrey and Zack, and she loathed the woman for it.

"They can cry?" Audrey asked. The sound became muted and muffled again, and the purple in her vision made Osgood feel like the room was spinning around her.

"They can."

"Does it mean she's—"

"As I'm sure Dr. Laghari has told you both, there really aren't enough cases of locked-in syndrome for us to call anything 'normal' or a 'sign.'"

Audrey's "thanks" was tinged with resentment for the woman who noisily departed.

With a *woosh*, the pressure changed, and it seemed to be the three of them again. Audrey leaned down over Osgood, tilting her head to the side, and slid her hand over Osgood's face. Her thumb caressed the cheek, and her fingertips met the back of Osgood's head. The momentary pleasure it gave her became overshadowed by ... something. She couldn't pinpoint why or how but felt like she might retch. Doing so in this state might kill her, she thought. Again. Maybe for good this time.

I may be hard to kill, she thought.

"That so?" The voice of a woman, smooth and clipped. Not irritated entirely, but not warm and inviting.

"What?" asked Zack. He moved out of Osgood's field of vision, and she longed for him, for both of them to just stay where she could see them.

When the woman peered down at her, Osgood recognized her but wasn't sure from where. The white coat meant doctor, and the woman established her place by again checking Osgood's pupillary response with a bright pen light.

Motherfucker! thought Osgood.

"She's crying," Audrey told the doctor.

"That can happen."

"Does it mean—"

"We really don't know," said the doctor. "But at this point, any new signs are worth being hopeful about."

"So you're saying we should be hopeful?" That was Zack, with an edge in his voice that Osgood wasn't sure she'd ever heard.

"I'm saying that it's not a *bad* sign."

The purple haze of the light's aftereffect began to dissipate, and Osgood looked into the deep brown eyes of the dark-skinned doctor. Her black hair was tied up on her head. She gave a slight, half smile, then looked up and away. Maybe at Zack? "You two have both been here so often, perhaps you should stagger—"

"I'll be here when she wakes up."

"Truly, the odds of—"

"I'll *be here* when she wakes up," repeated Audrey, firm, resolved.

Now, Osgood placed the woman above her. Dr. Laghari had seen her when she'd had that

(*My tumor had a face, and I want to see it!*)

thing removed from her head.

After I hurled myself out of a moving SUV into a snowbank, thought Osgood.

"Not wise," said Dr. Laghari.

Audrey stammered. "Excuse me?"

"Oh," said the doctor, "That wasn't to you. I, of course, fully support your desire to be here. I'm just telling you that it is improbable..." The doctor stopped, perhaps reading in Audrey's expression a conviction she wasn't in the mood to come up against. The women stared at each other, each drawing their own lines in the sand.

Then Zack put his hand on Audrey's shoulder and suggested they get some coffee. Audrey's eyes didn't waver from Dr. Laghari's. When he patted her shoulder and added a "c'mon," only then did Audrey let her intensity ebb.

Osgood felt a new tear roll down her cheek as her friends disappeared from her view entirely.

"Now we can be alone," said Dr. Laghari, staring down at Osgood. Her eyes looked a little wild as she nodded. "I'm curious about something." Osgood felt her chin get pulled down, her mouth forced open far wider than the breathing tube required, and then a hand was inside her. Her jaw ached as it was stretched far beyond its normal gape. When the Doctor's hand curled around her tongue, Osgood knew what she should've suspected earlier. Dr. Laghari wasn't the woman who had tried to shield her from seeing the teratoma that had been removed from her head. Oh, sure, they looked the same and had the same name embroidered on the same lab coat. But the woman squeezing and pulling on Osgood's tongue was—

"Coo coo cachew," said Yoko.

Osgood's head began to lift from the pillow as the thing wearing Dr. Laghari like clothing strained to pull her tongue farther.

Why are you doing this? asked Osgood.

Dr. Laghari stopped, let go of Osgood's tongue, and pulled back her hand, covered in a mix of saliva and watery blood. She put a finger to her lips and cocked her head, eyes toward the ceiling.

Fig 4b. The Thinking Monster, The Wretch in Repose.

"Because I can," the monster said finally, reaching back toward her mouth.

How can I make you stop?

"You know what I want."

To wear me like clothing.

A seemingly orgasmic shudder. "More than anything."

Why?

"We must have our little secrets," said Dr. Laghari.

But I don't have any, thought Osgood. *You've been inside my head.*

The smile on Laghari's lips was tight, an absurd look for someone with a blood print on their lip and a drip down their chin. Ignoring that, Laghari wiped her hand on Osgood's bed linens.

Or ... do I?

"Don't get cocky, you whelp." The Laghari mask had begun to slip. The browns of her eyes had gone orange.

Because what I know about you is interesting, thought Osgood, pushing through the throbbing pain of her tongue. She could feel the muscle swelling in her mouth, and for the first time was thankful she breathed courtesy of the ventilator. Otherwise, she might die.

"You won't," said Laghari, her tone tight.

I won't die? Tonight, or...?

Laghari, the monster, Yoko, just stared at her. Its eyes seemed to lose focus, and its irises drifted farther apart. Then, with a shudder, the lucidity returned to Dr. Laghari's eyes. The woman blinked a few times in confusion and looked down at Osgood. The tilt of her head was almost the same as the monster's, but Osgood could see that Yoko had gone. She was relieved, and more tears rolled down her cheeks.

Laghari leaned down and touched the tear, bringing it to her nose to smell. "I didn't know people with locked-in syndrome could cry," she whispered to Osgood. When she checked her watch, she laughed in surprise. "Wow, I don't know what I'm still doing here. I was off duty three hours ago!" Laghari's smile was genuine this time, and she patted Osgood's shoulder. "I'll see you tomorrow, Os."

Osgood felt her heart break, as this woman who was at least partially responsible for saving her life once before had not only remembered her among all of them (though it might be hard to forget the woman whose tumor had a face) but remembered to call her Os. She wanted to thank her. For everything. But couldn't. Because she was locked in. She wondered what had scared Yoko off, as Laghari exited the room, leaving Osgood alone with her thoughts. She willed Audrey and Zack to come back, but as the minutes passed, she became convinced they'd probably gone home. She wasn't sure how many days she'd been like this but couldn't imagine her friends visiting her daily after a week, two tops.

"God, Os."

Zack had returned. She wanted so badly to speak to him. To ask him how his relationship with ... Sally? Sandy! ... was going. To tell him how much he meant to her. Beyond calling him essential, of course. Because he was that. But when she'd said that, it had been about his place as her partner in the *Spectral Inspector* podcast and investigations. Now, though... Essential was the bare minimum he could be called.

He moved to the side of her bed. "They know absolutely nothing about this ... condition." He shook his head. "If I'd been in school longer, maybe...? But we only caught glimpses of LIS in elective classes about rare diseases." He shook his head again and covered his mouth with his hands. She saw him cry. She'd never seen him cry before. Barely noticed him worried. Like his father, Zack kept a pretty firm handle on his more vulnerable emotions.

Fuck, Zack, please don't cry. I'm going to get out of here, and then... More tears slid down her cheeks... *I'll never take your presence for granted—*

"It's very easy to say things like that," said Zack, eyes still closed, mouth covered by his hands. "Or *think 'em, I guess.*"

What? thought Osgood.

"'I'll never take your presence for granted again!'" said Zack in a macabre mimic. "Oh, I'll never have another cigarette. Never have another drop of liquor. I promise, honey, that was the last time, I won't see her again."

When Zack reopened his eyes, they were fire.

THIRTEEN

GET THE FUCK OUT of him!

Nothing.

I know you can hear me, Yoko, or whoever you are, thought Osgood. *If you hurt him, I swear to—*

"To what? God?" Zack laughed and slapped his hand to his cheek. He looked down at her, momentarily looking like Jack Benny from that TV show she'd watched with her father. "That show was the fucking *Jack Benny Show*, Ossy. That makes sense, right? Jack Benny, star of the *Jack Benny Show*. He actually *played* Jack Benny, too. Not like Dick Van Dyke. No, he was Rob Petrie on that show."

Osgood couldn't comprehend, couldn't respond. She had no idea how one should react to a shapeshifting or body-hopping deity talking about '50s and '60s television.

"No response needed," said Zack. "But I would like to hear your response to my offer."

She doesn't know what to say to that, either. *Offer? The thing about* being *me?*

Zack rolled his eyes. "Humans have such fragile *basic* minds. I can feel this one," Yoko tapped Zack's temple, "already losing focus. They wander off, and I'm left with— Anyway." He leaned down over her. "You won't like what's about to happen."

I don't like anything you do, thought Osgood. *What makes you think you can somehow outdo yourself?*

"Fine," he said, appearing glum. "Don't believe me." Zack brought both hands to her face, pressing his fingertips to her temples.

Going to read my mind now?

"I'd say I should've *cut out* your tongue, but that wouldn't have blocked your insipid mind from relaying your impotent rage."

I'd say it's hardly impotent if it makes you this angry.

"Anyway!" he screamed at her, and she heard Yoko's voice beneath Zack for just the briefest moment. His *true* voice. She marveled at that. She could barely do anything, so having a marvel would have to do for recreation. The marvel was short-lived, though, as she felt Yoko's fingers penetrating her temples. Zack's fingertips remained on the outside of her skin, but whatever was wearing him had begun to dig around in her brain.

"Get out of my—" Osgood yelled and then choked on her voice when she realized she'd said it aloud.

Not that *bit, clearly.* Yoko adjusted his fingers.

I can... began Osgood, but if she could have moved, her whole body would have sagged upon the realization that she'd only been thinking it, *...talk.*

"Nah," said Zack. "Can't have you just jabbering on, you might ruin— *There it is.*" He licked his lips, and some spittle flew forward and landed in her eye. She flinched, at least inwardly, but couldn't be sure outwardly she'd made any movement at all. "You know what's even rarer than locked-in syndrome? HSAM." His eyes met hers again, glee in them. She didn't know what HSAM was. "Right. Highly superior autobiographical memory. It's the ability, curse really, to be able to remember every moment of your life. Marilu Henner has it. From *Taxi*? Anyway. You, Prudence Osgood, you have *sorta* superior autobiographical memory. But with you, things kinda bunch together and get—"

Shuffled, thought Osgood.

"That's the perfect word for it," said Zack, his speech patterns both speeding up and beginning to slur. "You also like to snip out scenes you'd rather not deal with and leave them on the cutting room floor. Only the most traumatizing have the little tabs broken off, so you can't record 'I Think We're Alone Now' over them. Quick, was that Tiffany or Debbie Gibson?"

Tommy James and the Shondells, thought Osgood. *Go fuck yourself.*

"You're not gonna be so fucking funny in a minute," said Zack. "I assure you."

Bring it on, Yoko, thought Osgood.

And then ... he did. The spectral fingers seemed to push through a membrane in her mind and lodge deep, meeting at the center of her brain. The memory flooded in like a tidal wave. A real one, too, not like in the movies where rogue waves tower over skyscrapers, but the very real and somehow more horrifying relentless onrush of a *tide* doing what it usually does in twelve hours in a matter of seconds, and then throwing some more on top for good measure. At that moment, she was everywhere and nowhere. She was the Omni-Osgood, capable of seeing every moment of her life from the moment Cynthia's pussy had snapped open, and Prudence screamed her bloody way into the world.

Good news, Dad, it's a queerdo.

"Still joking," laughed Yoko, actual surprise in Zack's voice. "You are an extraordinary foe, Prudence Osgood."

She tried to thank it, if only to spit the compliment back in its face, but couldn't. Because once life finished reinstalling itself, then came the rest. The dreamlife. For so long, it had been centered on the crossroads of DeKalb, but now it contained so much more, from her very first nightmare about a cat with veins in its eyes to something that felt like it had just happened, but that couldn't be true. When would she have watched *Diff'rent Strokes* in her parent's basement recently? She hasn't been there... Well, since before the pandemic lockdown, that's for sure. And that's when she saw the Bicycle Man. He wasn't the *actual* Bicycle Man, of course, that'd been Gordon Jump as Mr. Horton (and how the fuck did she know that?), but *this* thing was Yoko. The Bicycle Man, like one of the extra jokers in a Bicycle deck, but this one with flaming eyes. She could see this one, printed in blue, the burning flames leaking from his face, melting the "air cushion finish" on the card.

He'd been there. Where? Everywhere. How had he—

That's not possible, thought Osgood.

"What isn't, Lamb?" asked Zack, resting his chin on his hands.

You couldn't have always been here.

"I *am*," said Zack. "Time is different for me, and your timestreams are so monotonously straight." The scowl of distaste caused his whole face to droop, and "straight" came out wet and sticky, sounding like there was a *sch* at the beginning.

At last, the rest filled in, bringing her up to date. All 192 days. She'd been present for all of them. Present and alert. When they'd rebroken and reset her bones, they hadn't been all that careful about her pain levels. They'd thought she was in a coma, then. Because when you hear hooves, you shouldn't think zebra, 'cuz it's never a zebra.

I'm a zebra, Osgood weeps.

Sure enough, Zack and Audrey had been there all along. Some days, though, Zack had kept vigil on his own. Osgood could understand that. Audrey had— *What? A life?*

"For someone you propose to love so much, you don't seem to think so highly of me!" yelled not-Zack, grinning down at her. The flames of his eyes had begun to singe his eyebrows, and she could smell it now. The acrid odor of burning hair.

I didn't mean that! Osgood's thoughts erupted in bursts, surrounded by new memories slotting themselves into place. They were coming faster now. A janitor who'd come in to ... look at her? Some nights, he'd stay for hours, but he never

(show me on the doll where he)

touched her. A pair of nurses, or a nurse and a young doctor, using the corner of her room to fondle and pet each other outside the view of the nurses' station. Every blood draw. Every time someone had jabbed what felt like a needle into her heel, it was harder each time because she didn't, couldn't flinch. She'd become "the vegetable" here, the one who didn't care or matter.

But Dr. Laghari...

"You think she still cares?"

She remembered my name.

"Your name's written on the board." Zack flicked his thumb dismissively.

Osgood's fury rose. For a moment, she thought that she even felt her teeth clench. *Get me the fucking board, and if my name isn't written as "Prudence Osgood" on there, you can have my—* she stopped, wondering what to call it *—my life.*

Zack didn't let his burning eyes leave hers. She knew she'd won the bet because he wouldn't look over. She'd called his bluff.

She remembered my name, thought Osgood again. *Because she cares.*

"*No one* cares," growled Yoko.

"It may feel that way," said Audrey, out of sight somewhere. "But it's not true."

Yoko whipped his head toward the source of the voice, and the Zack mask snapped back into place so quickly Osgood thought she could hear it.

"I got you coffee," said Audrey as she appeared in view. Osgood felt the softness of Audrey's hand in hers.

Don't, thought Osgood, but she wasn't sure what.

Don't!? You'll have to be more specific, came from Yoko in her head. Here, its voice was more profound as it needn't be produced by human vocal cords.

Don't hurt them, she pleaded, watching as Yoko-pretending-to-be-Zack made small talk with Audrey above her.

They really are what you truly *care about, aren't they?* Yoko sounded almost impressed. *Especially him. She may be the love of your life, but... He is essential.*

Osgood couldn't respond, could only watch them. Yoko winked down at her; Audrey didn't notice.

Do you remember it? asked Yoko. *What I asked for?*

Osgood did, now, and offered a weak, *Yes*, in return. She remembered both times, in fact. When he'd asked as Alice, and when he'd asked on the shore of some vast stygian sea. And as she thought further, she remembered him asking other times as well. After turning the corner in her bedroom on Summerdale. After reaching the basement landing on Elm Street. As she lay dying in that wreck. He'd asked before the Lord had asked his own question.

You don't actually believe that fucking Christmas decoration granted you resurrection, do you?

The question caused Osgood to halt her brain, almost like pulling the emergency brake. *What?*

Yoko-as-Zack grinned at her and put his hand atop Audrey's atop hers. The moment, which could've broken Osgood's heart with joy, instead made her skin crawl.

"Did you see that?" exclaimed Audrey. "She got goosebumps!" She leaned down to Osgood. "I knew it! You're still in there. Os, please come back! We need you!" Tears fell from Audrey's eyes and landed on Osgood's face. She wiped at them and apologized, then returned her hand to the pile. She squeezed Yoko's hand and Osgood's. "We will get you back." Her voice was intense and assertive. "We will *not* lose you."

"No, we'll *never* lose you," said Yoko-as-Zack, and he smiled. Then something happened, an electrical current moving through her hand. Now Audrey had ceased her tears and was smiling. Zack ... Well, he looked supportive but confused.

Stay away from her, insisted Osgood, but she knew it was in vain. What Yoko wanted, Yoko got.

"You're goddamn right," said Audrey.

Zack shook his head to clear the cobwebs and stepped out of Osgood's view.

"You alright?" Audrey asked him, but her voice held no concern for his well-being.

"Yeah," he said. "Just got lightheaded for a second."

Audrey walked around the bed, and Zack reappeared. Audrey stood behind him, massaging his shoulders. Osgood could tell the gesture made him uncomfortable. He really didn't like being touched much. She knew Zack was somewhere on the autism spectrum but wasn't exactly sure where. Then Audrey's hands moved to his neck.

"Um, Audrey," laughed Zack nervously. "You really don't have—"

If Osgood had had a voice, she'd have screamed, but since she didn't, all she could do was watch as her beloved Audrey squeezed the life out of the man who'd been there for her more than anyone else.

Alright! she screamed in her head. *You win! Take me!*

Fourteen

When Osgood tumbles from the gaping maw of the cave, it's as though the entire world has shifted. Below her his horizon, and she skirts across the rocky shore and over the sea. Maybe she'll fall around this fucking world, whatever it is.

"Oh, Zack," cries Osgood.

As she falls, she can feel her speed increasing, well beyond terminal velocity until—

She awakens.

She feels the soft Egyptian cotton linens. She hears the dull drone of the air conditioner. Cold in here now. In the night she seems to have pulled both the comforter and her leather coat over her in her sleep. Depending on the light and her mood, the coat often looks different shades of red. Today, it (and her mood) are crimson. She lies there, breathing along with the drone.

Just a dream. Just a...

No.

She bursts forth from bungalow 312 into the blinding sunlight of a new day on The Isle. Around her, couples mingle, and the rare stray single — someone who looks like she could be called a wealthy dowager — eats at a table with her, perhaps, three-pound dog whose boutique breed surely ends with -apoo. The *umph umph* music is back at the pool, and Osgood squints. Did she just have too much to drink last night? It wouldn't be the first time she's been caught in a dream that was both incredibly long and astonishingly vivid.

"No," she yells, defiant. "Because this isn't fucking real."

The woman with the dog looks up, and a red heat crawls up Osgood's cheeks. Because here she stands among people in their swimsuits and beach cover-ups, some topless here and there, and then there's Prudence *fucking* Osgood, storming around in a crimson leather trench coat atop a Fangoria t-shirt, torn black jeans, and yellow Chucks. But the embarrassment is short-lived because then comes fury. "Fuck all you people who don't exist." She shoves her way through the resort, first avoiding people and then shoving them out of the way.

She astonishes one dudebro so much he actually throws a punch, one that Osgood catches before it reaches her face. She pulls him in with his fist and spits into his perplexed face. "You're not real."

"Woah," says the dudebro, and he pushes his way backward off the path.

"Yeah, give space to the lunatic," says his broseph.

She rounds a last corner, her coat fluttering behind her like a cape, and stands directly in front of the courtyard bar.

"Hey motherfucker," she says as she slams her palm on the bar in front of Virgil. "What comes next?"

He stops wiping his glass and looks up at her with confusion. "Well, I could get you a drink," says Virgil. But ... His name isn't Virgil, is it? It's Victor. Stated clearly on his nametag. Victor is a far more common name, especially in this part of the world. Everything else though ... the same.

Minus the flaming eyes.

"Virgil," she tries.

It doesn't fit, and Victor introduces himself. He has an accent that Virgil doesn't. He may not be a local, but he is definitely not from her neck of the woods — though neither is Virgil for that matter.

"No no no," says Osgood, backing away from the bar. "I remember everything."

"That's good," Victor tells her, seeming perplexed. "Sometimes the morning gives folks hangover ... forgetfulness."

She looks around, seeing the other guests in the courtyard eyeing her with various levels of concern. Some in the lobby look through the sliding plate glass doors. In front of those doors stand the general manager, a large imposing man, and Maria. The heat hits Osgood's cheeks as embarrassment rises again, shoving itself through her body. She feels the words "I'm sorry" come to her mouth. Why not? She's said those words so many times. She's *needed* to say those words so many times. "I'm sorry, I'm a—"

She stops and looks down at her hand. On its own, it seems, it has riffled through Osgood's coat pocket and pulled out a folded sheet of The Isle's stationery. Her hands shake as she unfolds it, finding not Audrey's writing this time but Zack's. Small, in all caps: HE'S HURTING US.

The embarrassment drops back into her stomach as the sounds around her seem to all run together. Before she can think too long about it, she's vaulted over the bar, something she could never do if this was real, and has in hand a knife far too big for cutting limes. She holds the knife to him. "Virgil."

"I do not know a Virgil. *Por favor*. Please, *Señorita* Osgood."

"It's. Just. Fucking. Osgood. You. Psychotic. Fucking. God." Osgood punctuates each word with its own period, a stab of the knife into Victor or Virgil or Yoko or whoever-he-is's chest. The blood spurts, thick, soupy. It covers her. Dousing.

The courtyard full of spectators screeches to a halt in gasps of horror.

When she wipes the blood from her eyes, though, it's night. The music has ceased, and the horror of the crowd has ended as well as there no longer are any people. Just Prudence Osgood, covered in blood, brandishing a knife. The amorphous clump of viscera on the floor in front of her isn't a corpse because it's moving, pushing itself away from her. One of its eyes has popped and run down what was once its chin, but the other one, its flaming iris rimmed in blood, stares furiously up at her.

"See, I *thought* it was you," says Osgood. She reaches down and grabs its ankle, only apparent because of the shoe attached to it, and begins to drag the clump back toward her.

"I thought," it coughs, "you might want to forget."

She kneels atop it, her knees on its left hand and digging into its right side. *If it has kidneys,* she thinks, *Imma pop one.* "Forget?" she asks with an astonished laugh. "Then you shouldn't have made me remember!"

Her newfound memory comes up behind her. What she'd had for lunch on April 11, 1981: PBJ with the crusts cut off—she was only three, after all. She remembers the mileage on the Buick Skylark when she inherited it from her father: 82,453, and she'd put nearly one hundred thou on in the interim before the accident. She remembers the semi driver's head coming off and how it had stared at her as she died. And that time she'd tried to microwave a waffle and put 20 minutes instead of 20 seconds. Those plates weren't microwave-safe in the hands of a toddler. She remembers good things, too. The first time Audrey said "I love you" to her (months after Osgood had said it, of course) that night after stopping at the beach in Rogers Park, the furthest north neighborhood in Chicago. She knows every line of

Audrey's lips. She knows every inch of her body, from the tiny mole on her left breast to how her labia minora sticks out like a tongue on the right side.

"Memory is a superpower," she tells the pathetic thing whimpering before her. "And if you're a god, why don't you just get the fuck back up?"

She laughs, not at it, but at a weird, fleeting thought that had come with the cluster of other memories. "In kindergarten... Yoko, you can hear me, right?" Virgil's bloody remains nod at her. "We were coloring mimeographed pages of the Stations of the Cross." She widens her eyes. "I know, right? Can you imagine giving... What is kindergarten, five years old? ...giving them the timeline of an execution to use their fucking Crayolas on?" She crouches down to be sure Yoko can hear and see her. "And as a side note, if you give a child a bloody scene and a red crayon, they're going to give you a bloody mess. Mrs. Nosek was shocked all the way down to her stockings—they started the day up top but usually had reached her ankles by 2:30. Anyway, when presented with the Eleventh Station..." She poked at Yoko with the knife, causing a new spurt of blood. "If you're a god, you probably know number eleven. It was my favorite 'cuz it was the most violent thing I'd ever read. It's when they *nail* cool-dude-but-certainly-not-god Jesus to the fucking cross. And they showed us the nails. Not the actual nails, but replicas. I'm sure they bought them at a fucking religious surplus store in the 'let's traumatize the sinners' section. These were like railroad spikes." She held up her index finger to Yoko's face, which... *I thought I'd stabbed out one of those eyes.* Shakily Osgood continued. "But I remember as I colored in that right horrorshow, thinking about our Lord and Savior, which I actually *did* believe then, I wondered why he didn't kick the Romans as they tried to nail in his feet. Like, surely he could've knocked them down; then yanked each hand off his cross and went on his merry way, smiting the sinners."

Fewer holes in Yoko's face just now, and Osgood's voice wavers further. The waver seems to amuse Yoko.

"Of course, there's the version where he's nailed to the crossbar and hoisted up. I imagine he'd be in no physical shape to kick there. Oh and in that *Jesus of Nazareth* mini-series it wasn't even a crossbar, it was a fucking *log!* And there's the version where he's tied, then nailed, or nailed while the cross is flat. Mel Gibson did that one. Nail penetrating his hand, the wood, and the ground. And then there's the true believer bit. This man, this god, loved the world so much that he endured this pain to kick open the doors to heaven that his daddy had slammed shut when he was in a mood because the first people he made wanted to know stuff."

Sure enough, Yoko sits up, the blood on his face now superficial. "Because," he says with a gurgle as the hole in his throat hasn't entirely closed, "that's the sacrifice. Like... Like Odin ... hanging from the tree." Yoko turns his neck, and it snaps back into place, the hole now gone. The wounds in his chest and arms seem to be nearly gone too. He nods at the knife in her hand. "So, that was you kicking at the Romans?"

"Have to put up some sort of fight; what fun would it be otherwise?"

"Dear Prudence..."

"Fuck you."

"Your fight has been exquisite."

"Thank you," she assays a scornful curtsey.

"And I expected nothing less," Yoko smiles.

She hears triumph in his voice, and it infuriates her. *Are you in my head?* she thinks. But he doesn't answer. Maybe he'd made good on that deference at the cave. Maybe he's just cocky enough...

"Your sacrifice will not be in vain, I assure you. And millennia from now, your name will be in epic poems."

"Oh," she says cocking her head at him. "You know that I wasn't Jesus in that allegory, right?"

"You..." He snickers, then stops.

"No, you're the one sacrificing."

His smile vanishes, and he cocks his head, mirroring hers. She thinks at first he's doing it to mock her but then realizes he is actually confused.

"See, Yoko," she says. "You overplayed your hand."

There's a bubbling sound below, and the pool of blood beneath Yoko begins to rise, covering his feet. He looks down at it, confused.

"It was what you said about the Lord of the Hinterlands not resurrecting me..."

Yoko puts his hand on the bar to steady himself as the blood pool rises from the floor like a column, up to his calves.

"If he didn't do it... And *you* didn't..."

"How do you know I didn't?"

"Because you're a cocky fucking god who would've bragged about it if you had."

That silences Yoko.

"Then either I'm *really* fortunate to have survived that crash, which is what I always thought, or I'm special." She stares deep into his fiery eyes, and he glares back, looking both intimidating and a little like a fox caught in the henhouse. Sure, the fox can do damage, but when the farmer catches him... Osgood stabs the knife down, through Yoko's hand, into the bartop below and the creature produces an inhuman roar combined with a pained yowl.

"And since you, and The Lord of the Hinterlands, and even Cora fucking Ballard told me I'm ... well, you've all been kinda vague, but my aunt and great grandmother said I'm extraordinary. And while I may not always say, 'Damn, I feel like a woman,' I'm fucking grateful to be an Osgood woman." Osgood reaches under the bar and pulls out another knife, the kind of overlarge chef's knife that Michael Myers might weild to stalk around Haddonfield. It seems to surprise Yoko, and that look is all Osgood needs to confirm her suspicion...

I'm winning.

The blood reaches his knees, and the lowest bit has cured to a deep brick red.

"You are... So fucking cocky." Yoko laughs, but the fight has gone out of him.

"You're goddamned right I am," she tells him. She gets close to his face, nearly nose to nose. He reaches up to her throat, but she swats away his hand. "Stop that, you know you've lost." She presses the knife point to the side of his head and slides it into his temple.

"You can't kill me. I'm eternal."

"Gods like to say that," she says. "The Lord of the Hinterlands also claimed to be eternal. And then my girlfriend killed it." The knife is an inch deep, and she sees a fresh, bright red pool in the milky white surrounding Yoko's flaming iris. "But gods do die. Like everything else, they're forgotten in the sands of time. And you, Yoko, will be forgotten as well."

"You've got no right—"

"There's the anger! You're just confirming my suspicions. Why would you be mad if I *couldn't* do this to you?" She slams her palm on the butt of her knife, and the front half of his left eye tumbles forward and splats into the blood column, now up to his thighs. "You'd just ... stop me."

"Fucking useless fucking cunt..."

"Oh please!" Osgood laughs, shoving the knife again. She realizes she can see the blade move through the bloody hole of his eye cavity. "I've been called so much worse by far more pathetic men. Now pay attention, 'cuz I think this is important. So I can create worlds in the space between, the margins. That's sorta impressive. But not extraordinary. When the chips are down, it's pretty much lucid dreaming."

"It's—"

"Hush." She pinches open his lids and bisects his other eye. "And the tulpa thing. I mean, it's great, but Buddhists have done it for centuries." She thinks about when her aunt Eliza and great-grandmother Lil had joined her to destroy the thing inside Sam Goddard and close the gate. "And combining with the other Osgood women, I'm pretty sure that trick was theirs, not mine."

"What's ... your fucking ... point?"

"Well, you said two things the first time you spoke to me. Really spoke to me, I mean, instead of hiding behind the quasar or the eye in the sky." She yanks the knife out and cuts Yoko's throat. Blood pours out, joining the roiling and gurgling column of hardening blood that surrounds him, now consuming his hand knifed to the bartop. "I'm really fucking hard to kill, and this is *my* fucking kingdom."

She stands up and watches as the bloody mass consumes him, growing to a point like one of the stalagmites in Meramec Caverns she saw during a family road trip when she was very young. She laughs sardonically, recalling a joke her junior high science teacher, Mr. Budzich, had told them multiple times in their geology unit. She'd never known if he was repeating it because he'd forgotten he told them or because wanted to drill down the knowledge. She decides to tell Virgil the joke. He might appreciate it. "Stalagmites might hang from the cave ceiling..."

The final droplets of blood coalesce atop his head and form into a twisty spire on the column of resin containing the god, the quasar, the black hole, the red sun, the eye in the sky, the thing that had terrified her so.

She lifts her right hand and snaps her fingers. The Isle is gone. Only a black void remains. Prudence Osgood, the Spectral Inspector, stands before a stalagmite prison for a god, and as she thinks about it melting away to nothing, it does. Then it's just her. So she finishes the joke. "They *might* hang from the cave ceiling. But they don't."

She smiles, and when she looks down, she sees that her clothes are clean, with nary a drop of blood on her.

A moment later, the black was gone, people scrambled about, and Audrey Frost exclaimed tearily, "You're awake!"

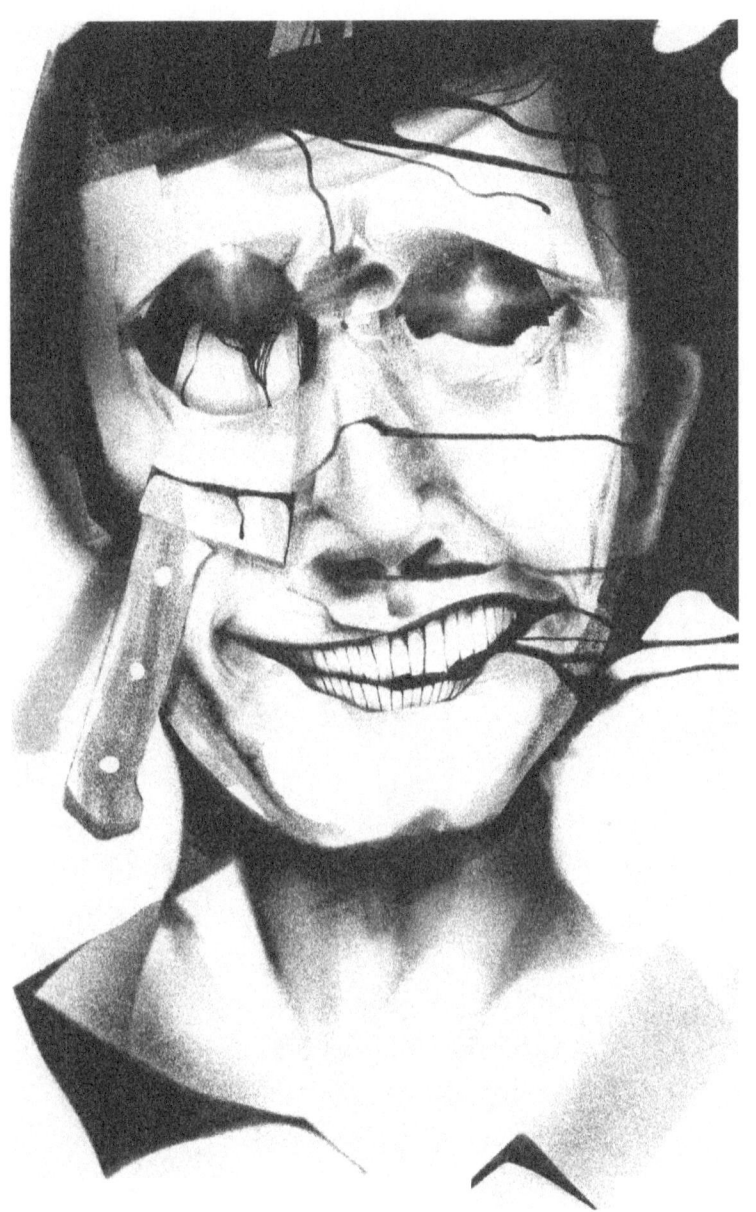

FIFTEEN

"Zack!" Osgood exclaimed, coughing her way through it, garbled by the ventilator.

"Fuck! Os!!" Audrey leaped up, dropping a hospital magazine, probably a months-old *People*, onto the floor. She rushed to Osgood's side.

Osgood only wanted the answer to one question: "Where's Zack?"

Audrey looked slightly confused and hurt but stammered, "He had to run some errands, but he'll be back."

"I need to..." Osgood stopped, feeling herself gagging on the ventilator tube. She took a deep breath. *This is gonna suck.* Grabbing it with both hands, she began to slide the tube out of her windpipe, then throat, then mouth, despite Audrey's slapping at her hands, desperate to stop her. With it out, finally able to breathe, she looked at Audrey and said, "Jesus Christ."

"You can say that again," said Audrey, hand on her chest.

"Zack's alive?"

"What?" asked Audrey. "Of course Zack's alive! Why would you—"

"It doesn't matter." How much of what she'd seen had been real? Osgood didn't know. She also wasn't entirely sure why she'd thought Zack might not be alive any longer. Or ... what she'd seen. But it didn't matter, really, did it? Zack was alive. Audrey was alive. Osgood was alive. "How many days?"

Audrey hemmed.

"You can tell me."

"Around two hundred," she said.

"Two hundred," Osgood said, astonished.

"Now, promise you won't leave again!" Audrey laughed, then put her fist before her mouth to stifle a sob.

"I can obviously make no promises."

"Os!"

Osgood whipped her head to the door where Zack stood. She was met with screaming fiery pain from her neck, and it felt as though her brain sloshed with the movement, but it, too, didn't matter. She tried to hold out her arms but was stymied by her IV and pulse monitors looped around the rail of her bed. She yanked them out and hugged Zack tightly amidst the screaming of the alarm for the nurses.

"They'll think you died," he said, and she saw the tears in his eyes. Audrey joined the hug, and they stayed that way, the Spectral Inspectors, until a nurse scrambled in and shoved them away.

The nurse, whose name was Cassie Bronson, did a cartoon double-take when she saw that not only was Osgood *not* dead, but had ripped out her breathing tube. Nurse Bronson stammered and said, "I'm gonna call Dr. Laghari," before disappearing out of the room again.

Zack and Audrey moved to return to the hug, but Osgood held up her hands. "I need— I need some air," she said and coughed, setting fire to her inflamed throat and making her wish she'd been *slightly* more careful when she'd removed that tube.

Her companions looked from each other to her and back. She knew what they wanted to ask, and she knew it made them nervous. "Yes," she said.

"Yes?" asked Zack.

"I was awake the whole time."

"You remember it?" asked Audrey. "All of it?"

Osgood thought about that. She wasn't sure, actually. Things were beginning to set in her mind like Jello, shuffling around and putting themselves into strange new orders. "Most?"

"What was it like?" asked Zack.

Osgood opened her mouth, then closed it again. She shook her head. "I don't know that I have the words at the moment."

They just stared back at her, blinking.

"Now, tell me, are my legs broken?"

"Well, they were," said Audrey, delicately.

Zack was decidedly less delicate. "You almost lost your left leg." He pointed at that leg in case she didn't know where to look. "It was hanging by a tendon."

Osgood nodded, letting her attention drift to the leg.

Audrey looked down, seeming to take multiple runups to her following comment. "Nora is…"

"I know," said Osgood. That she remembered for sure. When Nora became two. She didn't need to share that with them, not today anyway. No point, no benefit. Let two of the Spectral Inspectors live without that in their minds. In Osgood's, she's sure it's joined the pantheon of horrors alongside the semi driver's head and Goddard's martyr stare.

Step right up and see the bisected woman; she can do twice as much as you in half the time.

Osgood shook her head, feeling swimmy again. "Gotta stay awake."

"What?" asked Zack.

"I can't go back there," she said, reaching out and grabbing his shirt. "*The Isle* isn't real!"

The what?

"I..." he stammered. "You can sleep, Os. I don't think this sorta thing recurs without new injury."

"But you don't know!"

His face fell. "No, I, uh, you're right. I don't."

She watched him for a moment. "I love you, Zack."

Zack's dark eyes darted up to hers. He looked surprised. "Where did..."—"

"Audrey, too," said Osgood. "But she knows already."

"Thanks," said Audrey in a grousing tone. But she winked when Osgood glanced at her.

"I... Love you too, Os."

"Well. Aren't you resilient?" Dr. Laghari asked, though it was more of an astonished statement. "I'm happy to see you again, Os."

"You called me Os because you cared," said Osgood.

The doctor had a momentary marvel at her, then took a deep breath and put her pen behind her ear. It joined the two in the bun on the back of her head. Osgood wondered how often she went home with extra pens on days she didn't have to operate.

"You hafta take them out for surgery, right?"

Laghari's eyes narrowed as she tried to parse Osgood's meaning. Then she found it. "Oh!" Her hand went to her bun and nabbed the two pens. "Usually, they're grabbed by a nurse while I'm scrubbing in." With a laugh, Dr. Laghari pulled out a penlight and checked Osgood's pupils, ears, throat, and nose, then slapped on a blood pressure cuff.

"Will you be giving me a pelvic exam, too?"

"Will you be needing one?" asked the doctor, one eyebrow raised.

"Need?" Osgood tilted her hand from side to side.

"Osgood," snapped Audrey. "Boundaries!"

Laghari didn't look offended, but Osgood thought that was mostly because she was still marveling at Osgood's recovery.

"Can I go home?"

"Can you—" The doctor seemed stunned that this was even a question. "No!"

"Are you kidding?" asked Audrey.

"Then I'm committed?"

Audrey put her hand over her eyes, and Zack leaned down to Osgood, whispering. "That's not really how this works, Os."

"Your friend is right," said Dr. Laghari. "No one gets committed to a medical ward. But I absolutely, 150% — and as a woman of science, I generally refrain from going over 100 — think you must stay here while we observe you."

"Observe," repeated Osgood glumly.

She must have looked really crushed because the doctor sighed again. "That being said, if you want to sign the AMA release forms, I can do nothing to stop you. But I will emphasize that I believe it is a bad idea."

"AMA?" asked Osgood.

"It means Against Medical Advice," said Zack. Despite the confidence in his words, he looked to Dr. Laghari, who nodded in confirmation.

"Bring 'em," said Osgood. "Please."

"Os," said Audrey.

"That way, we have them if we need them," said Osgood.

Dr. Laghari turned to Zack and Audrey. "Please talk her out of this." Then she smiled a tight smile and left the room.

Zack quickly grasped the edge of Osgood's bed and got very close to her. "Osgood, you had a rare and misunderstood malady and spent over two hundred days locked inside your body."

"Yes," said Osgood.

"I..." Zack turned to Audrey. "Didn't think I'd need more reason than that."

"I would like..." said Osgood, looking at the ceiling, "a burger from Mary's. A glass of bourbon. A cigarette—"

"You don't smoke anymore!" said Audrey.

"Well, sure, but I may as well."

"You..." said Zack. "Why?"

Osgood smirked at them sure she must look crazy. "'Cuz I don't think I can die."

"That's quite a statement," said Audrey.

"I mean," said Zack, looking downward. "She has been through a lot of things that should've killed her." He snapped his eyes to Osgood. "Not. That. I *want* them. To have. Done that."

"Thank you, Zack," said Osgood.

"You can die, Os," said Audrey. "I assure you."

"And what data are you basing that on?"

Audrey looked to Zack, then back to Osgood. "I don't know, Os. The fact that people die."

"But I haven't."

"Well," said Zack. "If we're going by *that* logic."

"I've been in quite a few situations that kill people."

"I got shot!" offered Zack like a plea.

"Fair," said Osgood.

"I had cancer," said Audrey.

The trio looked at each other for a long, unbroken moment.

"How about instead," began Audrey. "We tell you about the ... stuff." She flicked her eyes to Zack, who took a deep breath.

"Stuff?" asked Osgood. "What stuff?"

"Something is..." Zack spent a long while taste-testing words before settling on, "...happening... in Chicago."

"Is it *strange*, Zack? Who're we gonna call?"

His look to Audrey was a plea, and she nodded, saying, "Life has been different since the subway incident."

"The subway crash that killed a girl I was dating, sure."

"Os." Zack looked down.

Osgood stopped. Maybe this wasn't the moment for her detached cynicism. Though she felt confident her friends would argue that there were no moments where it was ideal and many where it was vastly inappropriate. "Sorry."

"No," Audrey sent back. "You don't need to be. You experienced serious trauma that day."

"If I experience one more, I get the next one free." But even she couldn't laugh at her joke. There was Nora with a pane of glass sliding through her. Osgood suddenly envisioned cutting into a rare beef Wellington and felt sure she'd never eat that dish again, no matter how much she'd once loved it. "There's something strange in our neighborhood. I got it. Want to give me more details? I'm only filling the gaps in our conversation."

Zack handed Osgood a tablet, and in its dark mirror, she saw herself. Her curly hair covered her whole head, and she could see she'd gone almost entirely gray. She laughed sadly.

"What?" asked Audrey.

"I can't remember which side I used to leave long."

"The right," said Zack, without hesitation. Osgood looked at him. He'd moved back to the end of the bed but stared at her earnestly.

Osgood was touched that he knew.

"What?" he asked, shuffling his feet. "Tap the presentation app there."

Osgood did, and a photo filled the screen. It showed a green scene, trees and bushes, and an expanse of grass. In the distance, the lake cut an azure swath. "Is this Lakeside Trail?" asked Osgood, referencing Chicago's lakeside bike and jogging path.

"Yep," said Zack, then he waited.

Osgood looked up at him. "What?"

"Look again," he said.

She did. In the photo, a blonde woman in a crop top and leggings jogged with a terrier in pursuit. A man biked in full racing regalia. In the background, she saw the white triangles of a pair of sailboats on the water and, on the horizon, the dark smudge of one of Chicago's water crib pumping stations. She scanned the picture again, holding the tablet close to her face for good measure. "I don't know what you want me to see."

"That's kinda the point," said Audrey. "Keep looking." She and Zack just stared.

A laugh escaped Osgood, and she furrowed her brow suspiciously. "You're fucking with me. A little 'welcome back to the world' hazing?"

"Just..." Zack tapped the tablet's bezel with his finger. "Just look one more time."

Osgood's patience wore thin. "For *what*, Zack?"

"If you don't see it, I'll tell you," he said. "But I think you will."

Her photographic memory made this feel very routine, every object and person had already become old hat: bush, bush, tree, fallen branch, the edge of a tent, perhaps the residence of one of Chicago's many unhoused. Blonde, terrier. Biker. Sail— "Wait."

"Yeah," said Zack, "Chase that thought, whatever it is."

As she stared down at the image, she still saw all of those things, but somehow, the center of the screen showed something she'd missed entirely. It had just popped into view, like a Magic Eye picture. "What the fuck?" Front and center in the picture stood a wooden post the size of a railroad trestle, and a rough-hewn rectangle of old wood was nailed roughly into that post with a bent and twisty iron nail.

"You can see it?" asked Audrey.

Astonished, Osgood asked them, "How did I miss it?" Try as she might, though, Osgood couldn't read the words on the wooden rectangle. "I can't read it."

"No," said Audrey, "You probably won't be able to."

Osgood turned her head this way and that and looked under her glasses, but the words that she could clearly see existed didn't seem to want to resolve into ... anything. "I keep ... almost having it, I think."

"Don't try too hard," said Zack.

"You'll get a headache," said Audrey.

"So, what the hell?"

Zack told her to swipe, and she did. She found the following picture similar to the last, in that it revealed itself in stages. This one showed a beach on the north side. Hollywood, maybe, or Pratt. On the beach were figures in the distance throwing sticks and balls for dogs moving fast enough to be blurred. In the foreground was messy beach foliage and a broken-down hurricane fence. "Will it..." she started to ask, but then she saw. Again, a railroad trestle, an iron nail, and a wooden sign covered in words that refused to become anything, no matter how hard she stared at them. "Why can't I understand the words?" she asked finally.

"We don't know," said Audrey.

"They... the signs, I mean ...started showing up just after the crash. There's five in all." Zack reached out a finger to her and made a swiping gesture.

She mimicked the gesture and discovered more, each slow to be perceived. "This is trippy."

"The first one is just south of the Lincoln Park Zoo on the Lakefront Trail, as you noted; the second is Hollywood Beach. The other three are the end of Navy Pier, the Phoenix Garden just south of the Museum of Science and Industry, and then there's that one..." he pointed, and Osgood stared.

Unlike the others, this image had been shot at a weird angle and at night. It appeared to be an intersection, and police horses and bollards surrounded it. She found this sign much easier to see and wondered why that might be. She asked the question.

"Again," said Audrey, "we don't know."

"If we *had* to come up with an answer," said Zack, "I'd bet it's because it's not a dead-on view of the words."

"What *are* the words?" Osgood asked.

"Well," said Zack. "About this one first. That's the intersection of Monroe and State."

"That's right downtown," said Osgood.

"The city can't get rid of it," said Audrey.

"What?" asked Osgood.

"They tried," said Zack. "The bulldozer was nearly destroyed!" He made the swiping gesture again, and the tablet revealed a slightly out-of-focus photo of Zack, at night, pulling up a tarp to reveal a massive broken bulldozer roller. "Sandy took that."

"The two of them got arrested," said Audrey, a snap in her voice that amused Osgood.

"They arrested you for..."

"Professional photography without a permit," said Zack with a sigh. "Such bullshit, but what are they gonna say? 'Looking at bulldozer broken by mystery sign without permission?' By the time Audrey bailed us out, they'd moved the dozer."

Osgood chuckled, staring at her essential friend. "Done hard time."

Audrey rolled her eyes. "Well, two hours of—"

"In the clink," said Osgood. She giggled, then swayed. "I think the morphine is making me high." Two blinks, then a slower one. She shook her head to clear it. "Okay, y'all need to get to the home stretch, 'cuz I think I might crash."

"Good," said Zack. "It'll keep you here for another night."

"Only if a monster doesn't show up," said Osgood. She gave Audrey and Zack the finger guns, then dropped into a morose thought. "He killed them, yunno, the nurses."

"We know," said Zack, nodding, his face down.

"Let's wrap it up, Zack," Audrey told him.

He nodded. "The signs showed up one at a time, roughly every other week, each in the middle of the night. They can't seem to be knocked down or destroyed. And their messages have changed twice." The pause was excruciating, and then Zack impatiently gestured to the tablet.

Osgood looked down, swiped again, and another photo filled the screen. Rough. Butcher paper, maybe? Charcoal. "Is this a rubbing?" she asked, but she knew it was and didn't have to wait for the response. Here was the exact text she'd seen in the other photos, but somehow, it made sense. "'Eschaton due.'" She read aloud.

"Yeah," said Audrey. "After we... and everyone else, also, I'll point out ...weren't able to photograph the text, I snuck past surveillance and—"

"They're being surveilled?" asked Osgood.

"Keep swiping," said Audrey.

Osgood did as she was bid. The following image matched the first rubbing in style and coloring, but Osgood felt her humor leave her as she read it. "'Eschaton past due.'" She repeated the unfamiliar word to herself. *Eschaton*. It frightened her somehow. If she'd heard it before, her new memory trick wasn't telling, but something about it felt dark. "I'll bite," she said. "What does 'eschaton' mean?"

"Eschaton is..." said Zack. "The end of the world."

"Super," said Osgood.

Sixteen

"Really, Prudence, how many times are you going to try to die to get my attention?"

Osgood's eyelids fluttered, and she squinted at the light pouring through her hospital window. The sky outside looked angry, like charcoal smudged across paper. She couldn't see much beyond except the tops of buildings. She turned toward her mother, wondering if the voice was authentic or just the omnipresent version of Cynthia Osgood, who lived in her head. Sure enough, Cynthia, the *real* Cynthia, sat near the foot of her bed, several-month-old *Cosmo* in hand. Osgood's eyes narrowed, realizing that her mother had brought a prop from the waiting room. The woman looked thinner than Osgood could ever remember, wrists seeming to barely hold onto the bangles and platinum watch that adorned them. Her cheekbones were sharp beneath eyes that matched Osgood's, cycling from green to hazel to gray to brown. Today, their hazel was washed out, taking inspiration from the barren sky. Her tight lips sat below a nose as sharp as those cheekbones, wearing a permascowl that carved lines deep into her face. While Osgood's disdain for her mother was mainly fed by how different they were, there was no denying that of her two parents, Osgood had got the, ahem, motherlode of features from Cynthia.

"How many will it take?" asked Osgood, her voice raspy. She coughed. "Might have a few more in me."

Seemingly put out, Cynthia poured water from a beige pitcher into a clear plastic cup and snapped on a lid, puncturing it with a straw. She walked to Osgood's side and handed it to her. When Osgood took it, offering light thanks, Cynthia returned to the end of the bed. "Really, Prudence."

"Really, Mother," aped Osgood, uncertain if it had been a question, an admonishment, what? But she found the same tone regardless.

"Your father is flying home."

"From?" asked Osgood.

Cynthia's eyes hit hers from above the magazine. Osgood waited for the dig. But none came. "He went to your uncle's funeral in Buffalo."

"Uncle Randall died?"

"Wouldn't have been worth throwing a funeral had he not."

Osgood's lips tightened. "Can I do something for you, Mother?"

Finally, Cynthia closed the magazine and tossed it onto the chair by the window. She interlaced her fingers, each tipped with a pristine French manicure. She fixed Osgood with a look.

"Are you happy I'm alive?" asked Osgood, allowing the edge to creep into her voice.

"Of course, I'm happy you're alive. Don't be silly." She waved away *silly Osgood*.

"You're always so warm, Mother."

"The last time I saw you, you slapped me across the face, Prudence," said Cynthia. "Do you recall?"

I do, thought Osgood. *I now have total recall.* "Yes."

"So you'll forgive my distance and reticence."

"Whatever you need to feel better," said Osgood.

"And during seven months of chemo—"

"I was locked in," defended Osgood.

"You were most certainly sitting on your apartment couch, bemoaning the effects of long Covid as the reason you couldn't come by." She seemed to give each individual word its own punctuation, and some of them stung.

"So you had Dad call and pretend you were dying."

"You have my breasts, Prudence."

"Eew, Mother!"

"Don't be a child," said Cynthia. "I do hope you examine yourself regularly."

"Can we not?!"

"We. Can. Not."

"Are you..." Osgood began, but that was all she could get out.

"It is in remission, fully. My doctor says there are no signs of it," said Cynthia, as casually as she might mention a new brand of makeup she liked from the magazine in her lap. "Take care you don't miss signs."

"Again," said Osgood.

"You are a difficult ... person, Prudence."

Osgood found the pause interesting. When her mother wanted to put her in her place, she'd call her "little girl." Rarely did she say "woman," as though that would allow Osgood to actually be an adult in her eyes. Even rarer was the gender neutral. This one seemed intentional, though, a fact that Osgood didn't mention. "I am," she agreed instead.

Her mother examined her manicure. "I am a difficult woman, as well."

Again, Osgood noted the word choice. Also, the deferential glance. She waited for more, but none came. Was her mother actually apologizing in some barely recognizable way? Apologizing for the years and years of emotional torment when young Prudence had first tried very hard to be the little girl she'd wanted her to be and then nearly as hard to be an acceptable queerdo in a world where no amount of sapphic desire would ever be sufficient. As much as she yearned for more or had the urge to say, "Too little, too late," to Cynthia Osgood, she instead said nothing, just nodded.

Cynthia returned the nod, and her face changed mood entirely, going from severe and tense to... flighty? Clearly, that portion of their conversation had come to an end.

Probably all you're ever gonna get in the way of an apology, Os, Audrey's voice suggested in her head. *Better be grateful for it.*

"Maybe it's that I've been locked inside my head for six months, but..." She almost didn't say it. When she did, she surprised herself. "I'm glad you're here."

Was that a tear in her mother's eye? One that she collected with the pinky nail of her right hand. Osgood didn't know. What she did know, though, was that saying those words brought a rush of memories. She'd always held onto Cynthia's significant failings as a mother and ally. Of her parents, her mother had been the disciplinarian, while her father had tried to help her get away with things. Who knew? Maybe that had contributed to how they interacted as Prudence came of age. The memories flickered, kaleidoscopic. Tastes. Baking cookies in their kitchen in Chicago, standing on one of their wooden dining room chairs to reach the counter.

Further back, Cynthia reading *Mickey and the Beanstalk* to her, even doing a passable version of Giant Willie's voice. Cynthia comforting her after young Pru, maybe eleven or twelve, had a row with her father. Osgood found that if she held any memory front and center long enough, the entire day in which it had occurred would blossom behind it, and she could travel forward or backward in the memory. And the days that butted up against that one, while hazy and sketchy at first, would fill in the details as she focused her attention in their direction.

Fascinating, thought Osgood.

"I am, too." Her mother had said it almost inaudibly, but Osgood had heard it just the same.

"I'm sorry for slapping you," Osgood replied before realizing it was out.

"Let's not rehash the past," said Cynthia. "Let's leave it as both of us being happy that I am here."

"Of course," said Osgood with a smirk. "How much do you know about my last few years' work. The Spec—"

Her mother held up a hand. "Your father has told some... stories ...of your," she searched for words, then said it as though the phrase itself was preposterous, "fantastical adventures. Frankly, I don't know how he believes everything he tells me." Cynthia fixed her with an intense gaze. "Is any of it real?"

"Are you asking if the paranormal..."

Again, the hand. "Are your adventures, as spoken about on your..." She couldn't find this word either, and again, when it came, it sounded disdainful, "podcast. Are they true?"

Osgood sighed. This was likely to be as close as she'd get to her mother having any interest or engagement in her life as the Spectral Inspector. She nodded.

Cynthia nodded back, more to herself than to Osgood. "Then you are ... a hero. For saving children."

Thankfully, Cynthia had turned her gaze to her lap, smoothing out a wrinkle. She didn't see Osgood's gape

(*Close your mouth, Prudence!*)

or the tears that briefly swelled after it. Osgood tried to respond once, twice, three times, but couldn't find the words. Good enough, as Cynthia changed the subject.

"And that girl— woman you were with, on the El."

Is she actually asking about Nora?

"Was she special to you?"

"Do you mean, were we lovers?"

"Prudence." Her voice was flat but firm, not exclamatory, but certainly not calm. Osgood immediately understood that this meant Cynthia had chosen to engage up to a specific line and would not go further.

"Yes," Osgood told her quietly. The flash of Nora being bisected played vividly in her central cortex. It seemed Osgood could see every millisecond of it, including Nora's eye looking in her direction as it split. She felt about to retch but managed to rein it in. Thankfully, too, because otherwise, she might have missed her mother's following comment.

"I'm sorry for your loss." Cynthia still wouldn't look at her. "The pandemic and all that surrounded it have shown me how people who matter to you can be spirited away with alacrity. As was the case with your uncle Randall, and—"

"What did he die of?" asked Osgood.

Her mother's tone became the far more familiar chastising one. "Prudence, really."

"I was just asking."

Her mother shook her head, and the face recalled so many memories that flooded in. That look, that gesture. The one who couldn't believe *this* person had sprung forth from her loins. Then she checked her watch. "I really must go so as not to leave your father standing outside the terminal too long."

"Okay, Cyn— Mom."

Cynthia stopped at the honorific. She didn't acknowledge it with a look, but the slightest smile crossed her face. "I'm quite pleased that you are alright," she said as she stood. Without turning back to look at Osgood again, she waved a finger toward the table beside the bed. "Those were left for you while you were asleep."

"Thank you," Osgood said quietly.

With a *woosh* of the door, her mother left.

Osgood looked at the papers on the table. At first, she didn't understand them, but then she saw "AMA Form" written at the bottom. She looked back at the table and saw the Swedish Covenant Hospital pen. After a few circles to get the blue ink flowing, Osgood began to fill them out.

SEVENTEEN

"**I** WANT TO AGAIN emphasize how much I disagree with—"

Osgood stopped Audrey by holding up a hand. "Your concern is noted." She looked from Audrey's furrowed brow and frown to a mirror of it on Zack's face. "Zack, please note Aud's concern."

Zack noted it with grumbles. And expressed and noted his own. And Dr. Laghari's. And Audrey's again. But Osgood was vehement, grabbing her friends' wrists. "Listen, my loves. Please. I spent two hundred and eleven days in this room. I don't want to spend a second longer. Please." She felt the pleading in her voice. "Please take me home."

The moments passed as though in a dream: putting on her street clothes, signing out, climbing into Zack's Jeep Cherokee, and then they were home and climbing the stairs to the apartment above Mary's Diner and Bar in Chicago's Andersonville neighborhood. She watched as Audrey unlocked the door and let her in. Osgood felt like a guest in her own house, even more so than after her last walkabout jaunt when she'd tried on another world. Or, if not a world, the smudgy margin that lies between.

Why does this feel so different? she wondered. She ran her eyes over the room, stopping when she noticed her crimson leather trench coat hanging on a hook beside the door. Waiting for her. "Hello, old friend."

"It's been waiting there for you," said Audrey, giving Osgood's upper arm a light squeeze. Osgood reached up and put her hand atop Audrey's.

Osgood ran her fingers over the coat, and the shuffling deck showed her forty or so variants of her hanging it up or taking it down. The tangential rabbit holes led mostly nowhere, but there was something interesting every once in a while. She lingered on the moment she'd hung it with such force that she'd yanked the hook out of the wall. She'd left that old hook with the chunk of plaster on the floor for a while after; she'd had things to do, pussies to eat. That'd been BA, of course, before Audrey.

"You okay?"

Osgood looked at her. "I don't know what that means now."

"I know."

She turned to Audrey and saw that her friend's eyes were red and her cheeks were wet.

"I'm just so happy to have you here. Things feel ... dark, Os." Audrey wiped at her nose with the back of her hand.

"The signs," said Osgood with a nod. "That's really weird. Creepy. In a way—"

"No, Os," said Audrey. "The last few months have felt like the last horrible miles to that rest stop in Minnesota. The dread. Some days, it's so strong that it's hard to breathe. It's settled on Chicago like smog. And I feel like if we can't figure out what's happening... I dunno. Maybe we'll all die."

Osgood didn't know what to say, and when Audrey blurted a nervous laugh, Osgood laughed with her. "Sounds like a typical— What day is it?"

"Monday," said Audrey.

"*Feels* like a Monday," agreed Osgood with another laugh. "By the way, I seem to have total recall."

"You... what?"

Osgood only had to repeat it once before Audrey yelled for Zack. Her tone sounded concerned, a bit cautious of a loony-toons friend. When Zack appeared, she told him, and he said the words she expected.

"Okay, prove it."

So they sat in the living room. Osgood in her BarcaLounger, Zack in the chair across, Audrey on the couch. Osgood focused on Zack's face. She probably didn't need the visual marker, but in her mind, the shuffling imagery scrambled through years back to their first moment, hers and Zack's. A decade gone now.

"You had dark jeans and a black T-shirt. No logos or anything on the shirt. Your shoes were black, too. I didn't think you looked emo; I assumed you were either a backstage tech or someone who didn't want to get noticed. But standing around in the noon-bright summer day, you looked like you were baking. I assumed your sweat was from the heat, but it was from the conversation. I didn't know that until I got closer, of course. You were leaning on my car. Well, the tall guy with graying brown hair in a zip-up hoodie that wasn't appropriate for the weather had shoved you there. He had a box cutter. Not the little silver kind, but the orange work-style cutter. He had it open, and your eyes were almost crossed looking at it.

"I didn't *know* you because we hadn't yet met, but I knew you enough to know that you were the *Falcon48273* I was supposed to meet. I remember wondering if you'd researched me enough to know my car, and that's why you were there. But later, when we talked, you confirmed it was just a wild moment of happenstance. I heard you explaining yourself to the guy in the hoodie, and your explanation of why the parts you'd sold him were worth the price you'd sold them for sounded reasonable..."

"'Worth the price,'" began Zack. "Seems like you should know—"

Osgood cut him off. "He was rounding up what he'd paid from $4,381 to a full $5K that you now owed him for either faulty or just bad parts. I don't know which because he went back and forth between them, so it's not a fault in my memory, but in his explanation." She raised an eyebrow at Zack, whose mouth ticked up in the corners ever so slightly. "Anyway, despite not knowing the terms of your agreement, this guy felt like a douche being distinctly unfair to you."

"He was."

"What I knew, though, was no matter how much you owed this guy or why you owed it to him, I wasn't going to get the mixer you'd promised me if he cut your throat or something. Even if he just sent you to the hospital. And I had a feeling that you didn't have that five grand to reimburse him. Not like you were just waiting around for me to give you my $150, and then you'd be able to pay him."

"I did *not* have it," said Zack.

"Shush," said Osgood. "So, I weighed my options as he got that box cutter closer to your belly. And I thought it best to intervene. 'You outta stop,' I said, hoping my casual phrasing and nonchalant leaning on my cane would dial back the temperature of the conversation, if not the day, which had reached a sweltering 99 degrees, according to the American Chartered Bank sign that I'd passed on the way to the conference that morning. And the man in the hoodie gave me a smirk. Aud, you know, the one those weak boys do when they think they've retained the upper hand."

Audrey did know and nodded.

"As soon as I saw that fucking smirk, I knew that his next move would be to point that box cutter at me and call me a bitch or something and tell me to stay out of it. He surprised me by escalating all the way to 'cunt' and threatening to cut me, too. That was certainly enough for me to get involved, and I know he didn't expect me to swing my cane at him. You see someone leaning on a cane; you suppose they *need* to be leaning on that cane. But he didn't reckon with a decade of pushing through the pain, nor the upper body strength that comes with having hoisted oneself in and out of a wheelchair. I remember the *crack* when the head of my cane — that beautiful pewter jackal that was never the same after that — made contact with the back of his hand.

"He lost the box cutter under my car, of course, and swung his body toward me, but by that point, I'd already taken my second swing and hit him in the shin, causing another resounding crack, which, upon reflection, may have been when the jackal officially gave up the ghost, and he went down to the ground. There was a lot of 'What the fuck are you doing?' and 'I'll slit your throat, cunt,' and to be clear, I could tell you verbatim what was said, but it's really not important." Osgood pointed to Zack. "You seemed in awe. Though I thought you might be smitten with me at the time. And after the asshole stuck his *other* hand out to grab my ankle, looking up at me with fury, I knew I'd assessed him correctly, and I gave him a final smash on the top of his head."

"Jesus," said Audrey.

"Don't fuck with Osgood," said Zack. "And, yeah, that's exactly how it happened, including bits I'd forgotten."

"I mean, he sounds like an asshole, but were you scamming or stealing from—"

"Before you worry too much, Aud," said Zack, sidestepping the question. "When he tried to take cyber revenge on me for the incident, he left a hole in his firewall, exposing his collection of literal terabytes of child porn. A snapshot of the folder names was enough for the cops to get a warrant, and he's doing seventy-seven years down in Terra Haute."

"You didn't tell me that," said Osgood with a smile.

"Never came up," said Zack with a shrug. He gestured back to Osgood. "You were saying?"

"Not proof enough, yet?" asked Osgood.

"I mean," said Zack. "This is the good part."

Osgood smirked because, as grumpy as she could be and as un-nerving as her new gift felt, something about this story warmed her cold heart. "Then I suggested to you that we should go, and that you should knock fifty off the mixer because I probably just saved your life. You agreed and said, 'It's yours, FOC.' Then we drove to your car. Blah blah blah, you asked me if I knew what I was doing; it was clear that I didn't. You mansplained, then offered to do it for me, and a decade later, you basically live with me." Osgood looked at him, his youthful face starting to show the aging process, his days-old beard both scruffy and patchy. "And I put up with it," she said, locking eyes with him long enough that the deck shuffled for her, and she saw every bit of concern he'd ever shown for her. Especially those bad days before Audrey's return, when she drank herself stupid and nearly OD'ed on opiates time and time again. "Because you're essential, Zack. And I love your scammer ass."

The sentiment caused him to redden, and he looked away quickly.

"Now, can we agree I have something like total recall?"

"Yes, but can we call it by its real name: Superior Autobiographi-cal—"

"*Highly* superior," Osgood reminded him.

"Yes."

The three of them sat in silence for a bit. The feeling that it was all terribly unfair that her friends had gotten to exist in the world while she didn't, twice now, lingered with Osgood, but in the aftermath of telling the story of the day she'd met Zack, she felt rather content. Calm. The shuffling of her memory wasn't a constant. And with time, who knew, it could even be a benefit.

"We missed you," said Audrey with a choke in her voice. "So goddamned much. You have no idea how much you're needed—"

"Please don't," said Osgood. She put her hand to her face to dam up the tear ducts. "You keep saying you needed me. You don't need me. You two are the successful Spectral Inspectors, anyway!"

"Well, I mean," said Zack. "Not for the podcast or anything."

"Zack!" snapped Audrey.

"No! I just—" He scowled. "We *want* you on the podcast. We *need* you for other things. I guess when 844 people die, it kicks up some dust in the spirit world.

"844 people what?" asked Osgood.

"That's how many people died," said Zack.

"But...there couldn't have been that many people on the subway train."

"Oh," said Zack. "No, there were around seventy on the train."

"So where is that number—"

"You were the only survivor of the crash, Os," said Audrey.

Osgood couldn't help but laugh, deny the possibility, then laugh again. "How on earth was I—"

They looked at each other again, Zack and Audrey, but it didn't feel conspiratorial this time; it was more like it was a topic neither of them seemed eager to discuss.

"Um," said Zack, finally. "Here." He turned on the TV that hung above the painted-over fireplace that had been little more than a memory since she'd moved into the apartment. After a moment of booting, she saw Zack's home screen featuring a big-tittied cartoon woman in a pinup pose as the wallpaper. "Don't say—" began Zack, as he scrambled to open enough folders and windows to hide the woman. One of the windows was a video player. "This was made by one of my buddies. Most of the news stations bought it. Except for Fox, they still insist that the whole thing was a terrorist attack."

He slapped the spacebar, and a simple animation appeared on the screen. A white background with two sets of train tracks. A black-outlined subway train moved along the right track until it *very* abruptly stopped. The front car crumpled and turned around the axis that'd stopped it, jamming itself against the outside wall of the subway tunnel. The cars behind that one slammed in, one after another after another. Even in this crude animation, Osgood could hear the screaming of those in the car with her.

"Okay," said Zack, narrating the silent video. "Your train car, at the front, blocked the tunnel. The second one—" he rewound the video and pointed. After slamming in, the second car jutted off to the left. "This one shoved through the shockingly thin wall between tunnels and onto the northbound track. We'll come back to that one. Then, the remaining cars in your train crashed into that first car and slid along the second one onto the north track. The scraping damaged the doors enough that they wouldn't open, and by then, a fire had broken out, starting first in your car..."

"You keep saying my car; I was on the track at this point," snapped Osgood.

"Right, of course. The *front car*. As people began to panic and smash windows, they tried to climb into the other cars in the pileup; unfortunately, many of them were already burning, spreading the fire between cars. They were all so compact that it didn't take long to spread."

"Seventy people burned to death," whispered Osgood to herself. She thought she could remember that screaming when the horror and pain had turned into something altogether inhuman. The sound of pure agony. The sound of despair.

"Not..." He stopped, then looked back at the animation and let it speak for itself. "Okay, so the second car, the one that jumped to the other track. Well, it just happened to be immediately before a northbound train on that track, which plowed headfirst into that car."

The animation had expanded to a top-down view, showing the two subway tunnels beside each other as the carnage and crumpling cars piled up.

"Two trains," said Osgood.

Again, Zack hesitated and, this time, just pointed at the TV.

The two trains had fully crumpled onto each other, and both, to Osgood's astonishment, had cartoon fire poking out of them. But, of course, as deliriously simple as this animation was, Osgood knew that it hadn't been cartoon fire or little animated stick figures who'd died. They'd been people. Real people. "I still don't see how eight hundred and forty-four people could've..."

"Os," said Audrey. Her hand touched Osgood's gently. She'd moved down the couch and leaned toward Osgood, who hadn't noticed. Osgood nodded and waited.

"Okay, so the crash happened at Pike Street and Washington," said Zack. The screen shifted to a cross-section view, showing the pileup below the street and above it, a beehive-shaped building.

"Booth Tower." Osgood knew it immediately. Not because she had any connection to the condo complex, but because of its strange shape. *And my internal Yellow Pages,* she thought.

"Yeah," said Zack. "And the second crash weakened an already structurally unsound part of the foundation that the mayor had been campaigning to fix since—"

"1992," Osgood said, absently, as a fleeting image of the front page of the *Chicago Tribune* informed her of the date.

The tower on the screen was an illustration, but Osgood saw the reality in her mind. First, the beehive seemed to genuflect, but that was really just the collapse of the first two floors, a double-height lobby. The rest of the tower above stepped down after it as though stepping off a precipice, and the animation on the screen confirmed that Booth Tower, all of it, had crashed down onto the intersection of Pike Street and Washington.

"Eight hundred and forty-four," Osgood whispered.

"Eight hundred and forty-four," said Audrey.

"And I—" Osgood choked on the pronoun.

"You would've been eight hundred and forty-five," said Zack.

(you may be hard to kill)

The words echoed in her mind, reverberating and reverberating until they were nothing but a feedback loop that felt like it could blow out her eardrum. She would've been 845. Nora was 844. Or was she one? Had the driver perished first? Or had it been the cute girl standing next to her?

(but you can still fucking die)

The words careened around in her head until she began to grow dizzy. Just before she blacked out, she had the flicker of a thought, a response to the words in the ether.

Promise?

Darkness.

EIGHTEEN

"T HIS IS WHY WE wanted to ease you in," said Audrey. She dabbed at Osgood's forehead with a wet washcloth. The trickle of tepid water felt great against her skin.

"It's not fair," said Osgood.

"I know," said Audrey.

"No! I shouldn't be here," she pleaded. "I shouldn't be alive."

"That's not true," said Audrey.

Osgood slowly lifted her hand and wrapped her fingers around Audrey's wrist, stopping her. The washcloth dripped into her lap. They sat on the floor in the living room. Osgood had shoved herself back between the sidebar and the bookshelves that flanked the once-fireplace. It was the farthest she could go without being in another room. But it wasn't far enough. She wanted to run. To run to her room and seal herself in the way she had when her bout of Covid had hit: hermetically seal the room, lower the blackout curtains, and just exist in darkness.

"Look at me," said Audrey. When Osgood didn't, she repeated it more forcefully.

Osgood turned her head up.

"Here's what we're going to do," said Audrey. "Os!" she said more forcefully when Osgood's eyes drifted downward again. Their eyes met. Audrey's eyes had reddened, emboldening the icy blue of her irises. "That—what we talked about, the accident. That's just the beginning."

"Fuck," said Osgood. "I don't know how much more I can take."

"I do," said Audrey, her voice catching.

"What does that mean?" asked Osgood.

"It means you're Prudence *fucking* Osgood. The motherfucking Spectral *fucking* Inspector."

"You're giving a lot of fucks, Aud," said Osgood, making sure to pronounce it emphatically the old way, *their* old way, from when they'd been Pru and Odd.

"*All* the fucks, Os." Audrey plopped down on the floor opposite Osgood. She slid her legs in, enmeshing them with Osgood's. "Do you remember how we used to talk about maybe, someday, actually seeing a ghost? How it seemed the most far-fetched but greatest dream we could dream?"

Osgood nodded. Of all the indexes in Osgood's head, the ones that seemed to radiate the most strongly were those halcyon days without care. Before work, life, relationships, and the real world had ground them down. Lying in a tent in the backyard, listening to the cicadas and crickets, watching the lightning bugs in—

"Fuck," said Osgood, grabbing both of Audrey's hands. "Before the crash, I saw something."

"What?"

"It was..." She could see it through the View-Master in her head. The moment of the crash, with Nora falling to pieces and people screaming, was silent now. Just before she'd been ejected from the front car to become the sole survivor of the subway crash, which had apparently been far more than just a subway crash, the fireflies had turned into something. "It was an eye, Aud. And it *saw* me."

Audrey cocked her head and narrowed her eyes, in not a look of distrust but concern, maybe? Anticipation? "Was it that thing you've seen before? The black hole or—"

"I think they're the same." Osgood shuffled through her memory, opening the *eye in the sky* folder. "The quasar I saw in my dreams at the crossroads."

"Quasar, not a black hole, right," said Audrey.

"Do you remember the horrid red sun in the Hinterlands?"

Audrey frowned. "No," she said. "But I remember getting dizzy every time I looked at the sky."

"There were two stars in that sky, a small white sun, like ours, and a gigantic red burning thing. I thought it was another star, but I don't think so anymore." Osgood's mind began to race, and she felt the pace of her speech increase. "It was watching us. Watching to see what we'd do."

"To see if we'd survive?"

Suddenly, she could see that moment in a new way. The shriveled and diminished once-Lord of the Hinterlands, writhing and mewling on the ground, asking if she had no mercy. Then, when it had proclaimed this was not its end, Audrey had killed it. Stabbed it with a length of rebar she'd stolen from a piece of art that the oozing poison of this thing had helped to create. But something else had happened first. The white sun had eclipsed the red. And in that moment, the one it had tried to keep her from remembering, she'd seen the eye. Its pupil blazing white, its iris fiery red. The eye in the sky.

And it had been happy.

"I don't know how I know this, but I feel it deeply. Whatever it is, it has been watching. I saw it in the margins when I was gone; it watched the flanks of the monstrosities trying to get through the gate. It watched and, I think, encouraged me as I repeatedly tried to kill myself when we were up against that statue. And then, for good measure, it tried to kill me by crashing El car I was in and, apparently, dropping a building on me."

"That's..." Audrey began, her eyes downcast.

Osgood knew what Audrey was thinking. It was the same thing she would've been thinking herself had the roles been reversed. "Ridiculous."

"No," said Audrey.

Osgood coughed out a withered laugh. "No, it is. A giant eye has watched me for years and periodically tried to kill me."

"Well, if you say it that way..." said Audrey.

"Was my first way any better?" asked Osgood. She thought about the fireflies in her backyard and the same ones dancing in the subway tunnel, swirling eddies of sparks and insects and light. "I probably have brain damage."

"I mean, you've always probably had brain damage," said Audrey, so matter-of-factly that Osgood guffawed.

"Thanks, Aud."

"I needed to lighten the mood," she said.

"I remember something else," said Osgood, realizing she didn't remember something else after she said it. She recalled a memory that had vanished as though spliced out, omitted, red-penned out of her mind. "But I don't."

"What do you mean?"

"I remember the space of a memory. It's there, but it's not. Like...when you take a painting off a wall that's been there for years. You can see the accumulation of dust, grime, and life on the wall around the space that held the painting. So you *know* something was there, but only the approximate size, not the content."

Audrey nodded, but Osgood couldn't discern if it meant "go on" or "I understand."

"This one feels big. And it feels like the eye. Fiery irises." For a moment, Osgood thought she could see it. But then it was gone, and only a lyric remained, but from what song? "Does 'On The Isle' mean anything to you?"

"I don't understand the question."

"Is it from a song? Something creepy, or liminal, or..."

"All I can think of is the one by Madonna. *La Isla Bonita*."

"That's not it."

"How're you feeling?" asked Zack, appearing around the corner from the kitchen. He leaned down and handed Osgood a tall glass of water. As a hesitant afterthought, he gave her a second glass, short, with brown liquid inside. "Lagavulin. Neat. I bought the bottle while you were in the hospital. For when you..." his voice caught, and he coughed the emotion away. "For when you got home."

"Oh, Zack, I could kiss you," said Osgood. "No tongue, I promise."

"Raincheck," said Zack.

Osgood took the single finger of Scotch down in a gulp, then shook the glass at Zack. He cracked a smile. She smiled back.

And then he said some words that would change everything. "The mayor is on the phone."

Osgood coughed on her Scotch. "Excuse me?"

"*The* mayor?" asked Audrey.

Zack nodded. "He called the Spectral Inspector line."

"Why is he calling us?" Osgood turned to Audrey and whispered, "Is it still Mayor Augusta?"

Audrey nodded.

"He wants to talk to you," said Zack.

Osgood turned to Audrey with a grin. "The *mayor* wants to talk to you!"

"No, Os," said Zack. "You."

All Osgood could think to say was, "But I didn't vote for him."

Nineteen

"*T*HIS IS MAYOR AUGUSTA. *Who've I got there?*" asked the mayor from the phone propped up against a Kleenex box on the coffee table in the center of their living room. Sitting between Audrey and Zack on the couch next to the table, Osgood didn't know how to respond.

Luckily, Audrey, who'd always been better at PR, took it upon herself. "Hello, Mr. Mayor, this—"

"*Please, call me Tom.*"

Audrey hesitated, but then continued, "Tom. This is Audrey Frost, and I have Prudence Osgood and Zack Nguyen with me."

"*The Spectral Inspectors. At. Last.*"

"At last?" asked Osgood.

"*I have an aide, Constance Beauchamp, who says y'all have one of the most enjoyable podcasts about the weird and unknown in the US.*"

"Well," said Audrey. "We'll have to shout-out Constance next time we record."

"And send her a hat!" said Zack, leaning toward the phone.

"*I'm sure she'd love that,*" said the mayor.

A pause caused Osgood to feel the itch in her brain. Instead of wandering off into the memory index, she leaned herself forward. "So, why does Mayor Tom Augusta want to talk to me?"

"*Prudence. Osgood,*" said the mayor, emphasizing her first and last name separately before expelling a long deep breath that almost made him sound ... proud? Impressed?

"Just Osgood," said Osgood.

"*Very well. Osgood.*" They heard him suck in a breath, as though hesitant, and waited. "*First, I want you to know how happy I am to hear you've recovered.*"

Osgood considered sharing with him the true horror of locked-in syndrome, but she thought it best to keep that to herself. Instead, she said, "Thank you."

"*I sent flowers a few times.*" Another hesitation. "*Well, to be perfectly candid, Constance did.*"

Again, a pause. Osgood looked between Audrey and Zack. Audrey shrugged. Osgood was about to ask her question again when the mayor continued.

"*We'd like to give you the Key to the City.*"

Osgood bleated a laugh, then covered her mouth. "Seriously?" she asked through her fingers.

"*Very much so,*" said Mayor Augusta. "*As I'm sure you know by now, 12/17 was a horrible day for Chicago.*"

"Wasn't too great for me, either," said Osgood. "My girlfriend got cut in half."

That seemed to quiet the mayor for a moment, but they could hear him muffled, speaking to someone.

"*We're all very sorry about that,*" said the mayor. "*As you know, my administration considers itself a friend to the LBGT community.*"

"Us queers are very grateful," said Osgood. "It's come up at our meetings."

Audrey covered her eyes with her palm.

Osgood remembered the mayor also flipping the letters around during his campaign. He was a "friend to the LBGT community," like many politicians were "friends of the working man." In this case, though, being a friend was better than the alternative. The other candidate had used the word *fag* more than once in a single interview.

"Yes," said the mayor. *"Would you accept the Key to the City?"*

"Does it come with any perks?" asked Osgood. In the mayor's silence, Osgood continued. "I mean, I've been stuck in a hospital for two hundred and eleven days, so I've got a rather full dance card."

"You're quick," said the mayor, his voice a bit harder.

"I am," said Osgood, knowing it hadn't been a compliment. Maybe he'd rescind the offer. Perhaps she just wasn't "Key to the City" material.

"Well, we'd love to have a little ceremony, WGN will broadcast it. You'd be welcome to promote your book—"

"It's really Audrey's—" Osgood stopped when Audrey squeezed a pressure point just above her knee.

"—your podcast, whatever else. It'd be your show."

"My show?" asked Osgood, with a slight smile.

The hardness returned to the mayor's voice. Perhaps he'd begun to realize what a bad idea it might be to give Prudence Osgood a show. *"Ideally, it'd be Friday or Saturday evening."*

"Saturday," blurted Osgood. She didn't know why but felt that the further away, the better.

"Perfect. I'll have my staff contact yours."

"He's not staff," said Osgood, absently. "He's Zack. He's essential."

Zack smiled.

"Constance will contact Zack, then," said the mayor, the edge in his voice growing.

He didn't want to make Prudence Osgood into a hero, did he? After all, he was the mayor who'd let a great tragedy happen to his city. And then, of all people, to be the sole survivor, this weirdo queer ghost hunter. What a bad look. And in an election year! Osgood thought about saying so but thought better of it.

"Yes? Good?" asked the mayor, likely frustrated this conversation had gone on so long already.

"Mr. Mayor?" asked Audrey abruptly, her eyes wide as though she hadn't even thought she would say anything.

"Is that Miss Frost?"

"Yes," said Audrey. "If we're going to be doing an event—"

"My thought was not that the entire team would be 'doing the event,' just our miraculous survivor."

"She is quite miraculous," Audrey said, her playful tone amusing Osgood. "Do you have any comment on the signs?"

Silence. Some shuffling of papers.

"Did we lose you?"

"No, Miss Frost, you didn't lose me," sighed the mayor. *"If you're referring to—"*

Looking at her phone, with the image of her rubbing, Audrey read: "'Eschaton past due.'"

"If you have issues with graffiti, I suggest you contact public works or your alderman."

"Alderperson," corrected Osgood.

Again, a sigh. *"Yes. Ward 48. Miss ... Lehane."*

"But it's not graffiti, Mr. Mayor. Surely you've seen the signs that—"

"The City of Chicago supports public art."

"So, not graffiti now?"

"And we stand by that." The mayor cleared his throat. *"Now, if you'll excuse me, I must go."*

"One more question if—"

"You can give your questions to Miss Beauchamp. She will see that I get them." His cadence trembled, and he sped up. Osgood didn't think he could explain the signs and they sure seemed to unnerve him. Rather than transferring them to Miss Beauchamp, the mayor disconnected the call.

Osgood laughed. "Your journalism leviathan rose up."

"It's not every day I get to ask the mayor about something."

"Yeah, but what did you think he was going to do," asked Osgood. "Agree that they might be supernatural?"

"He did what I needed him to do."

"Which is?"

"Acknowledge they exist." Audrey sighed. "Ever since they showed up, there's been a flurry of confusion and curiosity, then silence."

"And since people can't seem to photograph them, they don't play well with the internet," said Zack. "In fact, when we posted the rubbing Audrey took, first the image file was corrupted, then the page on our site, then, for about 2 days, our entire hosting platform."

"Huh," offered Osgood.

Audrey nodded. "Whatever this is, it wants to be known but not remembered."

Osgood thought about that, trying to rev up her memory to *see* Audrey's rubbing in her head, but as they'd described, it also seemed to have corrupted its place in her mind. The corruption almost seemed to be leaking onto the memories beside it. One memory there did stand out, though it took her a moment to see it. Her. The living room. "Eight hundred and forty-four," she blurted, then tried to figure out why that stood out. The number pulsed in the back of her mind as she wound her way through her memory banks.

"Yes," said Zack. "That's how many people died in the—"

"Eastland," said Osgood, but it still wouldn't gel. Now she could see the number and that word inside her head, floating in the ether before her. "What is…"

"Eastland?" asked Audrey with a frown. It seemed to mean something to her as well, but what could—

"On a Chicago Dial-Up BBS board recommended by someone on Lunatic Fringe. No, the Nuclear Greenhouse…"

Audrey looked at Zack. He just shrugged and shook his head.

Then Osgood saw it in glowing green text on a black background. *SS Eastland.* Had she only had a monochrome monitor when she'd used the original dial-up communities on the internet? No. She'd had at least a few colors by then, but the early internet builders of the Nuclear Greenhouse chat system and the BBS boards had liked the aesthetic of monochrome. Osgood felt relieved. There'd been something almost painful about calling up the information.

"1915," said Osgood. "*SS Eastland.*"

Audrey's eyes flickered and then widened. "The capsizing!"

"What's this now?" asked Zack.

Osgood recalled the opening paragraph of the description and recited it verbatim. "'The *SS Eastland* was a Chicago-based passenger ship that offered tours. On July 24, 1915, while docked on the Chicago River, the ship unexpectedly tipped over onto its side. Tragically, eight hundred and forty-four people, including passengers and crew, lost their lives, marking it as the deadliest shipwreck in Great Lakes history.'"

"Eight hundred and forty-four people," repeated Audrey.

"That total recall is ... something." offered Zack. She couldn't tell if he was awed or disturbed, but he couldn't stop staring.

"Are you sure about your number, Zack?" asked Osgood.

"Well, it's not my—"

"The number of people who died when my El train crashed," said Osgood, impatience rising.

"Yeah," he confirmed. "Since my last data scrape, at least. Eight hundred and forty-four people died in or because of the crash."

"That's weird, yes?" asked Osgood, looking between them. "That the numbers match."

"Yeah, it's weird," said Audrey, carefully considering her answer. "But it's also a coincidence. And it doesn't really fit with—"

Zack had already gone head-down in his laptop, clacking away at the keys. Audrey sighed and looked at Osgood with worry.

"I'm fine, Aud," Osgood said.

"You've never been fine," said Audrey with a small smile.

"Bitch," said Osgood.

"Cunt," said Audrey.

"Alright," said Zack with a weird level of authority. "You done with that?"

"Feeling left out?" asked Osgood. "Dick?"

"Alright," Zack said again. "It looks like eight hundred and forty-four is a rare number of dead, yes. And for these both to have happened in Chicago, within a couple miles of each other. Yeah, that's objectively odd."

"But not related to the signs," Audrey reminded him.

"Well," said Zack. "Look." He pointed to the TV and flung his screen up there. On it was the front page of the *Chicago Tribune*, dated August 31, 1915. The headline screamed BOAT DISASTER RECOVERY STALLED.

"What stalled it?" asked Audrey.

"Stalled, what? It—" He looked up at the screen, then back, shaking his head. "No!" He scrolled to the bottom right of the page, where a small column read MYSTERIOUS PLAQUES.

Osgood squinted to read aloud. "'Mysterious plaques have…'" She trailed off. While her memory might be sharper than ever, her vision certainly wasn't. She'd have to make an appointment for a new glasses script. After all, her last had been in 2021. She counted on fingers in her mind. 3 years ago!

Zach looked from the TV to Osgood and back, then continued reading in her place. "'Mysterious plaques have begun to appear in the parks of our fair city, puzzling and alarming citizens who frequent these public spaces. The four plaques—" Below that, the scan was smudged. And below that, it said, "See pg 5."

"What's on page five?" asked Osgood.

"Well, gimme a sec!" said Zack, impatience growing. He zoomed back out of the paper and flipped through pages 2, 3, 4, and 6.

"Wait," said Audrey. "Go back."

He did—to 4, 3, 2, 1. "Huh," he said. Then he moved forward and backward again. Then he flipped to page 14, the last page of the section. "It's not here."

"The article?" asked Audrey.

"The whole damned page!" said Zack.

"What about the *Sun-Times*?" asked Osgood.

Audrey shook her head. "That didn't begin publication until the '40s. But Chicago had other papers."

New search results appeared on the screen, and Zack immediately jumped to another tab, typing furiously. Then, he slapped the enter key and shifted to the previous tab. On that page was a list of Chicago newspapers between 1915 and 1917. "'*Chicago American*, *Chicago Daily News*, *Chicago Defender*—'"

"Okay, there are a lot of papers," said Osgood, cutting him off. Did you search for strange signs or the eschaton thing?"

"Yes," he said, "But the *Trib* didn't use the word 'sign.'" His tone was defensive, and he folded his arms across his chest and stared at them. "And eschaton is like impossible to search because of all the biblical sites that mention it. Fucking Catholics."

"I wasn't doubting your diligence, Zack," said Osgood, putting her hand on his knee.

"Sure," he replied and jumped back to his other tab. A short list of search results showed multiple instances of headlines, including "Mysterious plaques" from Chicago newspapers in September and October 1915. As they watched, he clicked each link, only to arrive at a 404 error, a dead page, or a file not found notification. The final one just spun, and they waited until it resolved to "database not found" after a full six minutes.

"Corrupted files," said Osgood.

Zack nodded.

TWENTY

THE MOMENT THE DOORBELL rang, Osgood knew who waited downstairs. Possibly even before that. She'd felt a swell in her chest, first thinking it to be indigestion, but she hadn't eaten since the morning. Then, a sense of warmth had settled over her. When she buzzed the intercom, her aunt's voice confirmed her suspicion. Now, they sat in the restaurant below, at Mary's Diner and Bar. Aunt Eliza's stoic face and twitchy countenance didn't convey the same warmth her presence did. Osgood smiled nonetheless.

"I'm thrilled that you're awake," said Eliza. She pressed her fingertips to her temples, smoothing the hair. She didn't need to, though. Eliza's hair rose almost a full six inches off the top of her head, terminating in a wisp like a paintbrush dipped in glossy white. Her black-rimmed glasses and permanent ... not scowl, but something between smile and scowl ... added to the severity. Osgood may not have spent much time with her aunt, but she knew the severity was just a mask, Eliza's resting cunt face. She wasn't sure where, but Osgood was confident that Eliza fell somewhere on the spectrum, which had likely added to the whole "Eliza's weird" opinion that had caused the estrangement between her and Osgood's father. Or was that something else that could be blamed on Cynthia?

"Thank you," said Osgood.

"Somebody with some sense needs to look into what's going on in this awful city," said Eliza. She sipped water from her glass, then set it back exactly where it had been and smoothed down her napkin with her fingertips.

Osgood felt a momentary need to defend Chicago, a place she truly loved, but she let it go. "And you think I'm the one to do that?"

When Eliza's eyes *did* meet hers, their ferocious near-emerald intensity caused Osgood to jump. Her aunt didn't need to answer her question and didn't. Instead, she looked away again and mused, "Their mixed drinks are served in that Rubenesque plastic torso." She pointed a long finger at a shelf behind the bar, where a curvy plastic woman stood with a straw jutting from the top of her head.

Osgood didn't know if Eliza was asking or just commenting. "Well, the party ones are."

"Party," said Eliza as though she'd never heard that word before. Before Osgood could ask if she wanted one, Eliza turned her gaze back, not to Osgood's face, but to a spot near enough to see each other. "Prudence. What occurred in your dreams when you were in the hospital?"

"What do you mean?"

"Whatever occurred, I could feel it. Lil could as well." Eliza sipped her water again, then fastidiously dabbed at her lips with her napkin and smoothed it out on the table again.

Osgood thought about Lil, her great-grandmother. If not the *original* extraordinary Osgood woman, then certainly the most prominent. And the only one that seemed to be able to transcend time and space to be with her. But as to her aunt's question, Osgood didn't know about her dreams. The newfound shame she seemed to feel every time she *couldn't* remember something pissed her the hell off.

"It's alright if you don't remember," said Eliza. "But I'm here to relay our concerns."

"What are you concerned about?"

Again, Eliza's eyes wandered, and Osgood waited for her to speak. "There was a ... well, not a man ... but an entity in your dream. We know it wasn't a man because we could feel his ... essence."

"You could?"

Eliza's eyes met hers. "We were most concerned about you, Prudence. You are the tether. This family's final tether. Unless you plan to have children. But those days must be nearly behind you."

Shame and embarrassment welled in Osgood, and she felt tears in her eyes. She knew that her aunt's comment hadn't been meant to hurt her, but it felt strikingly similar to things Cynthia had often said to her, lamenting a lack of grandchildren. There had been the one time when she'd learned she was pregnant at seventeen and briefly considered what it might be like if she kept the child. She hadn't known who the father was. She knew she didn't want to be connected to any of the possibles for the next eighteen years. The abortion had been quick and easy, so much so that Osgood often forgot she'd ever had one. That was until someone mentioned the idea of her having children. Now, though, it'd be impossible; during the pandemic, she'd convinced the doctors to tie her tubes.

Perhaps seeing it on her face, Eliza shook her head. "Please don't take that personally. I, like you, chose not to have children, and I'm perfectly happy."

Osgood suppressed a laugh, noting that the woman in front of her might be happy, but she didn't appear so. "They're giving me a Key to the City. This weekend."

Pride welled on Eliza's face. "Well, I should think so, after all you've done for—"

"No," said Osgood. "Because I lived."

"Oh," said Eliza, her disdain apparent. "I thought perhaps they were finally thanking you for ending that dreadful epidemic with the children."

For a flash, Osgood again sat atop the Guardian statue in Rosehill Cemetery, sawing endlessly with a hacksaw, trying desperately to decapitate the cursed thing. "Well, they don't know we did that."

"You ought to tell them when they give you the Key to the City." Eliza nodded, then shook her head, contradicting her support of this plan. "Will there be a ceremony?"

"They're doing something on WGN," said Osgood. "Saturday night."

"I will be there," said Eliza. "I'm sorry I was unable to help you..." Her voice caught.

Osgood stared at her aunt, waiting, surprised by the sudden emotion. But as quickly as she noticed it, it was gone. Instead of mentioning it, Osgood said, "I don't know if I can bring guests..."

"If they are giving you a Key to the City, you should be able to do what you like," said Eliza, and without a pause, she said, "The entity."

Osgood felt the conversation lurch back. "Yes."

"I hesitated to tell you this because I wanted to hear from your memory. But you asked us to save you from 'the Bicycle Man,' while at the same time insisting he wasn't a man at all."

Frowning, Osgood thought about that. Scanning through her memory of her time

(in purgatory)

locked in, she still couldn't penetrate the fog surrounding her dreams. But another memory swam up, nibbled, then grabbed the hook. "The Bicycle Man," she said aloud. She thought she could hear static as an old television turned on in the recesses of her brain, in black and white, and through intermittent broadcast snow, she saw Mr. Horton trying to convince Arnold and Dudley to stay for ... wine and sadness? That couldn't be right. "He was a villain on *Diff'rent Strokes*."

"The program where the rich white man saved the poor black children."

It wasn't a question, so Osgood didn't confirm.

Eliza shook her head. "I see no reason you would need to be saved from him."

"He died in 2003," said Osgood without a thought, then wondered why on earth she could remember that. "Gordon Jump did, the actor who played him."

"That is inconsequential. I believe that Lil and I could help you remember," said Eliza. "If that's something you would like to do. It's distinctly possible you had recurring nightmares, and your subconscious called out to us."

"That's distinctly possible?" asked Osgood, amused.

"Yes," said her aunt. Flat.

"Alright."

"Then we should do that?"

"I..." Osgood looked up at Mary's ceiling. The pattern of the purple-pressed tin swam in and out of focus, again reminding Osgood that she needed new glasses. "I'm not sure I want to remember. I came out of my," she wasn't sure what word she wanted to use, but *prison* sounded apt, "syndrome, able to remember ... everything?"

"Everything?" asked Eliza.

"Everything," said Osgood.

Eliza waited a single beat before, "When you were four, your father invited me for—"

Osgood held up a hand to stop Eliza because the moment her aunt spoke of it, Osgood's memory had shuffled back and pulled it up. She'd looked up at a woman with long white-blonde hair. Eliza crouched before four-year-old Osgood and said, "Happy birthday, Prudence."

"My birthday," said Osgood. "You brought me a magic set."

"Remarkable," said Eliza. "One more exceptional talent for the exceptional Prudence Osgood."

Now, Osgood felt heat in her cheeks. She ducked her head down and told her aunt to, "Stoppit."

"The spectral activity in the City of Chicago is unprecedentedly high," said her aunt, again lurching Osgood with conversational whiplash.

"Zack and Audrey were—"

"The archdiocese is circulating a press release among higher level clergy and parishioners, asking for guidance on how to respond."

"The Catholics might respond to ghosts?" The very idea stunned Osgood.

"They would call it phenomena. But, yes, it is widespread enough that they are beginning to get questions about—"

"The eschaton. The end of the world."

"Yes," said Eliza. "So, you can see why I'm happy you are back."

Osgood opened her mouth, then closed it again. The very idea made her incredulous. "Zack and Audrey said something similar. I don't know what you all think I can do."

"You forget, Prudence," said Eliza. "I saw you tear a hole in the very fabric of time to save the world from a gateway of monsters, with no concern for yourself."

"I..." said Osgood. But why be modest? "I *did* do that."

"If the eschaton is afoot," said Eliza, "untold horrors await."

This surprised Osgood. "You believe the Catholics?"

Eliza stared directly into Osgood's eyes, long enough for Osgood to look away. When she spoke again, it was low, and her eyes returned to the table. "There isn't a society in history that hasn't wondered about when the world will end, when their kind will disappear. This earth is a machine that cycles around again and again to extinction. Planet Earth, as in the literal world, will not end until the sun, beginning to die, expands and consumes it. But us? People? As happened in the Ordovician, Devonian, Permian, Triassic, and the Cretaceous Era, mass extinction will come for the human race."

"Those were all natural cataclysms," said Osgood, but in truth, while aware of other mass extinctions, the only one she knew was the dinosaurs, and her memory textbook said that was the Cretaceous extinction. Much of the textbook was a literal blur. Smudged line after smudged line. *Damn,* she thought, *maybe I should've studied.* "Not supernatural."

"Science may tell us that, and it may be absolutely correct, but it's always been woefully behind when it comes to the astral plane. The paranormal isn't quantifiable, measurable, at least not with the instruments scientists prefer to use."

"Are you saying paranormal forces were at play in previous extinction events?"

"There are multiple types of extinction, Prudence. Extinction of physical beings and obliteration of the essence of those beings. You can call it the soul or the aura. Why do you think you've never seen the ghost of a compsognathus?"

Osgood had no response to that.

"Extinction echoes, building from space to space, from universe to universe, from life to afterlife. And that is the eschaton. While the Christians may believe it's the end of their god's divine plan, those of us who believe there are other gods—" Eliza leaned forward with a smile and a wink that astonished Osgood "—like the one you killed—"

"Audrey killed him," said Osgood absently, still shocked by Eliza's aside.

"Very well. We understand that the obnoxiously named God — which incidentally isn't terribly different than our planet being called *Terra*, meaning planet, and our star *Sol*, meaning star, humans are astoundingly uncreative when they think the universe revolves around them — *that* god has no divine plan. *That* god is nowhere near 'in charge' on the hierarchy. For all we know, the eschaton may also be His end."

Osgood pondered that, overwhelmed by the vastness of the implications. It was hard enough to think about the world ending, even when you knew an afterlife awaited, but that afterlife also ending — well, that felt downright bleak. "How do you know this?"

Eliza seemed surprised. "Shall I cite my sources?"

"What? No! I just wanted to—"

"There is a network throughout this world and the beyond that binds us. If Eschcaton is being presaged, it may be stoppable. And since it's beginning in Chicago and nowhere else, it may fall to you to attempt to stop it."

"I just got out of a ... hospital. How can it possibly fall to me to stop the end of the fucking world?" Osgood's rising voice drew looks, including two raised eyebrows from Terry at the bar.

"I don't see why you should raise your voice to me," said Eliza. She leaned back from the table and looked away.

"I'm sorry, no, I just meant—"

Eliza snatched Osgood's hand and looked directly into her eyes. She likely meant it as a comfort, but the rigidity made it awkward in execution. "It is what we do when needed that defines us, Prudence.

You have stood for this world multiple times. It is not up to you to save it. It is up to all of us who are extraordinary." She let go suddenly and stood, then, as an afterthought, added, "Because god knows the Catholics won't do shit."

TWENTY-ONE

OSGOOD, CANE IN HAND, stood in the vast, echoey, and dimly lit basement of the Chicago History Museum. The light spilling down the staircase behind her cast a circle of safety upon her, flanked by Audrey and Zack. Before them were rows upon rows upon rows of shelving, each with large gear-like handles on the ends so the shelves could move forward and back. Osgood felt herself sway on the cane. The morphine had definitely begun to wear off.

"Who are we meeting?" she asked.

Audrey held her phone up and lifted her glasses to scan the email. As she read, she whispered quietly. God, Osgood loved this woman. "Todd Sherfinski."

Zack looked around the area in front of them, "Should we ... shout?" he asked.

Audrey sighed. "I don't—"

Osgood shrugged and went for it. "Is there a Todd Sherfinski here?"

A small voice on the opposite side of the room indicated that someone was coming, and not too long after that, an impressively small women emerged from between two stacks.

"You're not Todd Sherfinski," said Osgood. Audrey swatted her shoulder.

The small woman wore several layers of clothing, her fragile body beneath barely filling them. An olive-green crocheted cardigan topped them all, most certainly handmade. Seeming to bristle, the woman's mouth formed a slit, and for a moment, she appeared to have no lips. "I am not," she said slowly. "I'm afraid Mr. Sherfinski has come down with a rather unfortunate case of food poisoning."

"In the last hour?" asked Audrey.

"I'm Tricia Dorsey," the woman said, ignoring Audrey's question and loosening her lips into a smile that seemed to take twenty years off her age. Now, Osgood would peg her at sixty-five, tops.

"Did Mr. Sherfinski tell you what we're after?"

Tricia Dorsey held up a waxy finger with a neon orange post-it stuck to the tip. The words "Easton" and "Tribune" were scrawled upon it in hasty chicken scratch, along with some off-color wet spots that Osgood felt oddly confident were vomit residue.

"Yes," confirmed Audrey.

"Well, c'mon!" Tricia turned and rushed down the central aisle between the rows. As she went, she spoke quietly to herself. "*SS Easton*. Chicago River tragedy. Eight hundred forty souls."

"She knows her stuff," whispered Osgood to Audrey. She looked over at Zack, who seemed visibly annoyed that they'd had to resort to paper. "I'm sure we'll return to the internet soon enough, Zack."

"I just wonder how much of this is digitized, and how much isn't," lamented Zack.

"Well, we saw how effective the digitizing of our particular concern was," said Osgood.

"One instance," said Zack, holding up his index finger. "One."

"This way!" Tricia waved a hand above her head and made an abrupt right turn down a row. By the time the trio had corrected to follow her, she'd already reached the far end and made a left.

"Is she teleporting?" asked Zack.

"I love when the able-bodied complain," said Osgood.

When they turned the next corner, Tricia stood, waiting. Next to her stood about a dozen rows all smashed together. "We have every existing *Chicago Tribune* issue printed since the first morning issue on June 10, 1847." Her voice lowered as she qualified her statement. "All extant issues anyway. Because of the fire. Some are reprints, others are recreations." She reached up to a panel on the wall and pressed a button. Slowly, the stacks slid apart, opening up one, two, four, and six new rows. "Todd thought that all issues should just be digitized to 'save room,'" said Tricia with disdain. "I said, 'We have plenty of room, you heretic.'"

Osgood nudged Zack; he nudged her back.

When the eighth row opened, Tricia stopped. "Not many people care about physical preservation these days." She waved them down the row, again crossing the floor far quicker than her legs should have been able to carry her. "There's magic in physically being able to touch these issues. An actual connection to the past. Knowing that back in ... well, in this case, 1915 ... that someone else, probably an archivist at the *Tribune*, pulled this same issue off the stack." She pointed to a shelf, flipped up one, two, three folios, then leaned to Zack. "Would you retrieve that for me, young man?"

Zack pulled a large artist's folio down and looked back. The small woman crooked her finger to beckon and then darted back up the row. They emerged to find a wide white lacquered table with multiple hanging LED lights above it. Tricia pointed, and Zack hoisted the folio onto the table. She unzipped it. Inside, sheets of vellum separated the *Chicago Tribune*'s yellowing pages. She slid her dexterous fingers down the sheaf and stopped, flipping, to expose the front page from August 31, 1915.

Audrey cocked her head. "How did you know that's the issue we—"

"I have an excellent memory. All Todd had time to write down was this..." Again, she showed them the Post-it, still sticking to that finger. "But between coughs, he told me this date. And this one *is* an original."

Osgood turned to the woman expectantly. "Okay, so, gloves?"

Tricia's face distorted in horror. "Gloves? Are you *insane?*" She gestured furtively at a stainless steel sink on the wall. "Just wash your hands, you maniacs!"

"I got it," said Zack, washing his hands in the basin. Osgood thought she could hear him humming "Happy Birthday" under his breath as he did so. Twice.

"And dry them thoroughly!" Tricia called to him.

When he returned, he showed Tricia Dorsey his hands. She nodded approvingly.

He flipped the newspaper pages delicately until he reached page five. He opened his mouth to read aloud but self-consciously looked in the woman's direction.

"I'll leave you all be, but you'll get bruised knuckles if any of you touch that paper without washing your hands."

"How will we—" began Audrey.

"She'll rap our knuckles," said Osgood.

"Right," said Audrey.

"I will," said Tricia.

"I assume with a ruler," continued Osgood.

"Can we focus?" asked Zack.

They looked over at him, and when they looked back, Tricia had already vanished into the stacks.

"Okay, continued from page 1. 'Three bear the single word 'Kaliyuga,' and the final and most recently reported, 'Pralaya.' These strange metal signs have drawn the attention of many a curious passerby, though most regard them as little more than an amusing oddity. Some have speculated that they may be the work of a prankster, while others ponder whether they are a form of public art meant to provoke thought or simply entertain. Yet, after a moment's curiosity, the hoi polloi tends to dismiss them and carry on with their day. Both of these inscriptions come from the Sanskrit language, spoken at the time of our Lord Jesus Christ.'"

"Huh," said Audrey. She quickly thumbed her phone. "Kaliyuga *is* a Sanskrit word and has a lot of definitions, but it translates literally to 'Kali Age' or the 'Age of Kali.'" She squinted and read a bit under her breath, then continued aloud. "...also taken to mean 'the age of darkness,' 'the age of vice and misery,' or 'the age of quarrel and hypocrisy,' but notably thought to refer to the present day, when virtue and dharma have disappeared, and the world is ruled by the unjust, Kalkin will appear to destroy the wicked and to usher in a new age."

"Hinduism is hardcore," said Osgood. "How about Pralaya."

"You have a phone too, you know," said Audrey with a smirk.

A snap and a flash of light startled them.

Zack held his phone above the paper and took another picture. When he noticed them looking his way, he shrugged, "Someone needs to document it, since it's not online anymore."

"I didn't say anything," said Osgood. "You do you."

"Oh, Jesus," said Audrey, and they both turned toward her. "Well, Pralaya is *also* Sanskrit and also has a ton of definitions, but is a 'concept in Hindu eschatology.'" Could refer to the continuous destruction of all animate and inanimate beings, or the dissolution of one's... Atman? Oh, self. Or, 'indicates a great flood that ends all of creation.'"

"So, basically the same sorta thing as eschaton," said Osgood.

"Except for the extra words on our signs," said Zack, then leaned back to the newsprint. "'The appearance of these plaques has not been without controversy. The Archdiocese of Chicago has denounced them, labeling them as heretical and a mockery of sacred scripture.' Interesting, since they're Hindu-related. 'While some share in the Church's alarm, many Chicagoans seem content to view the plaques as nothing more than an odd, fleeting novelty.'"

"The Christians can see it now," a sharp voice behind them said, causing the trio to jump. Tricia Dorsey stood holding an elegant saucer and teacup full nearly to the top with steaming liquid.

"See what?" asked Osgood.

"You're investigating the eschaton warnings."

The words seemed so matter-of-fact that they took a moment to register with Osgood. "The... art pieces, yes."

"Oh, they're not art pieces." Tricia sipped her tea, and Osgood caught a whiff of whiskey that made her mouth water. For a long moment, there seemed to be no follow-up. But the moment was broken when Zack's phone slid off the table and hit the floor.

"Crap," he said, snatching it back up and examining the screen.

"Do you know what they are?" asked Audrey.

"They've cropped up occasionally and are among this city's most poorly documented odd occurrences." Tricia smiled and blew across the top of her tea. "One might only see the pattern if one spends far too much time amongst the sheaves of dead trees and ink. They were seen after the Chicago Fire; they were noted at the World's Fair in '93, one outside the H.H. Holmes hotel; and when those eighty or so poor men perished on the water crib, but I don't remember the year for that one."

"They come after tragedy," said Osgood quietly.

"It seems so. I regret I can't tell you much more, as my memory pool is shallow these days. But all the words are religious, and all portended the world's end. However, these new ones are slightly different, as they appear to be a countdown."

Another long silence passed between them. Suddenly, Osgood felt a shiver run from her toes to the crown of her head. She wasn't sure why, but she felt a desperate need to escape. "Thank you, Miss Dorsey," she said.

"Oh, please," said the old woman. "No need to put on airs with me. *Mister* Sherfinski was pretentious like that."

"Well," said Audrey with a laugh, "wish him the best for his recovery. What was it he ate that made him sick, do you know?"

"Oh. I imagine the rat poison made him sick," said Tricia Dorsey. "The sandwich was fresh." With a tiny hop, the woman turned ninety degrees and vanished into the stacks.

After a moment, they could no longer hear her footsteps.

TWENTY-TWO

DRIVING BACK TO THE apartment on Clark Street brought little but silence. Osgood looked between her compatriots in the front seat and could see, almost smell their exhaustion. It radiated from them like an aura. It wasn't until they'd nearly reached the apartment above Mary's Diner and Bar that Osgood finally spoke. "So, that old woman poisoned her coworker, right?"

A moment passed, but Zack chuckled and nodded. "Definitely."

"Should we..." Osgood looked around. "I dunno, call someone?"

"She was helpful," Zack offered.

"That's not exactly..." Audrey began.

Osgood shook her head. "Zack's right. Not our circus, not our monkeys."

Zack snickered, and his eyes met hers in the rearview mirror. It was nice to see him smile. His face looked as young as ever when wearing happiness. Worry had aged Zack, and Osgood felt responsible for that.

"Do y'all want to..." began Osgood. She wasn't sure where to finish that question. What do you investigate after what Tricia Dorsey had told them? The only direct link she could think of was, "Want to drive out to see one of the signs?"

Audrey sighed. "It's been a really long..." She trailed off. "Long, long day, Os."

"Yeah."

"I'm exhausted," she added.

"Zack?" asked Osgood.

"I... I mean... I'd have to pound some Red Bulls just to..."

"Got it," said Osgood. "Either of you know if there's gas in my car?"

"There might be," he said. "But you should have a mechanic look over—"

"You probably should just take it easy, too, Os," said Audrey. She turned fully in her seat as Zack parked on a side street.

"I just took it easy for over a year," Osgood said with a light laugh.

"Well, you know, that was hardly—"

"I know what it was," snapped Osgood.

Audrey and Zack sat in silence. He met Osgood's eyes again in the mirror. She watched as those dark eyes darted between her and Audrey. "You can take the Jeep if you want. We can get your car tuned up tomorrow."

"Are you sure?"

"I know this one runs," he said. He looked into her eyes a moment longer. "You have your phone?"

Osgood unconsciously slid her hand into the pocket of her crimson leather coat on the seat beside her. In it was a phone. Not *her* phone. Who knew where that had wound up after the accident. Just as he'd done the last time she reemerged as if from nowhere, Zack had spun her up almost an entire suite of devices. "I do. Thank you, Zack."

"Please be careful," said Audrey. "And if you start to feel exhausted at all, don't drive, just call. One of us will come get you."

"I'm fine, guys," said Osgood. She grinned to emphasize the point.

"Not a guy," said Audrey.

"*Touché*," said Osgood.

Ten minutes later, she sat in St. Boniface Cemetery, just a few miles south of her apartment. The Jeep rumbled quietly, every once in a while kicking its power back up, then letting it fade again. Sitting in the passenger seat, Osgood read the obituary on her phone.

> Nora touched the lives of everyone she met with her warmth and compassion. She had a gift for bringing joy to those around her and was always ready to lend a helping hand. Her absence leaves a void in the hearts of her family and friends, but her memory will forever be a source of inspiration and love. Her light may have been extinguished too soon, but her legacy of love and faith will continue to shine in the hearts of all who knew her. May she rest in eternal peace, embraced by God's love.

She climbed out of the car.

After checking the directory, Osgood found herself at a simple flat stone bearing "Nora Vance" and "Beloved Daughter." She stood for a moment, then two. The light in the sky was fading. The cemetery would close soon. But for now, there were only the two of them, her and Nora. Osgood wondered if they'd stitched her body back together. Her face, maybe, though she couldn't quite imagine how they'd have done that. She knew funeral home makeup artists were the tops in their field. But the body. Maybe they'd just left it. Two slabs of meat, wrapped in human clothes.

"Isn't that all we are, after all?" Osgood asked Nora's grave and felt a rush of sadness. For Nora, for her, for everything. Over eight hundred people dead. She couldn't even fathom it. It felt so out of touch, so far from what she'd experienced.

What you *experienced?* asked her mother's sharp voice in her head. *Not everything is about you, Pru. You didn't die, after all!*

"Yunno," a voice behind her said. "As I drove up Clark, I *knew* you were here."

Osgood wiped the snot from her nose with the back of her hand, but nothing could quell the faucet of tears. She turned toward the voice. Standing, backlit by the deep blue of the darkening sky, stood Dr. Ramona Yeagher. She wore a satin blouse and tan slacks, the pockets of which hid her hands. Her once-longer curly hair had been cut short, almost in a pixie cut, and she'd let her natural grays show. Osgood's voice cracked when she said, "Hi, Remy."

"Hi, Os," said Remy. "Isn't it a little warm for a leather coat?"

Osgood looked down at her coat and shrugged. She didn't feel overly warm. She didn't feel much of anything, come to think of it. Remy didn't move further toward her, but perhaps that was to allow Osgood to decide. A counselor would understand how over-whelming all this must be, after all. A grief counselor. "I should've died," said Osgood, and she broke down again, crumpling onto her hands and knees.

Remy didn't wait any longer, rushing to Osgood's side and wrapping her long arms around her. She pulled Osgood's face to her chest and stroked her hair. "No," she said, a simple declarative statement. "No."

Her presence made Osgood feel lighter, and in a moment, the tears began to dry up. It was almost as though the pain was being removed from— "Wait!" exclaimed Osgood, shoving herself away from Remy Yeagher, whose eyes were wide and cheeks flushed. "You're doing it!"

"You don't deserve that responsibility you feel," she said. "You don't deserve to have that thrust upon—"

"You can't just *take the pain* away, Remy!" Osgood snapped, putting a greater distance between the two of them, only stopping when she butted up against another tombstone.

"I should've asked," said Remy. "I'm sorry."

"Yes," grumbled Osgood.

"Most people don't know I can—"

"Suck the poison out?" asked Osgood with a morbid laugh.

"Yeah," Remy said, mirroring the laugh. "So I kinda just do it."

"Well," said Osgood. "I don't want you to. I want to feel this."

Remy covered her mouth with her hand, and Osgood saw her eyes redden and water. "Why?" she asked finally.

What a question, thought Osgood. She looked at the darkening sky. "Because," she said, but she knew there was more. "That's two now." She held up her fingers in a V. "Two who actually died because of me. Goddard wouldn't have even been there if he hadn't been concerned about me. He wouldn't have been in that hotel room if I hadn't insisted he fuck me. He wouldn't—" The shadows beneath a nearby set of bushes yawned like a chasm, and should Osgood move toward it, she'd thought she'd fall down that rabbit hole to where Sam Goddard's desiccated body lay, his eyes rolled up to her. She shook her head to send the phantom away. "And Nora," she pointed at the stone. "I didn't even really care about her! I mean, I liked fucking her, but she was needy and, and... I..."

"You're trying to distance," said Remy.

"Fuck you," said Osgood.

"Okay," said Remy, holding up her hands. "You want to emotionally martyr yourself for this?"

"If I had just let her be..."

"Everybody died, Osgood," Remy said, her voice tight. "Everybody on that train. And the other train. Everybody died."

"Not everybody," said Osgood. She waved her hand in the air. "Nora died like everybody else. It had nothing to do with you."

"Why did I live?" she asked.

"I don't know, Os," said Remy. "But take it from someone who has lived a *very* long time ... Often, the capital R Reasons aren't reasons at all. Often, the only answer is 'because.' And when there *is* purpose, meaning? Sometimes, you must also live a long time to figure *that* out."

"To stop the apocalypse?" asked Osgood. She laughed without feeling.

"That would be a pretty great purpose, wouldn't it?"

"It's so big," said Osgood. "The accident, too. I spent every day in there thinking maybe a carload of people died, only to find out..."

"I was near that corner when the tower fell," said Remy. "I think about it a lot."

Osgood looked up at her.

"It looked like..." she laughed a bit self-consciously. "Like the building was trying to cross the street and didn't quite get there..."

"Why is it my responsibility, though?" demanded Osgood. "The Lord of the Hinterlands focusing on me. The thing in my brain using me as a vessel. Why was I the one that had to decapitate The Guardian? Why am I—"

"You're special."

"I don't *want* to be fucking special."

Remy sighed and stood. "Tough shit." She brushed the dirt off her pants and put her hands back in her pockets. From that vantage point, she looked at Osgood for a long time—not just in her eyes but all over, as though scanning.

"You're a shitty therapist," said Osgood.

"No," said Remy. "I'm an excellent therapist; my treatment is second to none."

"You can't have my pain," said Osgood.

"What do you think I am, Osgood?" asked Remy.

"A pain in the ass."

"But really," Remy's tone dropped, lower than Osgood had heard. Low enough to sound ... not masculine, but almost ... split? As though it was more than one voice in harmony. "Would you say that I'm special?"

"You can consume emotion," said Osgood. "Seems pretty damned special."

"Do you know how long it took me to accept that?"

"No idea. You said you're older than you look," said Osgood.

"Far older," said Remy.

"So maybe it took decades? A century?" When Remy didn't reply, Osgood looked up at her and saw the woman's eyes were red with tears, her cheeks wet. "More? Less? Millennia?"

"More," said Remy, pained. "Less." She wiped her face with a tissue from her coat pocket. "Millennia."

Osgood wanted to know more. Ramona Yeagher had been pretty cagy about how she'd become what she was, and Osgood hadn't pried, instead letting the woman share when she chose to. Maybe this was the moment.

Instead, after a long silence, Remy changed directions. "You know how the Christians say that God won't give you more than you can handle?"

Osgood snorted. "That's such bullshit."

"I agree," said Remy. "But you've more than proven you can handle your shit."

Again, Osgood laughed derisively.

Remy paid it no mind. "You told me that the Osgood women are exceptional."

"Don't start."

"If the Osgood women before you were exceptional, why wouldn't you be?"

"*So* exceptional," said Osgood. "I have the dubious honor of being able to sidestep between worlds."

"Sidestep, and build your own," said Remy.

Osgood shook her head. Her worlds weren't anything special. All variants on the one she'd built herself once upon a time, by accident, and made it look like the crossroads where she'd died. Not like she could create anything of

(And on The Isle...)

value.

"Stalagmites *might* hang from the ceiling," she whispered to herself.

Remy tilted her head almost entirely to the side. "What?"

"Something that's been on my mind for some reason. It's an old joke. Or, not even a joke, like a mnemonic device. 'Stalagmites *might* hang from the ceiling of the cave.'"

"But they don't," finished Remy.

"Yes!" exclaimed Osgood with a laugh.

"I've heard that one, too," Remy said. "Anyway. If you can sidestep between worlds, *and* build your own, couldn't it be, just maybe, that you can also save this one?"

Incredulously, Osgood looked back up. "How?"

"I don't know, Os," said Remy. "Besides, just because some signs show up saying the world is ending doesn't make it so."

"Can you remember them?" asked Osgood.

"What?"

"The signs?"

Again, confusion washed over Remy's face. "Of course."

"I can't."

"You brought them up," Remy countered.

"I can remember that they exist but not what they say or how they say it. Neither can other people. Some don't even seem to remember they exist."

"Interesting," said Remy.

"It *is*, isn't it?" asked Osgood. "That means they're probably supernatural."

"Probably," said Remy. "But Os, this isn't the first time I've heard that the world is ending. This isn't the first time I've seen signs proclaiming it. So far? The world hasn't ended. Probably won't this time, either."

"Let's hope," said Osgood. She tried vainly to get to her feet, then thought she'd settle for her knees, but even that didn't work. Finally, holding her pride in check, she held out her hands to Remy and said, "Up?" like a child.

"Of course," said Dr. Yeagher, grasping both of Osgood's wrists (and for a moment, Osgood could feel her running her fingers down the scars) and pulling her to a standing position.

"So, wait," said Osgood as they returned to the Jeep. Dr. Remy's Trans Am was parked so closely behind that it could almost kiss the Jeep's rear bumper. "You just *knew* I was here?"

Remy took a moment, nibbling on her lower lip. Then she nodded.

"Did you know I woke up?" Osgood asked.

Remy nodded again.

"Can you..." Osgood stopped. She wasn't sure what she wanted to ask, maybe only if Remy could see that blank space in her mind. "See inside my head?"

"No," said Remy. "Nothing so flashy. You have a ... I dunno ... sense profile? A smell, a taste."

"I have a taste?"

"It's all of that. There's a spot in my head, and in my..." Remy pressed her thumb and fingertips together, then pressed them to her abdomen just below her breasts. "And that spot is you."

"Do you have that for all the people you..." Osgood snickered at herself. "Suck?"

"Cute, Os."

"I try."

"No, not for all the people. Not for most. Only a few get retained."

"I guess I *am* special," said Osgood.

They stood, looking between each other's eyes and the ground. Each time one of them seemed to be about to talk, the other would open their eyes a little wider, but it went nowhere. Before long, the sun had disappeared entirely, and the world grew night-blue.

"I have total recall now," said Osgood. "Like, can remember everything from every moment of my life and shit."

"Sounds like a superpower."

"Yeah, I guess," Osgood looked away. "So, I remember every moment I was in the... I was locked in."

Remy nodded solemnly.

"But I don't remember my dreams. I remember dreaming, but I don't remember what they were."

"That's not exceptionally odd, it's—"

"But I think I need to remember. It feels important. And if I need to, and I really have total recall, why can't I?"

Again, Remy stared longer than was polite. She took her hands from her pockets and rubbed them together, moving forward toward Osgood.

Flinching, Osgood pulled back.

"I'm not going to hurt you," said Remy.

"I told you, you can't have the—"

"Hush," said Remy. She put her hands on Osgood's face.

Osgood nearly melted. The sensation of being touched. The coolness of Remy's soft hands. The gentleness. The— "Stalagmite." She almost didn't realize she'd said it, thought it might have come from elsewhere. But unlike before, now she knew why she'd said it, as she could see a massive stalagmite very clearly in her mind. Taller than her, its irregular cone shape became finer and finer until all that topped it was a rounded dome of wet calcium carbonate.

"Stalagmite," said Remy in reply.

Osgood leaned toward it, bringing up a hand. Her nails were cherry red, and her arm was freckled as though it'd been in the sun too long—a preposterous notion, considering how much time she'd just spent in the hospital. As she followed her arm, she noticed her breasts and body were bare. Was she back at the crossroads? What was this—

CRAAAAAACK!

The thunderous sound drew her eyes back immediately, and the accompanying crack split the stalagmite from its peak to about two feet down. The crack didn't spread wide, merely gaping a centimeter at most. The sound must've startled Remy something bad as she shoved herself away. The push knocked Osgood's head back on her neck, drawing pain from several locations. Her teeth clacked together as she tried to keep her balance. Remy, meanwhile, hit the Jeep and slid along the passenger door. She stared back, her eyes as wide as the newly risen moon above.

"What the fuck was that?" asked Remy, trying to catch her breath.

"I don't know!" Osgood cocked her head at the therapist, who looked utterly terrified. "What did you see?"

"Fire." Remy gasped a few more breaths before yanking an inhaler from her pocket and squeezing it twice. "I saw fire."

"In the stalagmite?"

"I didn't see a stalagmite, only the word. What I saw was fire, and, and, and a smile, and... We're going to burn!" A rush of tears poured out of Remy's eyes.

Osgood rushed forward to help, to comfort, to—

"No!" Remy stuck out a hand. "I'm fine. Just—"

"Has that ever happened before?"

"I don't even know what happened. I felt this rush of ... death. And then—" Remy stopped, as though her brain had hit a brick wall. Her face showed a terrible confusion. "Yocane," she said.

"Yo ... what?"

"I heard it? Or I said it. Or..."

"Remy, I need you to—"

Abruptly, Remy turned and vomited next to the front tire of the Jeep. A moment later, she did it again.

"Remy!"

Again, Remy held up a hand to stop Osgood, but this one was less convincing than the last.

"Are you afraid of me touching you?" Osgood asked, yanking back her hand.

"No," said Remy, as her breathing began to return to normal. "No, it's not you. It's... Have you ever eaten something that you immediately knew was off? Or drank sour milk?"

"You were feeding," said Osgood.

"I don't know how to do what I do without absorbing— That's unimportant. What *is* important is that whatever's radiating off you tastes rotten. And that rottenness had a name. And that name was Yocane, or Yocan... something." Remy stood and moved toward Osgood, who took the opportunity to mirror the other woman's recoil. "It's not you, Osgood. Whatever it is, it's not you."

Osgood didn't feel confident about Remy's assertion, and the itch in her brain, the one telling the joke about stalagmites, showed her a photo she'd seen when she was seven, on the wall in her father's office. The black and white photo depicted a naked couple: the man with long hair and glasses, the woman with even longer hair and a shocking amount of bush on display. The man's penis hung long and had confused young Prudence because she'd never seen an uncircumcised one before. All the boys she'd played doctor with had little mushroom caps. The memory didn't have names attached, but adult Osgood knew who they were, if not why they were in her mind. The photo was part of a series of images of John Lennon with his wife, Yoko, which Annie Leibovitz had shot for Rolling Stone magazine.

As Remy drove out of the cemetery without saying another word, Osgood thought about that photo and wondered why, of all people, she was focusing on Yoko Ono.

TWENTY-THREE

Osgood watched Lake Michigan turn a boiling orange as the sun peeked its first rays above the water. From her position on the very end of the peninsula where the Adler Planetarium sits, she had an unblocked view of the Great Lake, and to her left, the city's skyline also burned with the reflected sunlight. She'd shed her crimson coat and sat atop it on the concrete circle surrounding the planetarium. Her legs dangled, still five feet or so above the

(wine dark)

water, inky, and roiling. She'd been chilly as she sat, watching the deepest night settle on the city and slowly turn to the very first vestiges of day. Now, though, with the dominant portion of Sol having pulled itself over the horizon, the sunlight had begun to bake her. Here was the July she'd been thinking about, not the weirdly blustery and dim bit she'd experienced. To be fair, she'd only given July a day to thrill her.

Sitting here, she thought of all the times she'd been in that building behind her, watching the sky show, first with her father, then with school, and that one glorious time in high school where she and Audrey sat in the back row and their teacher, Ms. Belzer, had caught them with Audrey's hand in Osgood's shirt.

"Prudence, Audrey, hang back," she'd said, as the rest of their class filed out. Ms. Belzer had stared at them for a long while, and Pru had wondered whether to put up some excuse or argument. Something inside had told her to keep quiet — good advice, too, because that had been the day that Ms. Belzer had confided her sexuality to her two students and urged them to be careful, as the world could be unforgiving. Osgood hadn't thought about that moment in quite a while, but it'd been a defining exchange with a teacher she'd cared for. And it had offered the first notion that her interest in Audrey might be okay. The wiki of Osgood's mind threw out a small obituary she'd seen, reminding her that not so long ago, Diane Belzer had died. *August 1, 20—*

She shoved the thought from her brain; she didn't want to recall the date, the expanse of time, the fact that she'd spoken to Ms. Belz—Diane, just before the Covid lockdown had happened. Her former teacher had expressed a desire to get together for a drink. But then, lockdown, paranoia, illness, death. And before Osgood had got her head back above the Covid waters (at least partly), the woman had died, not of Covid, but of the other heinous C: Cunting cancer.

This morning wasn't a time to dwell on that sadness but to be thrilled that she could move, speak, and comprehend the world again. The long nightmare of being frozen had ended. Abruptly, sure, and there were still odd bits and pieces she couldn't quite reach in her mind. But movement had returned to Prudence Osgood.

"A stalagmite *might*..." mumbled Osgood under her breath. She squinted at the ball of fire that had crested the water and grew whiter in its ascent. She thought about Remy, her terror. About Yocan ... something. And again, her thoughts turned to Yoko Ono.

Her phone buzzed, and she lifted it after one more contemplative moment.

Oh God, Osgood, where are you?! asked Audrey, panic strong enough to be read through text.

Zack's text was broken into several lines.

Aud5ey said you dint come home last nite

I can6 reach finmyph

Damn keyboard

Call us a sap.

With the exception of the second line, she understood him perfectly. After a moment, even that line made sense. "Find my phone," she said. No wonder they were panicking; they'd been tracking her. She'd known that, of course, and the number of times the tracking had helped in the past made her bristle the slightest bit less.

She stood and hung her coat over her arm, taking in the sunlight. Looking back down at the glistening lake, she saw an interruption in the rays. A white triangle peak, followed by another and another. A regatta? Perhaps a sailing school, getting their class in before the day grew too hot.

mfine, Osgood thumbed into her phone on Zack's thread, then long-press copied and pasted the same single misspelled word into Audrey's, before sliding her phone back into her pocket. She should be tired, shouldn't she?

Osgood shrugged and began to walk west on the peninsula, back toward the city proper. "Maybe I slept enough," she suggested to herself. That sounded right. She looked back, seeing the domed planetarium, and froze in place. One moment, she stood in the bright morning sun, and in the next

the darkness envelops her. Her eyes see nothing but a blue-green negative afterimage of the sunlight burned into her eyes. Her stomach drops. She staggers and reels, dropping her coat and putting her hands to her face to check if her head is still on. She takes a step backward, then another and the morning sun began to shift from gold to white. The true dawn of the day over Chicago, behind the Adler.

Osgood stood, confused. Horrified. Unsettled, un—

She vomited in the grass beside the sidewalk. After that, she stood on shaky legs, her face parallel with the ground, breath heaving. One of her curls dripped puke, and she retched again. Her pragmatic mind (that never could read the fucking room) took that moment to suggest she find a place to get a haircut, as her hair at this length would be too unwieldy for electric clippers. When she felt steady again and her eyes returned to the appropriate brightness setting, she looked toward the city, then to the ground, where her coat lay a good six feet from her, bunched on the sidewalk. She stepped forward tentatively, reached down, and lifted the coat with her left thumb and pointer finger. She felt its heft and nearly dropped it, but once she confirmed she wasn't about to vanish into darkness again, she shook it out and tucked it under her right arm, wedging her hand into her pants pocket, feeling the looseness of her jeans. She'd lost weight while locked in there, hadn't she?

She looked forward again, willing herself to take those first steps, but her feet seemed to ignore her brain. She stood rooted as a squad car made a lazy loop around the peninsula, slowing and stopping beside her. The car's passenger window rolled down, and a plump woman with short, dark hair looked across the equipment in the passenger seat, a quizzical, if slightly bored, expression on her face.

"Good morning," said the cop.

"Good—"

(Fuck the police.)

Osgood snorted a laugh, then stifled it with her palm. She shook her head as she looked back through the squad car's passenger window. "I'm very sorry."

"You been drinking?"

Osgood shook her head more vehemently. "No, ma'am."

"And if I tested you, that would be confirmed."

"Yes, ma'am." The reply also struck her as funny, but she didn't know why. All she knew was that it was a pretty bad idea to keep laughing at a cop, regardless of the reason.

"Where are you headed?"

Osgood looked from the officer to downtown Chicago and back. "I actually don't know," she said after a few minutes.

The officer appeared to consider that, then scratched the back of her head. "Why don't I give you a ride home..."

"Am I doing something wrong?"

"I just watched you throw your coat, vomit, then stand motionless for maybe ten minutes..."

To Osgood, ten minutes seemed a very long time to have been standing motionless.

"...And I suppose I could go through all the crap of giving you a breathalyzer test, but it's a nice day, and I thought instead I'd just help you with your walk of shame." After a nod, the officer, whose name tag said S. Clarence, climbed out of the vehicle.

Osgood watched as S. Clarence circled around and opened the rear passenger door. She remained rooted in place. The officer waited for her, looking into the squad car's back seat, then at Osgood, then back.

The radio on the officer's shoulder squawked and spoke in a male voice. "Clarence, update?"

Quietly, Officer Clarence responded. "I have her attention." Apparently wanting *more* than just Osgood's attention, the woman stepped across the patch of grass and put her hand on Osgood's shoulder, tugging her ever so gently forward.

The equal and opposite reaction pulls Osgood back into darkness. When her eyes adjust, she's even more confused. She stands on a vast beach, moonlit waters and sand. Music comes from behind her. In the distance, over the water, she sees the silhouette of the Adler Planetarium—something that definitely doesn't belong.

But the hand on her shoulder!

Osgood spins toward the spot where the person who pulled her into this dream world of

(The Isle)

a seemingly endless beach would be standing. But there stands nobody. Only a red flag off in the distance, the kind intended to warn of rough waves. Something was printed on the flag, but she couldn't quite see it.

"This may be the least comfortable I've ever felt on a beach," says Osgood. At least she remains clothed, though she's dropped her crimson coat to the ground once more. As she's about to pick it up, the silence of this world is consumed by the space between noise. White noise. Television static. Snow. The kind you don't get anymore since everything's gone digital. She'd once heard that the snow is actually cosmic microwaves left over from the Big Bang. While total, her memory isn't encyclopedic, so all she can confirm is that she'd read it on a site called *Know More Stuff*, and it had come with no citation.

She closes her eyes, wondering, if this beach is akin to the crossroads of her dreams, if she was the one who created it, then

(as I built my kingdom)

she should be able to control it. A loud *thunk*, then another, then another, and the sound of the static ceases. There's only the blare of silence from an unbalanced audio recording. At the sound of a crash, tinny and overprocessed, Osgood's eyes snap open again, expecting to find herself at that crossroad to see the results of the duel between her Skylark and a semi, but she sees nothing but water.

"Oh no, do you have insurance?" asks a halting woman's voice.

"Oh no, I don't!" responds another one, fear in there, but also an undertone of *Isn't this stupid?* aloofness.

"The fuck?" Osgood croaks. Her vocal cords ache like they've not been used in years. She supposes the ones she has here may not have been. Noticing a shimmery light all around her draws her attention to the sky. It is no longer black with a bit of moon but replaced by an enormous domed screen. The disorientation is overwhelming, and Osgood falls backward onto the sand. On the screen, filling her field of vision, is a terribly reproduced copy of a copy of a VHS tape showing two over-permed women driving a late '80s car. Both act their best pretend concern, looking back and forth through the windshield at whatever lies ahead, whatever Osgood can't see.

"I know this one," says Osgood. "Now the *Jaws* music." Sure enough, a knockoff of John Williams' brilliant two-note score echoes. It's just different enough so no one would get sued. But who would sue over a local TV commercial?

"Don't worry, ladies! I can fix it!" The voice is scratchy and low like a teenager pretending to be a grownup. The women turn, thrilled, and see perhaps the worst great white shark costume ever produced by a costume shop. The mouth yawns open, the eyes are dark and unfocused, and most disturbingly, the actor's arms and hands are clad in spandex the same blue as the shark itself and emerge from the body in front of the fins.

"Shark Man!" exclaim the women in unison.

Shark Man repairs the car's bumper with a wave of his fin.

"Thanks—"

An audio glitch obscures something like *ocho* or *echo*?

"Next time, I'll have insurance," says the driver.

"I'll give you what you need!"

Osgood remembers that line, thinking of the first time she'd seen the Sharkins Insurance commercial, midday between a *Small Wonder* bumper and an Illinois Institute of Technology commercial. It felt dirty to her, as though the shark had unsavory plans for these women, perhaps planning to sodomize one and penetrate the other with its dorsal fin. She shudders at the thought, wondering why it was so graphic, but then reasons it had likely been on her mind then, or why would it be here now?

Shark Man stares at the women for seemingly endless minutes before they break eye contact and climb back into their fixed car like lobotomites. As the passenger crows about the low rates in the Sharkins Insurance pamphlet she's pulled from the ether (maybe that had been what Shark Man had given her), the driver starts the car and pulls away, but Shark Man's empty eyes never leave the camera. They linger and linger and linger some more before. Finally, the announcer breaks in with the name, some starting rates, and a seven-digit phone number from before Chicago added the area code requirement. Of course, Osgood doesn't need to be offered the number; she'll never forget it. Even before her new superpower, the sing-songy recitation had a way of sticking.

The screen returns to Shark Man, who continues staring down from the domed sky. Staring down at her. After five seconds, then ten, Osgood tries to look away but can't. Fifteen seconds, twenty, a minute, two, then, finally, Shark Man breaks the silence. "I'll give you what you need, too, Osgood," says the mascot. "The Key to the City." The key Shark Man produces from his... pocket? ...is small, not an oversized ceremonial *objet d'arte*. Shark Man thrusts the key forward, directly into Osgood's left eye. She feels the orb of her eye pop and ooze down her cheek. There's no pain, though. Maybe Shark Man can protect her from pain, maybe—

Electricity coursed through her, and Osgood fell to the sidewalk. The sun beamed down above her. Osgood shook and spasmed, looking up, pleading at the shark, the blue thing above her. But Officer Clarence pressed the button on the taser again, and Osgood fell on her face on the sidewalk.

"Just stay down," the officer said.

Osgood's eyes rolled into her head just as the blue flashing lights of another squad car approached. This time, the thought, "Fuck the police," came out of her mouth, slurred and sticky.

That'll teach 'em.

Darkness swallowed her.

Twenty-Four

A COLD DRIP ON her hand caused Osgood to stir. Everything before her was hazy, and her entire body seemed on fire. Typical, perhaps, but today, it felt itchy, as well.

A heavily shellacked bench extending away from her head filled Osgood's vision. The cold of the bench radiated into her cheek, another bone that screamed for attention. In the distance, she could hear the sounds of bureaucracy: phones ringing, keyboards clacking, angry conversations, and quiet. The bench stretched away from her about five feet, and cream-painted bars stood at the end.

"Thisss siz novel," thought Osgood. Or had she said it? The thought had been slurred, so she'd probably spoken it aloud. "Imma call Shurk'm." That was definitely aloud, but it felt like it had come from someone else entirely. Osgood confirmed to the other, "588-2—"

"Good morning," said a husky voice.

"Morn," said Osgood, but she couldn't get more to come out. She rolled her eyes upward past the bench and saw a figure in shadows on the other side of more painted bars. "M'in prison?"

The figure chuckled but clearly tried to keep it quiet. "Jail," they said, then cleared their throat.

"Ima lawyer," slurred Osgood.

"You're a lawyer?"

"No, dammit!" Fury and sadness joined Osgood's frustration at not being understood. "Wherscot."

The figure crouched, and when closer, Osgood could see the face, broad and tired, with a graying mustache. "Are you asking about your coat?"

Osgood nodded, rubbing her cheek against the bench, drawing forth more pain, first in her cheek, then her head.

"It's hung up."

"Occifer."

"Yes."

"Fuck the police." Osgood laughed as though she'd said the funniest thing that had ever been said in the entire history of the human race.

"They told me you'd say that."

"Fuckin' tased me, bro."

"They did," said the mustachioed man. "You punched one of my officers." He chuckled again. "Well, I would have punched her if she hadn't moved out of the path of your fist. You, Miss Osgood, were not very quick on your feet."

"Osgood," said Osgood.

"Yes," said the cop.

Conjuring a significant feat of strength, Osgood hurled herself upward and managed, for a moment, to sit upright on the bench before falling in the opposite direction, smashing her face against the bench and then rolling onto the painted concrete floor. Through the aching haze, she repeated, "Imma lawyer."

"I know you are not, in fact, a lawyer—"

"No!" complained Osgood, rolling onto her back, suddenly aware of how much shit was probably on this floor regularly. She hated when people didn't understand her. The light above blazed down at her, and she pushed her palm between it and her face. Now, what was she trying to say? "I. Am. Not. A. Lawyer," she parsed out to the man on the other side of the bars.

"I know that. And I also know who you are," said the man. "Your name comes up occasionally around here. Did you know that?"

"M'popular," said Osgood. "Why solitaire," she added, a statement instead of a question.

"You're not in solitary."

"Danger to myself and others," said Osgood. This also struck her as absurdly funny, and she giggled, curling up into a near fetal position, shaking and laughing and hurting.

"You should probably stop talking, Prudence."

"Tell me what to do," said Osgood with a scowl.

The man on the other side of the bars sighed. "As much fun as this is, I'm here to collect you."

"Collect this," said Osgood, flipping the bird, though she realized after a moment that she'd offered it to the back of the cell, and it had been her ring finger.

"That's wonderful," said the man. He jingled his keys and then unlocked the door to the cell, moving until he stood over her. His head, looking down, blocked the light, and his face went dark. "Are you able to stand on your own, or do I have to pull you up?"

"You wish," said Osgood. She put one palm flat on the ground, then the other, and pushed herself up, first in an arch that flared pain throughout her back, then forward to her knees. The man tried to help, but she yanked away her shoulder.

"You are a piece of work, aren't you?" asked the man.

Osgood saw a flash of gold and leaned in. Glenn. "Is Glenn...your first name or last."

"Glenn is my last name."

"What's your first name?"

Glenn sighed. "Captain."

Osgood snorted. When Captain Glenn reached out to guide her shoulder, she shrank from him and almost toppled again. He held up both his hands and shrugged his shoulder, then offered her the right of way to go first.

"Take a right, then the door on the left."

Osgood paused at the intersection of hallways and held up her hands to discern right from left.

"That way," said Captain Glenn, pointing.

Following his finger, she turned.

"Do you want anything to drink?"

"Gavulin."

"You have good taste, but I was thinking water. Soda, if you prefer."

"Boo," said Osgood, following it up with a raspberry that continued as she stepped through the first door on the left. The raspberry caught when she saw the back of a large man in the room.

"A Bronx cheer? For me?" the man asked slyly but didn't turn around.

Osgood heard the door click behind her and looked down at the brushed steel table with a ring in the center for handcuffs. She looked down at the folding chair on this side, then at the back of the man. His burnt umber blazer and dark pants seemed impeccably cleaned and pressed. She heard a page turn, then another. After a few moments of silence, Osgood knew she couldn't stand any longer and sat uncomfortably, shifting in the folding chair.

"My deputy *begged* me to look into your past more deeply before I offered you the key."

"Tooma cell?" asked Osgood.

The man's enormous head rotated nearly around to his back, and he looked at her with pale blue eyes. He gave her a confused chuckle. "To the city," he said. "Don't you know who I am?"

"Should I?" asked Osgood.

Now he turned, tossing a manilla folder teeming with papers and photographs onto the table. He might be the largest human she'd ever seen, both in height and weight. His suit and slacks, however, hung perfectly. A brilliant red and black damask tie and dark button-down shirt completed the ensemble. His face, broad and round, had hints of rosacea beneath those blue eyes. His hair was thinning, but he didn't seem bothered by it. She'd never met him and only knew him in the vaguest of ways, but she sure as hell hadn't voted for him.

"Mayor Om Taugusta," she said, blinking back the lingering haziness.

"And circle gets the square," he said, sitting awkwardly on the folding chair across from her. "'Fuck the police,'" he said with a dramatic flourish.

Osgood snorted. "Agree."

"I was quoting you," said Augusta. "Captain Glenn said you're a very odd firecracker."

Osgood blinked a few times, trying to get everything to line up in her head. "Decent description."

"Are you always this standoffish?" asked the mayor.

"Never imprisoned before."

"It's jail," said Augusta.

"Same difference."

"Slight difference," he said. "Prison is for long-term stays after conviction and sentencing. Jail is for stays until sentencing."

"When you can't afford bail," groused Osgood.

"Do you really want to talk policing and injustice?"

"How often am I gonna talk with the mayor?" She folded her arms tightly across her chest, growing increasingly miffed about how her morning had gone. "And now that I'm more lucid, I'd like to complain about that officer who tased me for walking while queer."

The mayor narrowed his eyes at her and sniffed what sounded like amusement. "I could litigate that with you, but that's not why I'm here."

"Why *is* the fucking mayor of Chicago here instead of my friends?"

"Because Constance, my aide, you remember, heard your name on the police radio, and I thought I'd come down here myself to ensure—"

"That your survivor girl isn't a psycho?"

He said nothing, only smiled at her.

Bingo, she thought.

"What was your involvement in the North Side Ripper case?" asked the mayor after a while.

Osgood blinked back at him, a growing heat in her chest. Jesus, what could she tell him?

You should tell the truth to the mayor, suggested her mother's stern voice. *And what truth would that be, mother? Don't worry, we killed the ancient woman whose statue was causing the murders...*

Instead, she said, "I don't know what you're talking about."

"Okay," said the mayor. He folded his hands on top of the folder. "You're often involved when strange things are happening. It took some digging, but I found a few references to you regarding the death of a Sam Goddard from Milwaukee."

Osgood coughed. "And what kind of references would those be."

The mayor didn't respond, only stared at her, hands folded. "As well as Laura Maroney and Adam Pollack."

Those names meant nothing to her, and she said as much.

"A receptionist and a nurse at Swedish Covenant Hospital."

There it was, Sam Goddard, yes, the Goddardmonster, killing to get to her as she'd made her escape. How long ago that felt now. She swallowed. "Are you accusing me of something?"

Again, he stared, searching her face. She held his stare, and he looked away first. "No. I'm not accusing you of anything, Miss Osgood."

"Osgood," said Osgood.

"Osgood," repeated Augusta.

"What's going on in Chicago, Mayor Tom?" asked Osgood, leaning forward and folding her hands opposite his.

"To what are you referring?" asked the mayor, leaning back from the table.

"Signs mentioning the end of the world, an uptick in supernatural activity."

"Chicago has suffered a massive loss, Miss Osgood—"

"Os—"

"—and as you well know, that type of trauma and loss, like your friend—"

"Girlfriend," said Osgood. She didn't like that word, never had, but the pit in her stomach wouldn't let this man get away with calling her only a friend.

"Girlfriend," he repeated. "Trauma and loss often give rise to multiple things, not always all at once, though; maybe we're lucky." He stuck out a giant pinky finger, holding it in the air before her. "An uptick in church attendance." A ring finger joined the pinky. "An uptick in superstition, conspiracies, and lies." His middle finger joined the party. "And the rush to conflate things that have no business being conflated."

"Is that your official position?" asked Osgood. "Trauma-induced mass hysteria?"

"I would never say to the press."

"I might."

"Be sure to mention that I said it when you got bailed out of prison after attacking a cop."

"Jail," corrected Osgood with a scowl.

"Jail," repeated the mayor. He stared at her for a long while, tapping his index finger on his folder. "Do I need to worry about you?"

"I don't know what you mean," said Osgood.

"Maybe you don't need to say 'fuck the police' *to* the police?" suggested the mayor.

"ACAB," said Osgood.

"That either."

She acquiesced.

He stood and moved to the door, leaving the folder on the table. She looked from it to him. With the door open, he filled the doorway to the extent that Osgood almost couldn't see how he could move through it. "Oh, your friend..."

Again, with the friend. "Nora was my girl—"

"Different friend. Patricia Dorsey."

The name hung in the air as Osgood's brain shuffled through notes. "The woman from the historical society?"

"Yes."

"She wasn't my friend, I hardly—"

"She's been arrested for the murder of her coworker. Thought you might want to know."

With a final nod, Mayor Tom Augusta turned, ducked, and then passed through the doorway with ease, vanishing down the hall. Osgood remained in the room for a moment longer, then snatched the folder from the table and left.

TWENTY-FIVE

T HE SUNLIGHT TEMPORARILY OVERWHELMED Osgood as she stepped out of the doors of Chicago's 1st District Police Station. Parked at the curb was, gloriously, Audrey's minivan. Inside the van were, also gloriously, Audrey and Zack. With the front passenger window open, Osgood leaned down. "So..." she said. "Come here often?"

Audrey's face looked disturbingly like her mother's *I'm not mad, just disappointed* face.

"You got tased," said Zack from the back seat. His tone did not indicate whether this was a question or a statement. "Did it hurt?"

"I did," said Osgood, leaning into the open window. "And I don't know. Probably? I passed out."

Zack nodded, processing the information. "Audrey got in trouble," said Zack.

Osgood looked to Audrey, who rolled her eyes and waved her into the passenger seat. When they were headed back north, presumably to their apartment, Osgood turned to face Audrey, smiling.

"What?" asked Audrey, not looking away from the road. She made a dramatic show of flipping on her left turn signal.

Osgood stared at her for another moment, then looked to Zack.

"She accosted the mayor," said Zack.

"I did not!" Audrey pounded her palm against the steering wheel for emphasis. Then, making her left turn, she took a deep breath and calmly repeated it. "I just wanted to ask him some questions, and since he was here, I—"

"Why did he bail you out?" asked Zack.

"I don't know," said Osgood. "I think to save embarrassment about that whole Key to the City nonsense." She handed Zack the folder. "He did oppo research on me. Didn't like what he found."

"Oh, shit," said Zack, paging through. His face went white. "They know about us blowing up the statue's head?"

"And Goddard's death," added Osgood. "And those people he killed at the hospital."

"Are we going to get..." Audrey started, with panic in her voice.

"In trouble?" asked Osgood. "I don't think so. Why would he give me the folder?"

"So we know that they know," said Zack. "And they know that we know that they know."

Osgood turned to look at Zack but had nothing more to add. Audrey eyed him in the rearview mirror.

"Why were you out all night?" asked Audrey.

Osgood shrugged.

"Really?" asked Audrey.

"What do you want from me, Aud? I needed to ... clear my head."

Zack put his hand on her shoulder. "Which you should, of course, be able to do."

"Thanks, Dad," said Osgood, then regretted it when Zack scowled.

"It's just," said Audrey with a pained sigh. "Your first night back. We..."

"I'm sorry I worried you," said Osgood. She remembered what Remy had said. "Does the word Yocane mean anything to you?"

"Use it in a sentence," said Audrey.

"If I could," said Osgood, "I wouldn't need to ask."

"Do you know how to spell it?" asked Zack, pulling his tablet out.

"No idea." Osgood shook her head. "Y-O-C-A-N-E?"

"Nothing," said Zack, turning his tablet toward her to show the "no results" screen.

Osgood squinted and read the text below it. "'Did you mean Yoko Ono?'"

"Did you?" asked Zack.

Osgood thought of that picture of John and Yoko again, then shook her head. "I don't *think* so."

"Where'd you hear it," asked Audrey.

"Remy saw ... or felt it ... from me."

"When did you see Remy?" asked Audrey.

"Yesterday," said Osgood. "Why?"

"Oh. Nothing. Just haven't seen her in a while."

"Do you remember Sharkins Insurance?" asked Osgood after a silence that ballooned.

"No," said Zack.

"Might be before your time," said Osgood.

Audrey pursed her lips, thinking. "Was that the commercial with the guy in the—"

"Shark costume," said Osgood, "Yeah. 'I'll give you what you need.'"

"Shark costume," laughed Zack. He tapped on his tablet. "What did you say it was called?"

"Sharkins Insurance," said Osgood. "K-I-N-S, I think. It was a local company."

"Their ads used to run on the high UHF channels," said Audrey. "I remember them on late-night programming."

"Or when you stayed home sick," said Osgood, flashing to lying in her bed on Summerdale, watching the black and white TV with the rabbit ears. In the middle of a *Diff'rent Strokes* commercial break, the guy in the shark costume would say he'd give the women in the ad what they needed. But Osgood thought now he might have been saying it to her.

"Must've had a different name," said Zack.

"Why?" asked Osgood.

"Nothing listed. No Chicago businesses." Again, as if to prove it, he offered his tablet.

"Well," said Osgood. "We're talking mid-to-late '80s, probably wouldn't still be around."

"Victory Auto Wreckers is," said Audrey. "Empire Carpet, too."

Osgood conceded that two other local companies from the same era were still around.

Zack returned to tapping on his tablet. "It must not have been locally based," he said. He turned the tablet to Osgood.

"You don't have to show me every time," said Osgood. "I *do* believe you, Zack."

Sheepishly, he pulled it back. "No company named Sharkins Insurance has ever been registered in Illinois. No company with the word Sharkins in the name, either. Of course, they could've used a different corporate name... Are you sure?"

Audrey looked over at Osgood, brow scrunched, as she stopped at a red light. "Why would you bring that up?"

"Oh," said Osgood, "When that cop tased me, I passed out and had a dream."

"Fuck, Os," said Audrey. "The crossroads?"

"No, actually, a beach!"

"Okay..."

"But there *was,* projected on the sky, that commercial. Just like it was before. Those terrible actresses, that horrible costume."

"I always hated his arms," said Audrey.

"Yeah, like, why fins *and* arms?"

"Nothing on the tube sites," said Zack.

"Okay, fine, Zack," snapped Audrey.

"What?" he asked, shoulders slumping in what seemed to be a cower.

"You can't find it, we get it."

Wide-eyed, Zack looked to Osgood. "I'm just..."

"Tense, Aud?" asked Osgood.

"There's ... a lot is happening," Audrey sighed. "Oh, I heard that woman from the History Museum—"

"Tricia Dorsey?" asked Osgood.

Audrey blinked at her. "Yes. She's been arrested."

"For poisoning her coworker," said Osgood. "I know."

"And they know, too," said Zack quietly from the back. "It's in the folder. So they know we went there."

"Great," said Audrey. "Not just poisoning, Os, killing. He died."

"Sheesh," said Osgood. "Shame, she knew a lot." After a short while, Osgood asked where they were going.

"Home?" said Audrey, pronouncing it as a question.

"Don't you want to rest?" asked Zack.

"Don't need to," said Osgood. "Wide awake."

"Where'd you sleep last night?" asked Audrey.

"I didn't."

Again, Audrey narrowed her eyes. "You haven't slept since..."

"Coming out of the syndrome... Nope."

"More than twenty-four hours," said Zack.

"Look," said Osgood. "Y'all said the end of the world is coming, so shouldn't we get on that?"

"I mean," said Audrey. "We're just worried—"

"About me," said Osgood. "I get it. I'm *fine*. And when I get tired, I'll sleep."

"You start hallucinating after 48 to 72 hours," offered Zack.

"I'll let you know," said Osgood.

"How could you tell?" grumbled Zack under his breath.

"Well, then," said Audrey after a deep breath. "*Spectral Inspector*."

"Don't do that," said Osgood.

"Really, that's what you are," insisted Audrey. "What would you like to look into?"

Osgood considered it. Various concepts shuffled through her mind. The rubbing of the sign, the wreck of the Eastland, the absence of a company whose commercial she had seen almost daily as a child. "Yoko," she said under her breath; it didn't come from her conscious mind, but from her unconscious.

"Yoko?" asked Audrey.

"She keeps coming up in my head. Yoko Ono."

"Because she was an alternate result?" asked Zack.

"No, before that," said Osgood. "Maybe not Yoko Ono, but the name Yoko."

"Yocane?" asked Zack.

She brought the letters up in her mind, the way she used to picture words when trying to memorize spelling mnemonically, as though it were written across the glove compartment in front of her. Yocane. Then something happened. The Y began to collapse, its left branch and base curving inward to the right. Then Osgood saw it. "Try E-O-C-A-N-E," she said.

"Like search for it?" asked Zack.

"Yeah," said Osgood. "E instead of Y."

"Huh," said Zack.

"What?" asked Osgood.

"Eocanemot," he said.

The pit in her stomach said something particular. "That's right."

"Okay," Zack scrolled and scrolled with his finger. "It's a footnote. Eocanemot is the Old English variant of the more common Latin, Locanemotus. Not terribly helpful."

"It's a *little* helpful," said Audrey.

"Can you search for—" began Osgood.

Zack stopped her. "Locanemotus. Got it." He tapped around on his screen, his eyes lighting up as he found his way into the search. "Um..." he squinted. "*Motus* seems to be about momentum or movement. *Locane* translates to locane."

"Helpful," said Osgood.

"Hold on." Some more rhythmic tapping. "Aha! I got a 'see:'!"

"A see what?" asked Osgood.

"No, like in an index. *Manos*, see: hands."

"Alright, see what?"

"Yoaganemotsa," said Zack, trying to sound it out as best he could. "Looks like it's... Sanskrit."

"Lovely," said Osgood.

"And it means ... well, this suggests 'the one who moves the world.' But the comments are a debate over whether or not it should actually be 'the one who moves the world *on*.'"

"Ominous," said Audrey.

"This may be another 'trip to the library' type thing," said Zack. "I'm not finding a whole lot here."

"I've got a better idea," said Osgood.

Roughly an hour later, the minivan pulled to a shady spot in the woods of St. Charles, approximately 40 miles west of Chicago. The trees surrounded a house where they'd once held, if not an exorcism, then the nearest thing to it. An exorcism that had killed Sam Goddard, and a house owned by Dr. Donald Albrecht, former teacher to Osgood, now mentor and, well, drinking buddy.

The old man had tears in his eyes as they climbed out of the car. He hugged Osgood so tightly that she worried he'd pull his fragile body apart. She felt the wetness of his tears on her neck, along with the bristly fibers of his snow-white mustache and curly gray hair. "I'm so glad you're okay," he said. "I have some Pappy Van Winkle that I've been saving for this moment." He stepped back, held her shoulders, and beamed at her. Older or not, when smiling, Donald Albrecht looked like a schoolboy.

"Alright, Albrecht," said Osgood. "Let's keep it together."

"I'll do my best," he said with a laugh, wiping his eye.

"We're here to ask you about... Yoga— I can hear it, but I can't pronounce it," she said and swung her head back to Zack.

He pressed a button, and in a computerized voice, the tablet offered, "Yo-ga-ne-mot-sa."

Albrecht's eyes narrowed. "Where on earth did you hear that name?"

"You know it?" asked Audrey.

Albrecht nodded. "Well, yes. It's Sanskrit. That version is, at least. I've heard Locanemotus, also Iocanemotus, and Yekanemots, which is proto ... proto Indo-European?"

"Are you asking?" Osgood laughed. "What does it mean? Or, who is it?"

"Well, since you've come as a trio, I assume this is Spectral Inspector business," he said.

"We visit sometimes," said Zack.

"And if it's business, and you're after Yoaganemotsa," he said, his pronunciation very fluid. "Then I have fear."

"Out with it, old man," said Osgood, elbowing him gently in the ribs.

Albrecht took a long sigh. "Yoaganemotsa is a god who ends the world as it is."

TWENTY-SIX

"I'VE BEEN FOLLOWING THE signs," said Albrecht as he shuffled into his living room. Despite the foliage outside, the cathedral ceiling and floor-to-ceiling windows on one side lit the room like mid-day. He set down a tray with four teacups, two rocks glasses, and a bottle of Van Winkle Special Reserve. "When I couldn't remember them after my first look, I took a rubbing." He reached into the breast pocket of his salmon button-down. His hand reemerged with a folded piece of paper.

"We did that too," said Audrey. She pointed to Zack, who already had the image on his screen showing "Eschaton past due."

Albrecht's unfolded paper had a different message on it. "'Eschaton is begun,'" he intoned.

"That's not ideal," said Osgood.

"Eschaton is an apocalyptic term," said Albrecht. "Common in Christianity especially, but has usage in other liturgy."

"The end of the world," said Osgood. "We know. Like our friend Yoga—" Again, she couldn't do it. "Yoga man." She laughed.

Albrecht's face was grave. "The world has had various apocalypses throughout the eons. What is a mass extinction, if not an apocalypse? Or Pompeii. When your world is small, an apocalypse could be as simple as the Nile flooding after a tidal wave, and those who wrote about it thought it covered the earth." He reached for his tea but, hesitating, bypassed it and poured himself nearly a full glass of whiskey.

Osgood laughed, but the professor didn't. He just poured her one and then offered to add it to the teacups in front of Zack and Audrey. Zack declined; Audrey held up her thumb and pointer finger to indicate a little bit.

He took a long sip of his whiskey and then wiped his hand over his mustache, brushing away the droplets.

"Why does this bother you so much?" asked Osgood. "I mean, it's eerie, yeah, with the signs, but—"

"Why can't anyone remember the signs?" he asked, his voice clipped. It was a rhetorical question, and the old man immediately continued. "Because the power that erected them doesn't want you to. There's no other reason I can comprehend. There's no discovered scientific thing that would induce memory loss only around a single visual point."

"So, they're supernatural," said Audrey.

"You don't think so?" asked Albrecht.

"No," Audrey stuttered a bit. "I... It's unusual. We can pretty much confirm that."

"Don't take my word as gospel, of course, but the only way it makes sense is that it wants to be seen, wants to be understood, but not remembered."

"We found instances of this happening other times as well," said Zack, going to pull them up on the tablet.

Albrecht nodded as if he didn't need to see them. "After tragedy?" he asked. "Great loss."

"Yeah," said Zack. "The USS Eastland..."

"Well," said Albrecht, pointing his papery finger toward Osgood. "You've spoken about the membrane between worlds being thin after mass death."

Osgood nodded. "So much energy passing through ... crossing over." She considered it as she said it, remembering the *Spectral Inspector* podcast episode number (312) and word-for-word the rest of her rambling talk from that day. As she did, the sun, peeking between the tree canopy, found the bottle of whiskey, refracted through the bottle and the brown liquid within, and caught her eye. "Pappy Van Winkle's Family Reserve," she said without thinking, and the light disappeared.

Albrecht stopped mid-sentence. "I can't afford that, I'm afraid," he said to her, his head cocked to the right. "This is just Special Reserve."

Bringing up the View-Master in her head, Osgood barely heard him. Questioning, she flipped through images, far more than the old toy could have held. But sure enough, she found Pappy Van Winkle's Family Reserve in one. In a pair of tan hands, on a bartop. And she was ... was she wearing a bikini?

"No," said Osgood. "I remember it. But not from—" She growled in frustration, flicking through more and more images in her head, unable to find it again. "Fuck!"

"What's wrong?" asked Albrecht.

Without looking at him, Audrey said, "She has something like Enhanced Autobiographical Memory. It's new since the accident."

"Or since the coma," said Zack.

"Locked-in syndrome," Osgood tossed out, without looking up from her internal memory Rolodex.

"Remarkable," said Albrecht.

"But what good is total recall if I can't remember the one thing I'm trying—"

"Remember an elephant," said Albrecht, his voice calm for the first time since they'd begun to talk about the end of the world.

"I... Okay," said Osgood.

"Describe it," he said, still calm.

"African elephant at the Lincoln Park Zoo. The guide said its ears are shaped like Africa, and that's how we should remember."

"Good," said Albrecht.

"But what does—"

He interrupted again, holding his palm down and slowly dropping his hand. "Remember an Art Deco style building."

Osgood opened her mouth to question it again. Instead, she said: "The Rookery, designed by Root and Burnham. Burnham was one of the architects of the Columbian Exposition in 1893."

"Ah, a World's Fair," said Albrecht, wistfully. "Remember the White City."

The blazing whites of the temporary city Chicago had built for that World's Fair filled her eyes. She'd never seen such a vivid picture, and tears fell from her eyes as she gasped at its beauty.

"Remember Lake Michigan," said Albrecht.

She lamented the loss of the White City. Its absence felt so visceral, as though something had punched a hole. *That wouldn't be the first hole punched in you, Pru,* offered her mother's voice from far away. "Easy," she said, "I was on the planetarium peninsula this morning."

"Remember the—"

"No, wait!" snapped Osgood. Albrecht did as he was bid. She could smell the lake, that mix of fresh air and sourness from when it hadn't rained in a while. She could hear the morning gulls. A boat out on the water, not a speedboat, but it did have a motor. "I'm there."

"Is it getting easier?" he asked.

Osgood didn't answer; she just stared at the lake in her mind. Stared past the boat, past the gulls, past the sailing class spreading out across the horizon. "This isn't a memory," whispered Osgood.

"Osgood?" asked Albrecht.

"Something's happening." She considered what that something might be, growing quiet. "And not out there."

"Out there?" asked Albrecht in confusion.

"Where?" asked Audrey. "If not on the lake."

Osgood shook her head violently and shushed the trio. They shushed. "Something," said Osgood, still quiet. "Something," she repeated, hoping it'd kick off the thought and tell her what that something was. She squinted and realized she was slowly moving out toward the water and circling around until the planetarium dome was in front of her. On top of that mighty dome, though, was something that very much did not belong. Looking right at it, she found it hard to see, but looking from the sides of her eyes, it was barely there, dark and bumpy, jutting from the arched roof like a finger pointing at the sky.

"Stalagmites *might* hang from the ceiling," she said.

"But they don't," said Albrecht. His rejoinder didn't come in the cadence of a joke, but more to express confusion. "Stalactites... well, of course, they don't hang from the ceiling either; they accumulate downward..."

"No," said Osgood forcefully, the image gone. "There's a stalagmite on top of the Adler Planetarium."

"That wouldn't be possible," said Albrecht.

"Yeah," agreed Zack. "Stalagmites grow from dripping above them, and above the planetarium is the sky."

"Not the real one!" exclaimed Osgood. "The one in my head!" But it wasn't in her head any longer, was it? Try as she might. She flung her glasses off and rubbed her eyes. "Why can't I fucking see this?"

"Adjusted memory would be hard, even for someone with perfect recall," said Albrecht.

Osgood couldn't tell if he'd been answering her question or sorting it through in his own mind. "Adjusted memory?" she asked.

Albrecht stayed in his own head a bit longer.

"Albrecht!" snapped Osgood.

"Sorry," he said. "I was just thinking that the mechanism is the same. You've seen something, somewhere, at some point—"

"Or dreamed it," said Osgood. "I don't remember my dreams from the hospital. Apparently, I asked Eliza and Lil for help. To save me from—"

"The Bicycle Man," said Albrecht. The look on his face was of a man who finally understood something he'd thought about for a while. "Eliza called me in the middle of the night a couple of months ago. Said she thought you needed to be saved from the Bicycle Man. Then she hung up. She didn't know what she'd meant when I asked her about it later."

"What *does* it mean?" asked Audrey.

"It's," Osgood couldn't think of how to explain it. "I don't know why. But the Bicycle Man is something that bothered me as a kid. And it was somehow connected to that 'very special episode' of *Diff'rent Strokes*."

"When Sam gets kidnapped?" asked Zack.

"When did *you* watch *Diff'rent Strokes*?" asked Audrey with a laugh.

"We didn't have cable," he said with a shrug. "Had to watch over the air."

"But you haven't seen the Shark Man commercial?" asked Osgood.

"No!" exclaimed Zack. Almost petulant, he added, "And honestly? I kinda think you're making it up now."

"The man who ran the bicycle shop tried to molest Arnold," said Osgood.

"On the sitcom?" asked Albrecht in surprise.

"Told ya," said Osgood. "*Very* special."

Albrecht took a long, slow sip of his whiskey, finishing off the glass, which he filled anew, making sure to top off Osgood's as he did. Then he wiped his mustache, holding his hand there for a moment. "Alright, there are signs that can be seen and understood but not remembered." He pointed at Osgood. "Your aunt worried that you needed saving from something but couldn't remember what..."

"She remembered it later when she told me about it," said Osgood.

"Perhaps it was Lilian that could remember," said Albrecht. "As she's not of this time."

Osgood found that idea fascinating. Her great-grandmother's involvement in her life had been limited to the occasional voice of comfort or comment that Osgood was never *really* sure wasn't just coming from her own head in the same fashion the voices of her mother and Audrey did. She wasn't able to converse with Lil the way her aunt Eliza seemed to. "We need to ask Eliza," she said finally.

"Well, yes," said Albrecht. "But if you'll let me finish, it's all the mechanism of memory. Seen but unseen. Heard but unheard."

"If you don't remember something, did it really happen to you?" Osgood asked. She'd pondered this question before, first as a child, when she'd likened it to a pill making humans forget the long duration of a trip to Mars, then again when she'd fallen out of reality for a bit. The lack of memory functionally erased much of that time. "Depending on how much of my locked-in life I spent dreaming, I may have forgotten an awful lot."

"And dream time is different," said Albrecht with a nod. "You may have spent lifetimes that you can't remember. But what's most important is how it connects to this. To the eschaton and to our new friend Yoaganemotsa."

Osgood picked up what he was putting down. "Because if gods are real..."

"We *did* meet one," said Zack.

"We met a demigod," said Audrey. "Maybe"

"Way to downplay the fact that you murdered the Lord of the Hinterlands," said Osgood with a laugh.

"Murdered is a weird word to use there," Audrey said.

"But again," Osgood continued. "If gods are real, and if Yoga... Yogan..."

"Yoaganemotsa," said Zack, seeming to have picked up Albrecht's effortless pronunciation.

"Him. If he's real and is an apocalyptic god, placing apocalyptic signs around Chicago after a huge number of people died and maybe rubbed raw the membrane between worlds..." Osgood trailed off, hoping someone would pick it up.

"Yoaganemotsa's transitory," said Albrecht.

"Okay," said Osgood. "If *they're* real."

"Really, Os?" asked Audrey.

"Transitory in that Yoaganemotsa ends the world for the current inhabitants," said Albrecht.

"I.e., us?" asked Osgood.

"*Id est*, us," confirmed Albrecht.

"I mean, if the human race dies, the planet itself would be better off," said Zack.

"Well, okay," said Audrey. "But let's not make that part central to our plan."

"Yeah," agreed Zack.

"Eliza thinks I have to save the world," said Osgood quietly. "So does Remy."

"Two perceptive people," said Albrecht.

"If I save the world, I'd better get more than a fucking Key to the City," grumbled Osgood.

TWENTY-SEVEN

T RAFFIC INHIBITED THEIR RETURN east to their apartment, adding forty minutes to their travel time. Sitting in the rear, Osgood stared at the headrest on the back of Zack's seat. Little tufts of his black hair poked above it. He and Audrey were conversing about ... something, but Osgood didn't pay much attention to it, as it felt like the type of conversation people had when there was a significant elephant in the room that they'd rather not discuss. Instead, Osgood had turned her attention inward, finding the various mechanics of memory becoming easier to sort and discard. It amused her that her brain wouldn't let go of such an old, silly skeuomorphism as the View-Master.

Using it, she could quickly locate the planetarium image topped with a deep maroon stalagmite. The color of blood. No, that wasn't quite right, though, was it? The color of dead blood. Clotted and coagulated. The view of the planetarium also felt odd, as though it wasn't a memory. Certainly, she'd never seen it from this angle, from the lake, above the building. She'd been to that place so many times, and never once had there been a stalagmite atop it. For such a vivid image to have come entirely from her mind, she felt she should be able to see further. Her frustration grew with every attempt, and her running leaps at the dreams and fantasies that had played out in her head the last six months only made them feel further away. The only thing that had turned up for her was a fleeting thought, like a sentence spoken by someone in another room.

"And on The Isle," she said, quietly enough that the two in front couldn't hear her above the travel noise.

The word conjured many things: resorts, turquoise water, white sand beaches, the white-painted buildings of Mykonos, and Madonna's *La Isla Bonita*. The last one intrigued her, mainly because the opening lyrics spoke about dreaming of a beautiful island. Though that rubbed her the wrong way, The Isle wasn't beautiful, was it? Maybe Madonna's San Pedro was beautiful, but something about this one, *her* Isle, was wrong. Broken.

Invented, suggested a voice deep within, a calm and tender voice, the voice of Lil.

"Lil!" Osgood exclaimed.

Zack turned to look at her, a puzzled expression on his face. She caught Audrey's eyes in the rearview mirror.

Osgood shook her head. "Sorry."

"You know," suggested Zack. "We've still probably got about an hour to go. You should take a nap."

"I'm not tired," said Osgood.

"Not at all?" asked Audrey.

Osgood considered. "No, not in the least."

"That's weird," said Zack.

"I mean, it's not like staying awake can kill you," said Osgood with a laugh. When her brain began to cycle back, looking for articles to support or deny her assertion, she pushed away the thoughts before they could arrive. "It can't, can it?"

"I don't think anyone dies from lack of sleep, but—"

"But it can lead to death," said Osgood. "Good thing I'm invincible."

You may be hard to kill, Prudence Osgood, but you can still fucking die.

The thought came loud enough that Osgood could hear it, and her eyes darted between her companions who, judging by their expressions, had not. She flicked through the View-Master, trying to find that moment in time: it was a memory, she knew that. It was too vivid to be a dream that had happened. Someone had leaned over and—

"Someone tried to kill me," she said, interrupting Zack and Audrey's conversation about how unlikely her invincibility was.

"Wait, what?" asked Audrey.

"When I was locked in."

"You're just remembering now?" asked Zack.

"Sorry I couldn't be quicker, Zack," snapped Osgood.

Audrey ignored the snark. "Do you remember who it was?"

Focusing on the View-Master slide in her mind produced the hospital room's ceiling, the tiles, the lights, and the sounds of the machines around her, and she couldn't breathe; why couldn't she breathe? Because someone held her oxygen tube between her thumb and forefinger. Osgood, in the back of Audrey's minivan, began to gasp and clutch her chest. She felt the oxygen vanish entirely, but not before someone leaned down over her.

"Yoko Ono tried to kill me," said Osgood.

Audrey quickly shot the minivan across two lanes of traffic to exit Route 88. She made a couple quick turns, and then there they sat, parked in a half-full Culver's parking lot. Cars and SUVs lined the blue and white restaurant, flanking the drive-through. The Spectral Inspectors didn't have food, though, only concern. Zack moved to the back seat next to Osgood, and Audrey leaned far out of her driver's seat toward Osgood.

"Obviously, Yoko Ono didn't try to kill me," assured Osgood. "'Cuz that would be crazy. And I'm not crazy."

"Eh," said Audrey, but the amusement in her face didn't reach her eyes.

"But something hiding behind that idea did. Or at least wanted my attention bad enough to cut off my oxygen."

"You were constantly monitored," said Zack. "If your oxygen levels ever dipped severely, there'd be a record of it."

"Would they have told you two? Or my dad?" she asked.

"Not if they were satisfied you were fine," said Audrey. "Maybe thought it was a glitch."

"I could probably break into the hospital's system to check that out for you," said Zack. He gave her a little smile.

She saw weariness in his eyes and on his face. She wondered if he was exhausted from the day or if all of this had emotionally aged him. She'd never forgive herself were that true. Looking down, though, below his smile, she saw ... bruising. Not recent, but there. All around his neck. How had she not noticed it before? Was she really so self-centered and worried about *her* situation?

"What happened?" she pointed. "And when?"

"What do you mean?" he asked.

Osgood cocked her head and pulled his shirt collar away from his neck. She yanked him toward her so she could look around at the back of his neck, too. "The bruising."

"Bruising?" asked Zack. He pulled back and away, then rubbed his hand around his neck.

As he did so, Audrey leaned closer, surprise filling her face. "Yeah," she said. "It looks like a ring around your neck. Except by your Adam's apple."

Osgood nodded. "Like someone came up behind you and strangled you with both hands."

Confused, Zack turned on the camera mode on his phone and then switched to the selfie camera. He examined his neck in the lens.

"Did you notice this before?" asked Osgood. "Is it new?"

"It doesn't look new," said Audrey. "No, I didn't."

Concern filled Zack's face. "What the hell?" he asked no one in particular.

"You have no idea how you got that?" asked Osgood. "You haven't been doing any BDSM recently with Sandy?"

"What? No!" asked Zack, seemingly horrified at the thought. "And Sandy and I thought it best that we keep our relationship on professional ghost hunter grounds."

"We'll unpack that later," said Osgood. "So, someone tried to kill me, and I didn't remember; maybe someone tried to kill you, too!" She swung her head toward Audrey, who immediately lifted her chin. Nothing on her friend's pale white skin except the light suggestion of veins and arteries beneath the surface. "I don't see anything," said Osgood.

Zack continued to stare into his phone, rubbing his neck.

"Does it hurt?" asked Audrey.

Zack shrugged and shook his head. "Maybe a little tender?"

"Osgood," said Audrey. "What's hiding behind Yoko Ono?"

Osgood thought again about that moment, the moment someone had cut off her oxygen supply in the hospital. "I don't know," she said. "But I want to find out."

TWENTY-EIGHT

T HE NEON OF MARY'S sign blinked outside their apartment's front windows, sending in alternating red and blue rays. Beyond that, there was the new distressing white-blue of the street lights. Every time Osgood saw them, she pined for earlier days' orange sodium street lights. Clark Street had gone quiet, as had the city beyond — not uncommon once midnight rolled around. Only a few late-night joggers and dog walkers were still out and moving.

"Os, are you ready?" Audrey asked.

Ready wasn't the right word for it. As Osgood looked through the front windows, she wanted to know, needed to know, to unpack that missing time, those missing dreams, to peel off the sticker of Yoko Ono and see who was really beneath it. She thought she knew. The name kept floating through her mind's eye. Yoaganemotsa. She could continue to stand here in the frigid air blowing out of their window-mounted air conditioner or go find out.

Well, she thought. *Why not pretend to be ready?*

Osgood turned back to the front room. All seats were taken, save her BarcaLounger. On the couch sat Audrey and Remy, with Zack squished into the middle between them. In the chair opposite hers sat Aunt Eliza. On the table had been set a candle, a watch, a metronome, some rocks, a feather, and two small branches with leaves still on them. "Quite a spread."

"We're not certain what will work," said her aunt without looking up from a spread of tarot cards in front of her. After a moment, she collected the cards and put them back atop her deck. "Are you going to sit?" she asked when she finally met Osgood's eyes with a fierce intensity.

Osgood sat. "Did I get a good card?"

"No," said Eliza. She didn't offer more.

"Oh," said Osgood.

"Yoaganemotsa," said Eliza.

No one around the table seemed to know if she'd asked a question, made a command, or called out to the potential god. After moments passed, Remy said, "Eocanemot is what I felt."

"It couldn't matter less what we call it," snapped Eliza. After a moment, though, she sighed and put her hand atop Remy's knee. "But thank you." The two women held eyes for a moment, then two, then Remy smiled and nodded. "Eocanemot, Locanemotus, Yekanemots, Yaqanemuts, Iokanemotzos, they're all the same."

"Yoko Ono," offered Osgood.

Eliza looked up at her, head tilted slightly to the left. "That's very funny," she said, though her face didn't suggest the same. "Yoaganemotsa is the oldest variant I've found, and..." she paused as though listening. "Lilian agrees."

"You can just talk to her," said Osgood. "Like that?"

"Yes," said Eliza. "Now, we're—"

"I wish I could," said Osgood.

Eliza stopped and folded her hands in her lap, now looking at Osgood with all her attention. "Your power is greater than ours; you should not wish for the power of others."

"I..." Osgood began but felt that it might be better to listen.

"I'm not sure of the religious practices of those on the couch, but it is worth noting that nearly every religious mythos is the same. There's the creation myth, the myth of the wrathful god — usually involving a great flood — the messiah myth, the martyrdom and resurrection, and the go-forth-and-spread-this-religion-like-wildfire ideal."

"Myth," said Zack.

"Are you a believer?" asked Eliza pointedly.

"What?" Zack seemed to shrink into the couch. "I— I just have never heard someone so casually reduce religion like that."

"When we look at individual religions, we look at this on a micro level. We need macro. The big picture is there's a concept called religion, and within that concept, we all tell pretty much the same stories." Eliza waited, perhaps wanting to see if there'd be any more interruptions. "But what exists with certainty? The earth; oxygen, our life force; water; fire; the moon; the sun; the—" She froze, her eyes wide. She stayed like that for a long moment before turning slowly to Remy. "You're a daughter of the sun," she said, sounding awed.

Tears filled Remy's eyes. She nodded.

"What does that mean?" asked Osgood. "Remy?"

Her aunt focused on Remy a moment longer before she returned her attention to the table. "When I say micro, I mean planetary."

"Wait," said Osgood. "What do you mean a 'daughter of the sun?'"

"Os," began Remy.

"We do not have time for that." Eliza snapped, then waved Osgood's attention back to her. "Suffice to say, she'll be an asset."

Osgood dropped it, but stared, perplexed, at Remy, who'd become very interested in her own knees.

"Alright," said Audrey. "Let's start pointing ourselves in a direction where—"

"Our planet is micro," said Eliza directly to Audrey. "The universe is macro."

"And the multiverse?" asked Zack.

"Irrelevant," said Eliza. "Our Goddess, Gaia, is also micro."

"Is Gaia the planet?" asked Zack.

Eliza continued to ignore questions she had no interest in answering. "The macro gods are eternal. Their cycle is only to wake and sleep."

"So gods are real, but not religion?" asked Audrey.

The question seemed to irritate Eliza, so much so that Remy leaned forward and put both hands on Eliza's legs. As Osgood watched, she saw frustration and stress leaving her aunt's face. When Remy leaned back, Eliza seemed to be rejuvenated. She looked at Remy, eyes wide with fascination. "We must talk."

Remy nodded.

"But not at this moment."

"Secrets, secrets are no fun," said Osgood. "Secrets, secrets—"

"Don't be a child, Prudence," said Eliza, firm and clipped. "Yoaganemotsa is a macro god. And it has, for some reason, connected itself to you."

Osgood snickered nervously. "What does that mean."

"Yoko Ono didn't try to kill you," said Eliza.

"How did you know I—"

"Lilian told me," said Eliza.

Osgood blinked in surprise. "Is she ... always listening?"

"No," said Eliza without further comment.

"Alright," laughed Osgood. "Well, I know that already."

"Yoaganemotsa seems to be a god of universal stability."

"Seems real stable, trying to kill some random people from Earth," said Osgood.

Audrey and Zack concurred.

"You are not random," said Eliza.

"I know, but..."

"*You are exceptional.*"

Something about her aunt's tight-lipped emphasis frightened Osgood. She put her head in her hands. "I really wish you'd stop saying things like that."

"What do you mean by 'universal stability?'" asked Zack.

"If you picture the universe as a great clock, a massive and ancient timepiece, every element within must function exactly right to keep the clock moving."

"To keep time moving," said Audrey with awe.

"Beyond time. Every dimension. The essence of life. Cosmic creation. Everything. Should any bit of this clock be broken or, seemingly in this case, pull itself out of whack, the entire clock would stop instantly." Eliza looked down at her fingers. "Based on what I've absorbed from Gaia, I think that Yoaganemotsa is trying to break this bit of the clockwork, this small little iota. Because even the smallest bits have great consequence to the whole."

"But he's a god of stability!" said Osgood.

"These areas and titles aren't really..." Eliza shook her head. "Doing his job ensures stability. Not doing his job..."

"Leads to chaos," said Audrey.

She returned her eyes to Osgood. "And this being you've called Yoko—"

"*He* called himself that," said Osgood in a whisper. Her eyes widened at her own comment. "I didn't know that."

"It's starting to return," said Remy.

"This is good," said Eliza. "This being that *calls itself* Yoko could be anything, true. Could be a trickster daemon. Could be a spirit wanting to mess about."

"Or could be a god literally trying to topple existence," said Audrey.

"Yes," said Eliza.

The room went quiet. What more was there to say?

"Why does everything want to end the world?" asked Zack. "I mean, really. And this thing wants to end the *universe*?"

"Again," said Eliza. "Micro/macro. The big picture is that beyond our perception of the 'universe' or even 'universes' is otherspace. What you've called the margins. Outside. Humans don't exist there. Life doesn't exist there. Only gods, daemons, creatures. Perhaps Yoaganemotsa regards this existence as a prison." The old woman shrugged, her black-clad shoulders making points that flanked her head.

"So," said Osgood. "Lemme just see if I understand you clearly. What you said earlier, what Remy said about me saving the world..."

"Yes," said Eliza.

"Now you're saying that this thing might be big enough—"

"Size is truly irrelevant," said Eliza. "Macro is more a concept than a measurement."

"Sure," said Osgood. "Powerful enough?"

"That would be accurate," said Eliza.

"That I need to stop it from destroying the universe? Not just our world, but the whole motherfucking universe?"

"Yes," said Eliza, as though Osgood had asked, "Are we in Chicago?"

Again, laughter came, and Osgood couldn't stop it this time. The absurdity of it all. That she, Prudence Osgood, might be standing between not humans and the world's end anymore, but between being and nothingness.

"I don't mean to put undue pressure on you," said Eliza.

"Oh, thanks," said Osgood through a momentary break in the laughter. "Then let me ask you why I'm the poor chosen one?"

"I thought that was obvious," said Eliza.

"Well, indulge me," said Osgood.

"You're able to sidestep between worlds," she said. "If Yoa-ganemotsa is genuinely making a play at destruction, it'll likely need a distraction, or ... a vessel."

"Like possession?" asked Audrey.

"Like inhabitation," said Remy, looking to Eliza for confirmation. After a moment, Eliza gave her that with a nod.

Again, a phrase reached Osgood, a fleeting thought that brought its own sound. "I wear them like clothing." A woman had said that to her, a woman in the hospital. Osgood squinted at the View-Master in her mind, willing it closer, sharper, willing it to— "Alice," she said. "Alice. A nurse. She— I mean, I don't know. But she said she wears them, humans, I think, like clothing."

The group didn't know what to make of that.

TWENTY-NINE

"O s?" asked Zack, startling her.

She looked away from the window, outside of which the city had just begun to grow light again. The neon Mary's sign had been snuffed out around four, and now the day had started to break. Osgood hadn't slept, of course. She'd tried: got in bed, pulled up the covers, turned off the lights, threw on some white noise. Nothing. At 2:40, she'd come to the living room and stood in the bay window, watching the sparse cars traverse Clark Street.

"Have you slept?" he asked.

She shook her head as she turned to him. His eyes registered concern again, but she could see immediately that wasn't why he was here.

"I haven't either," he said.

"You should sleep," said Osgood.

"Pot, kettle," said Zack.

Osgood shrugged with a smile.

"I found Alice Tremond. She was a nurse at Swedish Covenant and was on duty on a day your oxygen got cut off."

"How do you know that?" asked Osgood.

"I got into the records, found yours, found a few instances where your oxygen levels tanked, referenced nurses on duty, and found her."

Osgood smirked. "You're the exceptional one, Zack."

"Nah," he said. "I'll take essential. *Exceptional* seems to come with a lot of added risk and expectation and not much reward."

That made her genuinely laugh. She heard a grumble and shuffling and was surprised to see Remy asleep on their couch. "I didn't know she was there," said Osgood, hushed.

"Awake," said Zack. "But not observant."

"Shut up." Osgood shook her head, focusing back on Alice Tremond. "*'Was'* a nurse?"

"Yeah, she didn't show up again the day after that happened."

"What happened to her?"

"Nothing," he said. "I mean, I don't know. But there are no records of anything to do with her. She didn't move, didn't— I mean…"

"She didn't exist?" offered Osgood.

"Oh, no," said Zack. "She exists. She worked at Swedish Covenant ever since nursing school. Seven or eight years, I think. Lives off Foster and Ravenswood. At least, she did two months ago when she had her last day at the hospital. They sent her check there."

"No record of anything," asked Osgood. "That's weird."

"Yeah," said Zack. "People don't just vanish. I mean, you really *can't* just vanish anymore."

"I did," said Osgood.

"Well, yeah, but I don't think she *also* fell out of reality."

"Wanna find out?" asked Osgood.

"What, now?"

"You busy?"

"I mean, no, but—"

"Are you saying you'd rather we wake up Audrey and Remy and make them come with us?"

Zack glanced back to where Remy slept. "No, I… We couldn't wait until morning?"

"I could go myself," said Osgood.

"No," grumbled Zack. "Don't do that. Lemme get my shoes."

By 5:30 that morning, Zack and Osgood were heading west on Foster in his Jeep. The building, one of Chicago's older two flats, was less than a mile from them. He pulled up in front of it and then shut off the engine. "She lives in A." He pointed at the first-floor windows. The drapes were open, and the TV was on. Osgood couldn't tell what was on it, but it projected bright colors onto the ceiling.

"What's the plan?" he asked after a moment.

"What?" asked Osgood. "I don't know! What's the plan?"

"Why would I have one? This was your idea!" He pulled himself out of the Jeep and slammed the door behind him.

Climbing out of the passenger side, Osgood caught Zack as he came around. "You just usually have a plan," she said, rubbing his arms, hoping to offer comfort. He seemed mildly embarrassed.

"Well," he said, looking up at the windows with her. "If the TV's on, she might be up."

"So, just knock on the door?" asked Osgood.

"Why overcomplicate things?"

They rang the first-floor bell on the front stoop. No response. Ringing it again, Osgood realized she could hear the bell faintly from the apartment above. Osgood gave it two more quick presses, but there was still no response from Alice Tremond.

"Do you know if she has neighbors?" Osgood asked him.

He tapped on his phone a bit, then again, then again. She couldn't tell if he was searching or chatting, but finally, he came back with, "The Eastons lived upstairs in B, and U, which is, I guess, what they call the basement flat, is unoccupied."

"And she lived here alone?"

Zack shrugged and nodded.

"With the TV on and her not answering, she might be hurt," said Osgood.

It took Zack a minute, but he nodded. "Possibly needs some emergency medical help."

"It'd be a public service to break in and check on her," offered Osgood.

"Let's not give ourselves any civic awards," said Zack.

"I'm already getting the Key to the City," said Osgood.

Zack laughed. "If you're not seen as a liability for doing things like breaking into strangers' apartments at 5:40 in the morning."

This gave Osgood pause. "Should we not?"

"I don't know," said Zack. "Why do you want the Key to the City anyway?"

"Maybe it'll impress Cynthia," said Osgood after a moment. Such an honor might actually move the needle for someone as hard to please or impress as her mother.

"That's fair," he said. He reached down and tried the knob on the front door. It didn't move. "Always worth a try." Zack flipped open his satchel and dug around a moment before removing a device the size of a screwdriver. He indicated something to Osgood with his eyes, but she didn't know what. She made an educated guess and turned and stepped between Zack and the road to hide him from any onlookers, but the street was relatively quiet. He pressed his electric key against the lock, and she heard a tiny high-pitched whir, a *click*, and the sound of a door opening. Osgood turned back to see the door open to a small vestibule and a staircase leading up to the first-floor landing. More important than the stairs, as though screaming to be noticed, was a mass of letters, flyers, and catalogs that spilled out of a fully gorged mailbox onto the floor.

Zack stood slowly, closing his satchel again. "That's not a positive sign."

The two stood in the doorway, looking from the stairs to each other, trading flicks of their head into the building, both trying to will the other to take the lead. Finally, Osgood jammed the end of her cane into a pile of mail, shoved it aside, and led the way up the stairs to a small landing. She stepped aside and gestured at the locked door. Zack nodded and got to work.

A *creeeaaak* came from above, and Zack froze, eyes still glued to the lock. Osgood leaned around the corner and looked up the second flight of stairs, notably dusty, as though no one had used them for quite some time. Another *creeeaaak*, this time closer to the second-floor landing.

"How're we doin', Zack?" she whispered.

"Almost," he hissed back. And then followed the *click* they'd been waiting for.

"Let's get inside!" whispered Osgood as the slow sound of a door opening above them neared.

The smell that blew through the doorway as it opened knocked them back, a bloated mixture of dead flowers, rotted meat, the stale scent of liminality, and, below it all, human funk, the kind that takes days, maybe weeks, to build up.

A foot hit the landing above, and Osgood grabbed Zack's wrist and pulled him into the apartment, closing and locking the door behind them. Osgood coughed and brought her hand to her mouth to block the omnipresent odor. The TV was indeed on. Osgood knew what was on without even seeing the screen. A car crash, an actress' line, "Oh no, do you have insurance?"

"Zack!" she exclaimed.

"I need to open a window before I can—"

Osgood grabbed his chin with her free hand and turned his head toward the TV just in time to see a man in a poorly-made shark costume drop into the scene.

"Is that—"

"Sharkins Insurance," whispered Osgood, mesmerized by the screen. Outside of her dreams and nightmares, she hadn't seen this commercial in decades, maybe. "It looks different than I remember."

"Different, how?" asked Zack.

"The women in the car looked different. The shark costume..." She trailed off, looking at the arms emerging from either side just before the pectoral fins. They didn't seem to come from holes but were an extension of the base costume. "It's more realistic ... but also less realistic? I don't know how to explain it better than that."

The commercial ended with the shark looking into the camera and proclaiming that he'll give them what they needed. Then, as had happened in her dream, he simply stared.

"Is it paused?" asked Zack.

"No," said Osgood. "Look at the trees behind him."

Sure enough, the trees blew in the wind. The women in the car, who'd apparently been granted post-accident insurance by the chimera before them, were also frozen, staring at the shark. Their hair blew in the wind as well.

"He's just staring at us."

"Yeah," said Osgood, feeling her stomach beginning to clench.

"Look at those actresses, too," Zack said as he brought up his phone and snapped a picture of the TV. Sure enough, not only were the actresses frozen, but the expression on their faces looked like the shell-shocked returning from war. Vacant stares, not at the shark man but into the middle distance. Slack jaws. Was that even drool dropping down one's lip?

Osgood felt her mind's insistence that there was something there she needed to see, and she also stared. Zack, she knew, did as well. They might have remained that way for minutes, hours, days? Who knew? Their focus was interrupted when the door behind them opened, and in walked Alice Tremond, clad in pale blue scrubs covered in Winnie the Pooh characters, not from Disney but from the original Milne book art. The characters and the blue fabric were dirty, stained, and streaked, and Alice carried the same odor that seemed to have gotten into the building's bones. Her straight hair had gone from blond to almost brown, caked in oil and dirt. Whatever Alice had been doing, she'd not cleaned up afterward.

"Alice," began Osgood in a shaky start. "You might not remember me, but I'm the one who had…" Osgood realized talking was pointless, as Alice didn't even notice they were there.

They followed her down the apartment's main hall to the kitchen, where Alice went to the fridge and got out a nearly empty gallon of milk. A cup with caked white in the bottom awaited her on the kitchen table, and she poured chunky plops of rancid milk into it. She set the gallon down with a light thud and lifted the glass to her lips.

"Oh, no," said Zack. "You really shouldn't—" But he turned away as she choked the lumps into her mouth, swallowing hard. Osgood heard him dry heave.

"Alice," she tried again and gave the nurse a slow wave. "Can you hear us?"

Alice turned and, standing rigidly still, looked directly into Osgood's eyes. There they stood for a moment, Osgood uncertain if she should say more. When she finally decided she ought to, the moment had passed, and Alice turned away, moving back down the hall. She trailed her fingers along the wall as she walked, knocking into a few framed pictures and sending one to the ground. The grimy trails at the height of her fingers suggested she'd done this many times before.

Upon Alice's return to the living room, she sat on the floor mere inches from the television. Osgood noticed a dirty circle surrounding her, presumably from remaining in this spot. On the television, a shark man offered to fix the damage caused by the accident. Alice was riveted to the screen.

"Psst," hissed Zack. Osgood looked at him and saw him standing at the apartment's open front door. He pointed at the staircase leading up and again at the ceiling above him. Osgood followed his finger and saw that a nasty discoloration had spread across the ceiling above Alice. From that spot wafted the scent of death.

She took a deep breath. "Let's see what died upstairs."

THIRTY

THE RANK SCENT OF death built as they reached the upper landing. Amid the clutter of cardboard boxes and packaging, the door to apartment B was ajar. A pair of flies emerged from the gap, spiraled around each other, and disappeared down the staircase, possibly to find Alice.

Zack grasped the doorknob and then held it. He breathed in through his nose, out through his mouth, then swung the door open. Darkness beyond. Slits of light were visible from where the windows should be, but they seemed to have been covered by something. The hallway's own lack of light didn't help. Osgood felt along the wall to the right of the door, hoping for a switch, but her excitement at finding one was short-lived, as it did nothing. Neither did the two next to it.

"Phones," whispered Zack.

They turned their phones on simultaneously, casting harsh light into the room.

Osgood immediately saw the pile of gristle and bone. Blackening blood, teeming with maggots and flies swarming and writhing. It didn't resemble anything at first. "Oh... God."

Zack turned his light to focus further to the left of Osgood's. "Oh boy," he said. Osgood looked and saw a hand at the end of a long and uneven range of piles of meat. A human hand. A (hopefully) dead hand. The skin and muscle had been stripped from the middle to pinky fingers, and each was now merely bones and tendons. Beyond the hand on the floor, the finger meat and skin seemed to have been arranged in a mimicry of the skeletal vestiges before them. Zack retched into a corner while trying to keep his light pointed at the center of the room.

Osgood moved toward the body on the floor, feeling the carpet beneath her grow thick and sticky. The thickness, the tug of it — this scene wasn't recent. Old blood. Old body. How old, she didn't know, but more than days, likely more than weeks. As with the arm, the torso of whomever this was had been reduced to a pile of offal, rib bones strewn into a pile beside it. Another shift of the light revealed the stump of a neck, with a protruding spinal column, but no head. Finally, Osgood joined Zack in retching.

"What the fuck is this, Os?"

"I..." Not knowing what to say, Osgood repeated, "I."

"We should get out of here and call the police," said Zack, talking through a dry heave. "Anonymously, of course."

"In a minute," said Osgood.

"What more do you need?"

"If she did actually try to kill me," said Osgood, "I want to see if there might be an obvious reason why."

"Because she wanted to serve you on a deli platter like this?" asked Zack with a nervous titter that vanished when, this time, he clapped his hand to his mouth as he heaved.

"Vomit can contain DNA," said Osgood absently, running the light on her phone along the sparse furniture in the room.

Zack nodded and choked it back, then stood bent over with his hands on his knees for a while.

"Well," said Osgood. "I found the head."

Zack looked reluctantly at where her flashlight was aimed. Below the offal of the chest, the body's stomach had been slit and spilled forth food. Far from digested, though, this seemed to be an entire fruit bowl, grapes, a pear, two apples, and a strangely out-of-place onion spilling down the stomach to the bloody floor. Though uneaten, the food had begun to rot.

"Like some fucked up horn of plenty," said Osgood, looking down further to where she'd seen the outline of the head between the legs (as they were) of this creature. Moving closer, Osgood saw the head, upright on the stump of the neck, eyes open and staring, though not seeing, at the belly and viscera above. Immediately next to the head, Osgood saw that this once-man's penis had been fully flayed, as had the balls beneath.

"What the fuck."

"Zack," said Osgood, taking two steps back, widening the range of her light.

"I mean, this is so much more fucked up than we've—"

"Zack!"

"What?"

"Your light," she said, cocking her head, unsure if she'd seen what she thought. "No! Point it at the ceiling!"

Zack did as he was bid, and his phone's light pointed straight up from the phone held above his head. The light spread out on the white-painted ceiling and returned the barest amounts of light to the room. "Woah," he said.

"Yeah," said Osgood. While the grotesque once-human at the center of the room was horrific, the true breadth of it all sent chills through her body. Radiating from the body were brownish-red streaks along the hardwood floor.

"Is that a... Not a Zodiac. A rune?" asked Zack.

Even without seeing it in totality or being able to consider it objectively, Osgood felt that she knew it deep within her soul. It was no Zodiac, no pentagram or pentacle. At first, she thought it might be a smiley or emoticon. The arc and vertical lines certainly looked like the old =) she used to send her friends on those chat boards. But the third line between the others gave her pause.

"If that's an emoticon, it's alien," said Zack. "I don't recognize it. Not part of the ASCII code-set either."

"I've seen it before," said Osgood.

"Where?"

Osgood sensed that the memory she had was a mask for something bigger. "I saw it on a flag, on the beach, in that margin space before I got tased. But I've seen it much more than that. Somewhere deeper."

Zack looked back from the bloody alien smile to her, then opened his mouth to say something else, but he was interrupted.

"For hwon eart þū hēr?"

He unleashed a scream that would have made Jamie Lee Curtis proud, and he and Osgood swung their phone flashlights toward the door, toward Alice.

"For hwon eart þū hēr?" repeated Alice.

"What language is that?" Osgood whispered to Zack. He shrugged, still appearing sheepish after his scream. But turning his phone's screen to her, she again was reminded why he was essential. He'd started recording.

"Kasmin kāraṇe tvaṁ atra asi?" asked Alice. She directed her bloodshot eyes at Osgood and moved forward, closing the five-foot gap between them by an inch or so.

"Are you..." Osgood began, uncertain what would be best to ask. "...Yoaganemotsa?"

The name stopped Alice. She looked down at her hands and then back up to them. *"Yoaganemotsa chakrasya parivartanam asti."*

"Sure," said Osgood. She took a firm step toward the former nurse. "Why the fuck did you try to kill me?"

"Saḥ tvāṁ āvaśyakaṁ asti."

Osgood looked over at Zack, who shrugged.

He looked up from his phone's screen and asked. "Do you still speak English?"

"Ġēa."

"Was that 'yeah?'"

Alice nodded. Then she turned and walked out of the room.

Osgood shrugged at Zack, who shrugged back. As they followed down the stairs, Zack whispered to her, "There's an AI translation app on your phone. It's called TowerOfBabel."

"What makes it AI?" asked Osgood skeptically.

"Is that what you want to talk about?" snapped Zack. He reached out for her phone, and she handed it to him. He opened an app and handed it back. On the app was a blinking cursor. "It's set to translate into English. So I'll keep filming with mine, and you tell me what she's saying."

"Do you think she understands us?" asked Osgood.

"I don't think she's very aware of us," said Zack.

When they returned to Apartment A, they found Alice had returned to her seat on the floor in front of the TV, where the Sharkins commercial still played on a loop. She didn't look up from the TV. Zack moved slowly behind her, sitting on the couch at the room's back wall while Osgood crouched beside her. This close, the odor was unfathomable. Shit and piss and rot. Osgood nearly hurled herself backward when Alice turned to her and grinned, pointing at the TV. The woman's eyes were so bloodshot there appeared to be no white left, and she was missing several teeth in the front of her smile. Osgood found the breath emitted from behind that smile even more horrifying. Still, she grasped the floor with her palms and held steady.

"Hē wæs hæftling," said Alice, a near whisper.

Osgood was stunned when the sentence appeared on her phone, all accents and strange letters, along with the legend "Old English."

"It's Old English, Zack," said Osgood.

"We asked her to speak English."

Osgood read as large bold letters appeared below. "'He was a prisoner.'"

"Yoaganemotsa?" asked Osgood.

Alice nodded.

"Where was he a prisoner?"

Alice laughed at something on the television. Osgood was about to repeat the question, but Alice said, *"Ūtan."*

Off the screen, Osgood said, "'Outside.' But he's not a prisoner anymore?"

"Nā." **No.**

"I could've guessed that one," said Zack.

"What does he want?" asked Osgood.

"Hē wille þæt wiel brecan. Þone cycel ġeendian." **He wants to break the wheel. To end the cycle.**

"The Bicycle Man," whispered Osgood to herself.

"What?" asked Zack.

Osgood shook her head. "Can he be stopped?"

"Hē ne mæg gestilled bēon." **He cannot be stopped.**

"Great," said Osgood. "Can he be killed?"

"Hē ne mæg ofslægen bēon, hē drēamian wille and āwacan, and drēamian and āwacan." **He cannot be killed; he will dream and wake and dream and wake.**

"Os," whispered Zack.

"In a second," said Osgood.

"No, now," said Zack. "Look."

Osgood looked at Zack, whose finger pointed to the TV. The commercial was still Sharkins insurance, but the feed had gone wonky. Electrical noise was everywhere, but especially the Shark Man costume, which now appeared to be entirely made of television static, and within that static was embedded a single orange eye. Osgood looked back to Alice.

"Is that—" she indicated the eye "—is that him?"

"Ġēa," said Alice.

"How did he—"

Osgood stopped abruptly as Alice reached her right arm over her head and tucked her fingers inside her mouth.

"What's she doing?"

"How would I know, Zack?"

The nurse followed it with her left hand, this one taking hold of her lower jaw.

"Alice," said Osgood cautiously.

"Hē wille þæt þū gemunē." The words came out garbled because she had both hands in her mouth, but miraculously, TowerOfBabel understood them. **He wants you to remember.**

"Remember what?"

Alice just gripped harder.

"Alice? Remember what?"

Alice never told her what she was supposed to remember. In a shockingly quick move, the nurse yanked her jaw apart, pulling her entire head backward until her spine snapped.

"Jesus Christ!" Zack scrambled with his camera to make sure he filmed this.

The now (hopefully) deceased Alice remained upright, her body normal up until the hanging jaw and flung back head. Her tongue dangled from the side of her mouth, seeming longer than humanly possible. Then, thankfully, she fell to the ground.

"Should... Should we..." Zack stammered.

"Leave? Yes!"

"Yeah. Yeah," said Zack, then added a third yeah as good measure.

They drove in silence the few blocks back to the apartment, encountering few vehicles and fewer people as the day began on the north side of Chicago, trying desperately not to scream.

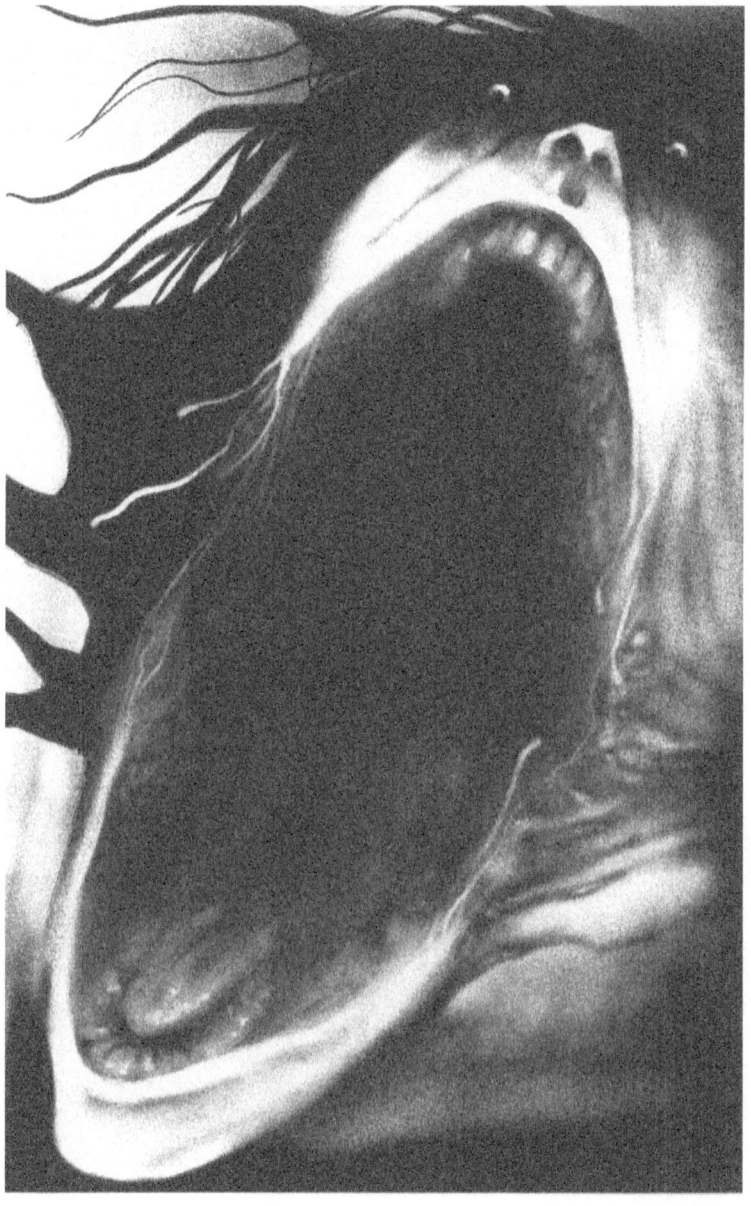

THIRTY-ONE

ARRIVING HOME, OSGOOD HAD been surprised to find her aunt still at the apartment. She was unsure where the woman had slept, as she hadn't taken Osgood's bed. Also, the black she wore today differed from the black she'd worn yesterday. Meanwhile, Remy had helped herself to some of Osgood's clothing and was rocking a pair of black jeans torn at the knees and a "Do You Read Sutter Cane?" tee. Osgood wondered if being attracted to someone dressed as oneself was narcissism. Well, what else was new? She already knew she was a narcissist.

The kitchen table was so full they had to bring over the stool Osgood used when she — rarely, since she couldn't stand long enough — washed dishes.

"Police would want to know why we were there," said Zack. He shook his head. "I'm thinking an anonymous tip."

Osgood looked at him, suddenly alarmed. "Won't they be able to..."

"I wiped down everything we touched as we went. You actually didn't touch much of anything."

Osgood thought about it and then couldn't remember if she'd touched *anything*. Surely she had; one couldn't just go someplace and not. "The light switches," she remembered.

"Got 'em. Trust me," said Zack. He held his eyes on Osgood until she returned his look. She nodded. "Everybody agree that's the best course of action?"

Some murmurs and nods from around the table.

"Right," said Zack. He tapped something out on his phone, and there was a woosh sound as it was being sent. He set the phone down.

"What did you do?" asked Remy.

"I asked a friend to filter it through some channels so it can't be directly connected to us. The cops should get the notice within the hour."

"Sounds like a good friend to have," said Remy.

"He's a crypto scammer." Zack shrugged. "But in this circumstance, yeah, good friend."

Osgood snorted a laugh and then choked on it, remembering the translated words from Alice. "He wants me to remember."

"Remember what," said Eliza, her voice stern and clipped. She was not asking a question.

"My question, too," said Osgood.

"In the interim since our last conversation," said Eliza, looking at no one in particular. "I've come up with a few thoughts. Oh," she added. "I also asked Donald to join us."

"Who's Donald?" asked Osgood, leaning in.

When Eliza looked at her, she laughed. Her aunt's face held the greatest *duh* expression she'd ever seen. "You call him Albrecht, but I refuse to believe you don't know his first name."

"Oh!" said Osgood. Of course, she knew his first name. It'd probably been a decade or more since she'd used it. "Okay, good. Putting together a crew."

"What are your thoughts, Eliza?" asked Audrey.

"Well, firstly, Yoko, which is what I suggest we call it for expediency's sake," said Eliza, her vocal clip becoming rapid, "and to be clear, I'm not saying that *our* Yoko is Yoaganemotsa. It may be a lesser demigod, or daemon, or even just an angry spirit that likes to swing its dick around."

Osgood chortled, then covered her mouth when Eliza side-eyed her. "Sorry."

"But given the appearance of the signs after the El crash and the tower's falling, I'm inclined to believe it's at least a bit more powerful than your average trickster daemon."

"Oh yes," said Audrey. "Those."

Eliza paid no mind to the interjection. "Therefore, I suggest we move through all avenues, but firstly, we explore the largest and most ludicrous: that Yoko *is* Yoaganemotsa and is making its play to misalign the universe, which may destroy it or may do something we can't even fathom. We've really no idea. But whatever it intends to do, it seems to want or need Osgood's attention to do it."

"Why would it wipe my memory, then?"

"Strength through adversity?" suggested Remy.

"Yeah!" said Zack. "Yoko knows you *can* be powerful, but you probably need to fight to get there, so the first obstacle is you actually breaking through your own brain fog."

Osgood nodded, hoping her eyes didn't show how overwhelmed she was becoming. "What about Shark Man?"

The table was quiet; either no one knew more than she did about Shark Man and Sharkins insurance, or they didn't want to be the first to share.

"Anyone?" asked Osgood.

"Well," said Zack. "My sources confirmed that there isn't now, nor ever was, a Sharkins or other Shark-named insurance company in Chicago, or even the greater Midwest."

"Then why did we always see the commercial?" asked Audrey. Osgood nodded to second the question.

"I saw the commercial before as well," said Remy. "Though you all seem to remember it more vividly."

"Not me," Zack pointed out. "Until this morning, I'd never seen it."

Audrey shook her head. "It's hard to forget! It was a ridiculous commercial and ran several times daily during rerun programming blocks."

Impatience rose on Zack's face, and Osgood knew he would throw a snit if they pushed it any further.

"If Zack's cadre of misfits and criminals say it doesn't exist, I'm inclined to believe them," she said, hoping to right his ship. He'd had a hard day. Watched a woman do ... what would that even be called? It wasn't decapitation.

"Some of them are neither misfits nor criminals," Zack groused.

"Okay," said Osgood.

"One of my fri—" He stopped, seeming to think better of his wording. "Criminal associates sent me this." He turned his tablet to the table. On it was Tom Baker, the Fourth Doctor, he of the ridiculously long scarf, curly hair, and oversized fedora. He appeared to be confronting a creature made almost entirely of spray-painted bubble wrap. The image quality was atrocious early video, with lights that burned their image onto the screen as the characters moved.

"Is this *Doctor Who*?" asked Remy.

"What?" asked Zack. "Oh, yes, give it a second."

"I am quite familiar with *The Ark in Space*," said Eliza.

Osgood raised an eyebrow at her.

"What?" she asked.

As if in answer, a glitch appeared, scan lines like something had been taped over the original program. Then back to The Doctor.

"Is there going to be more to it than that?" asked Audrey.

Zack threw her a look that seemed to plead she give him some credit.

A second glitch, this one containing a bar of snow and static, knocked out the audio from the *Doctor Who* episode. Now, all that played was a deafening room tone hum, the sound of everyday machines with nothing to distract from it, and a still image of ... well ... brown.

Osgood leaned toward the tablet, hoping to see what she was supposed to be seeing. "What are—"

A *blare* of static noise with something deeper below it, almost like a bass drum or a very low wind, then back to the quiet of near nothingness. They sat in that nothingness for so long that nearly everyone at the table jumped when the man in the shark costume popped up.

"Jesus Christ, Zack!" Audrey swatted him on the shoulder.

"What?" he pleaded in defense. "I haven't watched this!"

"What's it doing?" asked Osgood, tilting her head. The image on the screen felt so out of place and wrong that she wasn't sure how to process it.

The brown in the background was maybe a backdrop or a painted wall. The shark in the foreground looked so very much like the

(I'll give you)

man in the shark costume from the insurance commercial she'd seen

(what you need)

so many times growing up. Its eyes seemed similarly vacant. Though this one's skin was obviously made of felt, as were the eyes, felt oval whites with felt circular blacks, maybe only pinned on. She could see in the very back of the shark's open mouth, beyond two rows of felt triangle teeth, black mesh with the glint of eyes behind it.

"That's a person," she said. She had no doubt. "Not a monster or a demon or a god. Just... some guy."

Some mumbling could be heard just out of frame, and the shark whipped its head to the left, exposing its dorsal fin. A moment later, the blaring room tone and static returned, and then Tom Baker was grinning like a madman, perhaps having just beaten the bubble-wrap creature. Then, the tablet went dark.

The silence around the table was audible.

"Care to elaborate, Zack?" asked Osgood.

"Yes, well. So. This happened in January of 1983." He tapped the tablet, bringing up a still frame of the shark. "Someone hijacked the WTTW feed and broke in with... that ...during a broadcast of the *Doctor Who* episode *The Ark in Space*. A guy at the station caught it after a few seconds and forced the feedback out."

Remy rubbed her cheek. "Since you say 'someone,' I assume..."

"They've never been able to track down the source other than it was local. It literally overrode the broadcast transmissions, so it would have to be..." he shrugged, "...within the city limits."

"But there's no record of Sharkins Insurance," said Osgood.

"It isn't clear to me how this relates to our current situation, young man," said Eliza to Zack, then she leaned in, face full of genuine curiosity. "But I'm chuffed to hear more."

Osgood thought she'd never seen Zack beam so wide. "Um, well, no," he said. "But!"

"I hope it's a big but," said Audrey.

"Oh, do you like big buts?" Remy asked Audrey with a wink.

In Osgood's head, a soccer ref showed her a yellow card for jealousy. Fair.

"I cannot lie," said Audrey, winking back.

"But the internet is aware of it," Zack said, his smile remaining.

"I'm afraid you'll have to say more about that," said Eliza. "My knowledge of tomes may be extensive, but the internet remains a rather obtuse mystery."

"So, another one of my friends—"

"Criminals," said Osgood.

"They're not *all*—" Zack stopped himself and shook his head, now directing all his attention toward Eliza and Remy on the opposite side of the table. "He's really good at spreading things. He can simultaneously type a comment in one box and post it to thousands of sites and social networks." Perhaps sensing he was losing his audience, "He asked if anyone remembered Sharkins Insurance, the Shark Man mascot, or, *hopefully*, had a tape of the commercial."

"And you've found it?" Osgood asked, knowing the answer was likely no.

"No," said Zack. "But here's the *but*."

"The big but," said Osgood.

He ignored her. "Roughly thirteen hundred people remembered seeing it. Several could recite it from memory. A few remembered the phone number, though oddly, that number memory was very inconsistent."

"And no one had the video," Audrey sighed.

"No, but..."

"So many buts," said Remy.

"One *did* have something that, as far as I know, *no one* else has ever mentioned online." Zack swiped and tapped on his tablet. His brow furrowed as he looked, and his voice, though he tried to hide his frustration, betrayed him. "See, I'd heard about the PBS broadcast break-in. It's legendary that someone could do that and never be caught. But somehow, I had never heard of the second instance."

He tapped the tablet and turned it toward them. On the screen, *very* rough and blurry, was a commercial for West Coast Video, a store for which Osgood felt a dull ping of nostalgia. As the commercial ran, many image tracking issues — sliding from side to side, up and down, and popping color in and out — attacked it.

"What's doing this?" asked Remy.

"Oh," said Zack. "This is just because it's a copy of a copy of an old VHS tape transferred to digital via old cables and an old box. I don't think this bit is relevant. Just give it a second."

Sure enough, after a few moments of the West Coast Video commercial highlighting upcoming video releases, including the Rat Pack's *Oceans Eleven* in February, the blaring drone came, and the brown background appeared. Again, the shark stood up into the frame. It looked off to the right, then back. Then, very muffled by the costume, it spoke. *"I'll give you what you need. I'll give you what you need."*

"Turn it off," said Osgood, feeling a pulsing pain in her chest. She stared into the shark's eyes, and it stared back. She felt almost sure it could see her through the four decades since this had aired.

"I'll give you what you need. I'll give you—" But then the blare happened, and it was gone.

Back to the program already in progress. Canned laughter. A young woman came down a fancy set of stairs.

The cold ran through her entire body. "That's Dana Plato."

"Who's Dana Plato?" asked Zack.

Audrey squinted at the screen and asked, "Are you sure?"

The video cut off.

"Is there more?" asked Osgood. Pled, more like.

Zack cocked his head at her. "No, why?"

"Did your guy—"

"He's not *my* guy."

"—this *person* know when this aired?" Osgood felt a certainty that she already knew what seeing more of the video would've told her, what this instance of the shark had interrupted, but she needed to hold it back, to not taint what others thought and said with her until it wasn't a theory but a fact.

"She says the tape was prime-time from late February of 1983. Less than a month after the PBS break-in."

Osgood yanked her phone off the table and thumbed a messy request into the search bar: **Diffrnt Stokes ring schedule 1983.** Miraculously, the search engine understood her and gave her a list of episodes. She didn't have to scroll far to see February and confirm her hunch. She dropped her phone.

"What is it?" asked Eliza, showing the most concern she perhaps could through a dense layer of confusion.

Audrey put her hand on Osgood's. Osgood felt tears in her eyes, and a tightness in her chest had joined her other symptoms, each breath like she was taking in less. "I need some air." She pushed back from the table, banging her knee on its metal leg, then turned away from the group, all watching with concern, as she shoved open the back door, letting the hot daylight in. She stopped, staring out at the apartments across the alley from them, listening to the sounds of Chicago. A car alarm. A jackhammer working a few streets down. A dog bark. Someone driving by with their windows down blaring ranchera music. After a moment, she felt her pulse go back down. She turned back, and it was as if she were a TV show being watched by four other people with bated breath.

"Dana Plato was the older sister on *Diff'rent Strokes*," she said, then took a deep, soothing breath. "And if that break-in happened in late February of 1983, that episode there..." She pointed in the vague direction of Zack's tablet but wouldn't look directly at it despite the image being blank. "I'd bet anything that was part two of the very special episode: *The Bicycle Man*."

THIRTY-TWO

"**A**UDREY THINKS YOU SHOULD let me calm you down," said Remy as she came up next to Osgood on the small wooden porch that jutted out of their apartment. "Well, she said I should suck whatever it is that I suck. Then she blushed. Now she can't look me in the eye."

Osgood laughed. "Not because she doesn't want to face me?"

"What would give you that idea?" Remy put her hand on Osgood's.

"I told you not to feed on me," said Osgood, pulling her hand back.

"I *can* touch you without feeding, you know," said Remy.

"But will you?" asked Osgood, cocking her head toward Ramona Yeagher and squinting from the brightness. She regretted her tone, especially as she could see the momentary falter in Remy's eyes. "Standoffish is my love language."

Remy laughed. "I think your love language might actually be cunt."

Osgood cackled despite herself, then wiped tears from her eyes. "Alright, you dumb bitch, what're you doing out here? And it's not because Audrey thinks I should let you calm me down."

"Actually, it is, partly."

"And the rest?"

"I felt awful at the cemetery, that I pushed you away," Remy put both hands on the wooden rail and looked at alley beyond. "I've only occasionally felt something as strong as Eocan— Whatever y'all call it."

"Yoaganemotsa," said Osgood without hesitation.

"That," said Remy. "And I could've looked closer. Maybe could've seen what it actually is."

"But I'd have had to let you feed," said Osgood.

"What is it about me taking your pain that makes you so afraid?"

"Because it's mine!" Osgood beat her fist on her chest, a move she regretted instantly as she felt it all throughout her torso. She looked back at the door into the kitchen. "Because, as much as there is happening around me, as much as there is happening *to* me, my pain, my regret, my self-loathing is a choice."

"Then why don't you let it go?" asked Remy. "Why do you torture yourself with it?"

"Because it's *me*," she said, this time without force, quiet. A plea.

"It's not you, Os," said Remy. "And you are not it."

"How do you know that?"

"You'd be amazed what someone like me can learn when they watch a person come." Remy's smirk and wink made Osgood smile slyly, remembering the day on the side street when Remy had told her to masturbate and, well, hadn't had to ask twice.

"Yeah?" asked Osgood.

"I won't push you to release anything," said Remy. "And you're right; we all are products of our lives. Who knows what could happen if some pieces were removed."

"But you still want to take my pain."

"I want to help you, Os," said Remy.

"Sounds like we're both not getting what we want," said Osgood.

"Oh, really?"

"You know what I want," said Osgood, and to drive home the point, she ran a finger along Remy's shoulder.

"Tell you what," said Remy. "Let's stop this apocalypse, and then I'll fuck you."

Another snort-laugh from Osgood.

"I'm serious," said Remy. "And your aunt is, too."

Osgood blanched. "Don't bring up Eliza when talking about fucking!"

"You don't think she got busy in her day?"

"I think she gets busy right now," said Osgood. "I'm pretty sure she's fucking Albrecht."

"Well, there you go," said Remy. "But what I meant is Eliza and I think we might be able to get to the center of this Bicycle Man thing. Track it to its source."

"Oh?" Osgood's tone oozed skepticism.

"And I promise to only take the bare minimum of your pain," said Remy. She took Osgood's hand.

"It's not that I don't want to be free of it," said Osgood.

"I know," said Remy.

"I just—"

"I know," said Remy. "Shall we?"

"Before we do," said Osgood. "'Someone like you.'"

Remy turned back to her, repeating, "Someone like me."

"You said I'd be amazed what *someone like you* can learn..." Osgood narrowed her eyes, wanting to watch Remy's expression. The timing might be wrong, trying to get to the bottom of this, but on the other hand, maybe it was perfect. "And you said you've been called a being of light."

"Yes," said Remy, hesitant.

"And Eliza said that you're a daughter of the sun. And Cora Ballard said you shine. And that you're not a person."

A nervous laugh from Remy, a deflecting laugh. "Man, that total recall is something else, isn't it?"

"It is indeed, but I can't remember what I don't know." Osgood leaned back against the porch railing, looked at Remy, and waited. "Just as an aside, you look really fucking hot in my clothes. Is that narcissistic?"

"Probably just means you want to fuck yourself," said Remy.

Osgood nodded. "Oh, I definitely want to fuck myself."

Dr. Ramona Yeagher stood silently for a while, then seemed to have a few false starts. "Let me tell you a story."

"Why not," said Osgood.

As Remy told her tale, she picked at her cuticle and looked away, not meeting Osgood's eye. "There was a forgotten tribe in Africa. Long before it was Africa. The tribe had a name, but in their language, it was just 'the people.' And two girls were born just as a solar eclipse happened. And in those days, they had no idea why the sun just *went out* in the middle of the afternoon."

"That would be traumatic," said Osgood.

"Indeed," agreed Remy. "And why things like eclipses were seen as horrible omens and portents. But these two girls came out of their mother's womb entwined during this eclipse. Embracing each other. The mother wept as the tribe had been experiencing a vast famine and a horrendous drought. Most newborns died within minutes or hours. And here she was, not with one baby she could barely care for but two! But these girls hung on, literally and figuratively. They remained together throughout every moment. Holding hands as they slept. They rarely cried, but when they did, they *both* did."

Osgood wasn't sure how to take this. But Remy had never spoken about her history, and this might be the most she'd ever get, whatever it meant.

"It's not that the tribe was savage, because they weren't. They appreciated art and oral tradition. They resolved conflicts peacefully."

"Okay," said Osgood. "Did you get the sense I saw things differently?"

"No," said Remy. "But you're about to. The elders, after consulting a shaman, became convinced that these girls were the key to the survival of the tribe. The births, coming as they had during the eclipse, suggested their fates."

"Is a wicker man coming?" asked Osgood with a laugh. When Remy looked up, her eyes were red and her cheeks wet. "I'm sorry." She moved to go to Remy, to hug her, to calm her, to comfort, to—

But Remy stopped her with a palm.

"They brought the girls, still just babies, only weeks old, out to the highest peak in their area, a treacherous climb that they only made when the African wilds, which in those days were even more brutal, got too close to their fires." Remy wiped her nose with the back of her hand. "They viv—" Here she broke and held up a finger to beg for a moment. Osgood nodded. "They vivisected the girls, removing both of their hearts."

"Oh jeez," said Osgood.

"Then the shaman reached into the sky and plucked out the moon—"

"What?"

"—which he placed into the dark-haired one's chest. After holding together the flesh on either side and quietly saying the words his ancestors had taught him, the words of the gods, the girl's body was whole again, and she began to cry.

"Then the shaman pulled down the sun and placed it into the chest of the light-haired child, repeating the words and making the signs again.

"For weeks, there was darkness, and the people felt alone and forsaken. They prayed to their gods that they be spared, saved, treated with mercy. And on the fifteenth day, the girls awoke, and the light returned. The sun rose at dawn and the moon at dusk.

"From that day forward, the daughter of the moon's influence on the tides ensured there was never another drought. The daughter of the sun's influence on growth and warmth ensured there was never another famine. And those daughters saw to it that this tribe wasn't one of the thousands of proto-civilizations that never grew to viability, instead being among the peoples who'd cross land bridges, brave ice ages, and settle new worlds."

After she finished speaking, Remy gave a full-body sigh and covered her face with her hand. Her body shook with sobs. Osgood wrapped her arms around her. Why had this woman she trusted told her a myth? Surely, she couldn't think that she was descended from such an early tribe, at least in any more concrete a way than all of humankind was.

Remy wriggled a bit, uncomfortable in the affection, and smiled, meeting Osgood's eye only for a second. "It's just a story," she said.

"Remy," said Osgood. "Are you—"

The therapist put her finger over Osgood's lips and repeated, "It's just a story."

After a while where neither spoke, the two women went inside. There was work to do, after all.

Thirty-Three

A SINGLE CANDLE LIT the dark room, reminding Osgood of her gothy high-school days when she'd painted her walls black (much to Cynthia's chagrin, as it didn't match her New England Yachting Community aesthetic). Today, though, in her dark bedroom, privacy curtains drawn, one candle lit, she felt anything but safe. The others sat in a circle around her, Audrey to her right, then Zack, Eliza across from her, Albrecht very near to her aunt, then Remy. Remy reached out her hand, and Osgood took it. Audrey did the same.

"This is rather new to me," admitted Eliza. Osgood noted one of Albrecht's papery hands squeeze her aunt's shoulder.

"Me too," said Remy.

"Well, no time like the present to go on a fishing expedition in my head without guardrails," Osgood said with a chuckle. She felt Audrey squeeze her hand. Zack brought up his phone to document whatever was about to happen. "So, are you going to speak Latin? Do an incantation?"

"Modern witchcraft doesn't need a lot of that old bullshit," said Eliza.

"Instead," said Albrecht. "I'll tell you that you're getting very sleepy."

"I'm not, actually," said Osgood.

Audrey swatted her shoulder.

"Look at the candle flame," said her former professor, a distinct note of annoyance in his voice that she remembered often from classes.

Osgood did. She wanted this to work, too. *Then stop being combative,* suggested her mother in her head. For the first time in a long time, she felt her mother, or at least the simulacrum she carried around with her, was right. She closed her eyes, took a deep breath, and let it out through her nose. When she opened her eyes again, she focused only on the candle flame, sending it into sharp focus and everyone else into a blur. The flame flickered and danced. She watched as the wick inside grew redder and redder before giving way to the white-hot center. She yawned because, unbelievably, she *was* getting sleepy.

"Let it take you down. Let it draw you all the way down," said Albrecht. "Your conscious mind sits atop your unconscious, which is always churning, connecting neurons, bridging thoughts and concepts. Allow the conscious mind to open and allow Eliza entrance to the dark thoughts below."

Osgood felt wavy as she breathed, listing a bit to the right, then left. She must've gone too far to the left because Remy's hands gently squeezed her shoulder and propped her back upright.

"Remember," said Eliza. "Inside your subconscious mind, you are in charge of your dreamscape. You've built kingdoms. You have a rare talent so impressive that beings from other worlds have sought it out. If your subconscious doesn't want to let you see those dream moments, you can force it to, because you, Osgood, are in charge."

"I could count myself the queen of infinite space, were it not that I have bad dreams." Osgood felt the words leaving her lips and knew she'd paraphrased something, but even the encyclopedia in her head came up empty. She laughed, realizing her eyes were closed.

She opens them.

The darkness still surrounds her, but there's no longer any candle. Her hand isn't held, her shoulder isn't supported, and there's a chill in the air that isn't terribly cold but still crawls down her spine and sends her a-shiver. She stands and brushes fine dust off her knees. "Huh."

At a distance that she can't quite comprehend, she sees the vaguest impression of light and moves toward it. "I am the master of my fate," she says, not entirely understanding where that one came from either. She knows it's *Invictus* but doesn't know why she said it. "I am the captain of my soul."

"You are, my dear Prudence," comes a voice from the steadily brightening area before her.

Osgood rounds— could it even be called a corner? —in the dark, and finds a dimly-lit antechamber beyond, a silhouette on the threshold. "The dweller," she suggests.

"Lil," the woman corrects.

Osgood rushes forward and hugs her great-grandmother, her mind briefly rebelling against the title, as the woman in her arms is maybe nineteen or twenty, with long, flowing blonde curls. "You came! You came to help."

"I have come, yes," says Lil. "What good I can do here is... unknown." Lil waves her hand toward the antechamber. "There's more light this way."

Osgood the younger follows Osgood the elder through the chamber and another tunnel lined with stalactites and stalagmites. "We're in a cave."

"We are in your mind," Lil reminds her.

"Right," says Osgood. "Huh." She stops and looks over at a rock the size of an orange. "Cast light," she says to the rock, which erupts in a brilliant white light, illuminating the cave tunnel.

"That's good magick."

"I may only be a level three bard, but I have a plus three for charisma."

Lil smiles at her. "I haven't the faintest idea what that means."

"I only barely understand it myself," says Osgood. She takes the lead from Lil, holding her illuminated rock ahead as she moves into a large chamber bedecked in ornate carvings on the walls. "This is all from me?"

"I wish I could tell you more about how this works, but as Eliza explains it, this is from your mind."

Osgood moves toward the carvings, feeling like she's seen similar things. Perhaps in movies. A cosmic scene here with a flaming eye. Sauron's eye in *Fellowship of the Ring*? There's her quasar. Across the ceiling of the chamber is an enormous set of clockwork gears. "He wants to break the clock. Break the universe."

"They always want that," says Lil with a scowl. "It's not enough to be powerful, in charge; they must dismantle the status quo."

"We call that small dick energy." Osgood realizes Lil may not know and adds, "Penis."

"I am not a naive fool nor a prudish waif." Lil covers her mouth as she snickers. "Which way?"

Osgood looks up and sees various tunnels leading out of the cave. She picks one at random, but does she really? Is it random if she's controlling it, even just a little? As they move downward through the next tunnel, a tunnel that grows smaller and smaller, Osgood begins to worry she's made the wrong choice. "I don't know about this," she tells Lil behind her.

"Trust your feelings," Lil tells her.

"Well, my feelings tell me we're going to be crawling in a few minutes, and we should get the hell out of here before this turns into the Nutty Putty cave."

"You are a mystery to me," says Lil. "I must admit I find you fascinating."

Osgood looks back at her great-grandmother. "How old are you?"

"In here?"

"However you got here, on the outside, how old are you?"

"I'm twenty," says Lil. "And my transport is opium."

"Of course," says Osgood. "I'm happy to fascinate."

"You say you want to leave, but keep moving forward," Lil points out.

"I guess I'm trusting my feelings." Osgood begins to crawl. She can hear Lil doing the same behind her. The cave walls grow closer until she's shimmying forward, one arm outstretched to keep picking up and then chucking the illuminated rock further ahead. For a moment, she sticks in place. Panic rises. "Oh fuck. Oh god." She feels herself beginning to hyperventilate.

Then she feels Lil put a hand on her ankle, perhaps all her great-grandmother can reach. "It is not real; it is only phantasmagoria."

"It feels real!" Osgood's panic careens into overdrive; she can't breathe, and she can't move further.

"Eliza," says Lil. "We could use an assist."

Warm hands reach Osgood's face, and through the hazy light in front of her, she sees a shimmering image of Remy. "Will you let me take this?" the therapist asks, her voice sounding as though she's far away, in another room somewhere. Osgood nods, and Remy smiles, slowly beginning to vanish again and taking the panic with her.

"You have surrounded yourself with goodness," says Lil.

Osgood nods, bringing her breathing back in line. "I never thought that would be the case."

"You are good, Prudence," says Lil, taking the time to calmly emphasize each word.

"Agree to disagree," says Osgood, chucking the rock one more time and seeing that, just in front of her, is the mouth of the tunnel leading somewhere else. "Finally!" she exclaims, dragging herself forward across the rock-strewn floor, cutting jagged scrapes into her arms and legs. She stands up as soon as she's able and reaches back in to help Lil out. Lil looks horrified, and Osgood turns to see what she sees.

Before them, illuminated by what seems to be moonlight coming from an open crag above, is a bastardization of the scene on Golgotha, the scene she'd once colored so excessively gory. Except unlike that version with a very Caucasian Jesus and two thieves, this crucifixion scene is personal. In the center, nailed upside down to the cross, is Sam Goddard.

(*Upside down is how St. Peter was martyred*, offers the encyclopedia in her head.)

She can't tell if he's alive or dead, but his torso is split from neck to navel, and his intestines have slithered their way out to hang down before him. She puts her hand to her mouth to catch a gasping sob.

"Remember, it is only a thought," says Lil.

"I know it is," cries Osgood. "Because it's what I think about!" As she wipes tears from her eyes beneath her glasses, she remembers who the gory messes are in the thieves' places beside Goddard's abomination. "Dismas and Gesmas," she says to herself, then adding, at her memory's insistence, "though that's a gnostic thought."

"I would have thought Christian dogma would have run its course by the 21st century," says Lil.

"These are just scraps of a time when I believed in God."

"And now you must believe in gods." Lil touches Osgood's arm.

But the thieves aren't the penitent Dismas and the insolent Gesmas. They're not even entire people, are they? No, they mirror each other, the left hand and left foot nailed to the right cross and the right hand and right foot on the left. The body is bisected neatly in half. Not how it had happened, of course, but why split hairs. Nora plays both of the thieves in this tableau. Thankfully, both Nora and Goddard appear to be expired; she's not sure she could take hearing from them without going insane. She notices parchment nailed upside down above (below) Goddard's head. *"Rex stultorum."*

"It means 'King of the Fools,'" Lil tells her.

"How can it?" asks Osgood. "I don't know Latin."

"With your encyclopedic recall, perhaps you—"

"No!" Osgood is firm, shaking her head. She brushes Goddard's curls away from his eyes and immediately regrets it as his open eyes stare at her. "No, I don't know it. I didn't create this 'kingdom.' At least not by myself. I had a co-author."

THIRTY-FOUR

A FTER TWO MORE TUNNELS wriggled through, Osgood finds a door no higher than her knee. "Now someone's just fucking trolling me."

Lil's eyes narrow, but she doesn't ask what Osgood means. Perhaps context and the irritation in her voice say all Lil needs to know.

Osgood crouches down and puts her ear to the door. Strangely, she hears music on the other side, the sound of steel drums, maybe calypso? She crouches even further and presses her eye to the oversized keyhole in the door. Of all the things Osgood might expect to see on the other side of a Wonderland-style door, night sky, the ocean, and palm trees blowing in the breeze wouldn't come anywhere near her *number one answer, still on the board.* She tries the knob and is surprised to find it unlocked. She opens the porthole to someplace very much

(and on The Isle)

other. A night, but a false night. Wind and water, but both feel artificial. It's the beach of her momentary sidestep just before she got tased. The beach with a full-on Omnimax dome screen.

"How are we supposed to get through this?" asks Osgood. When her great-grandmother says nothing, Osgood turns to look at her, standing behind with a smile on her face. "You know, your habit of making me figure stuff out for myself isn't as endearing as you think it is."

Lil shrugs.

Osgood looks at the miniature door, which might be able to pass a basketball, max. She absently reaches into her pocket and finds her tincture. She pulls out the glass bottle, usually filled (or as full as she could get it) with the bootleg Oxycodone she needs to simply exist in the world, labeled with a silver Sharpie O. This one is full and still labeled in silver Sharpie, but it says Drink Me. She laughs, staring at it. "I thought that might be the solution."

"You thought so, and thus you made it the solution."

"Alright," grumbles Osgood. She uncaps the bottle and brings it up to her lips before stopping. "Do you need it too?"

"I'll be fine," says Lil, waving the question away.

"*L'chaim*," says Osgood.

"Up yours," says Lil with a wink.

Osgood knocks back the entire bottle and feels her body contort as if every bone is breaking. She hears ripping and realizes it's her skin tearing apart and coming back together tighter. Lil grows enormous behind her, and the door before her slowly becomes more and more manageable. When the horrific pain stops, Osgood feels a crushing weight above her, like that way-too-heavy weighted blanket she bought while high as a kite with Covid. Sniffing it, she smells her own armpit. She's inside her sleeve.

"It's wildly unfair that my pits should stink even in my head!" she calls through the cotton fabric that feels like a lead apron.

"I wondered if your clothes would also grow small." The fabric lifts and Osgood sees her 20-year-old great-grandmother towering over her.

Osgood looks down, and, of course, she's now naked. "Mother-fucker." After a moment, she shrugs. She spent decades naked at the crossroads in her mind; why not here, too? "You're good?" she shouts up to Lil.

Lil nods and shoos her through the doorway.

Knowing this place is fake, Osgood is quite impressed by the extent of it. She stands on a path outside a white stucco building in what seems to be a resort. People in various levels of dress and swimwear meander. "Looks like I'll fit right in." She reaches for her pocket, hoping to find the corresponding Eat Me cake, but quickly realizes that unless she wants to go digging in "nature's pocket," she'll have to find a plan B.

"Well, in the book, the Eat Me cake was on a table, wasn't it?" Her mind springs to life, this time visualizing a library, scanning down the books until she reaches *Alice's Adventures in Wonderland* (823.8 on the Dewey Decimal System), then flipping through the pages in the book until she finds this passage: "Soon her eye fell upon a little glass box lying underneath the table. She opened it and found in it a tiny cake, on which the words 'EAT ME' were beautifully marked in currants."

Osgood turns quickly and, sure enough, beside the door sits a glass box. In that glass box is a cake with the words Eat Me on it. "I bet Alice's cake didn't look like Audrey's vulva, though..." She chortles and pops the cake in her mouth. Again, the pain is excruciating and accompanied by more ripping, and a stretching sound like a balloon being squeezed, but before long, she is back to full size. Still naked, of course.

"I read that book, you know," says Lil, again standing behind her. "I found it so sad. Alice needed to go through her ordeal just to realize she had love in her life."

"Let's not make this a very special episode," says Osgood, turning her head to watch as a nude couple walk past. "Apparently, this place is clothing optional." She waves her hand in front of the face of a woman in a bikini, but the woman walks right by. "And metaphorical."

"Should we get your clothes?" asks Lil.

"Does it bother you?" asks Osgood.

"Why should it bother me?" Lil smirks, then pulls the tie on her peasant-style linen dress and drops it to the ground. Osgood does not stare but notes her great-grandmother's vast curly carpet, and a bosom not unlike her own, just twenty-five years younger.

"Alright, " Osgood says with a nervous chuckle. She looks down the path, which branches off in two directions. "Where should we go? What should I be looking for?"

"That I do not know," says Lil.

"Aren't you the guide?" asks Osgood.

Lil snickers. "I'm the support. Eliza called me your backup." She moved to Osgood and put her hands on her cheeks, looking deep into her eyes. "This world is yours."

Unexpectedly moved, Osgood wipes away a tear and then points toward the steel drum music. "That way." She walks, and Lil follows. At the end of the path, Osgood discovers an expansive courtyard with a fountain in the center and, to the right, a Tiki bar built of bamboo and thatch.

"Why don't we—" Her words die in her throat when she sees, where a bartender ought to be standing, a stalagmite, the color of bruises and dead blood. "But they don't," she mumbles. She swings her head back to Lil, who regards her with wide eyes. "That's it! That's why we're here!"

"The termite mound?" asks Lil.

Osgood leaps over the bar, her bare ass cheeks making a screeching sound as she slides across, then drops down into the well behind the bar. The stalagmite is massive, reaching from the floor almost to the peak of the vaulted thatch roof over the bar. She puts a hand on it. "It's warm!"

"Prudence," says Lil, caution in the word.

Osgood runs her hand down the side and finds the edge of a crack. She traces it, seeing it widen and widen until the gap spans nearly an inch. "I think I can reach inside it."

"No!" Lil rushes up behind her, and Osgood momentarily almost wishes she'd gotten a chance to see the other Osgood woman leap over the bar. "The energy coming off of this is horrid."

"Would make sense if the memories I've wiped away are awful, right?"

Lil quiets, stepping back. "I think we should go about this another way." She looks to the sky. "Eliza, darling, we need—"

"No!" exclaims Osgood. "You said this is all in my head: my kingdom, my place."

"I did, however—"

"And this thing, whatever it is, because it's not a fucking stalagmite, *might* be able to fill in some gaps for me."

"I think there is more than just information in there, Prudence." Lil moves back toward it, reaching both her arms out. "We must not be reckless."

A thunderous crack interrupts their deliberations, and the very tip of the stalagmite, a mound about a foot high, snaps off and tumbles down. Osgood looks from the stalagmite to Lil and back. "Okay, I feel that, too." She looks into the courtyard to see if anyone heard it. The resort seems empty. The music and the wind have stopped, and the lighting has snapped down to only this bar, only this point.

Osgood looks up at the vaulted roof of the bar. "Eliza? I think I made a mistake."

Another crack.

"She has not responded," says Lil.

"Okay," says Osgood. "Well, what should we do? Can I— Well, it's my world; I could glue it or something." Her eyes dart to the barback cooler. "Because, uh, there's *definitely* glue in there." She slides the aluminum lid up, and not only isn't there glue, but the bottles and cans within aren't real. Instead, only a picture affixed to cardboard shows the contents. "Yeah, that won't work."

The cracks begin to appear quicker and quicker, spidering across the stalagmite.

"Whatever's inside," says Osgood. "I think we're about to see it."

She has no sooner finished saying it when the stalagmite explodes outward in a shower of dust and chunks of wet rock. Osgood manages to keep most of the damage off her face with her arms, but her breasts, stomach, and legs take several pointy rocks, drawing small streams of blood.

When she uncrosses her arms, there stands a man in white linens, his shirt unbuttoned to his navel, sporting a square jaw and flowing blonde hair. He breathes like a bull, and in a guttural voice, he utters her name, "Pru-dence..." savoring its syllables like a prime cut of meat.

Osgood girds herself, standing tough despite her nudity. "And who the fuck are you?"

He laughs a single "Hah!" flicking his head up and back down; his irises are made of fire when he looks into her eyes again.

"Yoko," Osgood says. "Yoaganemotsa."

"Going all the way back to the Sanskrit, are we? I can give you some older ones if you'd like, but you'd have no concept of the tribes that voiced them. Nemot is one," he says, then offering a click of his tongue and a glottal stop, "is another. Some can't even be spoken with modern tongues. Isn't that fun?"

"You're in a good mood," says Osgood, "Didn't expect that."

"Well," says Yoko. "You pathetic foolish girl, you let me back out." He vaults the bar himself, a graceful leap without touching it, and lands with a gymnast's flair. "And you are such a fucking cunt of a pill, I don't wanna deal with you anymore. I'll find someone else who can do what you do."

"No one else can do what she does," says Lil.

He laughs. "Who's your friend?"

"You will halt, foul shade, and speak thy purpose." Her voice is powerful, and Osgood realizes it's because Eliza's voice is layered atop it, speaking in unison.

"Are you fucking kidding?" asks Yoko, slapping his thigh.

Osgood's momentary concern at his furious yet jovial tone shifts; that question held confusion. "He doesn't understand what you are," Osgood tells Lil. "What we are."

The half-smile on Yoko's face falters. He looks between the women, considering. "Alright, you just became interesting again," says Yoko. "Three of you? Connected through..." He sniffs the wind. "Genetic line powers. Oh, truly fabulous!" Again, the smallest of catches in his tone.

"Speak they purpose," says Liliza. "We will not ask again."

"I'm a fucking *god!*" Yoko's fury is palpable and seems to raise the temperature in the entire courtyard. "What is it you think you can do to me?"

Lil is silent for a long time and walks closer to him.

"Wait, Lil," says Osgood, holding out her hand.

Lil pays her no mind and walks until she stands directly before him. He's nearly a foot taller than her and clothed, but at this moment, he looks like the frightened weakling. "You're not a god," she whispers.

An orange sphere of fire erupts from Yoko, knocking Lil back and Osgood next. Osgood lands on her back, and the pain is excruciating. Her body hurts as it did after she was first denied opioids for her pain. When she opens her eyes again, the resort is gone, The Isle is gone. Everything is black, and now it's only her, Lil, and the monstrosity who has doubled in size yet still looks like a man.

Fuck me, thinks Osgood.

Thirty-Five

A s Osgood sits forward, she sees Lil standing before him again, defiant as ever, hands clenched in fists, staring up at his hulking body. "You are *not* a god," she repeats, with Eliza's voice upon hers once more. "You say you are a god to trick us, to get us to do something we would not otherwise do." As she speaks, Osgood can pick out other voices within. She hears Albrecht, Zack, Audrey, and Remy. They speak in unison. "But you are not a god. Daemon, reveal thyself."

"I'm not a demon," scoffs Yoko.

Lil screams in a chorus of voices, "Reveal thyself!"

This command has wounded Yoko, who staggers.

"Re—" Osgood coughs. "Reveal thyself." She tries her best to move from sitting to standing.

Another voice comes, not from Lil or Yoko, but from the darkness around them. *"Heeeeeeeeee eeeeeeeees assssspecccccct,"* it hisses.

"Aspect? Aspect of what?" demands Osgood. She turns around, unsure where she should be directing that demand.

The hissing voice says something incomprehensible that causes Osgood's head to ache.

"What the fuck was that?"

"He is an aspect of Yoaganemotsa," says Lil, her voice back to herself alone. She lowers her hands, and Yoko falls to his knees before her. He's returned to human size and breathes heavily. "Yes?" she asks him.

He nods between gasps.

"What does that mean?" asks Osgood.

"It's only theory," says Eliza, emerging from the darkness.

"How'd you get here?" asks Osgood, jumping, then attempting to cover her tits.

"Oh please," says Eliza, waving at Osgood's display of modesty. "If he's an aspect of the god, he's a piece of the god. A representative. An avatar."

"A harbinger," gasps Yoko in between heaving breaths.

Osgood shudders at the word that she herself had been called years ago when she had at least one monster inside her. "So, can we kill him?"

Yoko laughs. "Stupid, naive girl."

"No," says Eliza. "We can't even *really* hurt him."

"Don't tell *him* that!" exclaims Osgood.

"He knows," says Yoko, standing and brushing off his linen pants. "You're the buzzing of flies. No more."

"Then why are you still here?" demands Osgood. "In my head."

Yoko says nothing.

"You need me," suggests Osgood.

Yoko says nothing.

"What did you do to me?" asks Osgood.

Yoko says nothing.

"Hurt him anyway," demands Osgood.

Eliza and Lil look at each other, then hold out their hands toward him. His face grows redder and redder. He seems to choke. He grasps at his temples. His eyeballs pop, each erupting in a little ball of fire.

His head drops again, and his breathing is heavy. Osgood walks slowly toward him.

"Don't get too close," says Lil.

But Osgood does anyway, just as Yoko looks up. His face is still red, but his eyes are whole again, and the irises blaze. He grins. "See," he says. "You can't hurt me."

"My head, right?" asks Osgood.

He cocks his head at her. "Yes."

Osgood gives him her best banshee screech as she shoves her hand through his forehead and into a mass of gunk that makes her think nauseously of carving a jack-o-lantern. His wide eyes roll up, and Osgood can see, in milliseconds, all he's been keeping from her. She can see her life on The Isle. Weeks. Months maybe. Trapped here on this island resort, in her dreams. She sees the other people he was, as well. Rebecca and Simon, who'd fucked her, others she'd interacted and flirted with. Bartender Virgil.

"Virgil was your main avatar, wasn't he?" she asks, but Yoko doesn't answer. His jaw hangs slack, and drool oozes out. She remembers the text on each of the signs, despite having only seen them on Zack's tablet. She remembers him forcing her through her own timeline. Bouncing, careening from age to age, each moment terrified of— "You're the Bicycle Man," she says, yanking her hand back out.

He staggers backward, his eyes unfocused but both pointing at the yawning slit in his forehead with sparkling darkness within. "Yeshlth," he says.

Osgood turns to Lil and Eliza. "I remember it! All of it. He wants to wear me like a costume! He wants to—" Almost unbearable pain in her lower back, a tearing sound, a hacking sound, then Osgood's legs fall out from under her. She falls, unable to catch herself.

Yoko stands above her, the wound on his forehead gone, holding a serrated knife covered in, presumably, her blood. "I ought to lobotomize you right here. Eat every last moment of your life."

"We won't let you," say Eliza and Lil in unison.

"Yeah," says Yoko, throwing them a growling scowl. Then he turns back to Osgood and crouches low. "Listen. You're not unique, you're not special, and you are most certainly not exceptional. And I have other fucking people to see." He spits a horrid-smelling wad right onto Osgood's cheek, then raises his left hand, and with a single 360 spin, he grows smaller until he vanishes.

Osgood awoke.

Having immediately explained to her friends what she could remember of Yoko and The Isle, Osgood felt powerfully exhausted. Her eyelids hurt, drooping, and she slurred her words.

"I can help," offered Eliza. "Tell them what I know."

Osgood waved her on, nodding until she got dizzy. "Why'm I so tired?"

"You haven't slept in days, Os," said Audrey.

"Did he drug me?"

"No," said Eliza.

"Am I paralyzed?" asked Osgood, reaching around to feel her lower back, then laughing as she saw her hand moving. "Guess he couldn't do that."

"Why don't you lie down," suggested Zack, pulling his laptop and a microphone off her bed. He reached his hand out to her, and she swatted it away.

"I'm not an invalid."

"Yes, Os," said Zack. "I'm very aware of that."

Her thighs crashed into the side of her mattress, and she face-planted into her bunched jersey-knit sheet. She was vaguely aware of

Zack's hands on her ankles, sliding her all the way onto the mattress. "Thanszk," she said.

"Thanks, Zack," he repeated. "At least, I assume."

"Essence...shill."

Osgood's last conscious moment saw Zack herding their guests out of her bedroom and closing the door, but before it completely closed, he reached in and flipped the switch.

Turn on the dark.

THIRTY-SIX

"WHAT TIME IS IT?" asked Osgood, pressing the back of her wrist into her eye sockets one after the other.

"Four," said Audrey. She moved over and sat next to Osgood on the bed.

"Afternoon or in the morning?" asked Osgood.

"In the evening," said Audrey with a smile. "How do you feel?"

Osgood sized Audrey up and furrowed her brow. "Weren't you wearing jeans?" she asked, noting Audrey's sundress. "When'd you change?"

"I was wearing jeans three days ago, Os."

"Three days," Osgood repeated derisively. She spat a raspberry.

"I don't know how to respond to that."

Osgood grabbed Audrey's hand in hers, making her best out-of-it attempt at wooing. "Can't you see what I'm trying to tell you? I love you!"

"I love you, too, Os," said Audrey, but her tone was dismissive. She pulled Osgood to a sitting position.

"Why are you making me get up?" asked Osgood, petulance in her voice.

"Because in three and a half hours, you're receiving the Key to the City."

That couldn't be right. "It's Friday?"

"No, it's Saturday, Os."

Osgood smacked her lips, which felt ungodly dry. She put her hand to her stomach and could instantly feel it rumble. She grabbed the sheet and lifted it up, suddenly worried. "Did I piss the bed?"

"No," said Audrey, "You managed to stagger to the bathroom — still asleep, mind you. Sleepwalking Osgood uses a *lot* of toilet paper. I had to plunge the toilet several times."

"I'm sorry," said Osgood

"The more surprising thing was you walking into my bedroom while I was in the middle of coming with my Magic Wand."

"Aww," said Osgood with a smirk. "I missed that?"

"You watched for like thirty seconds, then turned around and left. I heard you snoring before I fully realized what had happened."

"Let's get married."

"As much as your mother would *love* that," said Audrey, "I think we should get ready for this event tonight."

Suddenly, lucidity descended on Osgood, and she grabbed Audrey's arm. "Yoko!"

"Has been quiet this whole time. Your aunt's got half the seers in Chicago attempting to locate him. Though, they're not sure what they're looking for at this point. We don't even know if he has a body."

Osgood looked down at her hands. "I let him out."

"You can't take that on."

"But I did, I was too curious to leave it—"

"Eliza said it was clear he was near breaking out anyway and that putting him in there in the first place postponed whatever he was trying to do for quite a long time." Audrey reached down and clasped Osgood's hand. "You are responsible for nothing." She smirked. "Well, nothing *here*, anyway."

"Bitch," said Osgood.

"Cunt," said Audrey.

They stared at each other for a moment, and Osgood thought she felt a spark jump between them, the first in a long time, the first since her lack of relationship self-control that led to their lack of relationship. She was about to say something to that effect when Audrey broke the spell.

"What color do you feel like?"

"For?" asked Osgood.

"Your hair, for tonight," Audrey smiled. "Gonna be on TV, figured you'd want to do an Osgood queer-do instead of..." Audrey waved her palm in circles at Osgood's head to indicate clearly: "this whole thing you've got going on."

"What are my options?"

"I've got Manic Panic's whole lineup," she said, holding up a drugstore bag.

First, they moved to the back porch, where Audrey went at the left side of Osgood's hair with clippers. As the curls fell, more salt than pepper, Osgood felt her heart swell; the last time Audrey had done this for her had been in the hospital when she'd shaved all of it. So they could remove a tumor with teeth and a face.

"Looks good," said Audrey after viewing her work from the front, tipping Osgood's head this way and that courtesy a single finger below her chin. "Have you picked a color?"

"What do you like?" asked Osgood.

"I loved when it was purple," said Audrey. "And I didn't get to enjoy that for long."

"Well," said Osgood. "Because you hated me."

"Sure," agreed Audrey. "But then you vanished into another dimension, so..."

Audrey walked into their tiny bathroom with her, situating Osgood in front of the mirror.

There stood Prudence Osgood in all her splendor. Crow's feet dug into the corners of her eyes, frown lines instead of laugh. "God, I look old," she said.

"The gray hair isn't helping with that," said Audrey. "But we *are* getting old, Os."

"You saying that doesn't help either," said Osgood.

Audrey pulled the shower curtain aside and reached down to turn on the water. It began to run into the claw-footed iron bathtub.

"Are you gonna wash my bits too?" asked Osgood.

"No," said Audrey with a sigh meant to sound irritated but a smile that suggested otherwise. "You're going to rinse your hair to get rid of the damned shavings, and then we can dye it. Besides, we have to have *a few* normal-people boundaries. If we don't, suddenly, you'll be pooping in front of me."

Osgood laughed. "I've pooped in front of you."

"When did you—" Audrey looked legitimately taken aback. "Never mind! I don't want to remember." She pointed to the shower and assumed a commanding voice. "Shower. I'll get the dye ready."

"I love you," said Osgood.

"Shower," said Audrey.

As the water fell down Osgood's body, she realized she felt lighter and happier than she'd felt for a long time. "I'll bet Remy took some of the junk away," said Osgood to herself, but she couldn't begrudge it. Holding onto her emotional pain was just as useless as her physical pain.

You also had an unwelcome tenant living in a corner of your brain that you didn't know about, suggested not the Audrey out there but the one in her head. "You'd marry me, head Audrey," said Osgood.

"Are you talking about getting married again?!" exclaimed real Audrey from the other side of the curtain.

"No!" said Osgood in the same tone she was confident she'd delivered to her mother when caught doing, well, dealer's choice.

Audrey didn't respond. Through the translucent curtain, Osgood could see the vague silhouette of her beloved prepping at the small bathroom sink. She felt a mighty swell of worry for her.

"I don't think we should go tonight!" Osgood said.

Audrey was silent, but a moment later yanked open the shower curtain. "You're getting the Key to the City."

"Who cares?" asked Osgood.

"If you were an avatar of a god—"

"Aspect."

"Sure." Audrey smiled. "Wouldn't you go to a big event featuring the person you're pissed at?"

"Does that mean I'm bait?" asked Osgood incredulously.

"No," said Audrey. "It means that we've spent the last three days trying to figure out what to do, and seeing if he shows up there is the best we've come up with."

"That's *so risky!*" Osgood shook her head and climbed out of the shower, wrapping a towel around herself. "What if he jumps into a guy with one of those AS-15s and shoots up the place?"

"AR-15," corrected Audrey.

"Why the hell are you so calm?"

"Eliza told me I worry too much," said Audrey.

Osgood stared. "Did she fucking *dose* you?"

"What?" asked Audrey, snapping out of her smile. "No! I took a Klonopin. You're not the only one who takes drugs, Pru."

"Pru?" exclaimed Osgood, shocked at the appearance of the name that really only her mother called her, and even then, usually derisively.

"Why don't you sit on the side of the tub?" suggested Audrey.

"Why, what're you going to do?" asked Osgood.

"I'm going to dye your hair, you paranoid psycho!"

Osgood perched on the side of the tub, facing the tiled wall. "Please tell me why you're so calm about this plan."

Audrey began to brush the tangles out of Osgood's right side. "Lil thinks he's weaker than he's letting on."

"You're talking to my great-grandmother now?"

Audrey didn't dignify it with a response. "And if he's as weak as she thinks he is, he may be unable to entirely take hold of someone, maybe only moments. Besides, he *wants* you and can't seem to have you without permission."

Osgood sighed as Audrey brushed on the first gobs of Manic Panic Purple Haze. "He said he could; it'd just be messy and make me a vegetable."

"Do you think he was telling the truth?" asked Audrey.

"I—" Osgood thought about it. In all her time sharing a mind with him while unable to leave, he'd never taken her over. "He can make people do things. He made you do something," said Osgood, then regretted how pointed that seemed.

"I know," said Audrey, looking away. "And Zack knows. We had a long conversation about it."

"And you're cool?" asked Osgood.

"Yes," said Audrey. "Because, just like you, that wasn't my fault." She resumed painting the dye. "Eliza also thinks his power to manipulate was directly related to his proximity to you."

"Oh," said Osgood. "Great. It's not like anyone will be near me tonight."

Audrey stopped again. "We've really thought about this, Os. But if you're not on board, we will find another way."

Osgood reached her hand behind her, and after poking Audrey in the side (a well-toned side, Osgood noted), she found her friend's hand and held it. "No, you're right. It's probably the first thing I would've suggested anyway."

"You do tend to throw yourself *at* danger," said Audrey. "That's a personality flaw, you know."

Osgood gave her a little nod. "But when I do it, I try to throw only myself. I just don't want to get you all hurt."

"We've got a plan."

"Do you want to share it?" asked Osgood.

"Actually, no," said Audrey.

Osgood started. "Really?"

"We don't know if you're still connected," she said, taking Osgood's temples in hand and turning her face forward again.

"And if we are, he'd know," said Osgood.

"Yeah," said Audrey. "We all understand the danger. And it's not like this is the first time we've put ourselves in harm's way."

"Fine," said Osgood after a long while. "But the moment it looks like he's going to do something to you, I'm telling him he can wear me like a coat whenever he wants."

"Figured that'd be your reaction," said Audrey. "Done."

Dye applied, Audrey disappeared from the bathroom, leaving Osgood wondering about the brave face she'd been wearing. It wasn't like her friend to be blasé about danger, and Audrey was usually the one trying to talk Osgood out of doing something stupid. As Osgood picked her clothes out for the evening: black jeans that weren't ripped in the knees and a red and white ringer shirt with Zack's Spectral Inspector ghost logo on it — she worried. She'd meant it when she said she'd throw herself at him, but she couldn't even imagine what Yoko would do if given complete control over her. Or even what he *could* do.

"I *am* scared," said Audrey, appearing in the bathroom doorway as Osgood waited for the water to heat up again so she could rinse.

"Good," said Osgood. "I think we all should be."

"But let's say he actually is the avatar of a god, and he actually can break the clock and destabilize the universe…"

"Whew," said Osgood. "That's a biiiiig entry on the con list."

"Then we're going to go down swinging," finished Audrey. She reached out for the towel.

"I thought it'd be like you seeing me poop," said Osgood, handing Audrey the towel and standing naked before her.

"Rinse," said Audrey.

Osgood climbed back into the shower and stuck her head under the shower head. She watched as purple rivulets slid toward the drain before eddying down. A small blast of chilly air, and then she wasn't alone in the shower. She felt Audrey's fingers in her hair, squeezing out the dye. Osgood also felt Audrey's nipples on her back, her bush against Osgood's ass. "What're you doing?" asked Osgood in little more than a whisper.

"Look at me," said Audrey.

Slowly, Osgood turned to behold Audrey, naked before her. "What're you doing?" asked Osgood again.

"If the world's gonna end, I'm gonna fuck you one last time first."

"Deal," said Osgood, and she dove into a kiss. The warm water showered down both bodies as their hands moved across their backs and downward.

Audrey kissed up Osgood's chin to her ear. "I even have a new dick."

"When did you get a strap-on while preparing for the apocalypse?"

"Oh, I got it a while ago." Audrey looked away, amused and embarrassed. "I'd convinced myself that just purchasing it might snap you out of the locked-in syndrome. You didn't feel it, did you?"

"Nope," said Osgood. "But I *want* to lie and say I sensed a great disturbance in the sexuality force."

"I need to taste you," she said.

Osgood nodded greedily.

THIRTY-SEVEN

WHEN THE ELEVATOR DOORS opened onto the ballroom floor of the Harold Washington Library, the number of people milling about on the staircase up to the main ballroom left Osgood flabbergasted. What she'd assumed would be a small event seemed to have been elevated by a mayor whose goodwill had all but been used up.

"Nope," said Osgood. "I can't do this." She ducked back behind the side wall of the elevator and jammed her finger on the close-door button.

"Os!" Zack exclaimed. He stuck his foot in. "C'mon, before someone sees you."

When Osgood didn't move, he reached for her and grabbed her hand. Audrey took her other hand, and they darted left down a corridor and through a closed door. The room was decked out in bridal ephemera. Clearly, there'd been a wedding the night before or would be tomorrow. Right now, there was just Remy, nibbling her thumbnail, and a young woman with a headset and a clipboard.

"Remy, what's wrong?" asked Osgood. "I mean, aside from the obvious?"

The woman with the clipboard stuck out her hand. "Constance Beauchamp. I'm the mayor's aide and director of new media."

"Uh," said Osgood, shaking her hand. "I'm—"

"I know," said Constance, seeming thrilled. A closer look at her showed she was young but not as young as Osgood had assumed. Maybe late 30s. Every move she made seemed to have purpose. Constance Beauchamp was what society called a go-getter. "You're Prudence Osgood. The girl who lived. Your story is astonishing!"

"My story?" Osgood cocked her head. "You mean that I didn't die?"

"You say that as though it's something any old person can do," said Constance, wearing a showily perplexed expression.

"It's something my friends do every day." Osgood gestured toward them. "And can we talk about that *girl* part?"

"Woman, sorry!" Constance exclaimed, with a *mea culpa* face.

"I mean, I'd rather not be defined by my—"

"Oh, what are your preferred pronouns? They/them?"

Osgood took Constance's shoulders in her hands and pushed the woman further away. "You've got some really intense energy."

"I want to ensure we get this right," said Constance. "Anyway, you can talk to Dr. Yeagher about the details. We have about fifteen minutes 'til places."

Osgood nodded.

"Thank you, fifteen," said Constance. She waited. Waited. Waited. "Now you say it."

"Thank you, fifteen?" asked Osgood.

Constance grinned and left.

"Yep, she's Yoko," said Osgood to Audrey and Zack. "Go kill her." Osgood turned to Remy. "Now, what am I talking to Dr. Yeagher about?"

"Well, there's been a change of plans," said Remy. "I'm doing the interview now."

"What interview?" asked Osgood.

"I was told you agreed to an interview after the key ceremony?"

Osgood thought about it, surprised that her answer was, "I— Do not remember that."

"Well, Carl Mallory from WGN Nightly News was supposed to do it, but no one can reach him. Since I have..." She exhaled sharply. "...broadcast experience. And since I know you. And I'm here. They asked me."

"Well, that makes me less nervous about being interviewed in front of all these people and maybe a god."

"He's not a god," said Audrey.

"He's an aspect," said Zack.

Osgood whirled around. "Don't pretend you're any less scared of an aspect of a god, Zack!"

Zack seemed to cower, and Osgood immediately regretted it.

"So, no one will tell me this plan?" asked Osgood.

"Then you'd know," said Zack.

"That's kinda the point," said Osgood.

"We have ... contingencies." Remy moved to Osgood and put her hands on her shoulders.

Looking into Remy's eyes, Osgood sighed. Why fight? She'd feel so much better, wouldn't she? "Go ahead, take what you need." Remy did. And like the sun coming out on a rainy day, Osgood felt lighter. "Why don't I let you do that more?" she asked with a laugh.

"I have no idea," said Remy.

"Are Eliza and Albrecht somewhere safe?" asked Osgood.

"Well," Zack said. "If by 'somewhere safe' you mean the ballroom..."

"Jesus Christ," Osgood said, then turned to Remy. "Did you suck out everybody's nervousness?"

"Yeah," said Zack. "It was great. I almost came."

"Okay, I liked you more with a bit of a filter," said Osgood. "Anyone else here I should worry about? I don't know many other people."

Audrey looked at Zack, who nodded with his eyes closed. "We thought they might come," she said.

"They did ask us for parking information," said Zack to Audrey.

"I'm guessing Basil and Cynthia are here." They said nothing, but Osgood knew. "Well, whoop-di-shit."

"Dr. Laghari, too," said Zack. "I don't know how she even knows about this."

"Don't you know I'm famous now, Zack?" asked Osgood, grabbing his chin. "I'm the fucking girl who fucking lived."

"I liked you better with a filter, too," said Zack.

"When has she *ever* had a filter?" asked Audrey.

"Okay," said Osgood. She took a deep breath and lifted her hands, palms down, to quiet the room.

"You're wearing that?" asked Zack.

"Zip it," said Osgood.

"No, I mean, you know I love it when you wear our merch!" said Zack. "But your mother will have thoughts."

"Alright, I need everybody to focus with me here for a minute," Osgood took a long, slow breath. In through the nose, out through the mouth. Then again. The second time, everyone mirrored her lead. "I get why you won't tell me *your* parts of the plan. But is there something I'm expected to do? Or that I should know?"

"You're going to have the best view of the audience from the dais," said Zack.

"Sure."

"And we kinda assumed you could sense him," he continued.

"There's no reason whatsoever to assume that," said Osgood.

"Okay," he said.

"Look, Os," said Audrey. She took Osgood's hands and looked into her eyes.

Osgood was instantly lost in the blue for the second time that day. The first had been when they had their arms wrapped around each other, and Audrey's big purple silicone dick was inside her. "Yes," she said, blinking through the memory.

"What you said you'd do…" Audrey continued. "Let him in…"

"That's what we all figured you'd do," said Zack.

"And we didn't think there was any way to talk you out of it," said Remy.

"That's right," said Osgood. "There's nothing you can say."

"So, we've planned for that," said Audrey.

There came a knock at the door. "Five minutes!"

"Thank you, five," said Zack, his heart not in it.

"So, I *am* bait," said Osgood.

"No," said Remy. "You're the trap."

"Oh, I don't like that," said Osgood.

"We need to go get into place," said Audrey.

"No, don't go!" pleaded Osgood.

"We've got this," said Audrey. She took Osgood's face in her hands and kissed her deeply. Then looked into her eyes again. "We've got this." Then Audrey walked out.

Zack turned to Osgood. "What she said." He looked at her and then away. Then he leaned in and gave her the lightest peck on the cheek. Even that seemed to embarrass him, though, and he cleared his throat.

Osgood pulled him into a bear hug. "I love you, Zack."

"Yeah, um, love you too." Zack coughed. "Be careful."

Osgood laughed. "Haven't the foggiest idea of what to be careful of, so…"

Zack gave her one last nod and then left as well, leaving Osgood and Remy alone.

"Do we really have this?" Osgood asked Remy.

"You know in heist movies like *Ocean's Eleven* where plan A is meant to fail, so plan B can succeed under the radar?"

"Yeah?"

"We have plan A." Remy grinned nervously. "Hopefully, we don't need a B."

"Oh god," said Osgood.

"Oh, one weird thing," Remy said, holding her finger up. "If you see ... me ... out there ... don't freak out."

"Why would I freak out?" asked Osgood. "You're interviewing me."

"Just," Remy rubbed her arms. "Just promise you won't."

"I won't." Osgood wanted to follow up, but Remy left, leaving her alone in the bridal suite. The wedding must've been last night because the floor hadn't been completely cleared of confetti, and under the black couch was ... Osgood looked closer.

"Fuckin' A," she said, picking up the travel-sized Jack Daniels bottle, still sealed. She opened it and poured it down her throat, gasping at the burn.

You have this, said that melodic, calm voice within, the voice of Lil.

"I'm glad you're here with me," said Osgood. "'Cuz I'm feeling kinda alone right now."

You aren't.

Osgood took another deep breath: in through the nose and out through the mouth.

Suddenly, the door swung open, and a far more frazzled and wide-eyed Constance stood there. "We're at one minute! You need to get up there!"

"Thank you, one?" asked Osgood, before being yanked after the surprisingly strong woman seemingly half her size.

Constance pulled her up the staircase into the main ballroom, past people Osgood thought she knew from TV, past the weatherman who'd been doing channel 32's broadcasts since Osgood could remember comprehending what weather even was.

"Is that—" began Osgood.

"No time," said Constance. She pressed her finger to her earpiece. "Thank you, thirty seconds!"

Osgood saw her mother and father in a throng of people. They waved. She waved back.

Then she stood behind a sheer scrim, and someone was already on stage introducing, "Mayor Tom Augusta!"

Constance pointed at a blue tape line on the floor. "That's your spot until he calls you out. Then you're at the podium. Speak directly into the mic. Like an inch away, okay?" She held up her fingers to demonstrate the distance. "So many people stand like a foot away, and no one can hear."

Osgood looked at her.

"Do. You. Understand. Me?"

Osgood nodded.

"You're gonna be great," Constance told Osgood. "This is gonna be great," a far less confident Constance told herself.

"—remarkable woman," came Mayor Augusta's booming voice from the stage. Osgood leaned around the scrim and saw him; his massive frame dwarfed the podium. "Some have called her the girl who lived, but I've been told she doesn't like that." A chuckle in the crowd.

"Would you wanna be called girl?" Osgood whispered toward the audience.

"But regardless of what we call her, she's a *survivor*." The mayor nodded at the crowd, and some nodded back. "When she was eighteen, she was in a car accident out in DeKalb county and was dead for a record eight minutes."

Murmurs from the crowd.

"Nineteen." Osgood shuffled her feet. She hadn't known he would talk about that.

"And not long ago, she had an enormous brain tumor removed. Her doctor, the esteemed Dr. Nithya Laghari, is here in the crowd."

Osgood definitely hadn't known he'd talk about that.

"But most tragic, and it was tragic, on the day this city lost so many, Prudence Osgood lost the love of her life, Eleanor Vance, who was one of the eight hundred and forty-four souls lost on 12/17."

Osgood felt tears. That was to be expected, sure. And it would play well for the audience. But, "love of her life?" Also, he'd called her Eleanor. She'd always preferred Nora, and Osgood knew a little something about chosen names.

"Now, let's bring her out, the girl who lived—"

"Oh, for fuck's sake," said Osgood under her breath.

"—Prudence Osgood!"

Osgood took one more deep breath, then stepped onto the stage.

Thirty-Eight

OSGOOD STEPPED OUT FROM behind the scrim onto the dais. From this viewpoint, the room felt even more overwhelming. This ballroom's windows lined the walls from floor to ceiling, and the roof gave way to a massive skylight. The skyscrapers of Chicago were all around them, windows lighting up as another day ended, and all these Chicagoans were here. For her. Why the applause? What had she done? She only didn't die. Which, she'd be the first to admit, might seem somewhat challenging under the circumstances. She looked out at the crowd as she walked to where the mayor towered over the podium.

Her parents, Cynthia and Basil, stood, applauding. Basil, with his mustache freshly combed, wore his corduroy sport coat and turtle neck, his Carl Sagan cosplay, as she'd always called it. Her mother wore pearls and a dress. She'd dressed up for this. And she was smiling! Osgood felt a pressure in her chest that she couldn't identify. Was she really this excited that her mother seemed *proud* of her?

Hold up, kiddo, she told herself, feeling her eyes begin to leak. Then Audrey's voice added, *You need to get through this, yes, but you need to be fucking alert!*

That's right! Because, in all likelihood, somewhere in that crowd was the avatar, or aspect, or whatever, of a god who wanted to use her to end the world. No, even that was selfish thinking. Yoko wanted to break the universe. Her eyes darted between people clapping in the crowd as she moved to the podium, seemingly in slow motion.

No flaming eyes yet.

But she knew he could hide that. At least in her dreams, he could. She didn't remember the ones he wore as costumes always having flaming eyes. If he couldn't hide that tell, it'd be tough to fit in; perhaps he would wear sunglasses. Sunglasses, like that man standing near the back on the right-hand side. Or the woman three rows from the front, off center. Though with the massive windows and wide-open ceiling, the setting sun still bore down on this little greenhouse, casting everything in a perhaps timely orange glow.

As she neared the podium, the mayor opened his massive arms wide and, without waiting, wrapped her in a hug. "Oh, we're doing this?" she asked under her breath. But as she said it into Augusta's chest, he didn't seem to hear her. She felt a kiss on the side of her head that had been freshly shorn, and she shuddered. Why did people think they had the right to do that? Why did men—

The mayor released her, then leaned down, seeming to bend in half to reach the microphone. "Please, keep clapping, she deserves it!" The audience roared in reply. Then he leaned to her, bringing his lips entirely too close to her ear, the heat of his breath radiating. "They're all yours."

Osgood laughed self-consciously and turned to the microphone as the mayor stepped back, but not away. He grasped his hands together and bowed his head as though in prayer or observing a moment of silence. The gesture certainly couldn't have been an attempt to fade away in importance, as he dwarfed everything else on stage.

"I didn't do anything," said Osgood. She was too quiet and too far from the microphone. She saw Constance's eyes widen near the back of the audience, and she mimed pulling the mic closer, but all

Osgood saw was her pulling on a dick and then opening her mouth. She snickered, then adjusted the microphone. "I don't deserve to be here," said Osgood, this time into the microphone. She heard her words careen around the room. There were a smattering of rejections of the concept from the audience. "No, really. It's not self-deprecation. Though that is a specialty of mine..." She thought she saw her mother smirk. "But the fact is that eight hundred and forty-four people died, and somehow I lived. I watched as my girlfriend was literally cut in half by the El's front window. Yet somehow, I lived. But Nora didn't deserve her fate, and neither did those eight hundred and forty-three other people, as wild and Rube Goldbergian as that fate seemed." She stared at the audience, and they stared back. This wasn't what they wanted to hear.

"I think I know what you want from me," she said. "You want the feel-good story. You want to feel the miracle that I survived. Especially since our mayor was nice enough to tell you about my personal medical history—" An uncomfortable murmur rippled through. "Especially as I seem to be a miracle ... girl. A survivor girl. The girl who lived. And that's what you want. You want to hear that my outlook on life has—" The words died in her throat as she saw a tall, slender woman winding her way into the crowd. First, she moved so methodically and deliberately that Osgood was sure she'd found Yoko's new host, but then the woman turned to face her dead on, and Osgood gasped. Remy! But Remy with black hair reaching her waist. Was she going incognito before the interview? She'd changed clothes as well, what the fuck?

If you see me out there ... don't freak out.

But Osgood felt the freak-out coming. Perhaps best to look away, as the woman who was *almost* Remy Yeagher had begun to smile at her, nearly leer, and there was no joy whatsoever behind it.

"Some of you may know me as the Spectral Inspector," Osgood continued, beginning to find her footing after a shaky beginning. "But all I've ever wanted is to discover the unknown. And I'll say you have a *lot* of time to think when you're locked in."

Another crowd murmur. Sympathy for her plight.

"I'm not special. That's not why I lived. And that's not why any of your family members, loved ones, or friends died. This was unpredictable happenstance. This was random. Sometimes there *isn't* a reason."

Constance also grinned at her from the audience, but the jittery woman's smile felt different. First, that manic woman should still be rushing about, stressed out of her mind until this event was over. Second, her face didn't seem to fit with the grin, and her eyes seemed hot.

"I think we have a candidate," said Osgood quietly, but it came out booming through the speakers. "Um. A— A candidate for the most important person in this terrible tragedy."

She caught Zack's eye and flicked her head toward Constance. He stood on his tiptoes and looked around. He shrugged, wide-eyed.

"And that's our mayor," said Osgood.

She saw Albrecht and Eliza standing very close together. Did he have his arm around her? Were they dating? When Eliza saw the look, she pointed it out to Albrecht and quickly found Osgood's target. Good thing, too, as Constance had done an about-face heading toward the back of the crowd. Now Zack had seen her as well.

"Because while I was in the hospital, Mayor Augusta got to work rebuilding this city. And I think he deserves a round of applause!"

The mayor mimed bashfulness in the inauthentic way that only a politician can. He leaned down, pressing his bulk uncomfortably against her shoulder, and said a simple "Thank you" before returning the mic to Osgood. The applause continued, and the mayor moved from bashfulness to a request to stop applauding by giving them "let's all quiet down now" hands.

The applause had been a good cover, though, because while it continued, Osgood had seen Albrecht and Zack straining to hold a rag

(does this rag smell like ether?)

to Constance's mouth. It didn't take long, but her thrashing stopped, and she went limp, seemingly without drawing much attention.

Osgood felt two kielbasa-sized fingers press against her back and shove her back to the microphone. *More?* she thought. *What more could they possibly want to hear me say.*

"Things are strange in this city right now," she said, unsure where to go from here. She couldn't just unleash stream-of-consciousness podcast Osgood. She watched Zack, Albrecht, and Eliza carry stiff-as-a-board Constance in a Marx Brothers-esque madcap dash toward the bridal room. "Jesus, I hope they didn't kill her." The audience's sudden quiet surprised Osgood until she realized what she'd said into the mic. "The spirit of this city can't be killed by one accident or tragedy. When the Great Fire happened, we rebuilt it bigger and better than ever. And now we're..." she looked to the mayor for confirmation. "Rebuilding the Booth Tower? And the subway." He nodded in assurance, though he, too, seemed to be scanning the crowd. Perhaps he was looking for his aide.

Wrap it up, Pru; this is not you at your most eloquent. She admonished her mother's voice with an internal, *I know,* and leaned back to the mic, then thought, *What the hell?* "Until this city is back on her feet, you can count on your survivor girl here to be with you and my beloved hometown Chicago every step of the way!"

Applause erupted again. *That's* all they'd wanted. The old razzle-dazzle. A little rah-rah.

Zack appeared from the hallway and gave a thumbs-up.

Okay, she thought, *but what does that mean?*

The mayor reached to a stand beside him and lifted a surprisingly large redwood case with red velvet lining. "With that, I am exceptionally proud to give our Girl ... ahem ... *Woman* Who Lived this Key to the City of Chicago." He opened the case and lifted out the key. It looked gold, but Osgood was sure it wasn't. What it *was*, though, was ridiculous. Two feet long, and when he handed it over, she realized it felt like twenty pounds of steel. Lots of applause as she struggled to hoist it. She wondered what on earth she'd do with this thing? Does one hang it?

Be gracious, Pru, her mother's voice suggested snidely.

You may want to figure out how to display it in place of that junior year high-femme picture of me in the living room, Osgood volleyed back, also snide.

Several photographers stepped forward, and lights started flashing in their faces. The mayor put his arm around her and pulled her into his body, too close, but *smile for the camera, Pru!* She did. The closed-lipped smile that Cynthia hated. The one that hid the damage she had done to her teeth through neglect, through smoking, through bulimia in high school... She felt the mayor swaying next to her and looked up to see him pinching the bridge of his nose. Perhaps he also hated shit like this and wanted to get back to governing.

"Alright, um," he said, leaning down over the podium but now seeming to use it for support. "Let's give Miss Osgood—"

"Just Osgood," said Osgood.

"What?" he asked.

"Never mind."

"Let's give Miss Osgood a chance to mingle and get some appetizers. I saw that Saviano's brought their famous meatballs." He looked down at her with a weary smile. "To die for."

Osgood smiled back, tight-lipped still. She had no intention of mingling. She wanted to get off this stage and return to the bridal room to figure out what was happening with Yoko. If you knocked out the host, did you knock out the parasite? She gave the audience one last thank you, rushed off stage to safety behind the scrim, and slammed into Audrey. Both women careened backward, and Osgood fell on her ass. A pair of black-clad stagehands rushed to her side. "Why don't you help her, too?" asked Osgood, irritated.

"I'm okay," said Audrey, waving them off.

"Was it her?" Osgood asked Audrey.

"Maybe?" said Audrey.

"Maybe?!"

"She's lucid again and doesn't seem to remember the ceremony." Audrey sighed. "Of course, that could be a side effect of the fucking ether Zack used. Did you know he'd use ether?"

"I try to *not* know what Zack is doing at any given time unless he thinks I should," said Osgood.

"She's insisting that she needs to get back out here for the talk show portion and that the mayor cannot cope without her."

Osgood sighed. "What do you think?"

"I don't know, Os," said Audrey.

"By the way, there's a woman that looks exactly like Remy out there, except she has long—"

Suddenly, Constance Beauchamp barreled toward Osgood with a manic look. "Shit," said Osgood, bracing herself for a fight.

"I'm *so* sorry," said Constance, panting heavily. She bent over and put her hands on her knees.

"For?" asked Osgood.

"I must've gotten lightheaded out there," said Constance, pointing vaguely in the direction of the crowd. "Thankfully, your friends caught me before I cracked my head on the marble!"

"We do what we can," said Audrey.

"Constance," said Osgood.

"Yeah?" said the manic woman, smiling, hazel eyes wide. Not a hint of fire.

Osgood's mind was blank. *Just get rid of her.* "Could you get me a small plate of those meatballs and a whiskey?"

"Oh, I—" Constance nodded uncomfortably. "Sure." She scrambled with her clipboard and a binder, then set them on a speaker and disappeared.

"If he *was* in her, I don't think he is now," said Osgood.

"Fuck," said Audrey.

"What about Eliza?" asked Osgood. "Can she triangulate or something?"

"We're doing our best out there, Os," said Audrey. "Don't panic."

"I'm not panicking."

"Good."

"Yet."

Audrey quickly kissed Osgood's lips and disappeared without another word.

Osgood sighed and looked around the modest backstage area, clearly an ad hoc version of an actual presentation-quality event. But not so bad. She looked at the engraved brass plate on the box, now with the massive key reseated within its velvet lining. "'Prudence Osgood – The Girl Who Lived.'" Osgood sighed; not only was it bad enough being infantilized as *girl*, but, "Now I'll be forever tied in Google searches to that little wizard and his transphobic cunt of an author."

"Were you speaking to me?"

Osgood turned and saw Mayor Tom Augusta's hulking frame.

"That was fun out there," he said, standing close enough that Osgood had to crane her neck almost entirely upward.

"Yeah," Osgood said. "Fun."

He put his hand on her shoulder. "I know this sort of thing can be a pain, but generally, this helps to keep individual interview requests at bay. Because you've got so much more important work to do, Pru."

"That's—" she stopped. "You're right, I do."

"I know," he said. "And we can do so much of that together. Just think about it."

His hand moved from her shoulder to her back, then slid down the small of her back … into her jeans.

THIRTY-NINE

Astonished wouldn't be a big enough word for what Osgood felt as Chicago's mayor Tom Augusta slid his hand not only beneath her jeans but down the crack of her ass, as she'd gone without panties today. She'd been so busy looking for aspects of gods she'd utterly forgotten about regular everyday fucking creeps.

"What the fuck are you doing?" she asked, shoving herself away from the mayor. He moved toward her again, and that was when she saw his eyes. The irises were orange, not brown as before. "Yoko."

"I think you ought to continue calling me Mr. Mayor," said Yoko.

"Why do you need me if you have the fucking mayor?"

"I don't need," said Yoko in Augusta's voice. "I want. I crave. I yearn. I covet." He grabbed her shoulders in such a flash that Osgood couldn't get away. His hands squeezed, causing her left shoulder to pop right out of the socket and sending scorching pain up and down her body. The monster licked his lips.

Use the rape whistle hex, suggested her great-grandmother, but fuck if Osgood could remember it. Her aunt had even simplified it for her neophyte niece, taking it from arcane forgotten words to a memorable phrase. But what was that phrase? Then she heard Eliza in her head, *I created it for you, Prudence!* She scanned through her internal databases. It had to be here. How could she have lost something so essential? What good was total fucking recall if she couldn't—

"We're on in one!" shouted Constance without looking at them. She juggled the plate of meatballs and the whiskey.

"Thank you, one," sneered Yoko.

There!

On a mental scrap of paper, strewn in the margins of her mind were the words. She slapped her hand to the mayor's red cheek and sneered as she said, "I eat men like air!" When nothing happened, Osgood wondered if she'd gotten it wrong. Yoko's confused expression compounded her concern. But he did let go and step away from her.

"Okay. See you out there," he said with a wink. He sniffed his hand and walked away.

"Why are you making me crazy?" lamented Constance, dragging Remy by the arm into the backstage area.

This was the Remy Osgood knew, business dress and pixie-cut blonde hair. "Just give me one moment with Osgood before I go out."

"I'll give you *literally* a moment." She pressed on her headset and began angrily whispering into it.

"It's him," said Osgood in her own harsh whisper.

"Who him?" asked Remy.

"Mayor Tom Augusta is Yoko."

"Well," said Remy. "Fuck."

"Does that mean plan A has already failed?" pleaded Osgood. "I wish someone would just tell me what the plan is. Let me in on something. I feel alone in the dark."

Remy put her hand to Osgood's face, and Osgood's mood lifted almost immediately.

"That's not fair," said Osgood.

"Just until we're done with this interview," said Remy, grabbing Osgood's hand.

"Wait, I'm not doing the interview with him! He fucking grabbed me!" Osgood shook her head. "He's also fucking Yoko!"

"Plan A is still a go, Os," said Remy.

Osgood stared at her for a long while, then nodded. "Well, let's let the end of the universe be televised, I guess."

"That's the spirit."

Moments later, Remy stepped out from behind the scrim and sat in a single chair opposite two. Mayor Augusta took up the chair directly across, and the third sat empty, waiting for Osgood.

About to step out, Osgood saw a small plate with three meatballs and two glasses of brown liquid. She sniffed the first glass and felt the slight burn in her nose. *Strong. Bottoms up!* She grabbed the second one, debating taking it out on stage with her, but instead just poured it down her throat. "I really hope you're with me, Lil," she whispered. "And I really hope plan A is decent."

She walked out feeling light and calm, even though the drinks had not yet settled in enough to take off the edge, despite her lack of food today ... or yesterday, even. This was Remy's illusion. Or, maybe it wasn't. If Remy had actually *taken* the pain and the panic, then feeling better wasn't an illusion. But when the mayor winked at her with one of Yoko's blazing eyes, she still felt the urge to turn and run.

"You can do this, you can do this, you can do this," she whispered quietly, crossing the dais to the interview set. Of course, she could do this. She'd stuffed down her true feelings about so many people for so many years; what were 15 more minutes sitting on stage with an aspect of a vengeful god?

The audience's applause grew as she waved and smiled at them, again clocking audience members. Her parents, her mother still beaming. There was Dr. Laghari with a broad smile on her face. In the back stood Eliza and Albrecht. And Zack and Audrey had taken up on opposite sides of the crowd.

"Plan A," she said to herself as she sat next to this monster of a man. He put his arm around her chair, making her cringe something fierce. *Can't take away repulsion, can you*, she asked Remy in her mind, smiling at the woman before her. Remy's concern was evident at this distance, but Osgood doubted the audience could tell. It'd be down to vocal performance.

Remy's first question was a dramatic softball. "How do you feel after all that's gone on?"

Osgood couldn't think of what to say. Just *Fine*? That didn't make for a good interview. Instead, she repeated the question. "How do I feel? And by 'all that's gone on,' I assume you mean the crash and the rebuilding."

"You can probably interpret that question however you'd like," said Augusta, squeezing the shoulder opposite him. "Huh," he said, withdrawing his arm as she felt something drip down her shoulder.

Osgood turned entirely away from him; only she and Remy were in the world. "I feel lied to," she said. "If I'm being honest."

Augusta leaned in. "I think what Miss Osgood is—"

"*Osgood*," snapped Osgood. "Just Osgood."

She could hear many people tapping their phones in the audience. And there were the journalists and influencers. They sure liked that moment, didn't they?

"How do you mean?" asked Remy, putting her hand to her chin like the confidently hacky journalist she most certainly wasn't.

"Why isn't anyone talking about the signs?" Osgood asked.

The audience seemed confused.

"You probably don't remember seeing them, but I'll bet you did."

The mayor leaned into her. "Perhaps, Miss Osgood—"

"What part of '*just Osgood*' don't you understand?" Osgood demanded of the mayor, of Yoko.

Osgood was impressed that Yoko actually reared back from her intensity. He didn't correct himself, though.

"I think," began Remy, perhaps trying to win back the audience. "I think she's referring to the uptick in supernatural occurrences. Surely you've noticed that."

"Talk about survival!" shouted someone in the audience.

"Yes," said Yoko, pointing his finger toward that person. But his finger wasn't pointed.

Osgood thought he must be making that politician point where the fingers are all tucked. That was until someone screamed. Then she realized that his finger wasn't folded; it was missing. She flung her head toward the crowd where a woman with a small paintball splat of red on her forehead held up ... a finger.

"What the *fuck?*" yelled Osgood, and chaos descended.

"What did you do to me?" roared Yoko, his mouth thick with...not saliva...blood. It stained his lips and dribbled down his chin. He sneered, and she saw that the two left-of-center front teeth had fallen out. She wondered if they were in his lap or if he'd swallowed them.

"I. I," Osgood stammered. "I legit don't know!"

At that moment, she caught the fountain of white hair that rose off Aunt Eliza's head. Eliza wore a serene smirk in the middle of the panicking audience.

Augusta-Yoko pawed at Osgood's throat but couldn't find purchase, and she reached up to his face and pressed her fingers into it like clay. She pulled back in shock and took his right cheek with her. His jawbone and tongue were exposed to the world via that WGN Camera just down there, the one that the cameraman looked desperate to abandon but held tight because someone had to have some journalistic integrity, goddammit.

Augusta's fiery eyes darted back and forth in their sockets, between the camera and Osgood, and then he careened off the stage into the crowd like a bull in Spain.

Osgood turned to Remy, wide-eyed. Pale as a ghost, Remy said, "I think Plan A has failed."

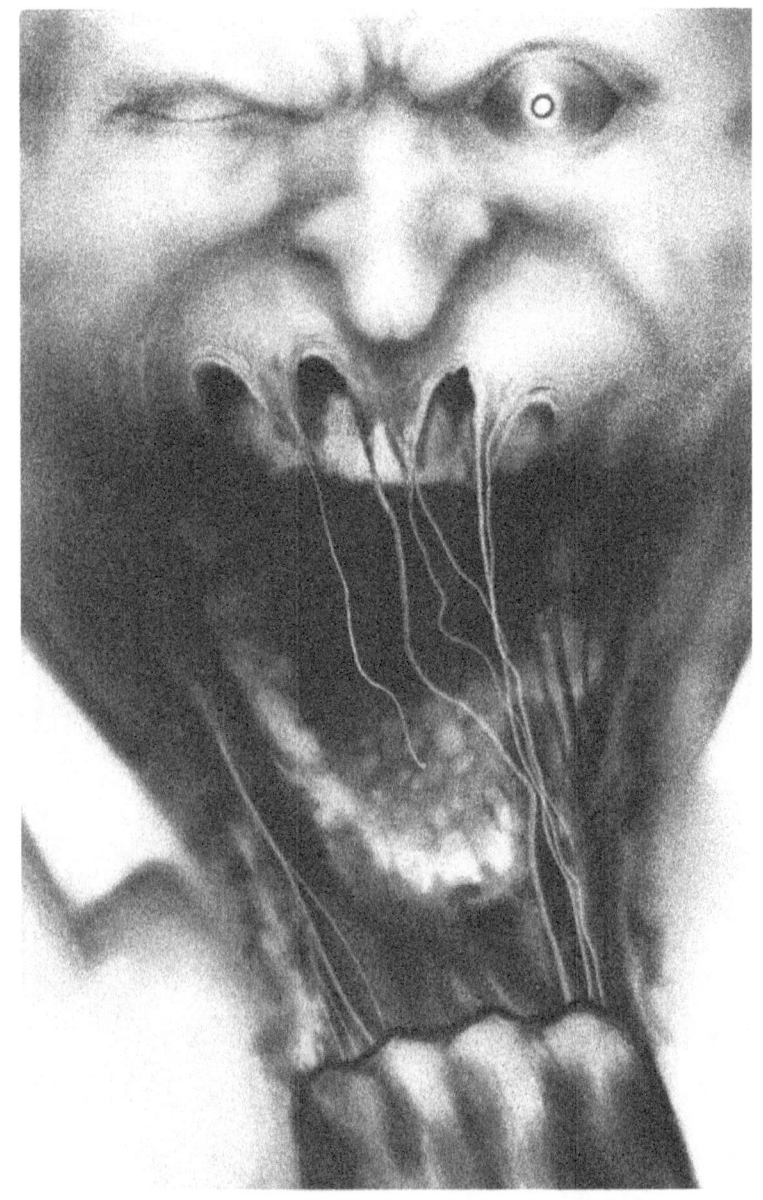

FORTY

"We have to think about containment," said Audrey.

"But also, we need to get these people out of here," pleaded Zack.

"He's a body jumper; how can we be sure any of them aren't him?" asked Remy.

Eliza and Albrecht joined them from the chaos, Albrecht breathing heavily. "I chased," he said as he tried to catch his breath, bent over, hands on his knees. "I chased down by the offices." Albrecht held up his finger, pointing the way.

Eliza took over for him. "Next to the elevator blocks is a hallway leading to offices. There wasn't anyone over there, so he may be isolated."

"And the audience?" Osgood asked.

"Are desperately trying to cram into the two elevators," said Zack, his face awash in worry. "There's a good chance they're going to overload one or both. At least some people have found the stairs."

"Now that plan A has failed, does anyone have a plan B?" asked Osgood.

"More like plan A contingencies," said Audrey. "First, we need to find the mayor."

"Alright, then let's do that," said Osgood. "Oh, and if he gets too close to you, his skin pulls off like taffy." She swung her eyes to Eliza. "Which is a bit overkill, don't you think?"

"Not for rapists," said Eliza, a smile in her voice.

Osgood conceded that.

The expanded Spectral Inspector team rushed toward the throng of people still trying to fit through the single door and six-foot wide staircase leading out of the ballroom. "Wait!" exclaimed Osgood. They did. "Stick with a buddy! No one alone!"

Now, they did disperse, leaving Osgood and Remy together. A scream came from the middle of the ballroom, and harsh footsteps clapped away, clamoring over folding chairs. Remy and Osgood moved toward the source of the sound. Lying on the floor, with her throat cut so deeply that she was nearly decapitated, was Mayor Augusta's poor aide, Constance.

"At least it looks like it was quick," said Osgood. "And by the look on her face, she never saw it coming."

Osgood looked around and saw that Remy was sobbing. The woman had a hand on her stomach and was heaving breaths.

"Oh my god, are you okay?"

"So much energy here!" She grabbed at Osgood's arm. "It's overwhelming."

"Can you do this?" asked Osgood.

Remy sniffed and shrugged, then nodded. Seeming to absorb the emotions back into herself as she stood again.

"Let's go toward the offices," said Osgood. "I don't want him to fall apart before I can rip him apart!"

"That was your aunt's hex?" Remy asked.

Osgood nodded.

"Bitchin'."

Crossing the room, now almost empty of audience members, Osgood saw the refreshments table, covered with drinks, serving trays, and a cake missing the bottom third. "The knife's gone," she told Remy.

"I saw frosting on Constance's throat," Remy told her in a small voice.

Osgood heaved. "Did plan A involve any weapons?"

Remy's eyes widened. "Oh, yes!" She reached into her bag and pulled out two plastic gun-shaped devices.

Osgood sighed, remembering how barely effective their tasers had been when Albrecht's house came under siege from the Goddard-monster. "I guess that'll have to do."

"Zack didn't think we could get guns in here," said Remy.

"I'm surprised you got these in."

As they moved into the corridor next to the ballroom, Osgood first saw a tiny trickle, then larger and larger droplets of blood. The larger pools were more brown than red. "He's gotta know we can follow him this way."

Remy nodded.

"Oh, and what the fuck was up with your costume change?" asked Osgood.

Remy cocked her head.

"The black wig?"

"She's here," said Remy, suddenly concerned about something entirely new.

"Who?" asked Osgood.

"That's Alexis," said Remy. "She's my sister."

"Your sister." Osgood blinked, taking that in. "And can she do what you do?"

"Yes," said Remy. "But it's ... different."

"Was she part of plan A?" asked Osgood.

"She's one of the only parts of plan B I have," said Remy.

"You'll need more than that," bellowed Mayor Tom Augusta as he charged out of a dark office, crossing the hallway before Osgood could recognize what was happening and bulldozed directly into Ramona Yeagher.

Osgood fired the taser, contacts flying. They hit him in the grotesquely bloody shoulder of his dress shirt. Without looking, he grabbed the contacts, yanked them off, and threw them to the ground. Then he turned to Osgood. Remy slumped out of the enormous wall divot, sliding to the ground. Osgood hoped beyond hope she was only unconscious.

Plan A. Last ditch.

"You can have me," said Osgood. "You can have me!"

"Oh, yes," said Yoko, one of the mayor's eyes blazing fire and the other clouded almost entirely with blood. "I will. But first—"

"Are you gonna tell me all about the horrible things you're going to do to me?" demanded Osgood, stepping up before him. "You need a new routine, 'cuz I've heard that one before." She clenched her fists and stood defiant in front of him.

Augusta reared up, straightening himself. He rolled his head around, and his neck's cracking sounds were horrid.

"Admit it," said Osgood. "You need me."

Yoko stared, then seemed to laugh, but it came out like a wet choke. "I'm rather astonished," he said. He rubbed his hand over the mayor's face and took both lips and the frenulum below his nose off with it. Now, the bottom of Tom Augusta's face was a gory grinning skull, though most of the teeth had vanished. "You seem to have no sense of self-preservation at all."

"People tell me that."

"What is it that you think *you* are, Pru?" asked Yoko. "Are you here? Your heart? Your emotion?" He poked a finger into her left tit, and when he pulled it away, the tip hung by a slender piece of flesh. Then he poked the same finger into her forehead, the remaining digit splitting and falling away. "Or here? Are you a mind, or are you a soul? Are you just a fucking walking ego?" He took a step forward.

Osgood, despite wanting to remain firm, stepped back in tandem.

"Well, let me tell you, you pathetic ape. You're not a soul. You're not a mind. There's no little flame of creation within you. You are just electricity. Descended from pure air. And that electricity doesn't need trivial things like a mind or a soul. Doesn't even need a heart anymore, with your various medical advances." He leaned closer to her until their faces nearly touched. "I told you I didn't need you willingly; it would just be messy the other way. And it's about to become messy."

On instinct, Osgood flung her head forward and latched her teeth onto his nose, biting as far back on his face as she could and thinking in that moment about the time her mother had told her she had an enormous mouth. Yoko hadn't expected the lunge or the attack, and when she bit down with all her might, she took the nose right off. She spat it to the ground between them.

Apparently, that move pushed them past Yoko's last bit of restraint, and he wrapped his massive hands around Osgood's throat, pressing hard against her windpipe with his two intact thumbs. She could feel the flesh breaking up and sloughing off his hands, but she also couldn't breathe. Her knees buckled, and he followed her down, his body atop hers, throttling harder and harder. Osgood saw spots in her vision, and she could feel capillaries bursting as her lungs demanded that she find a way to get air. She beat against his arms and shoulders, her limbs growing weaker and less effectual. She felt her eyes bulge in their sockets. The fact that he'd said that he had no intention of killing her didn't exactly make her feel better.

"Get the fuck away from my daughter."

Osgood heard a *slam!* and *clang!*, and suddenly, the mayor's bulk was beside her instead of atop. She could breathe again! But each breath felt like flames in her throat. When her vision swam back into focus, she saw ... Cynthia Osgood, her perfect coiffure mussed beyond measure, the sleeve of her blouse ripped open, and a look of fury on her face that Osgood knew well but that fury had never been *on behalf of* Osgood. The Key to the City was in her mother's hands, liberated from its box, blood, hair, and scalp caked on one of its two large teeth.

Cynthia looked down and met her daughter's eyes, and they matched their heaving breaths, passing a bit of a laughing grin between them. Then, her mother dropped the key to the ground with a metallic thud that cracked the marble tile. A spatter of viscera shot from under it. She rushed forward, crouching over Osgood. "Are you hurt? Beyond being choked, I mean, that's obvious. Can you believe this building can't get the fire department and ambulance crews up here for thirty more minutes? Outrageous!"

Osgood smiled, having a sudden vision of her mother going full Karen at the front desk of the Harold Washington Library. She rasped out something resembling, "Thanks, Mom."

Cynthia Osgood took her daughter's hands and slowly helped her stand. But in the middle of it, Osgood's pants grew wet.

Fuck, thought Osgood, *Even a supportive mom won't be happy about a* faux pas *as bad as pissing yourself.*

But wait, her shirt was wet, too. And Cynthia no longer held Osgood's forearms. Osgood staggered backward again, slamming her butt back into the ground. Her pain overwhelmed her adrenaline. Looking up, moments felt like an eternity as the reality before her gradually replaced what she still thought was happening. Her mother stood in front of her, but her eyes were unfocused. Below her chin was a new smile, wide, gaping, gushing red. And behind her stood Mayor Tom Augusta, almost entirely red himself now, missing a hand but holding the cake knife in his other hand. His horrid skeletal grin gaped over Cynthia's shoulder. Then Yoko pushed Cynthia forward, sending her crashing into Osgood, and both went to the floor.

Lying there, her mother's head against her shoulder, Osgood finally recognized what had happened. Cynthia Osgood, her mother, the most formidable woman she'd ever known, was dead. She'd been murdered by that thing standing above them. It seemed Yoko was also waiting for her to have this moment of clarity. He twirled the knife around in his hand, from cutting mode to stabbing, then he raised it and swung it down.

And Osgood suddenly doubted that she couldn't be killed.

Yoko's wrist thudded against Osgood's chin, and he seemed as confused as she was about what had happened. He turned to look over his shoulder. Remy stood behind him — battered, yes — not holding the knife, but holding Mayor Augusta's other hand, which still tightly clutched the knife.

"Fuck me," said Yoko, his voice incredibly wet and sticky, and Remy swung the hand and the knife around and put it through Augusta's head. "Fuck—" he tried to say again, but his face went completely slack, and the fire in his eyes went out.

Remy gave him a hard sideways shove, and he fell away from Osgood and her mother's ... she couldn't bring herself to think it, but the word was there anyway ... corpse.

"Get away from him, Remy!" said Osgood.

"I think he's dead," she said but moved away anyway.

"Mayor Augusta might be dead, but Yoko is ... who the fuck knows?"

FORTY-ONE

FOUR DAYS HAD PASSED since the event that journalists had deemed "Yet another horrifying tragedy for the city of Chicago." Osgood didn't know how exactly the city was spinning that, as to her, it seemed like the mayor going nuts and killing people (six that she knew of) on the evening news wasn't so much a tragedy as a horror. Her personal horror, though, was compounded by the fact that her mother, the oft-icy Cynthia Osgood, was dead.

She raised a finger to the barback with the dark hair, lip ring, and full-sleeve tattoos. The woman brought back the bottle of Johnny Walker Blue Osgood had been steadily wearing away.

"It's 2:40, you know," said the barback.

"What's your name?" Osgood asked.

"Cinthia," the woman said. "With an I."

"Doesn't Cynthia *always* have an I?"

"Okay," Cinthia said. "With *another* I where there's usually a Y."

"Ahh, parents thought they were being clever?"

"Great-grandparents did, actually," said Cinthia. "I'm the *third* Cinthia."

"Well, I'll be damned, I'm the second Prudence."

Cinthia smirked.

"What?"

"Just, nothing about you screams... 'Prudence.'"

Osgood knocked back the rocks glass she'd been provided and nodded at it for another.

"Let's do a water in between," said Cinthia.

"Boo," said Osgood. "Your tip will be adjusted to reflect that."

"Nothing about you screams, 'I tip less than a fiver per drink.'"

"You'd be surprised; I'm quite poor."

Cinthia put a glass of ice water in front of Osgood, who reluctantly slammed all twelve or so ounces of it. When it was done, she showed Cinthia the bottom of the glass.

"Fair enough," Cinthia said, refilling the rocks glass.

"Cynthia was my mother's name."

"Oh," said Cinthia, flirty demeanor draining away.

"I'm not saying you remind me of her because you don't," said Osgood. "She's on my mind because she just died."

"I'm sorry." Cinthia did what any skilled bartender would: she put on the mask of concern and understanding and pulled out the therapist's playbook. "Are you pre- or post-funeral?"

"Hmm?"

Cinthia pointed toward Osgood's chest, and she looked down, realizing that, against all odds, she was sitting here at the bar wearing a long black dress. "Oh. The wake." She flicked her thumb toward the door.

"At Chalfont's?"

Osgood nodded and sipped her drink like a normal person. "Not before or after, during."

"And you're—"

"Surviving."

Cinthia nodded. A bell rang far in the back of the dive bar, and the woman lightly touched Osgood's hand for the most minute of seconds. "That's a delivery. Are you gonna be—"

"I'm fine."

"Don't steal anything," Cinthia said playfully. "Remember, I have your credit card."

Osgood murmured in reply, and Cinthia disappeared into the back, leaving Osgood alone with her thoughts and herself. Across the bar, she saw herself in the mirror. Her mascara had run — so much for waterproof. Her cheeks were red and puffy, and the new layer of black dye on her curls hadn't had the staying power she'd hoped, bringing her hair to a very dark and patchy purple.

"Hey," Audrey said, pulling up on the stool beside her.

Without asking, Osgood shoved one of the empty rocks glasses over until it sat in front of Audrey and poured an overflowing drink for her, then another for herself. Perhaps Cinthia would regret leaving the bottle on her honor.

"People are asking..." said Audrey.

Unable to properly articulate what she thought they should tell said people doing said asking, Osgood just let out a grumble, knocked her drink back, and poured herself another. She looked over at Audrey, recognizing that her friend and sometimes lover had gone back into her own depression mode. Her hair was pulled up in a messy bun, tied with a simple black band. Her makeup was neat but sparse. Her skirt and blouse were dark, demure, and understated.

"Os, you have to—"

"Fuck off," said Osgood.

"You don't mean that," said Audrey.

"I don't?"

"You can be mean to me," said Audrey. "We fucked up. We should've told you the plan from the beginning. It was my idea to keep it from you. It was my call. It's my fault that Cyn— Your mother..."

"Nah. Fuck that," said Osgood. "I tried to get him to take me. He didn't want me anymore. Well, he wanted my electricity or whatever that means. Damaged goods for a god."

"What do you want, Pru?" asked Audrey. "Do you want me to wallow with you? 'Cuz I will. We can drink ourselves stupid here."

"Please don't call me Pru," said Osgood.

"Do you need a cheerleader, a get-back-on-the-horse type?"

Osgood answered that by taking a shot and then pouring another.

"Is it tough love time? Where I slap sense into you?"

Osgood grumbled at that question, too, and drank Audrey's drink.

"Please, just tell me what you want, and I'll do it!"

She tapped her empty on the bar a few times, then turned and looked deep into Audrey's eyes. "I want to die."

The intensity must've scared Audrey, as her friend gulped before whispering, "You don't."

"I absolutely do," said Osgood.

"Well," said Audrey with a deep sigh. "What you want doesn't really matter right now. Because your father needs you."

"She should've let Yoko kill me," said Osgood. "Then she'd be alive. Basil. Dad would be... It'd hurt less if it was me, instead of her." A fresh tear rolled down Osgood's cheek, bringing with it a trail of black.

Audrey stared at Osgood, seeming unable to speak. Perhaps she knew she couldn't dissuade the thought in the end, so she changed the subject. "I promised to retrieve you, so you and he could have a moment with Cyn— Your mother, before everybody else."

"That's not Cynthia. That's meat."

"Your father needs catharsis," said Audrey. "But ... What do you need?"

Osgood thought about it for a long time. She went to pour another drink but didn't. "I'll go over."

"Good," said Audrey, climbing off the stool.

"But first," Osgood stabbed a finger in the air and didn't move her butt, "I want you to tell me what your fucking plan was."

"No, Os, that won't—"

"See, you won't do *anything* I want."

"Fine," said Audrey, her cheeks wet with tears. "We knew we probably couldn't kill him, that we'd probably just wind up killing his host. So we tried to contain him. Eliza and Zack put down a digital ring of salt using the office's phone and Cat6 lines. I don't know what those are."

"I do," said Osgood quietly.

"The plan was to debilitate the host with the tasers, keep him inside the circle after we got everybody else out, and then let Eliza, Albrecht, and Lil work on him. Real him, I mean. The aspect. The avatar."

"Decent plan," said Osgood after a while.

"We figured you'd be strong enough to hold onto him while we did." Audrey looked at her hands in her lap. "We should've considered the mayor. I don't know why we didn't."

"And Remy's sister?"

"Sister?" asked Audrey.

"Plan B," said Osgood.

"We didn't have a plan B," said Audrey, confusion in her voice.

"Shoulda had a plan B," griped Osgood. She grabbed the nearly-empty Johnny Walker bottle, yanked out the pour spout, and held it up. "And for my next trick, Imma make all this whiskey disappear."

"Please don't."

Osgood paid her no mind, tipping it back.

Audrey snatched the bottle out of her hand, looked around furtively for what she ought to do with it, and finally, with a deep breath, poured it down her throat.

Osgood was astonished and frankly a little impressed. "You drinking like that gets my pussy pulsin'."

"You are a sick woman, " Audrey said, unleashing a short coughing fit. "Do they have your credit card?"

"Yeah," said Osgood. "I opened a tab."

"Good," said Audrey. "Let's go."

She yanked Osgood through the padded door of Patton's below the Schlitz neon sign and into the sunlight. Osgood held her hand before her eyes, desperate to shield them as her pupils adjusted. However, she hadn't needed to, as moments later, they stood inside the dim vestibule of Chalfont's Funeral Services.

Below her, faded floral carpeting ran in taupes and teals and dirty gray-pinks left over from the faded days of Miami chic. She walked, stumbling on her heels and wishing she'd worn her all-black Chucks. Off to the side in a cluster were her friends, her team, her ... plan A. Osgood sighed; that wasn't fair to them. They had just as much experience destroying demigods as she did, and Audrey even had one up on her with that. She raised her hand toward them but didn't wave entirely. Zack, Albrecht, and Remy all returned the same expression: "I'm sorry for your loss." She knew they truly were, that they felt for her, but humans have rarely been very good at comforting survivors of the dead.

Her father stood alone, lanky and awkward. He had a sheet of paper folded in half, which she recognized as the program for this event.

"Dad," she said, putting her hand on the back of his rough woolen blazer. He turned, his face gaunt and ashen, his mustache seeming almost entirely gray. He'd aged years in just the four days since the ...incident. The thought of that statistic — where when one half of a couple dies, the other does shortly after — swam into her mind, but she shoved it away with all the power she could muster.

"Osgood," he said.

"You can call me Pru today," she said.

He broke down, hugging her, heaving tears into her shoulder. She held him tight, patting his back a few times. He nodded at her when he stood again and gave her that famous British stiff upper lip. "I'm happy that you're here."

"I wish we both were elsewhere," said Osgood. "Where's Eliza?"

Basil Osgood waved in the direction of a hallway. "They added all sorts of new charges to the bill. She said she would handle things."

Osgood laughed half-heartedly. "I bet she will." She looked past her father to a room with closed doors. On an easel in front of the doors stood a picture of Cynthia Osgood from maybe fifteen years ago, with just the barest hint of a smile. "Do you really want to do this? With it open, I mean?" asked Osgood, thinking of what Cynthia had looked like when last she saw her.

Basil nodded. "Please." He put out his hand, and she took it.

They stepped through the doors into a small room with a mahogany coffin, lid open. He squeezed her hand harder as they moved up the aisle, which was dreadfully short, only ten rows. There should definitely be more rows. These rooms should be longer than wide! She took a deep breath when Cynthia's nose came into view and hesitated.

Now, it was her father's turn to squeeze her hand. They stepped up to the coffin, each putting a hand on the edge and looking down at an impressively repaired Cynthia Osgood.

"Your mother never liked that scarf," her father said, pointing to the silk scarf wrapped around her throat.

"Yeah." Osgood nodded at the purple and blue nebula pattern. "I got her that one."

"Oh," said Basil. "I'm sorry, Darling."

"Nah." Osgood shook her head. "Feels right."

Right indeed. Small, petty, likely unintentional microaggressions. From her father, it *was* unintentional. But it felt like a typical Osgood family gathering for her.

Under the circumstances.

FORTY-TWO

AFTER HER FATHER HAD gone to greet friends and well-wishers, Osgood stood alone beside the coffin.

The last memorial event she'd been to had been the tenth anniversary of Caroline's disappearance. She'd worn a dress. Audrey had still hated her then, and Osgood left without speaking to anyone. Standing here in the Autumn room at the Chalfont funeral home, she wondered if she could somehow make it out of the building without speaking to any relatives, her father's friends, or worse, her mother's friends, who would surely comment — as Cynthia always had — on her half-shaved head and steadfast refusal to grow up.

She leaned down toward her mother and smelled her perfume. At her father's suggestion, Osgood had bought it once for her when she was very young. She'd been happy enough to receive it but hadn't neglected to mention that she'd also just purchased some for herself.

"Well, now you have plenty, dear," her father had suggested.

"I suppose I do," Cynthia had said, not hiding the hesitation in her voice. "Thank you ... love."

"Why couldn't you just have been nicer to me?" asked Osgood of the corpse, fighting the urge to cry in big heaving sobs. "You wouldn't have had to approve. Just be fucking nice." She slammed her hand down on the coffin's edge, and the whole thing shook.

Osgood stepped back and took a seat in the first pew. Otherwise, she might have made one last huge impression on Cynthia's friends by knocking over the coffin.

"She loved you," her father said as he sat in the pew beside her.

"Yeah," was all Osgood could say to that.

"And you loved her."

Osgood turned to him. "Why are we doing this, Dad? Why are..." but the words weren't there. What she'd initially thought was a twinkle in Basil Osgood's eye turned out to be something else altogether.

"Shh, shh, shh, shh, shh..." said her father, Basil Osgood.

Yoko.

He lifted a finger to his mouth to emphasize the quiet. "I'm not here to fight."

Osgood scrambled for her purse; surely, she had something in there. Mace? Her keys? But her father, eyes ablaze, snatched the bag from her and put it on his far side.

His voice was low, and his accent odd, as if only part of Basil's British sound was coming through. "If you hurt me, you hurt your father, and you've already lost one parent." Yoko pointed at the coffin.

Sitting straight as a rail, Osgood contemplated her next move and slumped in the pew upon realizing she had nothing.

"Good," he said.

"What do you want?" Osgood asked, her voice tight and clipped.

"You know what I want."

"You told me you didn't need me anymore."

"Hey," said Yoko, holding up his hands in an almost *mea culpa* gesture. "We all said and did a lot of things the other day. Some true, some not. Some vicious. The mayor of Chicago did some especially repulsive things."

Osgood snorted.

"See," said Yoko, "There's no reason we can't figure this out amicably." He leaned over until his lips were close enough that his mustache brushed Osgood's ear. "Because if we don't, you will watch everyone you love die." As he leaned back away, Osgood clenched her jaw tightly and shuddered.

"An idle threat," said Osgood.

"There's nothing idle about it," said Yoko. He checked her father's watch. "Now, as there's not much time before this shindig begins, I thought we'd get down to brass tacks."

"What about the shark?" asked Osgood, wondering what Yoko would do if she simply refused.

"Excuse me?"

"Sharkins Insurance."

Yoko frowned and furrowed her father's brow in the exact way he always had. She could see him inside Yoko, just beneath the surface. Then his eyes widened. "Oh, the television thing!"

"Yes," said Osgood, irritated. "The television thing."

"Right before then, there'd been some murders." Yoko again mimicked her father, leaning his head against his hand as he did when he'd tell a "back in the day" story. "Not many. Usually, it takes a lot of death for the thinning, so I found it quite unusual. Something to do with Tylenol, I think. But it was the reaction to the murders. The outcry. The fear." He grinned, clearly enjoying explaining. "And I felt a weak point in the wall."

"The membrane between reality and non," said Osgood.

Yoko shrugged. "Call it what you want. I saw an opportunity."

"So you created an insurance commercial?" asked Osgood, incredulous.

"What? No!" Basil shook his head and smoothed his mustache. "I could push through only briefly; the membrane wasn't as flexible as

I thought. I hadn't seen television transmitters before, and when I explored, I saw that thing with the shark costume."

"The commercial?"

"No!" His irritation was evident, as the flames in his eyes flickered. "Those students that broke in." He held up his finger, making a corkscrew gesture. "So I tunneled through the signal, right into them. They were just fools with a camera, by the way, nothing clever at all. But the second time I broke through..." He chuckled. "Honestly, Pru—"

"Don't call me that," she said. "Not in his voice."

"Honestly, I don't even know what happened," he grinned. "A glitch? A tear. People became aware of me. But only in that stupid shark costume."

"So you made a commercial?"

"No!" he said, firm, anger coming through along with more of the British accent. "I'm not easy to see. And when people do see ... me, they can't understand. So, in a twist I find truly astonishing, you people invented a narrative to explain what you'd seen, and that narrative cohesed over the years, convincing you it'd been there your whole life." His chuckle turned to a full-blown laugh. "If I didn't have so much I needed to do, and such little time to do it, I probably would've just let you enjoy another millennium. You humans are fascinating."

"Thank you," said Osgood. "You kinda are, too."

The way he reacted to her statement made her feel ill. His mouth turned to a sneer, and suddenly, her father was every boy she'd ever given any amount of attention to, who suddenly thought he'd get lucky that night.

"You don't need to remain in the back, you know," he said, pointing to the back of her head, then poking the crown with her father's finger. "You could sit in the front seat with me."

"And what," asked Osgood, "watch as you tear the world apart?"

"You saw me at a bad moment the other day," he said. "That's not who I am."

"I think you're one drink away from asking me why I make you do it."

He tilted his head. "I don't understand."

"For my amusement, not yours."

He ignored it. "You've spent your whole life trying to *know* and have seen more than any human will ever see. Any corporeal being!" He smiled, working up his pitch. "You've even seen ... me. The real me. Not Yoko. Not Yoaganemotsa. I'd share my real name, but your father's vocal cords don't have the range. It's a shame, too, as I think you'd find it beautiful."

"You're talking about this like a romance," said Osgood. "And I heard it in the void. It was hideous."

Yoko scowled. "It doesn't have to be contentious, we can have a partnership," said Yoko. "Or if you'd rather, you can return to The Isle or any other creation you'd like."

"So you can fuck me again?" asked Osgood. "I consented to *that* guy fucking me, not a god."

"True, yes." Again came the *mea culpa* gesture. "I did resort to subterfuge."

"Then how can I know that *anything* you're saying is real?" she asked him, leaning forward. Though not interested in what he was selling, Osgood was still insanely intrigued by the sell itself.

"All I can give you is my word," he said. He put his hand atop hers on her knee, and she yanked it away. "Fair enough, not ready for that. But I know you don't want to be here. You've never wanted to be here." He grabbed her hand this time, yanking it to him and flipping it over to show a jagged and angry scar on her wrist. "As these lines can attest."

"That was another powerful being lying to me," said Osgood.

"Also fair," he said. "But you, Prudence Osgood, who has at least a pint of whiskey in your belly without food, you are already not long for this world."

"Funny, I can't seem to die," she said.

"You don't want to keep testing that theory. Remember what the cat who was too busy to count his lives said..."

"What?"

"Nothing, he was fucking dead."

Osgood stared at him. "If you hadn't revealed yourself, you could've just held onto my father and stuck around here with me."

"No," he said. He brushed something off her father's pant leg. "These minds can't hold the signal long enough for me to accomplish anything substantial."

"What will it do to him?"

"To your father?"

"Yes," she snapped. Her patience with Yoko had reached its very last thread. "To. My. Father."

"Nothing. I've only been in here for ten minutes." He tapped his temple. "Mrs. Chalfont, however, will be eating her meals with a straw from now on."

"Like Alice," said Osgood.

"Alice?" asked Yoko.

"You don't even remember," she said, standing. "How can you think that's okay? That I'd let you take me when you literally destroy people for no reason other than they get in your way?"

Slowly, Basil stood as well. His face seemed to be sliding down his skull. "I think you'll let me take you *because* I literally destroy people for no reason other than they get in my way."

"But you can't destroy me," said Osgood.

"I'll admit, you found your loophole."

"So what if I kill myself?" she asked.

Basil shrugged. "I'd still have a few minutes before the electricity dies. That's all I'd need to start the slippage."

"Then why can't you just jump in, do what you need to, and then get the fuck out?"

"*I can*," said Basil in a voice Osgood recognized from rare moments in her youth when her father, not her mother, had been the disciplinarian. "But I'm not going to. Because when I was in there before, I saw your controls. Whole areas you've never touched. Vast expanses of talents and abilities that you haven't the faintest clue about. I want to see what happens when those come online."

"So my options are to let you ... have me."

He said, "Yes," with a ferocious hunger.

"Or..."

"I don't want the or," he snapped. At Osgood's defiant look, he sighed. "Or, I decimate those you care about. Audrey. Little Zacky. I find Ramona especially intriguing — What's her deal?"

"She's a daughter of the sun."

"I don't know what that means."

"You decimate them," repeated Osgood.

"Yeah, I'll kinda let myself freeform improv their destruction. Maybe I'll crawl inside Zack's head and cut off his capacity for deep thought. Or take away Audrey's empathy. Maybe I'll just consume that 'daughter of the sun' or whatever she is whole." He shrugged. "That is if I'm feeling playful. I might just kill each and every one of them, quickly, yes, painfully, also yes. Maybe everyone else out there, too." He flicked his thumb toward the back door. "Hell, I might want your pale beloved Audrey to vivisect herself. Come to think of it, that little Beth Garcia got off a bit too easily. Some of those other kids, too. I could pick up where old Cora Ballard fell apart." He grabbed her hand, not letting her take it back this time. "I even know where the 'lord' of the Hinterlands flock went. If you think it was heaven, have I got news for you. All these are hypotheticals, of course. I don't *need* Earth intact to break the wheel. Maybe I'll give them all that biblical apocalypse they so desperately want. Trumpets, ashes from the sky, seas boiling, blood moon." He looked at her with a smile that didn't look evil, rather genuinely excited, and on her father's face, that scared Osgood the most. "It all sounds like fun." He wiped at the side of Basil's face, squishing it about on top of his skull.

"Alright," he said. "So that's the limited-time offer if you want Daddy to be okay. I will need an answer, and we won't postpone or sleep on it any longer. Yes, I can have you and the world ends in centuries and doesn't hurt your friends at all, or no, I can't, and I absolutely destroy everyone and everything you love until you're so depressed you cut your wrists again because I know..." He held up her wrist and pointed to the scar lines, "These are far more than two cuts." He shrugged. "Then, I'll take you anyway."

Osgood couldn't speak, looking into the flickering flames in her father's eyes. She didn't know how much time had passed, but it was longer than she'd wanted and clearly longer than Yoko was willing to wait as he stood and began to walk back up the aisle toward the doors in the back.

"Wait," she said, finally.

He stopped and gave a gloating turn.

"Okay," she said.

"I'm going to need a much louder and more confident acquiescence."

"Okay," she said, in her oration voice, "You can have my brain and body to spare my friends and family."

He clapped his hands together. "Well, now, this is cause for a celebration." He walked toward her.

"But!"

He stopped.

"Not until midnight tonight."

He looked put out for a moment but then shrugged. "Sure, whatever."

"And we go where we met."

"Which time?" he asked gleefully.

"The most important one," said Osgood. "And I think you know where that is."

"I do."

"So," said Osgood. "Deal?"

"Deal."

FORTY-THREE

O SGOOD IS ALONE. THAT'S by design. Having anyone else, anyone she cares about here with her would make them an instant target. Worse, they'd insist there are other ways to do this that won't hurt her as much.

While the City of Chicago has done a decent job in its debris removal and rebuilding efforts, the El trains are still redirected onto a single-line pass beside the mess that *her* train and the other had made. She knows this place, Pike Street station, from the drone footage she'd discovered on Zack's tablet when he left her alone with it. Astonishingly, several fluorescent fixtures still glow, producing enough light to see but not enough to see *into* shadows. It's been partially cleaned up, but hazard warnings remain. Wires still hang. Debris piles abound. Rebar pokes through the floor where once there'd been pillars.

She hears an El train rumble through the walls and looks down the tunnel to where the crash happened. Water obscures the rails, making Osgood think an "It's A Small World" boat might come for her. She laughs when she finds herself humming the tune.

A deep voice intones in echoey bass, "It's a small. Small. World."

She looks around but remains alone. "Oh, god, you are just the most irritating—" Her voice fails her as the lights in the station go out. Osgood scrambles in her pocket for her phone.

Illumination comes, though; thousands upon thousands of fireflies stream from the tunnel where she lay dying not so long ago. The yellow-green illumination from their blinks isn't intense, but as they begin to sync up and the lights blink together. The fireflies spread out wide, a gap appearing across the center of their spread.

"I thought this most appropriate," says Yoko, from the buzzing of the fireflies, the drippings of the water, and the rumbling of the trains far away. From everywhere. "As we've reached endgame."

The firefly mouth syncs perfectly with the speech, and Osgood forces herself to remember that this *is* a single being.

"Yes," Yoko says. "I am me. And I am we."

"So, how does this work?" Osgood asks, folding her arms across her gray tee shirt, the one with a black five-pointed star in the center. *David Bowie, give me strength.*

"What's that, dear?" he asks, and she is amazed how a voice not created by vocal cords can hold the amount of amusement and tone it does.

"Do I have to do anything," she shrugs. "You know, for you to have me?"

"I already have you, silly girl."

"Don't call me girl."

"You fight *so hard* against things without any meaning at all, but then you acquiesce to a god without another thought."

"I had plenty of thoughts."

The swarm of fireflies grows and comes together to form a humanoid shape, a flickering silhouette of a man who then appears to walk toward her. "I don't want you," he says. This time, the fireflies don't attempt to lip-sync.

"What?" Osgood feels her stomach lurch.

"That's why we're here alone," says Yoko. "I'm going to eat you. Like consume. In a way that I haven't eaten a being in centuries. Your world is so difficult to get into. But the membrane was *especially* fragile after the Black Death. The people, back then, though, tasted like shit."

"Aww," says Osgood, putting up a show of defiance in her voice. "Our world is tough? Boo fucking hoo."

Yoko laughs, but there's surprise in it. "You have always had that defiance, haven't you? I stopped in a few times after I first saw you. Well, before I saw your accident. I wanted to see what this Osgood woman was like."

"Am I foretold?" asks Osgood. "Prophesied? I am the girl who lived, after all."

"Don't be so conceited. You're nothing. Intriguing, sure, and your brain has some interesting wiring, but it's not like we talk about you around the water cooler of the gods. I found your childhood *mildly* interesting. You scare easily, about such odd things."

"Okay," says Osgood. "Bicycle Man."

The fireflies make a smile on the face, just a gap in the swarm.

"So..." she shrugs. "We're not doing this together?"

"You're not doing *anything*," he says, his voice growing dangerous. "You're not leaving this station. Because poetically, you're going to die—" The firefly man extends his arm and a finger toward the tunnel. "—right where you hoped. Right where you've lamented you didn't. They'll find your body and assume some wild animal got to it while you were down here exploring. Or, hell, maybe they won't find it at all. That would upset Audrey, wouldn't it? You disappearing again. There's been so much unexplained disappearance in her life."

"Don't," says Osgood, trying to appear firm.

"Are you commanding me?" he asks. The fireflies snap down to a point, then spread out again, becoming the enormous eye.

"Have I hit a nerve?"

"You beg me." Its pupil shrinks to a pinpoint. "You get on your fucking knees and *beg* me to make it quick for you."

"But you needed me," says Osgood, slowly lowering herself to painful knees. "Or was that a lie, too?"

"I. Need. Nothing."

"Then why the song and dance, Yoko?" Osgood asks, looking up at it. "Why are we even doing this?"

"I want you to suffer," he says with a sneer.

Osgood extends her arms to the sides

(the better to crucify you, my dear)

and sticks her chin out to him. "Then bring it the fuck on."

In a flash, the eye becomes the man, and the man punches her dead in the face. An almost deafening crack. A wail.

Osgood smiles.

Yoko staggers backward, clutching his hand. "How ... how did you do that? Another hex? Another—"

"Your bugs suck, Yoko."

The swarm reconfigures to the head again.

"As I visited your creation in my head, now you visit mine," Osgood says, striding toward him. "It's the prestige, motherfucker!"

The look on this composited face is oddly hilarious to Osgood, knowing that she's just confused the fuck out of a god and getting to see its perplexed look. She takes a step back and lifts her hands. An immediate woosh, and a clear acrylic box surrounds Yoko, a cell incongruently in the middle of this subway station. Yoko roars and bursts, the swarm growing larger and louder, no longer forming anything but a cloud of insects that fill the box.

"I didn't poke air holes," shouts Osgood over the din. "Didn't think you needed any; none of this is real, after all."

"You don't trap me," he seethes in his insect voices. "You can't trap me."

"I do," says Osgood. "And I did."

The firefly swarm resolidifies as the massive face within the box. "You can't hurt me."

Osgood smirks, ever so slightly. "I saw what happened to you as the mayor fell apart. I can hurt the thing you inhabit, and that weakens you!"

"Barely!" The firefly face scoffs. "And if we're in your head, *you are* the thing I inhabit, you stupid girl! You've hobbled yourself." Yoko laughs.

"Have I?" asks Osgood. "I'm not gonna monologue because I detest talking to you, but thank you for the idea. When you told me how badly I hurt myself. You were right. I do. I probably hurt myself more than I could ever hurt someone else."

The face of Yoko doesn't react, though its lips part ever so slightly. "So?"

"Did you forget where you are?"

Still no reaction. Osgood wonders if he's planning something if he's intended to do something bigger if this whole idea was stupid and ill-informed.

"What is this?" he asks, finally.

Osgood grins, enjoying this most momentary and fleeting of victories before the true horror starts.

"This is Plan B. YoaGo Fuck Yourself."

Forty-Four

T HE WOMAN'S BAREFOOT STEPS are nearly silent, without a single footfall echoing across their stage, their private subway station, replete with a massive box of bugs that make up the panicking aspect of a sleeping god. Osgood is wary of this woman, especially knowing what their plan involves, but still cannot take her eyes off the spitting image of Dr. Ramona Yeagher. She wears a pale blue sundress, worn and faded, dark hasty makeup on her eyes, the same grayish silver as Remy's, and her face is framed with long dark hair.

"You are girl," says Alexis Yeagher.

Osgood laughs. "Sure."

"My English is … I have not spoke English in long time." The accent sounds Slavic, Eastern European.

Osgood nods.

"You do not fuck with me," says the woman, pressing a long fingernail under Osgood's chin, hard enough to draw blood.

"I have no intention of fucking with you," says Osgood.

"This is not trap." The woman spins on her bare feet to look at the box of fireflies in the shape of a human. Her long black hair swirls around her like a goth flamenco dress.

"It is not," says Osgood. "Well, not for you. For him, it's a trap."

Alexis looks over the box, and the swarm seems more solid. "Okay. Bug man is trapped." She turns back to Osgood. "Now you."

Osgood takes a deep breath and reaches beyond one of the square pylons that hold up the station's ceiling, reinforced here with rebar. When her hands reemerge, they hold a pair of leather cuffs that she'd used with Audrey once upon a time, before they'd realized that these things weren't toys and they would hold you exactly as tight as they wanted to. She slipped them on and offered her wrists to Alexis.

"You are strange girl," says Alexis.

"I am," agrees Osgood. She hears the whimper in her voice but tries to hide it.

"Ramona tell you about me?" asks Alexis.

"Very recently."

"She does not like me," says Alexis. "I am surprised she call."

"I was surprised, too, when I saw you at the event."

"Is that fat man?" Alexis points again at the box.

"Yes," says Osgood as Alexis lifts her arms above her head and hooks the cuffs on a rebar hook, high above the ground, high enough that only Osgood's toes can reach the cement floor. For the first time, but not the last, Osgood wonders, not if she's made a terrible mistake, but exactly how terrible said mistake is.

We are here, says Lil's voice in her head, and comfort immediately descends upon her.

"Okay," says Yoko, his voice a combination of crabby and snarky that calls to mind the MAGA phase James Woods. "What the fuck are we doing here? Who the fuck is that? Why can't I see her in your head?"

"She's a daughter of the moon," says Osgood.

"*The* daughter of the moon," says Alexis without looking up.

"Any other questions?" Osgood asks him, a polite lilt in her voice.

"Another one. What the fuck does that mean?" he asks with a white-hot fury that Osgood can almost feel. He changes the subject without waiting for an answer that won't come. "How the fuck did you put me in your head?"

"I guess I really am exceptional."

"Are you sure you want naked?" asks Alexis, holding a giant pair of gleaming scissors.

Osgood nods. "Anything worth doing is worth overdoing, right?"

Alexis looks at her with confusion, then shrugs. "Okay." Quickly, she slides the scissors up, cutting Osgood's shirt and splitting the Black Star in two. Bowie would understand. Two more snips and Osgood's arms are unadorned; Alexis yanks the shirt away. She laughs. "We are match." On Osgood's confusion, she points to Osgood's armpit, where she'd allowed her hair to flourish. Then Alexis lifts her own and shows similar black curls. "Man love. They fuck."

"Not in my experience," says Osgood, remembering all the men who'd asked her if she had to be *that* queer. *Like, sure, but could you at least shave your pits?*

"Woman then?" asks Alexis.

"Far more often," says Osgood.

"Give me pants," says Alexis.

Osgood laughs, the nerves returning. "I ... can't. You're gonna have to take them."

"That. Yes. I take pants now." Again, Alexis's scissors make quick work of Osgood's jeans. Osgood cringes when Alexis leans forward briefly to sniff her bush, but the woman doesn't indicate the purpose or if she feels one way or another about it. Instead, she yanks off Osgood's Chucks, tossing them one at a time at the box. "Bug man is wery angry."

"I'm a god," demands Yoko.

"He's an aspect of a god," says Osgood to Alexis, who lifts her hands in a *wowee* gesture that seems to infuriate Yoko further.

Alexis stands before Osgood, puts down the scissors, and strokes her chin. Again, Osgood sees Remy in there, but without any of the peace, the love, the compassion. Every emotion radiating from this woman is cold and dark.

"Usually, I kill," says Alexis.

"Well, we appreciate you making an exception."

"*If* I make exception," Alexis says with a wink, then laughs and elbows Osgood in the ribs.

Osgood laughs back warily. *I really hope y'all are looking out for me out there,* she thinks.

Both Lil and Eliza respond in the affirmative.

"What the fuck am I doing?" Osgood asks the fluorescent light flickering above her.

"I would also like to know that," says Yoko.

"Quiet, bug man," says Alexis. She walks away from Osgood hanging on the pylon over to a table covered in shiny instruments. She picks up a scalpel and walks back to Osgood. Without another word and astonishingly fast, she slices a chunk out of Osgood's left side.

Osgood screams in pain, and the pain awakens her body's excruciating greatest hits.

"What the fuck are you doing?" Yoko asks again, seeming panicked this time.

Alexis walks over to the box and sticks the patch of Osgood flesh to the outside. The fireflies immediately swarm it, perhaps to get a better look as it slowly slides down the glass.

Osgood pushes through the tears pouring down her face, noting that Yoko's voice is higher and his panic seems real. When Alexis returns and looks into her eyes, the woman still questions. Osgood nods vigorously, even though it hurts like hell.

Alexis draws the scalpel in a straight line down Osgood's upper arm, through the hair in her armpit, and down the side of her chest. She's surprised as the blade moves that it isn't more painful, but it's when the blood starts to breach the cut that Osgood's nerves carry it to her brain. She wants to retreat so badly, to go to a place of safety, to go to her kingdom. Hide within. Down that entire bottle of Morphine that Zack's been hoarding. But this *is* her kingdom, this is her mind, and she's allowing herself to be tortured both here and out there. There's nowhere to go. Nowhere to hide.

She feels warmth on her back and turns her head. When she sees Audrey's face, she gasps a sob. "No, Aud! No, please!"

"Os," says Audrey. "You can't make me go."

"How are you even here?"

"Your aunt."

Osgood calls to the ceiling. "Fuck! Eliza! I don't want her to see this!"

Eliza's voice comes back in her head. *She refused to leave your side up here; we felt that at least down there, you would know she is with you.*

"I can handle it, Os," says Audrey.

"No," Osgood sobs further.

Alexis has returned with a small metal device. "You again," she says to Audrey. "You get in my way?"

Audrey shakes her head, but looking at the device, she says in desperation, "No, not that."

Osgood strains her neck, but she can't get a good view, and the movement's pull on her arms makes her chest tighten. She finds it hard to breathe.

"Is Pear of Anguish," says Alexis. "Is my favorite."

"That may be," says Audrey, yanking it away. "But we don't want permanent damage ... there."

"Pear of Anguish," repeats Yoko, actually sounding impressed.

"Ahh," says Alexis. She extends a finger toward Audrey. "You eat *pyča*."

"Uh," says Audrey. "Yes?"

"Wery well," says Alexis, snatching back the Pear of Anguish.

"You know," says Yoko, "Letting me watch her torture you isn't the deterrent you might think it is." He makes an aside to Audrey, "Pru's kinda been grating on me for a while."

"Yeah?" asks Audrey. She walks slowly over to the box. "You should check the bottom of your little cell there."

He does. "Huh."

Osgood can't see what they're referring to because her head is tipped back. Alexis has her hands and a pair of pliers in Osgood's mouth, and "Wugh" is the best she can muster.

"The bug man is losing bugs," says Alexis, giving a yank and taking Osgood's lower left back molar with her.

Osgood howls in pain, and Audrey rushes back. "I'm here," she says, rubbing her arm. Through tears and sweat, Osgood looks from Audrey to Yoko to Alexis. Alexis is grinning.

"You're enjoying this too much," says Audrey.

"I enjoy exactly right amount," says Alexis. "You fear ecstasy of pain."

"Ecstasy!?" demands Audrey.

"Aud, please," begs Osgood. "This is hard enough."

"We need to stop," says Audrey. "This is a terrible idea." She grabs Alexis's wrist as the woman comes back with the pliers. "And you are insane."

"Yeah," says Yoko. "Let's stop. We're a little out of control here." His voice wavers as it tries to be solid.

For a lunatic moment, Osgood thinks he sounds like her junior high guidance counselor Mr. Jung, one of the most ineffectual men she's ever met, and she knows that Yoko is afraid. "No," she says. "Keep. Going."

Alexis yanks her wrist from Audrey's hand. "You invite me; I did not just come."

"*I* didn't invite you," Audrey screams at Alexis. "This wasn't *my* plan!" Audrey begins to sob, great shaking sobs. "I don't understand the plan, Os, I really don't!"

"I know," says Osgood, just before Alexis pries her mouth back open to go for her lower right molar. This yank produces a wet scream.

Alexis leans forward, as close as she can, to Osgood's face. "This working," she says. Osgood is unable to make any sounds other than sobs and nods. "Good," says the woman, and she returns to her table.

"So you hurt me, so what?" Yoko attempts to bring some swagger back to his voice, but it's unconvincing. "Not like you can kill me."

"May...be...we...c...can," says Osgood.

"I'm a god!" he roars.

"Assss...pect," says Osgood.

"Okay," says Alexis, returning to Osgood with a hammer. "Now I break you."

Osgood gives a little laugh, astonished at where she finds herself. BDSM has never appealed to her. Mainly because when you're already in pain most of the time, what's the point in planned pain that, so often, can accidentally

(Alexis breaks Osgood's right kneecap)

have ripple effects through the rest of the body. Like now, actually. The best way to look at this, she thinks, is like her cutting habit. When life became especially tough, but not enough to tip her into being

(and the left)

suicidal, slicing a razor down her inner thigh gave her control over the pain. She caused it, she ended it, she healed it. Control. That's what this is, isn't it? Her Plan B: A plan so outrageous that Remy fell to her knees when she heard it. Fell to her knees and begged Osgood to reconsider. Fell to her knees, whispering, "She's a psychopath,"

(the top of Osgood's right foot, shattering god knows how many bones within)

but ultimately had to concede, as did Eliza and Lil, that there was no sane plan. And when there's nothing sane, sometimes you have to go with the insane.

(then the left)

Osgood, unable to hold them any further, feels her feet dangle. The pain radiating up her legs is so white-hot she almost doesn't feel it, as though it's nearly burned out her receptors. Still, she remembers, just before they'd begun — after begging Remy and Eliza not to share her plan with Audrey or Zack, who'd never let her do it — Remy telling her that Alexis knows how to make sure you keep ... feeling.

A feeling of being unzipped draws another scream from Osgood's lips, and she feels woozy. She doesn't look down but can hear Alexis rooting around in her innards, humming an unfamiliar song as she goes. There's a tug, a tug from within, and the pain reaches another level. Then the tugging stops, as though something has just been cauterized. She looks down and sees Alexis smiling up at her, a kidney in her hand. The woman grins and takes a bite out of it.

Osgood laughs.

"Os," Audrey whispers, eyes closed, head against Osgood's unsliced arm.

The laughter won't stop, though; it just grows and grows. She laughs louder and louder because she knows now, for a fact, that alongside her screams are the screams of an aspect of a god keeping harmony. Between laughs, Osgood turns to Audrey. "Aud ... How we doin'?"

"Bad!" says Audrey. "We're doing bad, Os!"

"No," says Osgood, finding it harder and harder to hold her head up. "Yoko?"

"Really?"

"This is ... plan, Aud," says Osgood through clenched teeth, her mouth full of pennies. "You need ... trust me."

"Plan is epic," says Alexis. "Delicious."

Osgood hears ripping and her left arm is being tugged. Of course, her laugh returns with the prickly cold pain, the tugging, the ripping. She thinks, *It's degloving for a hand, but what is the whole arm?*

"I fillet you," says Alexis, who, in a tremendous yank with a flourish, throws the opera glove of skin she just removed. It splats against the window of the box.

Audrey screams and rushes away from it.

"Bug man is small," Alexis whispers to her.

"How ... small?" asks Osgood.

"Perhaps small enough," says the woman. "And perhaps you not want me to continue."

"If you ... hafta," says Osgood.

"No!" screams Audrey, "We're good! You can stop!"

"You go way," says Alexis. "I eat bug man."

Slowly, Osgood nods, feeling like she's moving in stuttery, staccato slow motion. She turns her head to the box and sees Alexis approach it. The fireflies aren't in the shape of anything any longer, mostly dead on the box floor. What remain beat their cluster against the far side of the box, trying to get away. Their lights pulse rhythmically, like a heartbeat, increasing in speed and intensity as Alexis nears. The woman puts a bloody hand on the box and begins to sing some nursery rhyme in a language Osgood doesn't know.

With that sound and Audrey's screams ringing in her ears, Osgood drifts away from pain to a black hole of velvety sleep.

Forty-Five

"**N**o. Stop!"

The voice was harsh but feminine.

"Can I get help in here?"

Blurry, Osgood saw shapes surrounding her, holding her in place.

"She's trying to tear out her stitches again."

"Gimme..." said Osgood, a hoarse rasp. She smacked her lips, feeling her cheeks swollen. "Whas in mumouth?"

"Gauze, Os," said Audrey, the blurry form on her upper right.

"Gulses," said Osgood.

"What?" There was Zack.

"Glasses," snapped Audrey. "C'mon, Zack!"

"She fucking said 'gulses,'" he griped but slid her glasses onto her face.

"I had the strangest dream," slurred Osgood, far slower than usual. "And you were there," she said, pointing to Audrey. "You weren't," she added, pointing at the Indian woman she now recognized, "Dr. Laghari."

"No," said the doctor. "I was *here*."

"Here," said Osgood, closing her eyes again briefly.

"Listen, Osgood," said Dr. Laghari. "You are on an exceptionally high dose of morphine at the moment."

"I knew you'd gimme ... good stuff, Doc," said Osgood.

"Yeah, well, if anyone at the hospital ever found out. Or the AMA. Or the police, I guess…"

"I won't tell," Osgood said, lifting a hand to her mouth to add, "Sthh."

"Don't!" yelped Audrey.

Osgood stared, dumbfounded, at her hand, which was wrapped in scales. "Whadafuk?"

"It's fish skin," said Audrey.

"Atlantic cod, to be precise," added Dr. Laghari.

Osgood turned her hand and saw it went all the way up her arm.

"I did my best," lamented the doctor. "But I've never had to repair an entire arm's worth of skin."

"Good god." A laugh escaped Osgood. "Weresa psycho?"

"The psycho?" asked Audrey. "She's gone."

"'Lexis," said Osgood.

"Yes, Alexis is absolutely psychotic," said Audrey.

"Did she do it?" asked Osgood.

"I think she did," said Remy, entering the room that Osgood now realized was her bedroom. She made eye contact with Dr. Laghari, who shook her head and waved her onto Osgood.

"I'm going to give you some privacy," said Laghari. "But so help me, if she tears out those stitches one more time, I'm going to let her bleed to death."

"No, you won't," said Osgood playfully, feeling a wide grin on her face. "You like me."

"Don't test that theory." With a firm slam of the door, perhaps to put a point on it, Dr. Laghari left.

"So," said Zack pointedly. "Can we talk about not sharing plans now?"

"You didn't share yours first," said Osgood.

"Ours didn't involve you getting tortured and flayed."

"Would've been a pretty mean plan if it had," said Osgood.

Remy reached out, and Osgood said, "Don't."

It didn't deter her, though. "I'm sick of your martyrdom," said Remy. Pushing Osgood's fish-skin-covered hand away, Remy put her hand on Osgood's head, and the euphoric sensation of weight being lifted flowed through her body. "And now that you've tried to play Joan of Arc: The Home Game, I'm not listening to you anymore."

"Yeah, Os," said Zack, "Why don't you let her suck you off." He giggled.

"He's been doing that for days now," said Remy.

"Okay, okay," said Osgood, again feeling woozy. "Do you ... think it worked?"

Remy sighed and nodded. "Judging by how my sister nearly floated out of this apartment, I'd say her meal included something very substantial."

"Why are you difnit?"

"I didn't get that, Os."

"Diffni...differnet."

"Diff'rent?" asked Remy.

Osgood put one bandaged finger on her nose and extended her fish-skinned arm at Remy.

"Okay," said Audrey. "Stop that."

Remy sighed. "I love my ... ability. When I relieve someone of their pain, I feel joy. It fills me up. Alexis is different. She doesn't take emotional pain, she takes physical. And..." The therapist cleared her throat. "She feels every bit of it."

"Of their pain?" asked Audrey.

Remy nodded. "It's made her ... hard. Rough. Mean. Over time, the pain stopped hurting so much for her. Over time, she began to find—"

"Comfort in it," said Osgood.

Tears filled Remy's eyes, and she couldn't look away from Osgood. The women stared at each other. "I love my sister." She drifts away, just for a moment. "But she's ... she's a monster. I can't have her around me. I can't have her around people I love." Choking back a sob with a laugh, Remy feigned a smile. "And I still miss her like crazy. It's different being a twin."

"Yes, it is," said Audrey. "Like a tether."

Remy pointed a sad finger at Audrey and nodded. "When I went to track her down for this, she was already on a plane to Chicago. She knew I needed her." Remy chuckled. "And before she left, she pulled me close and said, 'Bugman ees delicious.'"

"That's uncanny," said Osgood. "Don't ever do that voice around me again."

A knock came on the door.

"Who else is here?" asked Osgood.

"It's just me again," said Dr. Laghari, poking her head in.

"More'n merrier," said Osgood.

Laghari held a tablet in her hands. "Got some results back, and your body is holding up incredibly well, considering the ... extensive trauma."

"I told you, Doc, I'm immortal," said Osgood with a laugh. Then her voice became grave as she realized, "I'm going to have to feel all this pain, aren't I?"

Laghari hedged, "Yes? But I mean, the upside of having your skin ripped off is that it definitely damaged some pain receptors."

"Bonus!" said Osgood.

"We will medicate," said the doctor.

"I'm not allowed to anymore," said Osgood.

"You'll notice I'm wearing my yoga clothes, not scrubs, right?" Laghari laughed to herself and then covered her eyes, shaking her head. "I'm not here as an official doctor."

"Why *are* you here?" asked Osgood.

"After you checked yourself out against my recommendations, I looked into you deeper than before."

"Ahh, a Specterino conversion," said Osgood with a laugh.

"Let's just say: What you do... I want to help," said Laghari. "Where and when I can."

"It's nice to bask in greatness," said Osgood.

"She means 'thank you,'" said Audrey.

Dr. Laghari smiled. "I'm counting on you to make sure she doesn't OD on the morphine."

"Me?" asked Zack in a panic.

"Me, I think," said Audrey.

"Yes, please, Audrey." The doctor scrolled on the tablet once more. She shook her head. "That's ... odd."

"Wha?" asked Osgood, feeling the morphine begin to double up on her, helping her fly.

"It, just..." Laghari turned to Osgood, looking into her eyes, and asked with a laugh, "There's no way you could be pregnant, is there?"

Audrey laughed.

"Not unless her silicone dick's got little sperms in it," said Osgood flicking her head in Audrey's direction. "But I'm happy to pee on a stick if you're concerned."

"No," said Dr. Laghari. "We ran the test along with the others. And, well..." She turned the tablet to them and pointed to the result in a small box on the lower right that boldly, in all caps, said: **PREG-NANT.**

"Oh," said Osgood. She looked from Audrey to Zack and back, then Laghari and back. "But I haven't had sex with a man since... Oh, fuck me."

PRUDENCE OSGOOD WILL RETURN

IN THE

SPECTRAL INSPECTOR V

Acknowledgements

A huge thank you to those who alpha'd and beta'd this book through all its growing pains, especially *Osgood's Specterinos* on Bookstagram, y'all know who you are.

The same goes for all the outstanding reviewers who took a chance on advanced copies, even having not read the earlier books. Brave and bold.

I would not have been able to get away with my Old English nonsense without first *Minerat27* on Reddit. Then Dr. Danny Bate, who patiently took my internet translated slop and massaged it into actual legitimate language, even telling me roughly how it would be spoken for the future audiobook.

It's weird thanking someone I've never met, let alone someone who's died, but I cannot begin to explain the impact David Lynch has had on me and my writing ever since I was exposed to his work far too young. (*Blue Velvet* is not for high school freshmen.) To other fans of Lynch, I've no doubt you've seen his echoes everywhere in my work. Despite showcasing some of the darkest evils, he was a force for good in an insane world. He was the robins. He was the mystery of love. He was the fish in the percolator, the gift given every day. There will never be another like him. And somehow, I owe him everything.

As always, I could not do these silly things without the unending support of my partners, Elle and Wren. They keep me moving forward despite the dark times we live in. My love for them is paramount.

And to y'all, I say thankee sai!

Cooper S. Beckett

January 30, 2025

About the author

In *Trump's America II: The Quickening*, Cooper S. Beckett remains both defiantly queer and non-monogamous, creating works of silly paranormal fiction that entire states would ban outright. In truth, he believes that creating art is most important when it is hard, and that art *means* most when it is defiant, especially when it reflects the diverse lifestyles of his friends, his partners, and himself. While Cooper is one of a privileged few on the queer spectrum who has great relationships with his immediate family, he also has a beloved chosen family, and could not survive and navigate this hellscape without them. He is incredibly lucky to have a nesting partner who believes in him and supports him in Elle, a satellite partner who stands with him always in Wren, a ghost hunting terrier named Egon who, while he may be tiny, will defend him with his mighty bark, and a black cat named Willow who ultimately cannot be bothered and will probably eat him after he dies.

He lives in Chicago, and cannot or seemingly *will not* write about elsewhere ... unless it's a nebulous swinger resort (in Mexico or inside someone's head), cuz he's done that *three* times.

BOOKS BY
COOPER S. BECKETT